This is a book about finding reasons to push on, even in our darkest hours.

It is for Eleanor, who is my reason to push on, in every hour.

Will you marry me, Sugarplum?

DAYS 4–5

It was like riding the fastest roller coaster he had ever been on, falling out of the sky like that. The kind of roller coaster that has a rickety wooden frame and rusty metal bars that hammer the bones and bruise soft tissue on every bend and twist; the kind that would be better suited to a museum than a carnival. The kind that has no lighting and no end, the kind that blinds you with terror. The fall had been fast but felt like a lifetime and it had made him feel as hot as being boiled alive and he had been sure beyond sureness that he was going to die, but he refused to be taken without a fight so forced his eyes to stay open until the craft reached the ground and everything went black and all that followed was darkness and silence.

But then he had woken, alive, in a desert. And only now, three sleeps later, was the constant reliving of it in James Verne's mind beginning to fade.

He stared out at the expanse of rock, dirt, and weeds, so incredibly immense that it appeared endless, as the star at the centre of this system crept over the horizon, drenching the desert in orange light. There was a breeze, a breeze that never seemed to become wind or to fade away completely, which was so light that only the top layer of earth – the lightest, thinnest dust on the surface of this desert – was even slightly disturbed by it; and yet, far off, through telescopic lenses, it always seemed to have enough strength to blow great dust phantoms across the landscape with little effort.

The sky, as usual, was completely clear of clouds. The orange and purple and blue went on forever, only stopping to meet the desert at the vanishing point.

Far away, not too far to see but definitely too far to make out clearly, something crawled across the floor in rodentesque scuttles, stopping here, running a little further, pausing there; but however much it seemed like it might be life, it was not. It was another pebble, another weed, another leaf, fooling the eyes, teasing the mind.

To the west, far beyond the crash site, there were mountains. A rust-coloured formation of ridges poked out of the landscape and put on a beautiful show in the morning, as the shadow of sunrise crept down their sides, gloriously revealing these intricately carved sculptures of nature inch by inch, as if a curtain had been drawn to hide them until then. But they were the only feature in a brown and orange and yellow and grey sea of nothingness, infinitely smaller but just as empty as space.

On Earth, this was the kind of place one would hope to be passing through, not ending up.

But here, the Conquerors woke, still groggy from the journey, three days after landing in one of this planet's many skin-peeling deserts. They had been sure they would reach civilisation within two days, walking at a brisk pace, sharing the load of their supplies between them; but they had not counted on the heat, the storms, the terrain, the crippling lag of cryosleep.

Cryosleep. Waking from it was like waking from a deep slumber very suddenly, in that disorienting way in which the brain first assumes it has not been asleep at all, but is forced to rethink its theory when it cannot account for its absence in the last few hours. Cryosleep was a total void, a colourless nothingness into which the mind disintegrated, losing all hope of returning to a conscious world again; so emerging from it was like waking from anaesthesia, completely unaware that the surgeon's knife has paid a visit until the pain returns.

Like waking from the dead.

So, none of the crew had yet adjusted to the shorter days, or the unpredictable temperature of the nights. Their weary bodies were not yet accustomed to the way this system's star, so huge in the white-blue sky, cooked the ground the instant it rose on the horizon. They had not known how their suits would weigh them down, their muscles would seize, their throats would dry to dust every ten steps. They left the wreck of the landing craft with their supplies tied to sleds and their guns strapped to their backs, and they stepped out into the desert before they knew anything about the world they had entered.

But now, they knew too well that the world they had entered was a cruel and barren one. Their sleds were gone, taken in the night by no one knew what; their supplies were dwindling; their ship was too far away and too damaged from the crash-landing to be worth returning to; and their destination was still unknown. They knew where a city should be – the ship had mapped some, but not all, of this area before it had prematurely launched their landing craft – but no matter how far they struggled, they never seemed to reach it.

However, one redeeming fact remained: they were still Conquerors. This world, this prize so far from the reach of any other humans who had ever existed, was theirs. They had made it. And it was this fact which held their morale together, as they peeled their sweaty bodies out of their sleeping bags and began to prepare for another day of trekking.

James Verne had been awake for some time before the others rose, and had watched this system's sun peek over the horizon from atop a boulder a short walk away from the camp, his overalls unzipped to the waist and his huge feet resting on top of his discarded boots, enjoying the only cool air the day would offer. He now sat cleaning and inspecting his gun, his large, thick, calloused hands working over the body of the automatic rifle with the delicacy and precision of a brain surgeon. The concentration he devoted to the task was more religious than practical; the cleaning of the weapon and the deconstruction and reconstruction of all of its parts, just to check once again that they were all healthy and in full working order should they ever be needed, more meditation than precaution. A daily deconstruction and reconstruction of himself, to check he was all working.

After the inspection – the ritual – was complete, Verne slid his feet into his boots and walked back toward the camp, to find the group sitting in a triangle, heads hung in hangover emulation, slurping hyper-nutritious gruel from foil sachets. Movements sheepish and gazes lowered, shaven apes cowering from the blows of a cruel, invisible master. Verne smirked upon the scene as he cast his long, broad shadow across it, and for a while, none could even find the energy or the will to look up and acknowledge his smug grin.

Jon Ballard, the Brit, rubbed his eyes with his dry, chapped palms before pausing to examine the cuts and sores that plagued the dark skin on the backs of his hands, each one filled with stinging desert dust because he had forgotten to dress them. Stella Kojima, the tall, skinny mission commander who had expressed a reluctance to actually do any commanding now that they had arrived and were eight light years away from Mission Control, was already climbing out of her sleeping bag, stretching her body and cracking her spine. Wednesday Shelley, the youngest of the crew, was always happiest to be awake, and when she noticed Verne standing over her she gave a wide smile and held a sachet up for him to take, squinting at him in the sunlight. Verne ripped the top off the packet and gulped it down in one movement, crushing the thing in his shovel hand and mounting his heavy rucksack on his back.

'Let's move out,' he said, half to himself, as he began to march away from camp.

They had been walking for an hour when they found the bones. There were two broken long bones, thick and beastly, snapped into spikes with their other halves missing; a curved piece of a flat bone, much like part of a skull, also broken into a jagged ashtray shape on the desert floor; and a section of what appeared to be a ribcage, half buried in sand and giving the impression that the complete chest would be bigger than any the crew had ever seen. The entire display lay strewn across an area of a few square metres, next to a dry desert shrub that stood impossibly still in the breeze, as if making an effort not to incriminate itself in the creature's murder.

Shelley dropped everything and ran to the remains, forgetting her aching muscles and unbearable body temperature and tapping her temple to engage the camera mode of her implant.

'Amazing,' she whispered, the twitch of her finger against her temple a constant accompaniment to her wonder. Kneeling, twisting her head this way and then that way and then this way once more, she took tens of photographs each second, trying to capture every angle of the scene as quickly as she possibly could. She looked like a woman crazed by scenes of death. A crash-site groupie, obsessed with chalk outlines.

Verne graced the bones with only a short glance, before going back to scanning the horizon.

Jon Ballard put his rucksack on the ground and joined Shelley in her close-up examination of the bones. Unlike

Shelley, he seemed unsure of what to do with their discovery – he knelt on the floor and stared at each bone in turn, his mouth gaping and his eyes wide as wells, but he took no action to capture the moment. After a while, he reached out to touch one of the ribs, and received a sharp slap to the back of his hand.

'Don't touch it,' Shelley snapped, shooting yet another angle of the display from over his shoulder.

Kojima took the chance to rest her legs, placing her rucksack on the floor and sitting on top of it and pulling out a tiny bottle of synthesised water with which to moisten her tongue. She rolled her eyes at the desert ahead of them as if to ask it what the fuss was about, and then she sat staring out at it in silence.

Shelley was now scraping a sample of matter from each bone and placing the samples inside sealed plastic containers. 'When the computer is repaired,' she mumbled, mostly to herself, 'we can analyse these.'

She had mentioned repairing the computer several times since the crew had arrived, but none of the other crew members were so sure that it would ever come to be. The computer had malfunctioned well before the crash had damaged it, that much was certain – it had initiated their waking from cryosleep when it was already in this planet's orbit, when it should have woken them days earlier; and just hours later, without having fully mapped the terrain below or provided the crew with logs to review or even any kind of information on why it was doing so, it announced that it was preparing their landing craft for launch and that this launch was in emergency mode and could not be overridden. They had been forced to rush through their checks and preparations and strap themselves in, feeling flustered and panicked, and then they had been ejected into the atmosphere of this planet to find that the computer's miscalculation of the distance to the ground and location of a safe landing site had hurled them into a crash course with hard ground and hot fire that could have left them just as damaged as the computer. Only a few small parts of it – the storage, a couple of sensors, a portable scanning unit – remained, and they sat useless, dented and scratched in Shelley's bag, waiting for someone with the know-how and will to save them and find out what had happened.

Being a computer scientist by trade, Ballard could probably have done it on Earth, but where he would find the tools and the power and the resources to do so on this planet was anyone's guess. Verne would not have known where to start. It was unclear whether Kojima cared if the computer was saved or not – when asked, she seemed to have no opinion whether it should be brought with them or left behind in the wreckage.

Either because he forgot his previous instruction or because he thought it no longer applied, Ballard reached out once again to lift one of the long bones, curious to feel its weight in his hand. But again, Shelley's hand hit his away.

'I said don't touch,' she hissed, 'you'll contaminate it. Besides, we don't know why it's here or how it died. Treat this like a crime scene.'

Ballard laughed nervously. Had the crew been given more time to get to know each other before they departed, he might have known that she was at most only half serious, and would not have felt so embarrassed. But he did not know this, so he sat feeling scolded and meek, like a child on the naughty step, while Shelley continued to scrape bone matter into her tubes.

'We should move on,' said Kojima, receiving an agreeing nod from Verne; so Shelley stood and closed her eyes tightly, sliding her finger along her temple, cycling through a slideshow behind her eyelids of the photographs she had taken. Satisfied that she had captured the scene sufficiently, she swiped down her skin to close the camera and opened her eyes once again. She added the vials she had just filled to the collection in her rucksack and followed excitedly, her slim legs skipping with the glee of finding something in this endless desert that was not just a rock or a weed.

When the rest began to walk on, Ballard was still kneeling by the bones. Before he stood to catch up, he picked up the skull-bone ashtray and slid the tips of his fingers over its surface, feeling its flawless smoothness, taking it in like a blind man might take in words embossed into paper. The bone had so much history, such a story to tell; and now it was his. He shoved it into one of the many side pockets of his backpack, and followed the team east.

Before evening had arrived, another storm began. They had survived two since they arrived, one bad, one not so bad; and both times, they could never have predicted it. Sun and clear skies gave way in an instant to a wall of hot, blowing sand stretched from floor to sky as far as the eye could see, and this wall tore through the landscape, scratching the face and hands and threatening to rip out the eyeballs and take them on its merry way. Not there, and then there in a second, and then an hour or so later not there again, like a natural marauder storming through desert villages. On and then off, like a switch. During the first storm, the bad one, they had still had their sleds, so they built a makeshift wall of defence behind which to shield themselves. The second, not so bad, they had slept through, and woken to find their sleeping bags filled with sand, dried leaves and sweat.

But this one looked like it might become worse than the worst that they had seen. The sand was coarser, its speed greater, its rage fiercer. The roar of it was deafening. They had been looking north at a large building that stood alone in the vast desert, wondering if they should expend energy trying to reach it when from here it just looked like ruins; and out of nowhere, before any of them had even had time to point at it on the horizon, the storm had been on them, around them, against them, trying its hardest to get inside them; and then they were running against it, trying to reach shelter, somewhere to rest and not drown in dust and sand.

Running, running, as close to running as they could get, each of them holding on to the closest body, a human chain shielding its eyes and forever pushing forward, forward, forward, they searched for a wall, a crevice, a rock to hide behind. One arm held against their foreheads, one holding on to the person in front, they followed Verne into the stream of hot dust, yelling instructions to each other, suggestions, directions, anything, and none were heard above the scream of the storm. Ghosts in the boiling blizzard, barely touching the ground as they howled toward safety.

Safety was a crack in the ground, twenty feet long and three feet wide, partially covered by a boulder the size of a minibus.

Verne stood at the mouth of that crevice, ushering them in, as the others climbed one by one into its darkness, allowing themselves to be swallowed by that rocky womb, dropping to the hard floor below where the storm above was just a gushing roar like a furious waterfall and a soft trickle of dirt down the walls within. Once inside the gap, so much more spacious underground than it appeared on the surface, the crew fell to their knees or buttocks, panting and thanking their gods or luck or nature for saving them. Verne stood with his hands on his knees for a long time, staring at the floor, seeming comatose, before sitting on a jut out of the stone wall and setting about emptying his rucksack of items and dust and then refilling it.

Shelley seemed to be taking the storm personally, huffing and puffing as she brushed the grey coating off her skin and clothes as if it had all been sent to inconvenience her. 'I am fuckin' sick of this desert,' she said, her Australian accent thickening with frustration.

Kojima smiled darkly and said, 'Well, if it keeps going like this, we'll be leaving it soon, and meeting up in the afterlife instead.'

Ballard considered the possibility that they might die here, and was filled with a feeling of dread like none he had ever felt before.

Shelley smiled too. 'Bullshit,' she said, 'we'll find the city tomorrow. I'd put money on it.'

'Your money is no good to me here.'

Shelley laughed. 'Good point,' she said. Her eyes were closed, her finger swiping across her temple.

That night, Verne woke alert, as if satisfied by the sleep he'd had, and after his eyes had adjusted to the darkness he watched a great long arm reach down into the crevice from above. It had fingers like yardsticks and an elbow as thick as a mechanical digger's, and the entire arm was covered in a thin, black, matted fur. Its claws scratching the air, unable to grasp anything below, the owner withdrew, held its face to the crack, shone its deep black eyes like polished coal into the mouth of the Conquerors' cave. The storm raged on, battering the creature at gale force with red-hot rock, but the hairy thing remained unfazed, eyeing the visitors to its land like it might be curious to find out how their skin would tear. Verne slowly, silently reached for his gun and raised it to point at the mouth of the cave as the animal stood on its hind legs, and from what Verne could see at this angle, it was ten feet tall and built bigger than five polar bears.

A chest the size of those ribs that lay half buried not five miles gone. A skull as thick as that cranium.

James Verne's finger rested on the trigger of his gun, ready to bring this alien species one specimen closer to extinction, and the animal watched him do it without seeming to care. It stared down the barrel for a few seconds, most likely trying to work out what exactly it was looking at; but before it had reached a conclusion, its head jerked off to its right, suddenly alarmed, and then it was gone, bounding off in a huge stride that took it away so fast that it seemed as if it had dissolved into the sandstorm.

And then Verne was waking again, to find that his gun was still exactly where he had left it before he fell asleep, propped against the wall of the cave.

When the crew emerged from the crack in the ground the next morning, the sky and the land around them were so serene that one would seem insane suggesting that a storm had ever hit. Shelley stood in the sun, stretching her aching body, craning this way and that, looking up at the white-blue sky and sighing softly, as Ballard and Kojima climbed out in silence, heads hanging low with great post-storm exhaustion. Verne inspected his weapon, his face wearing the deep frown that his disturbing dream of giant monsters had plastered there. The crew wandered in spirographic patterns separately, aimlessly, for some time, looking like cats sniffing for food, licking their wounds, seeking warm spots in which to sit and not move again for the rest of the day.

Until.

'Well,' called Kojima over the implants, after a while, from behind the jagged boulder that topped the crack the crew had slept in, 'I've found something you'll all want to see.'

Joining her on the other side of the huge rock, the crew saw what looked like a half-buried, ill-maintained, but undoubtedly real road, which stretched for miles from this spot, the thick black snake of its form sneaking all the way to the brow of a hill in the distance, where it disappeared into a maze of large rocks that lined the horizon. The crack in which they had slept had been a central reservation in this motorway, before it had collapsed into the ground; and the boulder that covered it was a collection of whichever rock this civilisation had used to build the surface, bunched into a jagged lump as if a giant had squeezed the road like pastry and torn off the rest of it. Beyond the crack, back in the direction from which they had come, there was no road. Just grey and brown and red dirt. Shrubs and dirt and rocks, as far as the implant could capture.

They had found signs of civilisation scattered in the desert already. A scrap of woven fabric here, a broken pipe or severed wire there. Most remarkably, that building in the distance, big as an aeroplane hangar, the memory of which was now almost completely washed away by the drama of the dust storm. But those discoveries had all led nowhere. Roads, on the other hand, always led somewhere. To cities, life, society.

Shelley considered crying, but instead engaged her implant to record the sight. Ballard just stared, grinning. Kojima and Verne, with no time for this sentimentality, started walking toward the horizon.

Suddenly, things did not seem so hopeless. They were here at last, here as they had intended to be, and not here as God's unwanted children, left to die in an alien desert. A black carpet had been laid, and this disused road would be their victory mile, leading them up to the civilisation they had come to visit, come to integrate into, come to experience like no other man could. The trivia of Earth, with its birth certificates and road tax and warring nations and beach towels and organised religion and homophobia and carpentry and adultery and financial markets and virtual reality and bukkake and insurance and gender inequality and Lou Gehrig's disease and every other little thing, suddenly seemed so far below them; for now, more than ever, they were Conquerors, and all the infinite wonders of this world were just one road away.

It was forty-six degrees in the shade, and the road was long. Whatever it had once been topped with had melted away in the heat of a myriad of middays, and what was left behind was an uneven, rocky surface as dry and sharp as the heat that burned into their soaked foreheads; but the crew did not tire. They walked on, slowly, with purpose, sipping water from their synthesisers as fast as it could be created, forever soldiering on toward that hill on the horizon, over which they could already smell, but not yet see, civilisation.

Walking until it felt like they were being cooked in their clothing, potatoes in an oven, legs like lead.

Pushing on because the prize was in reach, over a hill, past some rocks, and all would be revealed today. Not tomorrow, and not at some unknown point in the distant future, but today.

When it was revealed, the brow of the hill and the rock formations that sat atop it conspired to reveal the visitors' prize in stages. First, through a small gap in the top of the wall of stone that surrounded their path, came the tips and tops of buildings. Black and grey and midnight blue spires, wonky points and jagged corners, the dead-straight tops of flat roofs. Touching the sky with their immense height, lifting the spirits with their presence. Then, as a twist in the road left a foot-wide gap in the rocks through which their path snaked, smoke, and rising dust. Smog. Signs of life and activity, pollution and energy. All the ugliness of civilisation, so beautiful to the Conquerors who feared they would never see it again.

Next, as the road turned sharply and the boulders to their right were passed by, the edge of the city exposed itself to them, revealing sprawling suburbs. Smaller buildings, houses, bungalows, huts, as far as one could make out. The city was huge, spread like a quilt over a seventy- or eighty-mile plot. The grid of roads cut lines through the tiny roofs and vehicles and landmarks and who knew what else, all of those just dots from where the Conquerors walked, all patiently waiting for their arrival.

And finally, as they passed the final rock, the huge boulder which sat atop the hill and had, so far, obstructed their view of the city centre and the rest of the suburbs that surrounded it, the last marabou fan was lifted, and the sickening truth was revealed.

The buildings of which they had seen the tops were crumbling, falling, some of them tipping at odd angles and seemingly just waiting for a light wind to come and blow them the rest of the way to the ground. The dust they had seen was rising from buildings which had collapsed, which were collapsing, kicking up earth that would never settle until the city was a heap of dirt and gone forever. The smoke that they thought was man's red fire was really God's black death, rising from the windows of skyscrapers and the wrecks of vehicles and the back yards of suburban homes and drifting into the sky, unseen by any but the Conquerors and of no concern to any who had ever lived here. The towers that still stood were so covered in climbing plant life that they appeared to be great trees, grown hundreds of times bigger than they should have been. Though clearly once inhabited, this place no longer seemed inhabitable. The desolation of what looked to have once been a very large capital stretched as far as light could travel.

Civilisation had left this city decades, if not centuries, ago.

'No,' said Ballard, his throat tight, his stomach somewhere near his ankles.

Verne stood silent, expressionless, without movement.

'I'm sorry,' Kojima said, sitting on her rucksack once again and placing her hands on her knees and hanging her head as if she bore the blame for the wasteland they had found. 'I'm so sorry.'

Shelley sank to her knees, and then to her buttocks, and wept on the hot ground.

DAY 10

A thin sheet of rain trickled down on the town from a sulky grey sky, doing nothing to dull the oppressive heat. The stifling air smelt of smoke and rusted metal, even where there was none of either nearby. Broken machines and dead vehicles, all of them inoperable even if their controls had been decipherable, lay destroyed or damaged across the sides and the middle of the road, or half hanging out of the fronts of buildings, eternally stationary and waiting to be reclaimed by the planet and turned back into rock. Bones lay strewn here and there, stripped of meat and growing from the ground like weeds but more common than weeds, a constant reminder that that skeleton in the desert was not as rare as they had thought, back when they had been so thrilled to find it. Just like all the buildings and shacks they had entered so far – and they had entered many – the road was devoid of reward or comfort, dark and empty like the desert they had left to be here.

The town was not their salvation.

But still, for want of something better to do, the Conquerors kept walking. Feeling, now, less like Conquerors, and more like victims of a cruel prank.

With supplies near enough exhausted, water synthesisers struggling to keep up with demand, stomachs collapsing inward and moods darkening further by the day, the company were desperate to find in this suburb on the outskirts of the city a dwelling which still contained food or drink. This planet had all the ingredients for life, they knew that, but so far, it had kept them mostly hidden. None of the buildings had taps the crew could work out, all of the cupboards and containers had been bare, there was not a stick of furniture in the town, and nothing looked anything like it had been at home. Some of the homes here could seem so familiar, so similar in structure to Earth's, if a little ricketier; and yet, the whole town remained so undeniably alien. Like a picture with something missing. An Uncanny Valley.

So, with hope that each next house would deliver the supplies they needed or the answers they wanted, or both, they walked. And walked. And kept on walking, until they found the hostel.

They did not know it was a hostel at first. It was just a large building on a corner of an intersection, out of place among the smaller houses that surrounded it and decidedly different in style; but with the crew not yet familiar with the architecture or fashion of the world, it could have been a department store or a car showroom or a funeral home as far as they knew. It was four storeys high and no less than sixty metres across, and built from the same material as many of the houses they had entered so far – huge sheets of a very thick wood, taken from a tree that grew many times larger than Earth's average, a living example of which they had yet to find. It wore a metal sign written in a language they had seen only on crumpled road signs, and the sign had been half eaten away by rust. The façade of the hostel looked charred as if recently licked by flames, but there seemed to be no visible structural damage.

'This looks promising,' mumbled Kojima, looking back

at her colleagues for agreement.

Ballard smiled politely, a tired and forced smile which fell within seconds to make way for that sulky expression he wore more and more now that the grim truth had sunk in. Verne gave a single nod of absolute agreement, and then walked past Kojima. Shelley was grinning, engaging her implant's camera, forever excited about the next discovery.

The crew forced open the door and stepped inside the dark entrance hall. While Shelley hunted along the walls and floor for a gadget which might activate some lights, if there was still a power supply at all, Kojima performed a trick of her own: slashing all of the window blinds and ripping down any boards that had been nailed up to replace them, to let the natural light flood in, in the absence of its electrical substitute.

The lines of light that sliced their way through the floating dust and lint in the entrance hall of the hostel landed on a floor painted in neon colours, a gaudy and scattered pattern, dusty and chipped now, but still retaining some small amount of the glory it must once have had. The floors above them looked down onto the reception hall from balconies with intricately carved wooden handrails, taller than they would have been on Earth, as were all the ceilings, doors and walls of this planet. The foyer had a plant in a container in the centre which received light from a hole in the roof which may or may not have been in the building's design; and after such a long time without anyone to control it, the plant had grown out of the container and now its spindly green-black arms crawled along the painted floor and up the walls and across the windows like veins spreading under the skin, reaching out to grab the heart and drain it of all its contents.

This foyer, with its darkened screens and its useless input devices that had never existed on twenty-second century Earth, seemed like something from The Future, to this crew from The Past.

Following the days of endless destroyed and deserted homes, empty of everything but walls and dust and piles of decaying waste, the hostel was intensely exciting to the Conquerors, who immediately and excitedly fanned out, searching for sustenance or treasure.

Ballard climbed a ramp – there had been no stairs in any of the buildings so far – to explore the first floor, treading carefully as if loud noises would wake the building from its slumber and spell disaster for everybody. The first door he found was jammed shut from within, objects piled up against it so heavy and tall that the door was reluctant to budge more than a few inches, and even when it did, he could see nothing through the darkness within. Even if he had been able to slide it open, he suspected that the objects pushing it against its frame would fall and kill him. He wondered what could be in there, whether there was a dead inhabitant who had barricaded themselves in and never left. More disturbing, he wondered if they were still alive and could sense him standing there. He imagined this alien creature slowing its breath, freezing in position on the other side of the door, listening to Ballard doing exactly the same thing. His heart rate climbed and his brow moistened and it was almost a minute before he thought to remind himself that the situation was an imaginary one, and that he should move on before he fell any further down that hole.

The door to the next room was half open, so Ballard slid straight through the gap it left. The room was a perfect cube with a window covered by shredded blinds and hanging fittings which let enough light in so that Ballard could see a bed, much larger than any he had seen before, with no mattress or covering of any kind. It looked like a simple rectangular block of wood, heavy and hard in the corner of the room. Apart from the bed, there seemed to be nothing else in the room but space – an automatic sliding door in the opposite wall sat tilted and broken, partially revealing empty storage space behind it, and there was a similar sliding door to Ballard's left which was closed, but led only to another, smaller, emptier room. The only detail of note was the art, which lined every square inch of the walls and floor. Some of it beautiful, some of it dull, some of it confusing, it was faded and dusty but just like the floor in the lobby, he found it somewhat moving to see. Someone or something had painted this here, and now that someone or something was probably dead.

'I've made a discovery,' said Shelley, over the implants. 'Furniture. Or maybe just some big cubes of wood.'

Ballard smiled. 'Me too,' he replied.

'Have you tried moving it? This is heavy stuff,' said Kojima, joining in from downstairs.

Shelley had stumbled across what might have been the hostel's bar or canteen, a large hall with furniture scattered and beaten and rotting away, and a stage at the front in an even worse state of disrepair. The room was black with dust and folding inwards – much of the ceiling was dipping in the centre by several metres, ready to fall for good at any moment, and the banners and decorations hung drab and brown from the walls and ceiling like branches of a willow tree, decomposing or already decomposed. Still, Shelley felt that same once-upon-a-time feeling Ballard was experiencing in the art-covered hostel rooms above, as she imagined this room full of people (for without having seen any examples of this planet's dominant species, she had only people to imagine), heaving with life and activity, music and laughter, before whatever the event was that drove them from here stomped its angry feet, and the structures they had built and the city they had inhabited were all left to rot away. They might have laughed in here, been angry in here, had love affairs and squabbles and dreams come true in here, and now they were gone. The image was as captivating as it was depressing.

But somewhere in the back of her mind, she still felt quite glad that, unlike those lost souls, she was going to be remembered by her planet. That now, she had made sure of it.

She walked slowly, recording everything, and running her finger over the surface of a hip-high round table, sweeping through a layer of dust and rock an inch thick. It was only a couple of steps before her index finger snagged on something, brushed a corner that did not feel as hard as rock or as soft as dust. She stopped walking and brushed the table with both hands, sweeping the smaller debris and grit onto the floor and searching underneath for what she might have touched. Once found, she lifted it and held it up to a beam of light that was pouring through one of the floor-to-ceiling windows that lined the west side of the room.

It was a trinket, a tiny toy perhaps, carved from some kind of wood, no bigger than a human thumb. It had intricate markings and so many edges that Shelley could hardly guess whether it was a figurine of an animal or a strange sort of die, but its mere presence was enough to fill her with a satisfying kind of wonder.

She began excitedly brushing all of the tables, her hands quickly turning black with the dust, looking for more lost tokens of the missing civilisation. None of the other tables had anything of the sort sitting atop them, but still, she was exhilarated. She felt like she had found something which would reveal some enlightening fact just by being held, as if the toy had some mystical power, and the voice in her head that was saying this spoke louder than the one that told her it was just a piece of carved wood with nothing to say. Wandering further across the room, she reached the stage, and sat on its edge, examining her prize with joy. She was about to radio the others, when the ceiling fell down in the centre of the room, crushing several tables and creating a cloud of dust which instantly reclaimed the hands she had just brushed clean.

'What's your status?' said Kojima, her voice stern and

invasive over the implants. 'I heard a crash.'

'That was in here,' replied Shelley, still coughing from the dust. 'Roof collapsed. Christ. Fuckin' hell.'

'But you're okay?'

'Erm…' Shelley said, pausing. 'Yeah. I suppose. Apart from a lungful of shit, it's all fine.'

'Roger that. Watch your step.'

Kojima was exploring the rooms behind the hostel foyer, having kicked in a door behind the reception desk and found her way into the maintenance corridors. There were rooms that had an obvious use and rooms whose purpose was a mystery, but even those in the former category seemed like they must be red herrings – it was equally logical and unthinkable that this race's building design would be so easily decipherable, that they would build things for the same reasons that humans did, as if these things were not decided *by* humanity but *for* it. Logical, because man only built, say, toilets in separate rooms in order to preserve their privacy and keep the smell and the waste out of the other rooms, so it followed that an intelligent species on another planet would make the same kind of sensible decisions; but unthinkable, because surely the Conquerors had not come three hundred light years to look at such familiar mundanities as ill-maintained roads and staff common rooms. Surely, if there was justice in the universe, there would be some deeper discovery than that.

And these were things that Kojima thought about, as she searched through empty storage units in alien linen closets, unknowingly working her way toward the food store.

Below her, in the well-hidden basement of the hostel, James Verne found himself in what seemed to be a large room used for storing the remains of burned and partially shredded books and scrolls. The books could not have been burned here – the flames would have licked the ceiling and swallowed the building with the books – but this was where they were stored, in five piles, as if by someone who wanted to be rid of them but did not want them to be gone forever. The piles stood as high as Verne's chest, books and scrolls and who knew what else – some of them still almost completely intact – just waiting to be discovered.

He took a book from the top of the nearest pile and opened it up to find a kind of cloth-like paper of which there had been no example he had ever seen on Earth. The words were tiny and did not follow a straight line either across or down the page, so Verne had no inkling how it should be read; he just allowed his eyes to wander over the pages, seeing what they would, trying his hardest to imagine what these people might write about. And, obviously, failing.

He did this with a few more books, and he took a few scrolls and unravelled those too, not really looking for anything but feeling a childlike excitement deep in his chest that he had not felt in years and of which he did not really know the origin. Like Ballard with his empty hostel rooms and Shelley with her useless trinket, Verne felt privileged to have discovered something that nobody else knew, down here: that the people who lived here had written, and written much, and read and learned and passed on all their knowledge and stories and instructions and superstitions just like Verne's people did, before he jumped on a spaceship and left them forever. He wondered what secrets could be uncovered from these volumes, how many words and ideas and lives were wrapped up in these pages and documents and leaflets. This room, to his mind, held the key to this entire world, and he was sure that Shelley, when shown, would be the one to turn it.

But soon there was an interruption. A voice, calling his name.

'Verne!'

For a moment, his mind was lost in the piles and the scrolls and the dimness of the basement, and he barely recognised the sound. He kept on browsing the book he had in his hand, kept his shoddy little torch pointed at those indecipherable words scrawled on its pages.

'Verne, where are you?'

He recognised it this time, but like a child with a video game or a sports fan with a play-off, he did not want to be dragged away, and though he said, 'Hmm?' as if that alone would be a satisfactory reply, he made no effort to make himself known to whoever was calling his name. He wanted to take in as much as he could. Before he left the basement, he wanted to find and pocket the most intriguing book he could find, to entice Shelley into returning with him. For she was the one who wanted to crack the code of this lost civilisation, she was the one with the passion and the fire and the knowledge.

'*Verne!* What are you *doing*, man?!'

'Verne?'

'Verne, are you in the building?'

With the pressure of all three of his colleagues calling his name, Verne gave up and decided he would just take the book in his hand. But as he did so, slapping it shut in his big paw and turning to walk toward the entrance to the basement, he suddenly felt a peculiar feeling, as if he had caught sight of someone he knew, or had seen something in the middle of the books that did not belong. That feeling of seeing a relative in a crowd, then realising that that particular relative has been dead for years.

He looked back, but he could not find the feeling's source, so he gave up and climbed the ramp to the entrance of the basement. He could return later to find that which had rattled his cage.

'I wish you had an implant,' said Kojima, far down the corridor. The two others were standing with her, Ballard mimicking Kojima's faux-exasperation and Shelley almost vibrating with excitement.

'Come through here,' said Shelley. 'We have food!'

Kojima began to walk off, and Ballard followed at a slower pace. Shelley grinned, looking at Verne with wide eyes.

'Come *on*, Verne!' she said, like an impatient child.

Verne replied with a grunt and a nod, and when the rest had wandered off, he looked back down the ramp at those piles of damaged books. Unsettled, wondering exactly what had triggered that feeling of familiarity in that deeply unfamiliar place, he lifted his gun and looked it over, turning it around in his hand as if he might have mistaken it for a thing that should not have been there. But that wasn't it. He scanned the piles and the room one more time, standing and looking and breathing and doing not much of anything else, but without having the strange thing jump once again into his eyeline, he only had his imagination to put it down to, and so he ascended to join the others.

Stella Kojima had found a cold room filled with more food than the crew could ever have hoped to find in one place, completely clean of the dust and detritus that filled the rest of the building. Piled and stacked and portioned on the floor, tables and shelves, the food waited for them in cans and sachets and on blocks of wood from floor to ceiling. They felt like they had stumbled across Aladdin's cave for the starving. Ballard and Shelley were already eating; whether or not they had tested the food for toxins or contaminants before diving in, Verne did not know. They knew more than he did about using the gadgets with which their backpacks were filled, so he decided they deserved some small amount of trust. However, this did little to suppress the rest of his doubts.

'That looks fresh,' he said, pointing at the bright purple fruit out of which Shelley was taking a huge, dripping bite. 'How has fresh fruit lasted in here?'

They all looked at Shelley, who frowned, but did not stop eating.

'This could be a collection that someone or something is coming back for,' Kojima replied slowly, finishing Verne's thought for him.

'It's a strong possibility. In which case, do we want to be here when it returns?'

Shelley shrugged, and spoke with her mouth full. 'I haven't eaten properly for days. If it's a choice between dying of starvation because we were polite or risking *possible* death by eating a few pieces of fruit, I'll chance the latter.'

They all stood in silence, considering their options; the only sound that of Shelley and Ballard's chewing.

'She has a point,' said Kojima, shrugging her shoulders and filling her backpack with sachets of which she had no idea what the contents were. 'Let's take as much as we can, and move on when we're done.'

Verne stood watching for a while, and then he joined them, in lieu of beating them.

That night, they ate and they talked and at one or two moments they almost laughed, sitting in a circle in that room full of food. Ballard spoke of the room whose door he could not force open, and Shelley of her imaginary party in the hall with the falling roof. Verne gave Shelley her book, to her immense pleasure, and Kojima reiterated her disbelief that they were here, that this planet was so habitable without being inhabited, that any of the impossible things that had got them here were true and had happened. There was joviality in the air, though they were tired and their bones and heads ached, because something had finally gone their way. They had travelled for almost one thousand Earth years, frozen in a hurtling tomb, and landed on a planet that they thought would be heaving with life, only to find it empty and wide, with smoke in the air and ash on the ground. But now, their modest gifts were bringing them boundless joy. Now they had books, food, and a building that actually appeared lived-in. Evidence that there might have been life here, that there might *be* life here.

And when they were done, only James Verne and Stella Kojima remained awake. The excitement had died down, their stomachs were full, and they sat in silence for a long time.

Kojima sighed, as if she had been arguing with herself in her head and had been unable to reach a conclusion, so now she required Verne's intervention. 'What do we do now?' she asked.

'We just keep going,' he replied, speaking slowly and quietly, 'like we have been. We survive as long as we can, and we try to learn as much as we can, and the more we learn, the longer we'll survive.'

'And then?'

'And then one day we'll all die here.'

Kojima sighed again. 'We were supposed to find life here. Not just fight for survival until we can't fight any more.'

'Hey,' Verne replied, his tone flat, 'don't knock it. Some people on Earth can't hope for any more than that, and they didn't get to live the lives we did when we were back there. We're lucky enough. Besides, it could've been worse; we could have stepped off the shuttle and been shot for trespassing.'

Kojima smiled, and then there was a silence.

'Do you think they regret it?' Kojima asked, gesturing toward the two sleeping crew members.

'Not much they can do about it now.'

Kojima smiled. 'It's okay for us, we had sixty years on Earth before we left for this wasteland—'

'Seventy.'

'But these two are what, twenty-five? Thirty? And they took a one-way ticket to a distant planet, only to find it completely abandoned. I don't know if I could have handled it, at their age. If they had known…'

Verne was silent for a long time. He tried thinking about

himself at that age, but found that he could remember little to think about. He could not recall what he was doing or where he had lived, and this made him feel like something had been ripped out of him that he had not even realised was ever there. Like he had lost something, but could not rouse himself to miss it.

So he shrugged, and said again, 'Not much they can do about it now.'

Kojima chuckled. 'Go to sleep, Verne. I'll take the night shift.'

So he did. But as he rested his head after all the eating and all the listening, he still had a nagging feeling nibbling at his mind. What was it that had caught his eye, down there in that basement so full of an alien culture's history and fiction? What did he see that his eyes had not quite captured but his mind had wriggling in a bag that it refused to open up? Why was it bothering him so much?

And as his mind drifted away and his muscles gave in to the soft pull of deep sleep, the image at which he had glanced flashed before him once again, just when he was powerless to do anything about it. One of the piles of ashes and paper down there had a sketch of a hand, half open, a whole page wide, resting on top of its books as if it had been ripped from one of them and discarded by someone who did not believe in it. Verne realised, in that moment halfway between being awake and asleep, that he had seen a human hand, perfectly drawn, in a torn-out page of a book from another planet.

And then he was gone.

JANUARY 5TH, 2123

Stella Kojima threw her bag into the cab before she climbed in herself, hoping that the machine would be fooled by the weight of the rucksack and would finish its small talk before she decided to board. She leaned on the roof and closed her eyes and inhaled a heavy lungful of the warm night air, the vague hint of a breeze tickling her skin and her thin, short hair as if to mock her for having the hottest apartment on Earth. A dog barked in another street and somewhere in her own apartment block above her a young girl was cackling between bursts of such fast speech that it seemed as if she was a recording playing at double speed, and already Kojima felt a little better, a little less crowded by thoughts. It was true that her anxieties needed no trigger to enter her head, but loneliness, and that dank apartment of hers, were the conspirators that let them through the door.

Having finally had enough of the midnight air, still as humid and thick as it had been in mid-afternoon, Kojima let go of the dusty roof of the autocab and climbed in to sit on the long front seat.

The cab had not been fooled.

'Hello, Ms Kojima,' it said, and a smiling cartoon face

appeared on the dashboard screen in front of her as the doors locked either side. 'How are you this evening?'

Kojima hated being greeted by name by machines. This was, in part, due to articles she had read on the threat that a sentient AI would pose to its own creators, sensational and poorly researched prophecies written again and again over the last century or more which, despite remaining unfulfilled to this day, had made for themselves a permanent home in her mind, and which would make it their business to be the focus of her thoughts whenever a relevant topic was brought up in conversation; but mainly, it was that she found it rude for anyone to refer to her by name before ever having been introduced, so robots were no exception. It made her feel like some amount of privacy had been eroded, like she was being watched by someone or something somewhere and all this was being logged to be used against her one day. It was true that some of the things she thought and said would have people around her believing that she wore a tinfoil hat to bed, but they hadn't lived through the childhood she had, so they did not know like she did how precious their freedom and privacy were, how tightly they should be gripped.

'I'm fine. Let's get there quickly, please,' Kojima replied, tapping a panel on the door to open her window as wide as it would go.

'Certainly, Ms Kojima.'

The car pulled away from the kerb and started its journey silently, its smooth ride more like that of a travelator than the classic automobiles which still lined the streets of Kojima's country of birth.

'Hey,' it continued, 'would you like a summary of the day's headlines? In world news, we have at least forty killed by bombings in—'

'No chat,' Kojima interrupted, before the machine could list more terrible things she should dwell upon.

'Certainly, Ms Kojima.'

The cab was silent for a second, and then it said, 'Deactivating chat.'

Kojima sighed and leaned her head back and allowed the warm air to rush through the window against her face. There hadn't been a cool night in months, not a single evening with a refreshing breeze. Kojima found it impossible to sleep in a hot room; she could never seem to get cool enough for her mind to relax. Contorting amongst the sheets with swollen blood vessels and a sticky film of sweat on her skin, she would think about nothing but all of the war and the violence and the unfairness of the world and oppression and sadness and death and how it was all so impossible to escape and how it just seemed to be getting worse, and no matter how she tried to distract herself the thoughts would keep coming back like that big pink elephant you had been told not to think about but which you inevitably did and her scalp would grow hot and itchy and she would want to cry as if that would change anything, and in the end she would always end up in an autocab, cruising silently along Thiruvananthapuram's empty midnight roads, travelling back towards the empty laboratories of the India Space Research Organisation.

But tonight, it hadn't even been that. It had been the dream. The dream that she had had thrice this year already, the dream so vivid that it felt like she was right there, the thick rain trickling down her face, the world falling down around her—

'Hey,' said the cab suddenly, breaking Kojima out of her introspection with a start, 'would you like me to turn the screen off? I see you're trying to sleep.'

Kojima frowned at the grinning face on the dashboard and sighed heavily.

'I don't care,' she replied, 'and I said no chat. Stop talking to me.'

'Certainly, Ms Kojima,' replied the voice, and the screen turned off.

Kojima tried once again to put her head back and close her eyes, but she could not shake her frustration. After a few seconds, she sighed again and snapped, 'And stop watching me.'

'Certainly, Ms Kojima,' replied the machine.

Then, after too long a pause, the machine said, 'Disabling camera-based notifications.'

And she supposed that that was the best she could hope for.

When the autocab pulled up in front of the building, she climbed out before it could proudly announce that they had reached their destination safely (as if that should be cause for celebration and not just part of the routine), and before it had the opportunity to play an advertisement for deodorant or blackhead cream or body modification on its screens. She reached in and retrieved her rucksack, heavy with books and papers she would never get through, and strolled into the car park in front of the labs, wondering if any amount of work or distraction would take away that dark feeling in her gut, that thick weight around her neck left by the dream she had had, the state she was in.

She looked up at the building, once so grand and now so aged, and it all replayed in her mind once again.

She stood in a busy street, a steady stream of people brushing past her this way and that like fish down a river, seemingly unaware of her presence. A child's hand sat limply in her own, and the tiny girl to whom it belonged stood staring up at Kojima through eyes wide with expectation. Kojima had never seen the girl before – she had no children of her own, no nieces or cousins or friends with young children – but somehow, with the certainty one can only attain in dreams, she knew that the girl was her responsibility. That she alone had been trusted with keeping her safe, showing her the way.

She looked again across the road at the great building

opposite them, a red-brick palace like some huge countryside house in England that Kojima had only ever seen in films. It was a school, a good school, the best in the country; and the girl would start there today. Kojima swelled with pride, felt elated to play a part in the start of life's great adventure for this little girl she had never met before; and the girl shared this excitement, hopping and skipping along next to Kojima as they began to fight through the flow of people to cross the street and reach the school gates.

But a feeling of doubt grew within Kojima, that pride tainted by darkness, as they stood waiting for a gap in the traffic to allow them to cross. What if the school was not right for the girl? What if she was too smart, or not smart enough, and the speed of the teaching stifled her or left her far behind the rest? What if the other children were nasty, or the teachers inept? These worries flooded over Kojima like ice water poured over her head, so drenching and sudden that she would have missed the opportunity to cross the busy road, had the girl not pulled her along in her excitable rush.

She was being silly, she knew. These were worries every parent or guardian had on their child's first day at school, out there in the great unknown for the first time. *And it must be a lot worse for them*, she thought; *this girl isn't even my own blood. No, she'll be fine. This will be good for her.*

Still, she had trouble letting go of the girl's hand, once the fighting through crowds of people was done and they stood at the gates and the girl jumped from foot to foot, eager to leave Kojima and head inside. The worry had returned, but this time it was different: wider, more general. What did the future hold for this girl? What would the world look like when Kojima was too old to protect her from its darkness, or when she was gone entirely? How could Kojima let her go now, when she knew that one day she would have to leave her forever? Why waste this time, so precious and fleeting?

But she had to. If she loved the girl, if she wanted her to flourish and live and experience and survive on her own, she had to let her go. And she did love this girl, in her dream. She did want her to flourish, to live and love and invent and explore and survive, so she let her go, and watched as she skipped away, into the crowd of little boys and little girls, all running and walking and hopping excitedly toward their next big adventure.

However, as the girl merged into the heavy traffic of enthusiastic children, the clear sky turned grey, the sunshine dulled by clouds, and darkness and fear shrouded Kojima once again, stronger than ever. Suddenly, she knew without doubt that she had given the girl up to a fate somehow worse than death. She did not know exactly what awaited the children inside that building, but she knew that it would be painful and fearsome, that they would suffer and scream and feel sadness like never before, that this was no school at all. She had to stop the child, had to save her.

She forced her way into the throng, pushed past skipping girls and running boys, trying desperately to find the girl among the vast sea of dresses that looked the same, hairstyles that were identical. She called out to the girl, screamed her name into the flood of children, and none turned in response. The sky darkened and churned in a thick black stew of clouds above them and the building toward which they were rapidly making their way decayed, transforming gradually from a huge country manor into a crumbling, haunted mansion. Everything was falling apart, the sky was caving in, the future was misty and dark for these children; yet still, they ran toward it with excitement and joy, and Kojima could not save a single one of them, much less the whole lot.

Though she fought against the flow of the crowd, begged them all to turn back, searched for the face of her little girl on every passing body, the herd kept moving, and eventually, she reached the doors of the building. She accepted then, with grave disappointment, that her fight was lost, and she stood in front of the building in despair, tears running down her cheeks and children stepping on her feet as they ran past. The excitable crowd thinned to a trickle and then to nothing, and once every child had disappeared inside the building, Kojima dropped to her knees, drained, and sobbed on the ground in front of that dark, evil place. She sobbed for the children, for their blissful ignorance of the doom that lay ahead of them, for their souls which would gradually be worn down just like the building itself, and for the future, which seemed so bleak and inescapable.

Rain fell down upon her, and she sobbed into her lap, as the parents and guardians of all the other children walked away feeling proud of themselves and happy for their children, not seeing, or wilfully ignoring, the building rotting away in front of them or the sky falling in around them, and Kojima was alone in her devastation, just like all the times before.

Gazing up at the office building, with its corners and edges darkened by neglect and its windows grimy with dust and age, she wondered idly how long it would be before this building looked just as dishevelled as the one from that dream. If it was a dream at all – it had felt more like a broadcast, beamed directly to her brain. Like a virtual-reality video game that she could not control; the colours so vivid, the smells so close, everything as real as the air she felt around her right now.

She sighed. Her anxiety had taken hold again. She had known it for months now, but had not been willing to accept it. But now, with the dreams, and the sensitivity that left her wanting to cry at random times during the day for almost no reason at all, and the sleepless nights, and the obsessions that caused it all, there was too much evidence to ignore.

She and this anxiety were not strangers. She had lived with it in one form or another her entire life. Phases of deep depression would rise and fall like the empires of ambitious nations inside her head, taking over her every waking moment for months at a time and then going away to be replaced by bigger worries or, rarely, an inexplicable calm before the next storm. First, she had been worried that an automated car in which she was riding would hit someone and she would be blamed. That was in her teens. She had been so scared of being held responsible for the death of someone she could never have saved that she had avoided cars altogether, riding her bicycle everywhere and refusing to carpool with friends or colleagues even if it meant being spoken about behind her back or being thought of as strange. She had never spoken to another soul about that bout of anxiety, and after a couple of years of being ruled by it, it had gone away without her noticing.

Then it had been replaced by a fear of catching diseases from objects which had been touched by strangers. She would convince herself that there were ways that everyday situations could give her horrific illnesses, and that it was only a matter of time until she caught something terminal and there was no way it could be avoided. Worst was the time she saw a spot of red on a public toilet's tap, which she had just turned on. In her warped mental state, she imagined that this red spot was blood, and that this tap had recently been used by someone with HIV, who had a cut on their finger. Kojima had just used that tap; if she had between then and now unwittingly scratched a cut on her own skin, the droplet of blood she had picked up from the tap would end up in her bloodstream and before she knew it…

That fear was debilitating. She could not do anything outside of her own apartment without worrying about the consequences, or inventing terrifying deaths for herself as a result of tenuous, almost entirely imagined situations. She had no regard for science or statistics or rational thought – the only thing that felt real was that impending doom. The invention and fear and invention and fear formed a cycle that was never-ending and all-consuming and after nearly five years of living like that, she saw a counsellor and spoke about what she was feeling, and how it was taking over her life, and she felt close to normal again within months. She just needed to talk, she realised. She needed to hear how ridiculous her fears were when spoken out loud, and then she might manage to live without them.

But she had had other fears since then. Fears of having her identity stolen, fears of AI, fears of government surveillance and fears of hitmen hunting her down for crimes unknown. It was something that came and went, that she might never be free from – this much she had accepted by now. She could not afford to spend money on counselling each time, and she did not have the time to spare two hours a week to talk about her issues when all she wanted to do was spend that time moving forward, running on, hoping that none of her terrors could catch her.

So, here she was. She had recently celebrated her sixty-second birthday – if celebrating was the appropriate word, when she had only realised it had crept up the day after it had already passed – and it was three years now since she had developed her latest fear: that the world was ending soon, and humans were the ones ending it.

She feared nuclear war. She thought one was coming, that this latest Cold War that America and Russia were fighting – their fourth – would be the one to end up in their mutual destruction, with half of the rest of the world caught in the crossfire. She feared global warming, the climate change that humans were causing, and its effect on life on Earth. She feared mass migration and religious fanaticism, insane dictators and overpopulation. Sometimes, it felt like this new fear encompassed everything, that she was now scared of simply living on this planet; and just a few seconds of rolling news would convince her that this was the case without the need for any more persuasion.

Rolling news. The nemesis of a happy life. Designed to keep everyone in the civilised world terrified, so that they give the rich and powerful all of their money and support to do whatever they can to take away the fear. Kojima knew it was a trick, but still, it claimed her as its victim. Knowing she was under their control did not make their grip on her any weaker; it just piled self-loathing on top of that exhausting fear.

She wondered how there was anyone who was not as afraid as she was, when these twenty-four-hour news channels which had become such unstoppable villains in her head played on the screens in bars, in gyms, in airports. When even the places people went to relax were thickened with the tension of breaking news and special reports.

The world was obsessed; everyone else was desperate to be up-to-date on death and destruction all day every day, and Kojima was suffering from overexposure.

But she had not come here to stand and sulk over these facts; she had come to escape them. She sighed the thoughts out and entered the building and made herself a coffee in the cramped kitchen downstairs, then carried her oversized mug up the stairs to her desk. At her desk, she dropped her bag onto the floor next to her chair and placed her coffee on the desk and told her computer to turn on, the holographic screens unlocking as soon as they recognised her face and bringing up all the programs she had been using at home.

She stared at the screens without doing anything for a long time, her mind and body blank as if this was the first time that she had ever encountered a computer, so to be this close to one was baffling. She saw all the work she had left unfinished before she went to bed and she knew where she could pick it up again if she were to try, but there was no drive within her to do so. She had been performing calculations for fuel requirements for *Conqueror 23* – which had been her day job before she was asked to act as mission commander for the vessel, and was now just something she did because she wanted to fill every minute of her time – and she had data from other missions on one screen and simulations and adjustments running on the other and she did not know if she could be bothered to pick it up again; but nor did she want to sit there idle, allowing her mind to wander. She took a scalding mouthful of coffee and winced, and was set to place her hands on the projected keyboard on the desk surface when she heard a voice from the empty office ahead of her.

'What are you doing here so late, Commander Kojima?' it said.

Gregor Trusov, mission director of the *Conqueror* missions, stood by the noticeboard two banks of desks away from Kojima, a steaming mug in his hand and a black ISRO-branded *Conqueror* fleece wrapped around his bony frame. He was a short, thin man with no hair, characterised by a skeletal look that made one think he could drop dead at any moment, if he hadn't already; but tonight, he looked worse than ever. He was pale and hunched over, unshaven and wrinkled, his eyes black with exhaustion. He looked like he had not slept for a month.

Kojima stood and walked slowly to join him where he stood. 'Gregor,' she said, 'I thought I'd be here on my… are you okay?'

He smiled, a smile wrought from politeness rather than happiness. He nodded with his eyes closed, and when he opened them he continued to look at the noticeboard mounted on the wall he stood beside. When Kojima reached his side, she joined him in looking at the photograph pinned on the cork board of the mission's previous director, Mohammad Haque.

'Do you know it has been three years?' asked Trusov.

'Yeah,' replied Kojima, looking away from the photograph.

'I wonder what he would say, if he were here now.'

Kojima nodded. 'Me too,' she said.

Mohammad Haque was a genius. An unstoppable force, excitable and passionate and completely dedicated to everything that he did. Following the sale of his automated vehicle empire, he had taken over the abandoned work of NASA's Nexus for Exoplanet System Science, which had spent its time and resources looking at the habitability and characteristics of Earth's nearest exoplanets until it became a casualty of America's collapse in the 2050s, and he had extended this research with modern technology and expertise to look for far-flung exoplanets and study them in a depth that had never been conceived of before, let alone attempted; and all this, he had done with barely any external funding. This research exploded when he and his small team of enthusiasts had discovered planets which hosted life, life which was intelligent and civilised and of which he could prove the existence beyond all reasonable doubt, and within an hour of the publication of this discovery the India Space Research Organisation had offered him all the offices and resources and tools he would need, if he could only get a ship to one of those planets with their logo printed on the side.

Now equipped with adequate funding and space, his team found more exoplanets, and they put huge telescopes aboard satellites and sent them into orbit to image these new worlds, and they found more civilisations, and the people of Earth were captivated. Like the industrial revolution of the 1700s or the dinosaur renaissance of the 1960s, discovery of alien planets and races was the new obsession for any human with access to news and media. Haque was an overnight sensation, director of a mission he had never expected to lead, discoverer of worlds, a god among men. He turned down financial assistance from corporate sponsors almost daily, welcoming instead help from the European Space Agency and the China National Space Administration, and he was persuaded to send animals in place of robots to these alien lands, and all eyes were on this astonishing project that was the stuff of some far-off future come true today, never expected but dreamt of eternally.

But apart from any of this, he was Kojima's friend. He plucked her from the Japan Air Self-Defense Force in 2113, and gave her the opportunity of a lifetime to return to her passion for mathematics and work on the most incredible space mission the world had ever seen.

He had told her, with sweat running down his brow and his breath short with excitement, that this was the mission to which everything humanity had ever done had led. This was man's fate. It would unite a torn world, bring the warring people of this decaying planet back together and show them how beautiful the universe can be, and how far we all can reach when we work as one. How awesomely powerful humans are, how wonderfully insignificant. His vision had been childlike in its purity, astounding in its simple truth.

And then he had been killed by a roadside bomb on holiday in Thailand, on his way to the airport to come home. And his flame was snuffed out, as if it had never been there at all.

Now, Trusov was the director of the *Conqueror* missions, and he was as much in charge of them as Starbucks or Alphabet or MegaFon were, with their limitless sponsorship and constant pushing for more flights, more worlds, more exposure. The aim now was to get people into space, anyone, and aim them at those planets, and paint an advertisement down the side of their ship so huge that even the aliens they were going to visit would want to buy a grande skinny hazelnut latte and a cinnamon swirl. Now, there were going to be twenty-five *Conqueror* missions, all launching on one day, from launch sites around the world, heading not just for the five planets Haque had identified as definitely hosting intelligent life, but also the twenty he had identified as 'probably' hosting 'some form of life'. The vision that Haque once had had been lost in corporate deals and the desperate grab for column inches before his body had even been buried.

Kojima could imagine what Mohammad Haque would think of the missions now. Even through the blinding fog of her own excitement about commanding one of the *Conqueror* missions in just over a year's time, to the one planet which was populated by life so intelligent it had broadcast messages directly to Earth, she could tell he would not approve. She knew that he would be saddened that his vision had been diluted, that it was no longer pure achievement and was now partial advertisement, just like everything else.

'Have you heard about this explosion in Moscow?' asked Trusov, without looking away from the picture.

'I have,' Kojima lied. She supposed that it was probably the one the autocab had tried to tell her about, and she hoped that claiming to have heard about it would cut the conversation short.

'This world isn't what you think it is when you are a child,' said the Russian mission director, sipping from his MegaFon-branded mug, so big in his frail-looking hand.

'No.'

'It isn't what you think it is when you are an adult, either.'

'No. That's true enough.'

'I don't know what it is.'

Kojima nodded. She was not sure whether she should offer her sympathy for the bombing to Trusov – on one hand, he was a native of the country it had hit; but on the other, he had not lived there for twenty years, and she knew that he had never lived anywhere near Moscow. Offering her sympathy was surely the same, then, as offering it to any man in the street. The same as offering it to a mule, or a desk lamp. Plus, she did not want to extend the conversation on the matter – her thoughts were already darkening, the fear already setting in. What if talking about this violence brought it closer to home? What if she was next? What if…

'I was reading that they found no trace of any known explosives at the scene,' said Trusov. 'They say the bomber must have engineered something never seen before. He must have been a genius.'

'Oh.'

'I read that some people think that he was made in a laboratory, that he *was* the explosive.'

'I don't think—'

'It's possible. Here we are sending humans to live on other planets. It's possible that a man was made in a laboratory. He could have been made by anyone. A militia group, a mad scientist, a corporation, the government of some insane country, the government of Russia… It could have been anyone. It is so concerning. So concerning.'

Kojima loathed the conversation already, even having had so small a part in it; but she was bound by politeness not to change the subject without good cause or a better alternative, so she stayed silent, and felt her scalp grow warm from her thoughts of violence and bloodshed and hatred and genetically engineered human bombs. She thought once again of that crumbling school in her dreams, the way the future had darkened and fallen away with her every step forward.

'What do they want?' the small man next to her asked, demanding an answer as if he expected Haque to provide one from inside the photograph. 'Will they be happy when there is no one left? No one to argue with? Just their anger and their madness and their narrow world views? How can they enjoy that future when it comes, if they died creating it? Do they think about these things? They're insane, these people. Insane. It is so concerning.'

Kojima nodded, eyebrows raised. She wondered if Trusov would still be having this conversation if she were not even here, if he was alone in the office, as he had been before she entered. If he was having it with her, or the photograph of his predecessor.

Trusov sighed. 'I don't know,' he said. 'I don't know.'

Then, after a while, 'I don't know what's worse – that these madmen will murder your ideas or your people. What is a people without its ideas? What is an idea without people to believe in it? I don't see where all this killing gets us. Too much has been lost already, surely. A man should be free to do what he wants, he should not have his hands tied by other people's ideas, he should not be suffocated by what someone else thinks is right. One man should not have such a hold on another's fate. Not at all.'

The rambling man placed a couple of fingers on his neck, as if to feel for invisible hands which clasped his throat. He seemed to be unaware of Kojima's presence, so fully had he retreated into his philosophising, until he looked up at her and said, over the coffee which he brought to his lips, 'Anyway. This nonsense is not interesting to you. You are heading off in a year, to a brighter future.'

He sipped his coffee, and then turned his head away from the noticeboard and looked at the banks of empty desks in the office.

Kojima watched him for a few seconds, the frail man once again seeming to have disappeared, leaving a vacant body where his mind had once lived, and then she said, 'Are you okay, Gregor?'

Trusov jumped as if surprised by her voice, his head jolting upwards and his coffee swilling in his mug. 'Huh?' he asked, unsure of what he had been talking about before he had fallen back into his own head.

'Are you feeling okay?' Kojima repeated.

'Oh. Yes. Yes, of course. Yes, of course.' He waved his hand at her and forced an unconvincing grin. 'You go back to what you were doing. I'm sorry I disturbed you.'

'Can I help you with anything?'

Trusov paused, staring into Kojima's eyes. He seemed to be searching there for a sign that she could be trusted with a secret, or that she was ready to hear his problems, or that she would even care.

After a time, his gaze softened, and he sighed heavily. His gaze returned to the floor, and he said, 'The *Conqueror* missions can't continue.'

'I'm sorry?' Kojima asked. The words made her feel sick, and her heart began to spasm in her chest. For many months now, it had felt like the approaching launch day was the only thing holding her together, and to lose that would be to lose everything.

'I can't allow them to. Not knowing what I know. I have to stop it. I can't let you go there.'

'Why?' she asked. She was trying to hold him still, probing his tiny, dark eyes, trying to stare some sense out of him. When he met her gaze, he looked like he wanted her to save him from a beast that was already inside him.

'Do you want to see it?' he said. 'Do you want to see what I've found?'

'Yes,' Kojima replied. 'Show me.'

He sighed again, as if still unsure whether he should take her, and then he turned quickly toward his own office and waved over his shoulder for her to follow him.

'I should not be showing you this,' he said, shaking his head, 'but I must show someone. It weighs me down.'

She walked behind him with trembling knees and clammy hands, down the hall past the banks of desks which would be buzzing with activity during the day but were so eerily silent now, and then through the frosted glass door of his office at the end of the floor, which he closed behind them as if worried that someone might walk past and overhear them. He pointed to his desk without taking a step closer to it, keeping his distance for fear of what coming nearer might do to him, and Kojima walked toward the pile of papers there, picking up the top one and reading it frantically.

After she was done with the first, she read a second, and a third, and still could not quite grasp the meaning of what she was reading, did not know how this could be. But even without understanding, she knew that it was bad.

'See?' he said from the doorway, his voice trembling as much as Kojima's stomach seemed to be, 'I can't let you go. We have to call the missions off.'

DAY 11

Shelley was woken not by the heat or the smell, not by the cracking sound the walls made or by the roaring of the flames that tore them down, but by Verne grabbing her and running, throwing her over his shoulder like some strong man with a bag of sand, all the way from where she slept out into the street. She had barely woken up by the time they reached the road, so when he placed her on its dusty surface, nothing had been loaded into the cache of her brain other than simple fear and confusion.

The rain of the previous day had stopped, and a light breeze blew orange sand down the long grey road. Verne stood bent double with his hands on his knees above Shelley, panting, his face blackened by soot and the sweat that ran down it cutting slick lines like oil on a beach. Shelley lifted her face from the ground and looked at the other members of their company: Ballard coughing, retching, spitting thick black sputum onto the grey-orange rock; and Kojima reclining, leaning back on her hands as she sat on the floor facing the hostel, acting like nothing in the universe could possibly surprise her.

But that smell quickly overpowered Shelley's senses.

That black cloud billowing out from behind James Verne, so dark it looked like an ink spill spreading further and further across the sky, inevitably distracted her from her waking shock. It hit her right between the eyes, right in the belly; the headache of sleeping through a gas leak, the sickly feeling of smelling rotten flesh on an empty stomach. She looked past Verne, and saw exactly what she expected to see.

The hostel was no longer a hostel, but a ball of fire. A house of cards with a lighter on the inside, collapsing in on itself like flaming origami.

The building they thought had saved them was now a fiery cage of death.

Shelley gasped, and then she laughed, and then she began to cry. She knew not why she cried, but she cried all the same. And when she was done crying, the hostel was still burning down, and the rest of the crew were still silent.

'What happened?' she asked, sitting up, gripping her knees to her chest and shivering though she felt no cold.

Kojima shrugged. 'One minute we were asleep, the next the room was a furnace and Verne was shouting for us all to get out.'

Thirty metres away, a portion of the hostel roof collapsed inward, the building seeming to lose ten feet of its height in half a second. The building spat flames that dissolved into the cool morning air, and the faces of the crew felt touched by it for just a second.

'Do you think it was…?'

'No way to tell what it was.'

'Who was on guard duty?'

'It should have been me,' replied Kojima, standing and brushing her trousers down. 'It was my turn. But I went out like a light.'

'If it was something trying to kill us, it probably never came near us,' Verne said. 'It would have known where we were, where to hide, and how to get away before we'd choked to death on the smoke. It's at home; we're not.'

'Agreed. If it was something trying to *kill* us, I'm not so sure it would have failed.'

Shelley began to sob again, a little more loudly than before. She brushed hair away from her face with both hands and looked around at the crew with big, wet, wounded eyes and she said, 'Fuck. I could've died.'

Kojima frowned at Shelley. Verne put his hand on her shoulder.

Ballard laughed, then coughed from the smoke. 'You reckon this was aimed only at *you*?'

Shelley looked back at him, fury in her brow. 'You don't know that it wasn't. What do you know?'

'Are you fuckin' serious? What are the rest of us, bit players in *The Shelley Show*?'

Kojima cut in, reluctantly. 'Okay, all right. Both of you, shut up. This has done us a favour and woken us early, so get yourselves ready and let's head out, ASAP.'

The younger crewmates did as they were told, Shelley gathering her things sulkily with red cheeks and a mood in her step, and Ballard shaking his head and chuckling bitterly. They walked away slowly, tens of metres between them, Kojima leading the way.

But Verne was not done staring at the burning building. He felt hollowed by the collapsing hostel, as if he was watching his own business burning down and had no insurance to cover it. For the first time since the crew had crash-landed on this forsaken planet, the realisation was beginning to hit him that there was nothing for him here, just as there had been nothing for him on Earth. He was no fool – he had not expected there to be some ready-made life purpose boxed and wrapped up and waiting for him; but for a while, it had been nice to enjoy whatever small amount of hope his subconscious had decided to squirrel away for rainy days. And now, that hope was burning down before his eyes.

He felt furious that the books were gone, that that page he thought he had seen with the human hand drawn on it had been taken away forever. If it had ever existed. Which was, of course, what frustrated him most – he had woken in the night and thought about returning to the bookshelves to grab that page before it escaped him, but had instead lain there and stared into the blackness and wondered pointlessly if he had really seen it or if it was an imagining, an apparition, a trick of the mind. And now that was all it ever would be, because soon the whole building and everything in it would be ashes.

They had enough food in their bags to last a few days, and Shelley had her trinket that she had kept in her pocket, and they had their lives and all of their limbs, which was all they could have hoped for in an alien desert without hope of rescue; but Verne had spent a night wanting something for the first time in a long time, and what he had wanted was a number of answers, and they had just been snatched away.

DAY 11

Still streaked black and stinking from the smoke and the fire which had woken them, even after a whole day of walking in the drenching drizzle, Ballard and Verne sat in the doorway of a crumbling building, the women asleep inside. They had been sitting this way for a long time, staring out at the silhouettes of the buildings and the stars in the ever-darkening sky and not saying a word, just guarding against that rare breed of attackers who only planned to use the front door. It was in fact Ballard's turn to cover the night shift, but Verne had very little faith in his ability to cope under attack; so he would stay awake for most of his colleague's shifts, under the guise of an inability to sleep, which wasn't a complete lie, but wasn't absolutely true either.

Regardless, Ballard had never complained about having company. Being awake alone at night made him nervous. The darkness, and the way that even inanimate objects seemed to scream out their creaking sounds into the night, put him on edge, and the possibility that he might have to interact with an alien intruder, deal with an assault without assistance, was unthinkable. He had never been a fighting man, he did not have a military background like Verne or Kojima, and the inadequate firearms training they had received before embarking on this mission had been the first occasion on which he had ever held a gun, so to say he was unprepared would be to understate by quite a margin.

So, for most of Ballard's shifts, including this one, the two of them sat together in silence, guarding against life forms they had never encountered – the existence of which was not even a certainty – with all the enthusiasm of a pair of bed-bound pit bulls.

Until Verne stood, clicked his back, stretched long and high, a stretch that looked as satisfying as that of a cat just woken, and started to wander out into the road. Ballard watched as the older man strolled crookedly, one leg slightly less willing to move than the other, into the centre of the road and knelt on the floor, picking at its surface with his huge hands. He knelt there for a minute, first scratching at the road, and then holding something he had found up to his eyes, turning it to get a better look; and then he walked back to sit next to Ballard again, handing him the object.

It was a small blade, a knife without a handle or perhaps some kind of spearhead. Ballard turned it over in his hand and ran his finger along its blunt edge once, and rather than marvelling at Verne's find, inspecting it for clues or answers like Shelley might, Ballard just wondered how Verne had seen it sitting on the road from that distance, and in this darkness. He smiled, raised his eyebrows, handed the object back, all of this done in silence; then he went back to staring at the sky above them.

'Tell me,' Verne said, twisting the blade between his thick, dry fingers and looking at Ballard through one eye, the other winking as if the sun's absent rays were burning into it, 'what exactly were you trying to achieve, picking a fight with that girl this morning?'

Ballard looked at the ground between his knees, shrugging. 'I don't know,' he sighed.

'You crushing on her? Way you two act sometimes, it's like watching two kids pull each other's hair in a schoolyard.'

'I don't think so,' Ballard replied honestly. 'Women just seem so insane sometimes, y'know?'

Verne nodded slowly. A nod of acknowledgement more than agreement.

'They are,' he said. 'As insane as men are, that's for sure.'

Ballard smiled, shrugged. 'Sometimes I say things and then immediately regret them. But once you've started, you can't turn back, can you?'

Verne looked away. He nodded. 'Seems to me, best cure for that is to not start in the first place.'

'Yep,' said Ballard, and he sighed again, and then the conversation was done.

The road was so silent that the slow, deep breathing of the sleeping women was audible to the men from two rooms away. The kind of silence that swallowed a man. Like that which was so loud as to be deafening at Dante's Peak, where Verne and his wife had sat for hours, just looking out at the mountains and the mist that engulfed them, happy to be in the middle of nowhere as long as they were together. Which reminded him of Rhyolite too, the long road and its ruins in that never-ending desert, through which Verne and his wife had walked, hand in hand, miles away from any other human, feeling happier than they ever had before. So similar to this place, yet a whole universe and age away. Before their son, before the illness, before the drink.

But Verne did not want to think about that.

'One of those is our home,' Ballard said, after a time.

Verne followed his gaze up to the stars, now glistening brightly in the flat black ocean of space, clear of the clouds that had covered it all day. 'Not our home any more,' he replied.

Ballard smiled. 'I suppose not.'

Verne pulled his rucksack between his legs, and started

his occasional ritual of emptying and refilling it, his movements purposeful but lazy. Ballard watched him for a while, then went back to staring into space.

'Would you go back, if we could?'

Verne stopped what he was doing abruptly, and stared at the road as if thinking hard about his answer. Ballard had not expected him to need to think at all – Verne seemed like a strong, stubborn man who would stick by every decision he had ever made, regardless of its consequences. But thinking he was, and it seemed like a long time before he answered.

'Well,' he replied, 'if we could go back to the day before we left, yeah. Probably. Otherwise…' And then he shrugged, and went back to his reorganisation.

Ballard was surprised. He looked at Verne, hoping that he would elaborate, but knowing he would not. After watching him for a few seconds, he said, 'I wouldn't'; then continued looking at the sky. Unable, after several seconds of trying, to still the curiosity within him, he asked, 'Why would you?'

Again, Verne stopped his activities suddenly and thought long and hard about his answer. He smiled, a slight half-smile that would not have been visible if the stars were not so bright, and finally he lost that smile and said, 'Because we've come all this way and all I've realised so far is that there are a lot of things I wish I could go back and change.'

'Why?'

Verne continued his work now, speaking as he went. 'Because when I was young – like you – I'd make bad choices and think that it was okay to do that because I had a lot of time left to learn from them and one day, having learned from all of them, I'd be wise and well-adjusted and never again be a bastard – because sometimes, a lot of the time, that's what I was. But that day never came, and now I'm just an old man with a lifetime's memories of making bad choices and doing bad things and forever excusing myself with that voice that told me I wasn't a bad man and one day my actions would somehow automatically start to prove that. And I can't take any of that back now, so all I do is lug it around with me, everywhere I go. All the way here.'

Ballard watched Verne's stony gaze as he stopped his work and stared out into nowhere for many moments, his rucksack gaping between his legs and its contents strewn across the ground and his lap.

Then Ballard said, 'Why lug them around? How I try to look at my mistakes is like this: everything you did in the past – whether you regret it or you don't regret it, it doesn't matter – all of it led you to here. You could have done anything differently, but you wouldn't have learned what you learned and you wouldn't be who you are today. You had to have that yesterday if you ever wanted to have this today.'

'That's bullshit,' replied Verne, tearing his eyes away from nothing and staring instead at Ballard, 'and you know it. That's just another lie people tell to absolve themselves of the shitty and foolish things they did. Your mistakes are yours alone and they're yours to learn from or to regret, and if you're too cowardly to do either of those things then you've failed, and you deserve all the mistakes you're going to make from here till the grave. If all you're looking for is some reassurance that you did the right thing when you know that you didn't, then why not just… pretend? Most times, the only evidence anyone has that there *was* ever a yesterday is that our brains hold a dim recording of it that they decide to play back for us every now and then. If you're so determined to convince yourself you did okay, you can just edit out the parts of those recordings where you didn't. No one will correct you, especially not here.'

Verne paused, looking back down at his bag. He added, 'I do have to lug the weight of my mistakes around with me. It's my punishment for making them in the first place.'

'Hmm,' said Ballard, picking up a pinch of fine dirt and letting it trickle through the gap in his fingers back to the ground and repeating this movement several times. 'I suppose I see what you mean.'

Verne had grown frustrated as he talked because he had formed these strong opinions so many years ago now that he was no longer sure why he had formed them at all, but now it felt too late to change them; so he threw the remaining items back into his rucksack, zipped it up, stared further into nothing, and said to Ballard, 'Besides, even if all your yesterdays did add up to today, are you sure you wouldn't change anything about your yesterdays? Today isn't exactly the best day of my life.'

Ballard nodded. The older man had a point, even if it was one that Ballard had not really wanted to hear. He wondered how long he would stay sane if he thought like that, if he let the weight of his mistakes lie heavy on his own back and placed all the blame he really deserved squarely on his own shoulders, and he imagined himself crushed by it all, and wondered how Verne could handle it because he never could, and then he found that he did not want to think about such things any more because his scalp itched and there was a lump in his throat, so he stared at the stars again, and the two men sat in silence for the rest of the night.

DAY 18

Moving further east, the crew found that the towns through which they wandered became denser and taller with every block they passed, as if desperate to grow up to be part of the city, whose buildings were tallest and most spectacular at its very centre, most alive in the middle like rings of bacteria in a miles-wide Petri dish. The dwellings they passed had graduated from huts and houses and burnt-out hostels, bare and sorry buildings in tiny ghost towns, to apartment blocks and flats stacked five hundred feet high and often still furnished with all the flotsam of life, the belongings and accessories of occupants now long gone. And by investigating these apartments, exploring their innards, they had learned much about the civilisation that had once inhabited the city.

They had been intelligent, with a complex language and, seemingly, a passion for communication. The crew found as many books and scrolls and letters and signs in these empty apartments as lumps of debris and layers of dust; and for every word they had found written down, they had found two more works of art, painted on the walls and ceilings and floors, patterns and shapes etched in colours that were bright even in the dusty haze of the air, even through the cracks and dents and debris which also decorated these crumbling buildings.

They had also uncovered printed pictures and crumbling sculptures of the species, and found that they were tall bipeds, at least eight feet in adulthood, with long simian arms that almost touched the floor when the creatures stood upright; and their long, hairy faces and thin, wiry bodies made even their young look old to their human visitors, so that never having met a single one, the Conquerors had already reached the assumption that they had been a wise kind, a very wise and noble kind indeed.

Aside from this, and the fact that this species had possessed advanced and strange-looking technology which now refused to function, the visitors from Earth had learned very little. Without knowledge of the language they were reading and with no evidence of an extinction event to be found, they were finding it difficult to move beyond the basics: that which their eyes could see, and their brains comprehend.

They felt like toddlers exploring the world for the first time – willing and eager to learn all they could, but struggling to grasp even the simplest of concepts.

So, for the past few days, they had simply been gathering information. They had explored apartments wherever they found them accessible, and taken anything light enough to carry and important enough to keep. There was little method to their investigation, but with no deadline and no reason to establish a clear process, the system needed no improvement. They were happy just to be sheltered from the sandstorms that still occasionally tore through the towns, the rain that lashed down on a whim every few nights.

Shelley had been drawing a map on her implant, overlaying it onto the city as she looked out of high windows, trying to master the layout of the city, forever attempting to calculate the ideal route to this world's secrets. Ballard inspected the technology they came across, taking it apart and marvelling at its structure, understanding very little of it but making every effort to resurrect it. Verne, meanwhile, had spent his time pretending not to search for anything, while desperately searching for a book with diagrams of the human anatomy printed on its cover or within its pages – the absence of which had now led him to believe that the first one had simply been a creation of his mind. It was no great surprise; he'd had stranger dreams since then.

Kojima often wandered off, scouting rooms that the others had not yet reached, sniffing out trouble or seeking out treasure, or perhaps trying to gain a preview of the secrets the rest were yet to learn.

And it was for one or all of these reasons that she found herself today alone in a room filled with mummified bodies, some as tall as her and some eight or nine feet long, hanging and sprawled and decapitated carcasses crispy with age and left as a message of who knew what, addressed to who knew whom. There was writing on the walls, scratched over the art in the red-black blood of the victims, and even without the ability to read the words, Kojima could see that they bore only ill tidings. Death and hate and war and murder and never any mercy, here as much as anywhere. She was chilled to the core, stuck to the spot, and unable to breathe. So she just stood, staring at the bodies, the blood, the message, in silence.

One floor below, Ballard was looking out of a blown-out window at the city, having taken a break from prying open locked doors and dead gadgets. The sky was overcast, and the half-lit city was clouded by a thin grey mist of humidity and drifting ash. Something always seemed to be on fire, the sprawling metropolis forever burning and spewing out smoke from one of its roofs like a steam train that never moved, and today was no exception. A building far in the distance blazed furiously, red and orange and yellow and black, tossing its dark plumes into the sky like an allergy rash that would never stop spreading. This fire had been burning for two days now, and all Ballard had done was check up on it. How these fires started was a mystery to him, when there was no intelligent life other than the *Conqueror* crew to be found and no power source to cause explosions. He knew there must be an origin, probably that same arsonist who had tried to burn them in their sleep days before, but he refused to accept that some being was going around setting fire to things in a city already beyond repair without cause or discrimination, so he preferred to imagine it as an unsolvable mystery. He would just watch them for days, these flames on the horizon, watch them be born and watch them live and then watch them die, for a week or two or however long it took. What better was there to do?

The hostel had only stopped burning two days ago. And it wasn't a pile of ash, even now. There still stood a shell of a structure there, blackened and crooked, but standing all the same.

After a while, he turned to the rest of the crew – Verne turning a scroll over in his hands, putting it to his nose and close to his squinting eyes, trying to work out what material it was made from and unaware he was being watched, and Shelley lifting a locked chest way too heavy for her onto a table in the middle of the room – and said, 'Has anyone noticed that there aren't any birds?'

Verne dropped the scroll onto the block next to him (for the closest things to chairs, so far, had just been blocks of wood, huge cubes of tree placed sporadically around rooms, free of marking or colour or any difference at all from the last hundred other than, perhaps, size) and stared at Ballard in silence.

Shelley looked up from her locked box and stared too, blowing a strand of hair out of her eyes, and replied, 'You know what? I hadn't thought about it.'

She went back to struggling with the box's lock, a glass-fronted device which had presumably functioned as some biometric authenticator, but now sat lifeless, like all the screen-like units they had found. She was pushing a metal pole into the gap between the two portions of the box and putting all of her weight into bringing the free end down, but at fifty kilos, she had no hope of lifting the lid an inch.

She was pushing down for minutes, grunting and straining without assistance or success, before Ballard continued, 'It's so strange to look up at the sky and never see anything moving across it. Back on Earth, we had this tree in our garden, this huge tree, and every winter we'd have a flock of parakeets land in it, painting our decking with their turds. You'd hear them before you saw them, they were so loud. That was when I lived with Matilda. I remember it like it was yesterday; it's so strange. We'll probably never hear birdsong again now.'

'Matilda?' Shelley asked, as if that was the only detail she had heard.

Ballard sighed, shrugged. 'My ex-wife. The part I'd rather forget.'

Shelley raised her eyebrows and rolled her eyes. 'Jesus,' she said, 'why don't you just tell me your life story?' Ballard smiled, now a little more used to her humour, and Shelley grinned back at him. 'When you're done looking pensive, would you take the ship computer from my rucksack and keep it in yours? It'll be a nice project for you, getting that working for me.'

Shelley had developed a habit over the preceding couple of days of ordering Ballard to do things as if she thought he would otherwise be idle, and though she would probably be correct in that thought if indeed she had had it, he had still developed his own habit of showing reluctance to do the tasks she set him, as if he might complete them only if he could fit them into his busy schedule. If he decided he was going to start accepting tasks from her, and not otherwise.

'Hmm,' Ballard replied, frowning at her and sighing deeply, 'maybe later.'

While they had been talking, Verne had stood and slowly crossed the room. At this point, he gently pushed Shelley aside and popped two shots from his rifle into the front of the crate, destroying the lock and flipping the lid like a Jack-in-the-box with an invisible Jack. Verne walked back to his cube, back to his scrolls, and Ballard returned to his window and his silence.

Later, Shelley had assembled a collage of her favourite items from the chest on the table. She would pick each one up and tap her temple to record it before putting it down and moving on to the next, and she had excitedly taken shots of each of them three times before she realised she was duplicating and stopped. The box was filled with documents and photographs, the same kind of debris she had kept in a similar crate in her own house back on Earth, a scattered diary of the life of a native, and it was the first full collection of photographs they had found, blurrily printed on the same flexible, thick material from which the scrolls they had found everywhere had been made.

'Well, it looks like they had family units. This one… *person*… is the focus of all the pictures, so I'd say this apartment was probably theirs. They look to be a parent; there are so many photographs of them with children. Or, y'know, what *look* like children. Which is puzzling, because I can't imagine them living in this one-bed apartment with, say, three kids.'

'Perhaps divorce was a thing here,' said Ballard, as he slid a knife into the gap between two sections of casing around a small rectangular box he had found, twisting it to break the seal.

'Who says marriage was a thing? We don't have enough evidence yet to say they mated for life. There are several photographs here of two of them together, but who's to say they weren't all taken over one mating season, and the two never met again? It could be that these people had all this technology, had built this civilisation, and also respected nature's wish for them to live apart and only mate when necessary. I mean, it's not *too far* a stretch, even for our species.'

The box that Ballard was trying to break snapped open, and he cursed under his breath as the casing shattered onto the floor, exposing the wiring inside. 'Oh, I was only joking,' he said distractedly.

'No, I get it, but it's all worth considering. What we know about these people is that they'd built up a society that was, in many ways, very similar to ours. They had homes and they had cities and they had technology and art and all the rest; but it'd be foolish to assume that that means there weren't fundamental differences in our ways of life.'

Ballard smiled. 'What are you saying – we shouldn't be surprised if we find that they ate their young?'

'Well… yeah. Anything is possible at this point. We have to be open to everything, if we ever want to get to the bottom of what they were running from when they left this place.'

Shelley returned to the chest, which she was yet to fully empty, as Kojima entered the room wearing the face of a mourning insomniac. She forced a smile when the rest of the crew raised their heads to greet her, and her pain did not go unheeded.

'Where've you been?' asked Ballard.

Kojima attempted to affect nonchalance, wandering across the room with long, lazy strides and stopping at the window to lean back on the ledge, dropping her rucksack on the floor beside her and crossing her arms.

'I tried to go to the floor above,' she replied, 'but it's blocked.'

'No way up?'

'No. I tried clearing the path for a while, but no joy. Two floors up has collapsed, blocked the slope up to the next floor.'

Shelley sighed. 'That's a shame. These apartments were getting better the further up we went. I thought we might find the world's friendliest alien upstairs, ready for an interview.'

Kojima smiled and turned to look out of the window, scratching her arm to occupy her shaking hands. She still felt sick from what she had seen, but she had not yet thought far enough ahead to be worried that her lie would be exposed when another member of the crew checked the ramp.

'Sorry.'

And perhaps someone would have noticed her jitters, maybe someone would have smelt her fear, had there not come a loud noise from some distance below. A number of animal calls somewhere between a dog's bark and a seagull's yelp preceded a hefty thump and a terrifying squeal, and Kojima and Verne were out of the room, guns held high and ready to shoot, before the sounds had even finished echoing up the long ramps that linked each floor. Ballard ran to the door of the room, but did not follow them down.

Kojima tailed Verne closely, though she was unsure if she was ready to fire her weapon if it was needed. They would pause at doorways and turn into the large, empty rooms in synchronised movements, covering every inch with their weapons and checking every corner for hidden attackers. Their breath was shallow and loud, every sound a rumble in their sensitised ears, and Kojima felt so panicked that she was ready to faint by the time they saw the dogs.

They were not really dogs, but probably this planet's answer to them. Similar enough in size and appearance to earn the name, in lieu of earning any other. They had long, pointed snouts and jagged, sharp teeth that poked out at angles from their jaws and protruded from their lips when their mouths were closed. They had six legs each, and their backs curved steeply like those on cartoon hyenas. Their deep red hair seemed to grow in spots and tufts, uneven patches spreading sporadically across their bodies, revealing large areas of scarred, weathered skin beneath. They looked like demons from Hell, the three of them drooling and growling over their injured kin in the large corridor of this abandoned block.

Verne held up his fist, and Kojima stopped sharply behind him. They both had their weapons trained on the alpha of the pack, who was currently digging its teeth into the injured creature's neck, delivering the fatal wound to the animal it had chased here to murder.

Looking up, the hideous alien dog met eyes with Verne, and in the creature's glassy, deep black eyes, Verne saw no fear. Even in the eyes of the stray dogs of the abandoned railway yards in California, where he and his friends used to go to take drugs and set fires when they should have been at school, he had seen fear. Even those animals who had never had a predator, who ruled the tracks and sheds like kings of the rusting jungle, beheld humans with some degree of apprehension, some shake in confidence. But in these six-legged demons, James Verne saw nothing at all, and it stilled him.

As if they could see right through him. As if they already knew him.

Dark brown blood ran thick from the dog's teeth and its lips drew back into a hungry grin, as it slowly stepped over its dying enemy toward the two humans. Verne's knees shook and his heart palpitated and Kojima let out a barely audible whimper, but they held their ground, as the creature edged closer. Step by gradual step, it moved toward them, baring its teeth and clicking its long, curled claws loudly against the floor, and after a while, the other two beasts in the pack followed behind at the same pace. They growled deeply, a hoarse growl from right down into their chests, and suddenly, Verne was no longer sure that he would survive the encounter.

But still, he held his ground.

The dogs drew closer and their snarls grew wider and more murderous and Verne noticed through his cloud of terror how the two at the back would snap at each other, lashing out viciously whenever another got too close, ripping out chunks of fur and slicing tooth-marks through skin as easily as a sword cutting soft cheese. Beasts hungry for blood and death that they did not care from where they came. Verne knew he had to do something – standing and looking unafraid would not be enough. If he and Kojima were to walk away from this, he would have to take action to eliminate any possibility of winning in the beasts' minds.

But he was not sure what would happen if he killed one of them. He knew not whether they would care. He saw them approaching, united but disloyal and above all else indiscriminately violent, and he imagined the rest of the pack running past their slaughtered alpha to take the opportunity to kill before Verne had even had time to blink. He was sure that this was the kind of animal he had seen bolt off, in flashes of dark fur way off in the distance; and from this he knew that they could have their jaws around his neck before the sound of his shot had reached his ears.

He had to do something. They were no more than eight feet away, and he would not have ground to hold for much longer. So he took a step forward, a long, confident stride, and he fired a single shot at the floor in front of the pack leader, the bullet ricocheting past the animal and lodging itself in the ceiling beyond.

The dogs stopped and stood frozen like foxes in a street light, and one at a time, each of them shifted its weight to its hind legs and pointed its long, bony tail over its back at the shooter like a scorpion poising to pounce. Verne's hands shook and his heart beat in his throat so that his tongue felt like it was the only thing stopping it from escaping, and he thought of the dogs at the rail yard and the windy San Franciscan summers and the kiss of his wife and the touch of her hand, and he prepared himself mentally for this to be it.

And then the alpha decided, for whatever reason, that this was not worth its time. It lowered its rear and snapped at the air in front of it, before turning slowly and cockily loping off toward the exit. The other animals followed suit, turning and snapping and walking away with lives and pride intact, ready for another round whenever the opportunity arose.

The alpha hung behind as the others turned a corner out of sight, and turned to face the humans before it too left. From its face, directly between its cold black eyes, so still and soulless they may as well have been robotic, there opened a single wide hole, a slit that turned into a nostril that turned into a gaping orifice, from which came a spray of thick, clear liquid which the animal aimed at the wall, the floor, the ceiling, everything around, and which smelt like death and vomit. Done with its spraying, the creature closed its hole until it was no longer visible between those evil eyes, and licked its teeth clean with its forked tongue as it wandered casually out of sight.

Verne stood for a while longer with his gun held high and his eyes fixed on that corner, but Kojima let her guard down much sooner. She lowered her weapon and sighed long and loud, and she put her back to the wall and slid all the way down to the floor. After what felt like half an hour and might well have been, Verne helped her up and they climbed back up the ramps to join the others.

Ballard had fallen into the habit of reaching into his bag and stroking the skull bone whenever he grew nervous, and this was what he was doing when Shelley looked up from the contents of the chest.

'Are you okay?' she asked.

'Course,' he replied, pulling his hand out of his bag sharply, as if caught shoplifting.

'We really should have gone down there with them, you know,' she said, frowning at him as if he had persuaded her not to. 'Maybe we should go now.'

'I don't think so,' Ballard replied, a little too quickly. Realising his mistake, he cleared his throat and said casually, 'We don't know which floor they're on. They could be anywhere. We don't want to get lost. They know we're here, so we'll just wait.'

Shelley stared at him as if she was wondering what he was made of. He picked up his gun and returned to the doorway, keen to show that he was not a coward and that, if needed, he would be ready to fight off any intruders. However, his path was almost immediately blocked by their returning teammates.

'Pack your things,' Verne said, 'we're leaving.'

'Huh?' Shelley said, slightly panicked. 'What happened?'

'What did you find down there?' Ballard asked.

Kojima replied, 'Pack hunters. Vicious ones. Probable cannibals. We can study them another time. For now, it seems like they've marked this building with their scent and if they plan to return in greater numbers, we want to be somewhere else when they do.'

So Ballard and Shelley began to pack what they could into their rucksacks, and followed Kojima and Verne out of the building and into the street.

DAY 18

By the time they left the apartment block, delayed by the need to check every hallway and behind every obstacle for hungry monsters, the sun was starting to set. A glorious orange glow shot itself across the faces of buildings and painted the road with its barcode of sunset and shadow, and the air was still and warm as the team ran across the road, planning to find shelter in the nearest possible building and barricade themselves there for just one night.

The building into which they settled was in the next block, fourteen storeys high, chosen by Verne for its clear view of the previous apartment block and the brevity of their journey to it. The longer they spent outside, he said, the more likely they were to encounter a returning pack of demons. Once inside, they climbed the ramps to the fourth floor and found a room in which they could hide. With dusk falling rapidly, the room was dim and barely navigable, but the crew strained their eyes and made out a room filled with chairs, those featureless cubes of wood, these ones much smaller than the ones in the apartment they had just escaped. A size more suited to a human.

Verne barked an order, and the others started to push

some of those heavy chairs to the door. Ballard and Shelley managed only one each, either because their hearts were not in it or because they hadn't the strength; but Kojima pushed three more in the time it took the younger crew members to do their share, and they all watched breathlessly as Verne used his impressive strength to lift them and stack them in the doorway, blocking the entrance for any potential attacker. They were rushed and had grown tired, but the effort of pushing the blocks to Verne for stacking seemed tolerable when compared to the cruel death that would await them if the door remained unblocked all night.

Once done, they relaxed and admired their handiwork, Kojima sitting on one of the chairs that Verne had not stacked and Shelley wiping sweat from her brow as Ballard leant on the wall and panted. Verne strolled over to the window, where he would stay for the rest of the night, watching the apartment block opposite.

The implants gave Shelley, Ballard and Kojima night vision, if they decided to enable it; but since the things had so many features – half of which were never even used – only Shelley had remembered to activate it. Once the excitement had died down, she started to explore the room again, desperately fatigued but forever hungry for new experiences, more tastes of this world. Grinning, rushing from object to object with childlike amazement, she gave the impression of being insatiably excited about the planet and all the history and secrets it had to tell, as if the realisation that it was an abandoned wasteland and the rest of her life would be squandered here had not yet hit her. It had – she had already worn the shock on her face for days – but now she was over that hurdle, it appeared forgotten. When asked the secret to her eternal happiness, she would simply reply, 'There's always something to smile about.' And even this evening, after all they had been through to get here, it seemed that she believed it.

Ballard slumped onto another chair and, with his elbows

on his knees, ran his fingers through his hair, sighing loudly. 'How entertained we were when Hollywood showed us all those post-apocalyptic worlds in films twice a year,' he said.

'Huh?' asked Kojima.

'I'm just thinking. You'd never sit there in London or Vegas or… I dunno… Rome, and imagine what it would be like after a thousand years of neglect, would you? After everyone has died. You just assumed it would never happen, that it couldn't happen in our world.'

Kojima took a deep breath, and then sighed and looked at Ballard with tired eyes. 'I don't know,' she replied. She knew there were people who thought about those things every day, but she was too tired to say so.

Shelley was wiping thick layers of dust from the walls and surfaces with her hands, muttering to herself in amazement or shock with every new discovery. Her mumblings of wonder had by now become background noise that the rest of the crew had learned to tune out.

Verne watched the road intently. The dogs had not yet returned.

Ballard chuckled ruefully. 'I liked those films. Thought the world looked pretty when it was all torn down. Not so sure now.'

Kojima smiled humourlessly.

'Ugh,' said Ballard, twisting his back so that it clicked like pebbles in a bag, all the way up. 'I just want my mattress back.'

Shelley had been standing back and gazing at one wall for a long time. Though she had made no noise and was no more than a dark figure standing in an ever-darkening room, Kojima was intrigued.

'What's new?' she asked, standing but remaining by her seat.

'I think we're in a classroom,' Shelley replied, tearing her gaze from that one wall to look at Kojima, who looked as dirty, achy and exhausted as Shelley felt. She pointed around the room as she outlined the evidence for her claim. 'Over there, there are books in large print. Thin, easy to get through. Filled with paintings and pictures, the same way you'd find a lot more pictures in our kids' books. And there, on the wall, that's a painting of a really tall native lording it over the class, open-armed and dramatic, like a messiah leading his flock. The kids look less gangly than him, proportions more similar to ours. There's a glass screen over there, lining the far wall, attached to what is probably a computer of some sort. That's the smartboard. Then you have the other walls, which are lined with unfurled scrolls.'

'A is for abandoned, B is for barren…' Ballard muttered, his head sinking further into his hands.

'Exactly! Then there's this; my favourite find so far. A map of the world stuck to the wall, here. And next to it, a map of the city.'

Kojima strolled leisurely over to where Shelley was standing, and activated her night vision. 'Very cool,' she said, patting Shelley on the back, and stood next to her admiring the map that looked hand-drawn, hanging on its scroll which was hand-dusted, streaks of light grey smeared liberally over faded yellow.

'I'm guessing that this dark circle is where we are now, and from there, I've been trying to work out where we've been. Then we can work out where would be best to go…' Shelley began, and continued quickly and agitatedly, her excitement fitful and bursting through in waves like wine glugging through the neck of its bottle, all at once then none at all, over and over until all was gone, until Kojima was sold too and Ballard was fast asleep sitting up – head in his hands, elbows on his knees, snoring like a cake-stuffed child after a birthday party.

From the window, Verne watched as a pack of dogs approached the apartment block opposite, ten or fifteen strong and completely silent. He reached down to pick up his gun from its position on the floor leaning against the wall, knowing that even with a clean scope and a lit street, it would be very unlikely that his unsteady hands would hit a target from here, but gripping it all the same.

Shelley and Kojima continued to marvel at the map they had found, pointing and debating and plotting and planning from that few feet of distance, as if scared that it would disappear if they got closer. The further east they walked, the deeper they would progress into the city. Beyond that, they would reach the coast and the ocean. There was a river too, which wound its way from a mouth far south of the southernmost suburbs up in a sickle shape through the centre of the city, narrowing to a point as it reached the northernmost quarter. Many buildings were labelled and those which were labelled with larger text were guessed to be more important, so it was decided that they should be visited first. A route would need to be devised, a plan put in place, and they could decide it together in the morning, they said. They were lifted by this discovery, suddenly openly relieved though they had not previously been openly disappointed. In their excitement, they forgot all about their hunger, their fatigue, the fragility of their situation, the dogs and the loneliness, and just let their mouths wander off without them.

And then Kojima noticed something on the map. A building labelled like so many others, though in relatively small text, which could easily be missed but once noticed could not be unnoticed. It was small and dome-shaped (for all of these notable buildings had been drawn in three dimensions over this two-dimensional map), and above it hovered circles on the corners of a pentagon. Five tiny circles, with shapes drawn inside.

'Is that what it looks like?' Kojima asked, taking a step forward and using her implant to zoom in.

'What?'

'There,' Kojima said, pointing at the very top circle in the pentagon. Inside the circle, no bigger than a thumbnail, sat a chicken-scratch drawing of a tiny Africa, below a miniscule Europe. There were hints of Asia and America too. There was no doubting it. This tiny circle was not a circle at all, but a planet. Planet Earth. Drawn on a map, in a classroom, in a world that only four people from Earth were ever likely to visit.

'It's Earth,' Kojima said, 'and it's so close.'

Shelley just stared, her breath short and her knees twitching. She stood for a long time saying nothing at all, and then all she could find to say was, 'Fuck.' And then, 'Well, it's there next, I suppose.'

On the street, Verne saw the dogs leaving the building, loitering around outside it like a gang of teenage boys outside of a shopping centre. They were disappointed by losing their prize – that much was obvious from the way their formation had broken, and their loping was now lazy where it had been stealthy and bored where it had been aggressive – but it did not seem that they had picked up the scent of it in the school opposite. They walked in circles or nipped at each other's hind legs spitefully, or else just lay there in the street to sleep or stare into the distance, and Verne strained his eyes to make them out in the gloaming, and hoped with everything in him that they would never come close to the building in which he was hiding because he did not know if he would survive the next meeting, and so he stayed there all night and did not sleep for a second.

DAY 19

Kojima woke with the rumours of sunrise, and from her spot on the floor of the classroom she reached over to her heavy rucksack and dragged it towards her, careful to make no more than a light scratching sound against the gritty grey floor. In the blue morning half-light she took out a black book and a black pen and opened the book to the first blank page she could find, and drew a small, precise line on the corner of the page to check that the pen was working. Still wrapped in her coverings – sheets and rags they had found in apartments they had visited and what remained of her thin sleeping bag – she shuffled silently across the floor and propped herself up against a large wooden block near the window, where the light was slightly better, and began to draw.

She had not thought about checking for the number of bodies on the classroom floor. In her sluggish morning mind, distracted by its purpose, there had been no consideration that anyone might be awake or that she should direct her eyes anywhere other than at her immediate surroundings and the place on the floor where she intended to be. So she never noticed the silhouette of

Verne, still standing in the window behind her, now watching her sketching the scene of the bodies hanging from the ceiling in the apartment block opposite. Recreating, as best she could, the shapes of the scrawls on the walls and floor, while the room gradually brightened with each stroke of the pen.

When she was done, she sat looking at the drawing and sniffing. Her shoulders began to shake and she dropped the book so that she could wipe her eyes, and when Verne realised what she was doing he turned away to stare once again out of the window.

As he watched the long, slowly shifting shadows of the city's skyscrapers looming over the suburbs and flats to the west, and beyond those desolate suburbs, the unforgiving desert from which the Conquerors had come, fading now into the distance, trembling already from the heat in the air, he was sure he heard Kojima whisper, 'Why? Why did you do this? You're a fool. A damn fool.'

And by the time he turned to look at her again, she had fallen back to sleep.

DAYS 19–20

The crew from Earth spent their nineteenth day on the planet exploring further the classrooms and lunch halls and probable broom closets of this high-rise educational facility. Though they uncovered workbooks with jottings and doodles, keepsakes of probably long-dead civilians stashed away under chairs and behind smartboards, sackfuls of interesting material for the study of the missing kind that once walked this planet, their most prized possession remained the map that they had found in the classroom where they had first sought refuge. Shelley had carefully removed it from the wall and rolled it up to transport it in her rucksack, and she had jettisoned some vials of organic samples to make room for it. The mission to reach that building with the miniature planet Earth drawn above its roof was now the most important objective they had given themselves to date.

James Verne was the only member of the team distracted from achieving this goal. He had given up his search for books with human drawings, and was now more concerned with keeping watch for the six-legged dogs than looking for answers to questions nobody had asked. He would stand by the window of every room they entered, monitoring the empty roads below and pacing and checking and rechecking his weapon, ensuring he was ready at any moment for the beasts to come bounding across the street and up the ramps that linked each floor to murder the team like they did it for sport. He had dreamed about that exact thing, in the ever more common moments when his exhausted mind would slip into hibernation, while his body stood upright and on guard and poised for battle.

But the rest of the team were growing hungry and the supplies had once again been exhausted, and as much as Verne tried to warn them that he suspected the dogs would return and that it was unwise to exit to the road so soon, and that he was not sure they could deal with a pack of the number that he had seen two nights ago, they would not be contained any longer; and on day twenty, they left without regard for whether or not Verne was happy.

They soon found that the nerves that Verne felt and the resistance he had shown were not without cause, although he had been wrong about the reason. They had been on the road for barely half an hour and had made it just a couple of blocks, their wandering slow and deliberate, weighed down by their heavy supplies and barely suitable clothing (some of which Kojima had fashioned from rags and materials they had found in all of the buildings they had already explored) and the need to conserve energy, when their course was diverted by a wall of sand like a tsunami, pushing its way through the streets and between the buildings like an unstoppable stampede of sand monsters, roaring furiously towards them.

Like they had done in every similar situation before now, the crew followed the first one of their number to make a decisive movement, and ran in single file behind Kojima to the nearest shelter – a huge warehouse-looking building, wider than it was tall, caving in and charred at the corners as if the town arsonist had paid it a lazy visit and become disinterested before the flames had taken hold. But the storm too was using history as its example, and before they had even crossed the street to the front of the warehouse, in single-figure seconds, it was upon them, blasting them with coarser sand and more debris than they had experienced in any previous storm. They were bathing in sunlight one second and then drowning in a sea of orange and grey wind the next, the speeding dust scratching at their skin and eyes and wailing like a tortured ghoul thrilled by the chance to drag them away. Leaves and twigs and tiny stones joined it, tapping and slapping them on their way past, and the crew held tightly to one another as they waded through it so that no one would be lost.

Kojima reached the huge door of the building and found it ajar, wedged open at an angle that suggested it had fallen off its hinges, and she put all of her weight into her attempt to move it, which proved fruitless, so she decided instead to squeeze herself through the gap and drag her crew with her. Verne, at the back of the line, would have the strength to open it fully, she was sure.

But Verne did not follow. Shelley, her frame more petite than Kojima's, had no trouble squeezing through the gap, but of the two male members of the team, there was no sign.

From the dimness inside the building, the two who had entered peered out, seeking their friends, but they saw nothing but howling sand and the motion-blur of passing debris.

Ballard had been struck by a flying chunk of metal, the force of it against his skull throwing him out of the line as abruptly as if he had never been there at all, and now lay motionless in Verne's arms, bleeding hot blood from his brain onto Verne's clothing. Verne pushed forward, ducked head first, straining against the tide like a boy pushing a boulder; desperate to reach the door that he could not even see, but knew he would find if he just kept pushing.

The sand burned his eyes and the wind held him back so it felt like he was wading through oil and Ballard weighed him down like a rag doll filled with sand and more than once he stumbled and nearly dropped his passenger, but he pushed on because he had to. There was nothing but this struggle, nothing for which to keep pushing but hope.

And as he had hoped, after all the struggle and all the faith he had that it would be worth the fight, he emerged stronger than the dirt and the wind. The tall, dark door faded through the grey into view like a gift from God, and as Verne had done to the majority of gifts that God had given him back on Earth, he kicked it out of his way without a second thought.

But this was not the building that Kojima and Shelley now occupied. Verne had been knocked off course by the force of the wind and the steps he had taken to save his injured teammate, and now he found himself stumbling head first into a building that was falling apart, collapsing in on itself, folding helplessly into a sinkhole in the ground under the force of the storm.

Still holding Ballard like an overgrown baby, unable to put him down, Verne tried to find his footing on the tilting ground, tried to resist falling down as it tilted further; but the sinkhole was claiming him just as it had already claimed two of the four walls around him, and once the roof of the building began to cave inwards, he accepted that his only choice was to allow himself to be swallowed, fall into that hole and hope that the fate that awaited them below was better than being crushed by a falling building. So he fell onto his back, held Ballard tightly and slid down into the black, and the rest of the building collapsed on top of the hole like a matchstick model, and then there was nothing but the rubble and the storm and no trace of the men.

*

Stella Kojima and Wednesday Shelley waited for hours in

silence, hesitant to leave the building in case they put themselves in danger but also desperate to go out and find their teammates. They had not even assessed their surroundings, so busy were they with worrying, checking the gap in the door every ten minutes, hoping to see the great lumbering form of Verne or Ballard's dark skin and the bushy beard he had grown since they landed come out of the fog of sand and join them again.

Eventually, Shelley said, 'Do you think something's happened to them?'

The naivety of her query and the childlike way in which she asked it made Kojima pity her, and although the answer in her head was: *Of course something has happened to them, or else they'd be here*, she wanted to preserve her one remaining companion's sanity, so she shrugged, and replied, 'We'll find out when the storm is over. Maybe they found shelter somewhere else.'

Shelley nodded, but she kept staring at Kojima and tears appeared in her eyes, and she looked like a bullied little girl standing there afraid and alone, and Kojima became uncomfortable and began to feel scared also, so she walked away from the door and said, 'Let's see where we've ended up. No point waiting at the door when we could be gathering supplies.'

So Shelley walked away from the door too, and now she had a purpose, so she shook off her fears for a moment and looked around the room they found themselves in. Just as it had appeared outside, it was built like a warehouse or an aircraft hangar, a huge open space with four walls and a slanted roof and not a lot else; but at ground level, it was filled with large beds on thick wheels and machinery and bags and tools that looked medical in nature, and without knowing a lot else, the hall appeared to have been a hospital.

From the door to the back wall, uneven rows of beds covered in animal hide displayed varying degrees of dust and wear, as if some had been slept in just days ago and others had not been touched for centuries; and between them, cupboards and bins and shelves and tabletops were messy with blades, tongs, foul-smelling liquids, needles, forks, tools that had no equivalent that they had ever seen on Earth, personal possessions, and rarely, but most importantly, metallic sachets of food. These were packed immediately into Kojima's bag, and each one that they found was a gift that distracted them just a little more, so that before long they had almost forgotten that they were missing half their number.

By midnight, the women had worked their way to the last two beds against the far wall, and they sat on them with their backs against the wall, eating the last they had of a long, chewy plant of which they had found much in their previous dwellings. The sand continued to beat on the thin roof, and trickled through holes in the ceiling onto beds nearby.

'I hope they're okay,' Shelley said.

Kojima was silent.

'I mean, Verne's there, so they shouldn't get into too much trouble.'

Kojima smiled sadly at Shelley's understandable lack of faith in Ballard, but remained silent. Her eyes were fixed on her knees, her legs scuffed and bruised from all the trudging and hurting in places she had never before felt pain. Shelley watched her nervously, and once she had chewed up the bite of bitter vegetation she had in her mouth and managed to swallow it, she tried to open Kojima up once more.

'We're only a couple of blocks from the building with the drawing of Earth on it. I'm not sure if I feel excited or scared.'

'Shelley,' Kojima said distractedly, 'do you wish you'd never come here?'

Shelley looked as if she was surprised to hear the question. She took time formulating an answer.

'I wish it had been different. You know, that we'd made contact with this civilisation instead of arriving too late. But this is something most people could only dream of. There's so much to learn here, and we're only just beginning to scratch the surface. I wouldn't change that. I feel like Columbus.'

'You don't feel… I don't know… crushed? Like you've wasted your life, giving it up to a deserted planet? You've spent a millennium getting here, and now you've found it's a wasteland, you can't ever return. Even if you ever found a way to go back, you'd just waste a thousand more years.'

Shelley smiled condescendingly. 'That's the risk we signed up for. We all knew this was a possibility. They put one hundred idiots onto twenty-five ships and aimed us at a bunch of planets that may or may not have hosted intelligent life. It doesn't take a genius to work out that there are going to be a few that won't.'

Kojima raised her eyebrows and nodded, looking once again down at her aching feet, those dry, sore hands in her lap. 'Oh, okay,' she said, and she paused for a long time before asking, 'So if you'd known before you set off that yours would be one of the planets that no longer hosted life, would you have dropped out? Stayed on Earth?'

Shelley thought for a long time, pursing her lips and furrowing her brow. She ripped off a strand of the plant in her hand and raised it to her mouth a couple of times, each time thinking better of eating it, and then she looked at Kojima like the answer had always been there and she had only just found it.

'No,' she replied. 'I'd still be here. I tied up all my loose ends at home. I was ready for this. I didn't come here to meet an alien, I came here to find out a bit more about what it means to be human, to discover our place in the universe, to learn a little more about how it all works. This planet might have the answers to life's biggest questions – we just need to find them.'

Kojima was as comforted as she was baffled by Shelley's answer. On the one hand, it was comforting to know that Shelley was not being eaten up inside by regret, that she did not feel like she had made a mistake that she could never recover from. But on the other, it seemed absurd that Shelley thought she could decide in her twenties that her loose ends were all tied up, that she hadn't any more living to do, or that she had had enough of what Earth had to offer and was ready to move on. It seemed as silly to Kojima as a pre-schooler claiming they were ready to die. But the more she thought about it, the more she came to realise that, in a roundabout way, she must have made the same decision. That people make those decisions every day. How easy it is for humans to decide they are ready for something one can never be ready for.

'I guess, like me, you didn't leave much behind, then.' Kojima wore a smile of understanding, the sloped shoulders of relief.

'Oh, no,' Shelley replied, 'I had a wife. And we were gonna have a kid. But I'd said my goodbyes.'

'I see,' Kojima said. Then, after an unsuccessful attempt at understanding, 'Said your goodbyes?'

Shelley nodded. 'Mm-hmm.'

'And she just said, "Goodbye", and that was that?'

Shelley looked down at her plant, the stalk like a big green breadstick in her hand. 'No, y'know, there were tears, and she wanted me to stay, and it was hard and all that, but my mind was already made up. I couldn't have stayed when my head had already left.'

'She wanted you to stay, and you left anyway? Didn't you love her?'

'Of course I did,' said Shelley, frowning, her cheeks reddening, 'but I only get one life, just like she does. Why would I want to spend it with someone who wants me to change who I am, waste my life on a plan only she wants? That's no life. People with more powerful connections than ours have broken up over smaller things. That's just the way it is. I'll always love her, but I only live once, so I have to love myself more than anyone.'

'I see,' repeated Kojima, regretful that she had pursued the subject so far. She watched Shelley stretch theatrically, yawning and rubbing her eyes.

'I think I'm going to get some sleep. Wake me when you want to switch duties.'

Kojima nodded. Shelley turned away to lie on her side, and was sleeping peacefully within five minutes.

APRIL 26TH, 2124

There are facts about your lover that you will never be able to change, so it is best that you do not think about them.

First: someone else has enjoyed your lover's body.

Worse: *many others* have enjoyed your lover's body. And she probably enjoyed theirs too.

She dug her nails into their skin and she told them to push harder. She bit them and licked them and after they were done, she held them and told them that she loved them. She probably still thinks about them sometimes.

It is possible that some of these men would have shown her things you will never be able to. That some of them introduced her to worlds you would hope someone you love had never seen. It is likely, in this age, that she has dated dark, despicable people, and that far from being ashamed that she ever could have been so foolish, she is actually proud of this past, and she would not change a thing.

Your lover was once an idiot, and some of this idiocy still pumps through her veins, influencing her thoughts and decreasing the rationality of her choices. And nothing you can do now will ever change that, so you just have to pretend that all of that never happened at all. Or if you have enough skill in the art of fooling yourself, that it is *good* that all this happened, because without it, she would not be the person that she is today. The one you love.

These are the things that Ballard told himself. This is what Ballard believed about love and its meaning. And this is where Ballard failed.

He could not deal with exes, with fondly held memories, with all the keepsakes and baggage that his girlfriends would bring with them. He had never been able to, not since he was first old enough to develop crushes; his head just would not allow him. He would brace himself and take deep breaths and casually ask, 'Have you ever had your heart broken?' or, 'Tell me about your longest relationship', knowing that these were the kinds of things other couples could talk about without issue, but the answer, no matter what it was, would make him irritable and unhappy, every single time. Jealous to the point of sickness. He had an idea of how the world should be, how it would have been if it was perfect, and no answer could ever meet that imaginary land in his head.

But as he matured, he realised that if he wanted a shot at happiness, he would have to teach himself, somehow, to settle for *good enough* when *perfect* was unavailable; so he came up with these facts, this mantra which he could repeat to himself to remind him that love never came easy, and eventually, one of those girlfriends became a wife instead.

Which made his failure to accept these ideas all the more spectacular.

All of these things we must consider about finding love, he had considered; he knew that this was not something that was particular to him but something that almost every person who wishes to fall in love has to accept, and he knew that he too had a past and idiocy pumping through his own veins and former lovers whom he had fucked and whom he had held and to whom he had said, 'I love you';

so he had no right to resent anyone else for theirs, but once he and Matilda had built such a tall marriage on the slowly subsiding soil of Ballard's insecurities, the way that she had saved her darkest confessions for after their marriage, and the way that she had shrugged them off, and the way that she had giggled when he had gone silent with annoyance at hearing about them, all made it very hard to cover up the cracks that ripped through their walls.

They were watching a reality show called *Cuckolds*, which followed the lives of several wives who were cheating on their husbands, some openly and some in secret, when Ballard had said, 'What's wrong with people? How can they do this to someone? If you're not happy, just leave.'

Matilda had not even looked at him, such was her nonchalance, when she said, 'I slept with my supervisor at university once. He was married. He wasn't unhappy; he was just going through a really hard time. And I was lonely, so… y'know.'

And then she had shrugged.

'What?' Ballard said, pulling away from their embrace on the sofa, staring at his wife with a stinging hot scalp and fire in his eyes.

'It was years ago,' she replied, turning toward him slowly with a half-smile on her face as if she was surprised he would require more details. 'I was about nineteen; I was different back then. I wouldn't do it now.'

'How old was he?' Ballard asked, as if it mattered.

'Thirty-five, maybe. It's not a big deal. It was one night.' And she had giggled the issue away, and turned to face the hologram again without saying another word.

Ballard wanted to ask more questions, but he could not get words past the ball of anger in his throat. He was afraid that he would spit venom at her, say something nasty purely because he could not get his head around the situation she had so carelessly forgotten to mention until then. So he had stayed silent, and his heart beat hard and fast, and he felt hot and sulky for the rest of the evening.

But it had not ended then. From that night on, a resentment grew inside him. There were questions that would race through his mind when he was alone, and locked inside that dark cranium of his they would crawl up the walls and cover the ceiling until nothing he could do would block them from view and nowhere he turned was free of their black stare. Why had she waited this long to tell him such a character-defining fact? This woman was supposed to be the one he could always trust, and he the one she could; so what had stopped her from revealing such a huge crack in her judgement until they had already wed? The fact that she was capable of so thoughtlessly causing pain to someone else was deeply unsettling to him. And with someone so much older. A borderline pervert, by Ballard's standards. Could she not see that a man wanting to fuck a woman so much younger than he was was just… weird? That it said something deeper about what he was like as a person? Not to mention that he was supposed to be a figure of authority for her, never a fuck buddy.

Ballard could not understand it, refused to try. It made him feel sick, that she had had such terrible judgement. He also thought of the wife of this man, how she was probably still unaware of how many young girls her husband had fucked behind her back. What age he and his wife might have met, how long he might have been sleeping with young women while she sat at home. The whole thing was a rabbit hole that Ballard would fall down whenever he was given time to do so, and which he selfishly allowed to influence his every interaction with Matilda after that day.

He was angry that he had been fooled into thinking she was intelligent and caring, when there was such glaring evidence that she was not. He wanted answers to the questions in his mind, but did not have the courage to ask. He wanted to be reassured that she would never make this mistake again, that he was not going to be another victim of her whimsical betrayal. He wanted, at the very least, to see some regret in her eyes or her attitude. But of any of these things, there was none. There could be none, for Matilda did not owe it to him and he would not request it. So his anger just festered, and looped and looped in his mind like a soundboard on repeat, waiting for its battery to drain.

Which might have passed, its charge exhausted, if she had not then mentioned, in passing, her use of heroin at university.

'We took it once to see what it was like,' she said, 'just me and a few friends.'

And then, a few months later, that she'd sold it, too. Once or twice. A favour for a friend. No big deal.

Seemingly overnight, the woman he loved and thought he knew better than anyone he had ever met before became a stranger. She was no longer the clever, funny, sensitive soul he had fallen in love with, but a liar by omission, a cheat, a criminal. Ballard knew that he had led a sheltered life; that he judged people for things that most people tolerated but he just could not. He knew that these things would not matter to other people, that bigger men could laugh them off. He knew too that sometimes he could be unfair and shallow, and that if he looked deeper he might sometimes uncover a truth that explained away all the concerns he had; but he could not see past these things he had learned about his wife. He could not rouse the courage to stop them from having him treat her differently, from making him want to distance himself from her and allow the resentment to grow inside him instead of squashing it and moving on.

Which was probably the main reason that she cheated. Not, as he initially believed in that angry stage he had been through fresh from the break-up, because she was predestined to do so, or because some flaw in her personality had set her on a course for the beds of other men from day one, but because Ballard, seemingly overnight, turned from a doting husband into a resentful, judgemental, angry ogre who could not let go of the past, who would bring it up out of nowhere and let it stink out the flat like horrid incense and never let it waft away.

As if it had anything to do with him.

As if it would even exist in his mind, if she had never told him.

Because of Ballard's issues, and because of Ballard's inability to accept that what is done is done and move on, the relationship fell apart, and his wife – his *soulmate* – Matilda was driven into the arms of another man. And then, Ballard had no one to blame but himself.

That was why he had been alone for years. That was the one thing he would pay any price to take back.

So, as one who was always prone to dramatic gestures, and after a few more drinks than he should have had (which was itself a dramatic gesture – Ballard had never really been A Drinker, but drank to excess on nights when his depression took hold, mostly so that no one could doubt just how sad he felt), he ended up once again sitting in his car two streets away from Matilda's house, crying and remembering and attempting to build up the courage to call her or to drive away.

To calm himself down, he practised the conversation in his head, imagined her face on the screen in front of him.

'Tilly,' he would say, 'please don't hang up. I need to talk to you. I want to clear some things up while I still have a chance. Do you have time?'

And she would sigh long and hard, and the pause would feel too long, but then she would nod, because she was sweet and caring and deep down, she still loved him.

'I want to tell you that I love you. It's always been you. I was a waste of space when we were together, a selfish, bitter, angry prick, and I know now that I didn't deserve you. I treated you unfairly, I couldn't see past my own neuroses; I drove you away every day. And I'm so sorry. I love you, I always have, and I always will.'

By now, he imagined, she would probably be crying. He would, too. So he would pause, to let both of them compose themselves.

'I'm leaving next month, on *Conqueror 23*. I'm sure you've heard. I mentioned it in the messages I've sent you, too. Anyway, I won't be coming back. But all you have to do is say the word, and I'll drop out. It's not too late, Tilly. We can be together forever – all you have to do is tell me you want me here.'

And then, what would happen after that, he could not predict.

He took a long swig from the bottle in his passenger seat, the liquid hot and sharp in his throat, reaching right to the back of him like a greedy arm in a broken toy box, and once it had worked its way down, the alcohol and the dress rehearsal rejuvenated his confidence slightly, and in a moment of exhilarated madness he pressed *CALL* on the display in front of him.

The seconds of connecting felt like hours of waiting. But because he had withheld his ID, Matilda answered after a while, and her face appeared on the dashboard.

'Tilly,' he slurred, 'please don't hang up.'

But she already had.

He called again. And again, and again. And three more times, hoping that she would take pity on him and pick up, or else that if he harassed her enough she would answer just to stop him calling. But of course, she would not. She had better things to do than talk to her pathetic ex-husband about how hard it was for him to be without her, and she hadn't the patience to take pity on him again.

Through fresh, pathetic tears, he decided that he would try once more, and then give up and have his car take him home. But of course, he knew that if she did not pick up this time, he would probably have the energy for one more try.

She did pick up. She was in a different room this time, and her face was the colour of rage.

'Jon, what is it?'

'I want to talk to you—' he began.

'Yes,' she interrupted, 'I got that, Jon. What do you want?'

'I… I want to clear things up. I love you. Do you… have time to listen?'

Matilda sighed, long and loud. She closed her eyes and massaged the bridge of her nose with two fingers, her knuckles white and that familiar single blood vessel throbbing out of her left temple.

It was not the way he had expected it to be. Everything was wrong, not like he had imagined at all. He no longer felt prepared.

'Not really.'

'I just wanted to say that I was wrong. I was selfish and angry and… and bitter, when we were together. I didn't deserve you—'

'Oh, fuck off, Jon. We've had this a hundred times. You get drunk, you get sad; you call me begging for forgiveness. You need to sort your life out. Let go of this, it's never gonna happen.'

Flustered and hurt, Jon Ballard soldiered on. 'I-I'm leaving next month,' he stuttered. 'I won't be back. But all it'd take is for you to tell me to stay and I would.'

'Leaving for where?' she snapped, before stopping the answer with a raised hand and a turned head. 'Oh, I don't even care. Look, I've met someone else, and I told you that last time we spoke, and the time before that. You need to leave me alone. We're never getting back together. Next time you call me, I'm getting in touch with the police, okay? Goodbye, Jon.'

And then the screen in front of him was blank again. Ballard sat staring at it for a while, shell-shocked, wondering how it had gone so wrong. Flawed assumptions. Past mistakes. Poor planning. Why anything goes wrong. He wondered why he could not remember her telling him about her new lover, and then he wondered how many other conversations with her his mind had erased. And then he sobbed like his world had been destroyed.

Each sob shook his chest like a car rammed from behind, and they poured from him without restraint and without foreseeable end. He was lost, there was nothing left, and it was just as much his fault as not, and there was only one thing to feel from this and that was despair.

And all this, over a *marriage*.

How silly it would feel, when he was on another planet, with another civilisation, and all of this was a distant dream and everyone alive right now was long dead. How miniscule Earth would look from up there, how trivial all of human society would seem, after Ballard had joined the wise race of extra-terrestrial super-beings he imagined he would find. He laughed through his tears at these ludicrously high hopes, knowing somehow that they would be dashed to some degree, but knowing also that there was a lot of room for dashing before the situation could become worse than this. So it was what he would have to do.

The ultimate dramatic gesture: leaving the planet for eternity, to teach the world a lesson.

He looked up at the road, blurred by the thin film over his eyes. Only the windows with lights on stood out from the haze, little squares of other people's lives casting lens flare across the darkness of the night. Ballard watched as headlights turned the corner a few hundred yards ahead, the car skidding around the bend like no automated car could, and heading toward him at speed. The lights veered wildly and the car seemed to kick out its heels like a bucking demon bull storming down the street toward a foolish matador, kicking and flailing and breathing hot smoke from its flaring nostrils and caring for nothing but the impalement of the night and the death of its enemies. It rushed past Ballard and he heard crazed, angry laughter ring through the silence of the street like a lunatic's through a megaphone, and he shuddered. The way he imagined it, that was the laugh of a girl impressed by her boyfriend's daring, a young woman who was so deeply in love that she was willing to sit in a deathtrap vehicle on a road to destruction, as long as she could share it with her reckless, beautiful soulmate; and this made him suicidally jealous.

In reality, it was the laugh of four teenage boys who had had too much to drink or too weird a smoke and who had just worked out how to override the navigational and speed limits on their shitty old car. He knew that was most likely, but he wanted it to be the imagined love affair, so that he could feel envious and sorry for himself and wallow a little longer in the desperation of his situation. And this level of drunken self-awareness just depressed him further.

So, yes, perhaps another planet would do him some good.

Perhaps a thousand-year sleep would serve him well.

He sighed, and spoke an instruction, and had his car take him home.

Maybe there were a thousand other ways Ballard's life could have turned out. If he had had a thousand different yesterdays, it would have been anyone's guess what his today might have looked like. Perhaps there were alternate universes where his issues related to repressed sexual preference or addiction to chemicals or paranoia and anxiety. It was possible that there was a universe where Ballard was king, and these issues of his were the rod with which he beat his subjects, invading nations and outlawing subcultures to satisfy an urge for vengeance that would never be quenched. But this was not that universe, and this was not that time.

Ballard's obsession in this world was that his lover should be perfect, beyond reproach, better even than he was; and when he found out that this was not true, he hated her for it. He wanted to punish her, but never to lose her, and did not realise that doing the former would only ever cause the latter. And because it was an obsession, even once he had lost her it still haunted him. He lived and breathed that loss and it became in his head a monster that could never be slain, so that the only alternative left was to run away and to run away forever.

Unfortunately for Ballard, he was in the rare position of being able to do so.

DAY 22

'Ballard?'

  'Verne?'

  'Jon?'

  '*Veeeerne?*'

The women stood in the street, alternating between attempting to call Ballard over the implants and shouting Verne's name down the wide, empty road. They had been in this situation for an hour, waiting for the men to return for two days. How they could have disappeared like that was beyond the women. There was not a single trace left of their colleagues.

No footprints in the sand, no response on the implants, no dropped possessions or even movements on the horizon when they used the telescopic sight with which their implants had blessed them. The men had just vanished, into the hot, salty air of this new planet.

But still, neither of the women would mention the dogs or the storm or any of the bigger animals of which they had seen hints but which they had never seen in the flesh, in case speculation would make the worst come true. They remained hopeful that somehow, the men had made it out of that storm, and somewhere, they too were searching for their colleagues, calling their names and trying to think up ways to make their paths cross again.

Shouting in the street, painting a loud target on their own heads for hungry beasts to aim their teeth at, was not a good tactic. They both knew that. But it had been two days, and desperation had long since taken hold.

But Kojima was coming around to the idea that this would not do them any good, and she also knew that Shelley thrived on having something to occupy her mind; so eventually, she picked her rucksack up off the floor, deactivated the comms on her implant, and said to Shelley, 'Well, let's move on.'

Shelley stood looking at her, as if the instruction had not yet reached her brain, or it had, but she did not know what to do with it. 'To where?' she asked.

'Where we were headed before. Wherever they are, they know our destination. We were setting out for the building with the planets around it, so we should just keep going. For all we know, they're already there.'

Shelley considered protesting, but she too saw no sense in shouting names that would never be heard down an empty street, and she was reminded of the excitement she had felt when she first noticed the marking on the map in that school, so she also picked up her heavy rucksack, hooked it onto her aching back, and began to walk the dusty road with Kojima. Morning was quickly becoming noon, and the heat from the sun was merciless.

The building they reached was far less spectacular than the one they had imagined. There had been much debate over what purpose this building may have served when it was alive – an observatory, an educational facility, a centre for space exploration, a red herring – but whatever it had been was now clearly long forgotten. It was undoubtedly the one from the map – what remained of it certainly had the unusual dome-topped cube shape of that drawing – but fire and wind and years of neglect had proudly stamped their marks on it, leaving half of the building missing and the half that remained looking more like ancient ruins than any futuristic research facility. It stood black and broken against the clear blue sky, and it hadn't even the decency to be smoking, to be fresh from its destruction, when the women arrived. It just stood there, a shell of a building that might have held all the answers, had it lived long enough to tell them.

Shelley paused next to a toppled and beheaded statue of a native out front, once fifty feet high, tapping her temple and wearing mild disappointment on her sleeve.

'Well,' she sighed, 'at least there's still half of it left.'

'Exactly,' Kojima said, walking past her, 'so let's find out what the fuss was about.'

What was once the entrance hall was now a charred, empty square with only two complete walls and no roof. The floor was lined with debris and ash and dust, and they had to watch their steps so as not to trip on pieces of building or slip into potholes a foot or more deep. There were written signs on the walls which had survived the building's partial destruction, but none of them would be readable, even to a native. They were scratched and faded and, like the walls that held them, apt to crumble into dust at any moment. There were podiums too, perhaps former information desks or ticket barriers; but these too were weather-worn, slumped and broken, covered in dirt and detritus. It was clear that there was nothing here of use, but there were two doors on the right that led further into the surviving half of the building and two on the left that led to the open, mostly destroyed half; so Kojima took the leftmost of the intact doorways, and Shelley followed.

They entered a hallway lined with display cases, walls laden with exhibits bookended by empty metal frames which may once have held glass, or may have hosted some more advanced barrier, lasers or invisible shields or who knew what. Perhaps nothing at all. The exhibits were the bones and hair clippings and tools of some unknown species, all half hidden by more dust, more soot. Each sample had a label and in there with them were lifeless screens, some of them smashed or hanging at odd angles, which might once have shown animated information about the time and place from which these exhibits came. The women looked at these displays with more confusion than interest, lost among the language they could not read and the pieces of dead species they had not seen living. They stepped carefully, as if the floor might give way and the walls fold like paper if they were not gentle enough, as if this place was a moth on the skin and one wrong move could send it flitting away.

At the end of the room was another choice of doors, and though one was open and clearly led to another hallway filled with more broken and dusty display cabinets and screens, there was a locked one which interested Kojima more, so she kicked it open and went inside without consulting Shelley.

They found themselves in the mammoth hall at the centre of the building with the domed roof above it, part of it dented in like a stamped-on football, and five huge models of planets hanging from the ceiling, evenly spaced so that if it was the case that they hung above exhibits devoted to their study, then each of these exhibits covered a fifth of the room. Each planet hung above a wide door, which the women supposed probably led to a section of the building devoted to that world; and the hallway from which they had just come related to a planet which apparently had three moons, and loomed larger than any other hanging from this room's ceiling. They stood in the doorway of this hall in awe.

'Is this a museum?' asked Shelley, staring at the skeletons in glass cabinets, a souvenir of the life on this trimooned world.

'Looks like it,' replied Kojima, walking slowly through the maze of upright glass displays in the centre of the room, wanting but also not wanting to head straight to the section on Earth over the other side. Her knees shook and her heart thumped and she had to make an effort to regulate her breathing. She felt sick with the confusion of finding that these people had known so much about planets that might be light years away, that they somehow had skeletons and rocks and equipment from these worlds, to display in puzzling display cases. She was scared too, scared of what she might find in the section with the model Earth hanging above it, chilled by the prospect that she and her kind may have been spied on for centuries, studied by an alien race that would have her displayed in a glass case, if they had only got hold of her before their civilisation had been destroyed.

On the floor in the centre of the hall, there was a map of sorts, a painting of the position of all of these worlds in the universe. The planet they were on, 127-001, was right at the very centre, and painted lines extended from it to all the display cases and exhibits in the room, as if tracing a route from this room to all the inhabited worlds in the universe.

'A museum of life on other planets…?' Shelley mumbled, half to herself, tapping her temple to photograph the huge hall, the dusty bodies, the exhibits in various states of disrepair. 'This is spooky.'

Kojima was silent for a long time. Shelley wandered, captivated like a child at a funfair, snapping pictures of lizard men in chainmail from one planet, the exoskeleton of an insect the size of an Alsatian from another. She wondered how much of this was real, and how much was speculation. She could imagine seeing this kind of exhibition on Earth: the study of alien species that no one had seen but everyone who had seen a horror film could imagine. Unlike Kojima, who had instantly assumed that this exhibition was scientific and terrifying, Shelley found it amusing, and imagined that its native visitors would once have thought the same.

'You're telling me,' Kojima finally said, her voice echoing from the other side of the room, where she stood in front of a human skeleton, its right arm hung up in a waving position. Some of the bones were missing, fallen off or taken by something or crumbled away. She wanted to touch it to see if she was looking at the skeleton of a real human being or if this species had just replicated the bones of her kind remotely, but she was too afraid of the answer. She felt like she might faint.

'Oh shit,' Shelley said, joining her, 'where did they get this?'

'I don't know,' Kojima grunted, turning away from the exhibit and facing instead one of the cabinets that lined the wall, hoping for a break from the fear that cooked her scalp and weakened her joints. She found no such reprieve: along the wall, labelled and mounted, were guns and flags, coins and cards, passports, even a fire-damaged Bible. The species that inhabited this planet had not just looked through telescopes to study Kojima's planet; they had visited too. They had all this minutiae, all this indisputable evidence from Earth. They could have been watching Kojima's home planet for centuries. It was a terrifying thought that put a lump in her throat and a weight in her belly.

'Is this what sums our planet up?' Shelley asked, at Kojima's side. 'How depressing.'

'Hmm,' Kojima grunted in agreement.

What did this change, this sneaky visitation from humanity's intragalactic neighbour? What did it mean that they had crossed Earth's borders and taken some tiny souvenirs and no one had realised? Nothing had ever come of it, no one had been harmed that Kojima knew of, so why did it fill her with such crippling fear? Why did she feel so violated? If it was a matter of her privacy, that hope had been lost years ago. She had been watched since she was a girl, and she had always known it. What difference did it make that an alien race had joined the wide-eyed crowd around those CCTV screens, that crowd of governments and corporations and religions and cults? If it was that she feared they had been watching to one day attack, how would they attack now? Where were their armies, now that their cities were crumbling?

She did not know whose hands tied the knot in her intestines, what it was that made her knees quiver and her eyes well, but she had to get away from all of these reminders of her home planet, stand somewhere else and look at something so alien it might as well be fiction, so she did just that, while Shelley wiped the dust off an old pile of informational leaflets in the corner of the room, by the Earth door.

What had she expected? She knew that they could draw her home planet with some degree of accuracy, and she had shared Shelley's excitement to come straight to this building, to find out why the thing would have Earth drawn next to it; so why when she got here had she been so surprised that they could do a lot more than just draw the shapes of its continents? She was angry with herself for this self-inflicted terror. On Earth, she had known when something had the potential to make her feel this way, alarm bells had rung and she would take the steps required to steel herself or walk away and miss out on an experience for the sake of not losing sleep worrying about it later. But perhaps when they had landed, she had forgotten about all that, lost the ability or else discarded it thinking that now, being away from Earth, she would also be away from her worries, her fears, the things that crippled her life all those light years away. She felt foolish, disappointed. Trapped by the fears that she thought she had escaped.

'Do you think,' Shelley mumbled, almost too quietly for Kojima to hear from the other side of the hall, 'that this label is a translation of this page?'

Kojima took a deep breath, got a hold of herself. She turned from the exhibit at which she was standing but not really looking, and walked slowly over to Shelley. 'Sorry?' she said, now as ready as she thought she would ever be to face the rest of the museum. Which was, really, not ready at all.

'Well, look at the gun and the passport. Their labels are short, probably just a sentence long. But the Bible has a page torn out, mounted on the wall next to it, and next to *that* is a label the same size, writing all over it. I think it might be a translation of the page.'

'Oh, yes, I suppose so,' Kojima replied, hearing the cogs turning in Shelley's head. She did not suppose that Shelley could learn to read this city's language, having seen only a single page of a Bible, but nor was she about to mention this.

'I'm taking this,' Shelley said, reaching through the thin frame of the display case and plucking the Bible, its torn page and the translated page from the wall and squeezing them into her already bursting bag. 'Now, I propose that we tour the Earth section, find out what else they knew about us, see if we can learn anything we didn't know, then circle back and do the rest of the planets. But it's your call, boss.'

Shelley was still bouncy, excitable, grinning, while Kojima's spirits writhed in agony on the floor below her. If this was Earth, she would have walked away by now. She would have decided long ago that this was too much, that she would be better off not knowing, for the sake of not fearing; but she did not want to say this to Shelley, so she smiled, wrapped herself in imaginary armour, and said, 'Let's do it.'

But for the first time that day, she was handed a gift from whichever gods ruled this land. The door was locked, like all the others surrounding this great hall, and she had to kick it hard to move it even an inch. Three kicks, four kicks, kicking until her long, muscular legs shot pain down their joints, and she still had the door open only a foot; and then, suddenly, they were reminded just how dark the hall had been, for light poured in like water from a burst pipe, illuminating the drifting dust and ash that thickened the musty air in the hall and casting shadows of skeletons all across the painted floor.

Beyond the door, there was no hallway. No exhibitions and no more information. This door, they realised, led out to the west wing of the building, which meant it led out to only daylight and rubble, a flattened half of the building burned and crushed and never to be seen again.

Kojima, the recipient of this gift, showed only false disappointment, a sigh and a shrug and a barely convincing tut. Shelley's disappointment, on the other hand, was palpable.

'Ugh,' she sighed, her face glowing with a sheen of sweat reflecting the blinding sunlight, 'fuck it.'

Later that night, the women sat in a back room of the east wing of the museum, eating pureed food from silver sachets they had found in the hospital warehouse and preparing themselves for sleep. They had chosen this room not only for its remoteness in the building – a creature entering through any of the exterior-facing doors would gradually be led round to that main hall, and would have to go out of its way through a maze of narrow corridors to reach this room – but also because it had a hole in the ceiling which, unlike all of the holes they had seen in other ceilings in the abandoned buildings, was actually in the building's design, making this room a strange sort of maintenance closet with a skylight. So they intended to sleep among piled stools and stored relics from other lands, surplus stock and that same ever-present layer of black dust, under the light of the stars, the darkness of night so much blacker than it had ever seemed to be back home.

Kojima was writing a note in a little black notebook, its pages and cover tattered and worn. Shelley had not seen her do this before.

'What are you writing about?' she asked, looking up from the page of the Bible she was reading, comparing it to the jumbled, confusing alien translation.

Kojima felt somewhat caught out, blushing a little and closing the notepad slightly in an attempt to hide its contents. 'Oh, nothing really,' she replied. 'I have a bad memory, so I like to note down important things, so I can be sure I'll remember them.' And then she felt silly, telling such a weak lie.

In truth, writing things down made them small. They were on paper, a few inches wide, and she was towering over them, with the power to scribble them out or change them into something else entirely. So writing things down, drawing her memories, was what she did when something was playing on repeat in her mind, scaring her more with every passing second. When an idea or a memory was making her feel one inch tall, and she wanted to turn the tables.

Shelley smiled; either she had not noticed Kojima's awkwardness or she was too polite to mention it, or perhaps she did not care. She looked back down at her pages, comparing the two with deep concentration, frowning and sighing like a young child frustrated by basic maths.

Done with her jotting, Kojima watched her for a while, whole minutes, slouching back against the wall of the room and relaxing her aching muscles, and then she averted her gaze and looked up out of the skylight. The sky was deep and endless, blacker than black against stars that seemed too bright to just be stars; each one glowing like a tiny moon. She had never seen a sky like this, either because she had lived in brightly lit cities or because there were fewer stars in Earth's sky, or maybe because, she realised, she had never really taken the time to just look. She had now had the whole day to calm down, and she had written down her fears and made them manageable, so she was feeling more at ease. As she had been forced to do on Earth, she had spent a while telling herself that everything was going to be okay, and nothing was going to happen to her; and now, she was starting to feel it, too.

Shelley huffed loudly and slapped the papers down onto the floor beside her, breaking Kojima out of her reverie. 'I give up,' she muttered.

Kojima wore a half-smile, and took the opportunity to slip her notepad back into her bag. 'I'll be impressed if you can learn their language from a single page,' she said.

'I thought my implant would help me more than it does, to be honest,' the younger woman replied, tapping her temple and rolling her eyes. 'I learned Spanish before we left Earth, and it did most of the work. Now that I really want it to perform, it's as useful as a one-legged man in an arse-kicking competition.'

'It was helping you learn something it already knew that time,' Kojima said. And then, after a while, she added, 'You'll get it, if you devote a little time to it each day. We have all the time in the world.'

Shelley smiled gratefully, although she knew that Kojima did not truly believe that she would learn to read this land's language and, if she was honest, she was not entirely sure she believed it herself either. She was happy just to have something to work towards; so long had they been wandering aimlessly on an abandoned planet, hoping that the answer to this giant murder mystery would fall into their laps, that she had forgotten what it was like to have real purpose, an actual plan. Survival was not a purpose, wandering to the next milestone not a plan. She wanted a concrete aim, and an end to which this aim would be the means. And now, she had one. She could spend her time trying to learn this race's language, and once she had done that, their books would teach them of their culture, their history, exactly what it was that drove them from this land, be it death or terror or famine or war or something else entirely. Then, why they knew so much about so many other planets.

The two women sat in silence for a while, both staring in wonder at the stars. They were extremely tired – it had been a long day: first that walk in the sun with their heavy rucksacks, and then their world-changing discovery, and then that long walk around the winding corridors of this decaying museum, learning all about the civilisations of other planets in lieu of learning what this planet had known about their own, taking in so much information that their brains had felt clogged in the end, like too much had gone in and some needed to come out to make room for it all. And then there was the issue of their missing comrades, which was the seldom-mentioned weight they had both been carrying around their necks all day, wearing them down every time they thought of it.

'I keep thinking,' Shelley said, sighing, 'about that display. Guns, Bibles and flags. Is that really what characterises our species?'

Kojima watched her friend watching the stars, and she was surprised that Shelley would have anything so dreary play on her mind. In her almost-depression – or anxiety, or fear, or whatever one would call it when one cannot sleep and cannot eat and cannot function at all without feeling sick with worry – on Earth, almost a thousand years ago now, Kojima had thought those exact thoughts herself, in those moments when she had stumbled across the news headlines or overheard a conversation about the day's genocide, or terror attack, or the constant penis-measuring of world leaders.

Why, she had asked herself, *are humans so eager to kill each other? Why are our obsessions with war, nations, ideologies and power greater than our feelings of empathy, love, unity? Will there ever be a time when humans can just live their lives, seek to be happy rather than to kill or escape being killed? Where does all this killing get us, anyway?*

What was achieved, at the end of the day? They were all unanswerable questions, and their constant repetition in her head had clouded her world view, so that in the end, if she were to summarise planet Earth with a handful of items, her display would probably not have looked much different than the one they had seen today. But Shelley, any other day, would have scoffed at thoughts like that. She would grin, and wave her hand, and say that there was plenty that made Earth great, and that there was always something to smile about.

'Well,' Kojima replied, 'you lived on planet Earth. How would you sum it up?'

Shelley looked into her lap and her eyebrows furrowed. Her small frame and her concentrating face made her look childlike once again, and Kojima was reminded just how young she was, how much of a waste it was that someone with so much ahead of her could have thrown her life away like this.

'I don't know,' she said eventually. 'There must be something… nicer. I wish it had been our art, our books, our music; something like that. Love; something about love. That's a very human thing, isn't it?'

'It is,' Kojima said, though she was not sure. 'But so are a lot of things. The world we came from wouldn't have been the same if it hadn't been for war, or religion, or nations and empires rising and falling. It wouldn't have been the same at all.'

Shelley nodded, satisfied with the answer. She knew that these things were necessities, and really, they had not bothered her too much before; she was probably just tired, her spirit dulled by the disappointment of Earth's missing exhibits. She pulled her animal-skin quilt – one of which both of the women had taken from the hospital – over her, and shifted her weight on the hard, unforgiving floor.

'Yeah, I know,' she said. 'It could have been a lot worse.'

Kojima lay down and pulled her own cover over herself. 'Could've been a lot better,' she replied, closing her eyes and resting her head on the folded cloth she was using as a pillow.

Sleep came fast and heavy, like a fall into deep water.

DAY 23

Verne woke to the sound of a man's voice humming a song he had not heard since he was a child. So long ago now, that it barely registered in his head.

I'll tell a tale as old as nan, don't doubt I'll tell it true.
So gather round and hear my words, so you might know 'em too.
'Tis the story of McGraw, a hero young and brave,
Who saved the town of Chislehurst from collapsing into the caves.

His vision was blurred and his head felt like it was being operated on without anaesthetic. He tried to sit up, but he had no strength and his back shot with pain as soon as he moved. Had he woken before now? He was not sure. He thought he recalled waking a little while ago, but the memory was stuck in the traffic jam that was quickly building inside of his mind, weighing him down like a sack full of rocks.

No one dared to enter as the first rocks made to fall,
They thought it would be suicide to answer that sad call.
But McGraw was brave so he, having considered it at length,

Charged in and said, 'I'll hold the ceiling up if I've the strength!'

He looked at the ceiling. Curved concrete, cracked and chipped, ageing and ill-maintained, decaying like much of what he had seen before he fell down that hole.

The sinkhole. Of course. The city, the storm, Ballard and his injury, finding shelter and falling down, down, down. So, arriving on the planet had not been a dream, he at least knew that. Unless he was still dreaming now, which was possible.

No. Impossible. The pain in his head. No one could sleep through this.

And that song. Where the hell is that song coming from?
My head. Inside my head.
He turned his head to the right.

McGraw was never seen again, and the caves still stand today,
A monument to the bravery of the boy who saved the day,
Whose lover stood outside the caves awaiting his return,
Crying time away until her cheeks began to burn.

Ballard lay a few yards away on a bed of cushions, or foam, or a duvet, something like that, and he was motionless and had a bandage around his head that was grimy and wet, Verne could see the state of it from here. Yellow, brown. He was breathing, but his breaths were shallow and irregular. His face was more serene, more relaxed, than it had ever been when he had slept on previous nights.

Comatose. That was how he looked. Or dead.

But breathing.

At least he was alive.

She waited there to see his face every day and every night,
Until her bones were brittle, and her heart gave up the fight.
They buried her down in the caves so she could meet her lover,
And now through cracks in walls and floors they gaze at one another.

The song was so loud that Verne had trouble believing it was in his head any longer. It echoed off the curved walls and high ceiling of this giant pipe in which they found themselves, and it reached his ears before his mind, not the other way around. His memory was assigning the words to the tune as the sound came in; they were not part of a package he was imagining.

Verne did the only thing he could find the energy to do, and lifted his head from his pillow.

There was a man sitting two metres from the foot of his bed, stirring something in a pot and humming the tune, his back to Verne. He was of Ballard's build, lean and muscular but not stacked, and he wore clothes that looked like they would be assigned to him rather than chosen by him – filthy overalls and workman's boots. He broke from his humming only to hold the spoon with which he was stirring to his nose or mouth to sniff or lick it, and then his humming would continue when he was done. The dim electric lights lining the walls, which Verne had only just noticed, cast a long shadow of him all the way to Verne's bed.

Panicking, Verne's eyes darted from point to point along the floor and walls, looking for his rucksack, searching for his gun.

I've told a tale about the caves I'm sure I'll tell again,
Of how McGraw holds up the walls still now, as he did then.
He saved the town from falling, and he did it all for love,
For his darling, his home, and everyone who walks the streets above.

'Oh,' said the man, turning to face Verne with the pot in one hand and the spoon in the other, 'you're awake.' Though he stopped in his tracks for a second when he first noticed, after he had said these words he carried on with his movements, seemingly unperturbed by Verne's awakening, as if it had not spoiled his plans. Verne wondered if he had a plan, and what it was. More than that, he wondered if the man even existed, or if he was a hallucination.

Most of all, he wondered where his gun was. A shot between the eyes would be a sure way to tell if this man was real or not.

'I took your guns away,' the man said, as if having read Verne's mind, and in what he now recognised as a soft Scottish accent. 'I really hope you don't mind. I didn't know what you'd do when you woke up. I imagined you'd be shocked, and I didn't fancy getting shot.' The man laughed more than he should have, tickled somehow by his own honesty, and Verne tried once again to climb to his feet, but just ended up on his back, wincing. He looked at Ballard and he looked at the man and then he looked at Ballard again, and he tried to devise a plan for incapacitating the man and getting himself and his friend out of here without having to move more than a couple of inches, and came up with nothing.

'He's okay,' the man said, following Verne's gaze, 'we're out of the woods now. When I found you, I thought he was a goner for sure. But now, he seems stable.' The man walked over to Verne and sat cross-legged on the floor beside him, and Verne tried to back away but could not.

The tunnel they were in went on for miles beyond Ballard, the orange lighting glowing dimly down the same half-pipe-shaped walls for as far as Verne could see. He could not look to his left, his neck would not allow it, but he knew there was a wall there, that they were at the end of the tunnel.

The man's teeth were white and his nails well kept. His face was pockmarked and he had one eye that was blue and one eye that was green. Unlike Ballard and Verne, he was clean-shaven. His hair was blond and long and matted and tied back in a scruffy bun, but he was a handsome man. More handsome than Verne, anyway. He had a friendly face. Unfortunately, it had been Verne's experience that some of the friendliest faces hid the darkest hearts.

'I want you to eat something,' said the man. 'You've been sleeping for days. You need this.'

But when he held out the spoon, Verne just shook his head. He wanted to say no, to tell the man to step back before he broke his neck. He wanted to ask where he was, how he got here, who the man was, how the man got here; but mostly, he just wanted to kill him. The man was so out of place, it was so incredibly wrong for him to be here, that Verne could not handle it, and he just wanted to destroy him. But he could not move, and he could not speak, so all he did was shake his head.

'Please. You need to.' The man held the spoon out, dripping with something sloppy and lumpy, like brown porridge.

Verne shook his head again, and he tightened his lips, and he grunted and writhed, but the man pressed on, pushing the spoon to Verne's mouth, forcing that gloopy, slimy meal between his lips, the warm, gooey mixture strong and repugnant on Verne's tongue and sliding sickeningly slowly down his throat, filling his nostrils with its foul stench; and then Verne was vomiting, grunting and screaming in tongues at the man and at Ballard and at the endless tunnel, and then he was unconscious again.

Verne sipped the water that the man had handed him, and rested his back against the wall. He was now able to move, but he had to be slow and careful. Some of the pains that his body would give him were so intense that he thought he might vomit again as soon as they hit.

The man sat opposite, his face looking like he thought Verne was here to save him, or marry him, or otherwise make his day. Verne understood nothing; his mind was still swimming.

'How long have we been out?' he asked, rubbing his head and looking toward Ballard's body, still lying in the same position, breathing those awkward, irregular breaths.

Verne gave little thought to the fact that these were the first words he had spoken to the man, but the stranger took great pleasure in hearing them.

'Days,' he replied, 'two days. I mean, that's your friend here. He's been out for two days solid, but you've been waking to drink. I've given you water, sometimes with a little juice in it too, but I think today is the first time you've realised it was me. All the other times, you'd just take the cup and drain it and then fall back down to sleep like a log.'

Verne stared at the man through half-open eyes. He was still unsure if the man was real, even as he felt the metal cup in his hand and tasted the boiled water on his tongue. It would be a stretch to believe that he was imagining these experiences, that his mind was creating from scratch the bed that he had slept on and the covers that he was still using to keep warm and even the long, dimly lit tunnel; but it was still more believable than this man, this English-speaking human man, appearing out of nowhere to save them from certain death. He wanted to touch the man, just to reach out and feel his skin, to see how deep this insanity ran.

'My name is Alan,' said the man, clearly becoming uncomfortable, 'Alan Ellis. And yours is… Verne, right?' He gestured toward the name tag on Verne's filthy suit.

Verne just nodded. He was not yet ready to be on first-name terms with the human he had found living on an abandoned alien planet.

'How long have you been here?' asked Alan Ellis, his voice shaking and his leg vibrating. He had been waiting days for the opportunity to ask the question.

Verne was watching Ballard. He had heard Ellis's question, he simply had no interest in answering it yet. He felt like it was wrong of the man to ask him what he was doing here, to act as if he was the one who should be surprised, who would want answers, when it was Verne who had all the questions.

'He doesn't look good,' he said, his eyes on Ballard's bandages.

'Aye,' the man said, 'but he's through the worst of it. He just needs to repair. Something really took a chunk out of him, y'know?'

Verne grunted. He remembered Ballard's head, limp and cracked like a soft egg, resting on the crook of his elbow as he ran through that storm. He remembered thinking that Ballard was dead, that this was it. But he had run anyway, and he had found that warehouse, and he had thought they were saved, but then he had fallen, and then… Nothing.

'Where did you find us?' he asked, fixing his gaze once again on Ellis's eyes.

'You were in these tunnels, sticking out of a pile of rubble. I probably wouldn't have noticed you if you hadn't been groaning like a shot rhino. Took all my strength to pull you out. You're heavy, you know that?' Alan Ellis laughed his overenthusiastic laugh again.

Verne did not respond.

'Do you know where we are?' the stranger asked, after a silence.

Verne was interested to hear what Ellis would say, so he replied, 'Not exactly.'

'This is Planet 127-001.'

Verne waited for more, but it did not come. He sighed. 'Yeah.'

In his grogginess, he missed the significance of the name the man had given the planet. The same name they had given it on Earth, more like a code than a name.

'Right now, we're in a tunnel underneath a huge abandoned city. These tunnels stretch for miles in a grid under the city, and they connect the sewers, the underground transportation system and various maintenance and power access routes. Some of them even come out into bunkers or basements of buildings.'

'And you live here?'

Ellis smiled. He was excitable, pleased to have finally squeezed a little conversation out of one of his patients.

'I *exist* here, aye. I've been down here for most of the last ninety or so days.'

'And before that?'

'I lived up top.'

'In the skyscrapers?'

'Well, those and the smaller buildings. Wherever I could find shelter, before it became too dangerous and I had to leave. It's the same down here. This is a good spot, but within a day or two, we'll have to move on. You can't afford to settle down, not on this planet. Not any more.'

Verne finished the water in his cup and attempted to push himself further up the wall, to straighten his back; but it was no use. Though he would fight the sentence his body was giving him, he was unsure he would be released in time to move on when Ellis wanted to. He was not even sure he wanted to keep to this stranger's schedule. He slouched back down, wincing.

'How long have you been here?' Ellis repeated, after a time.

'Where are my things?' Verne asked, careful not to give a name to what he really wanted.

'I have them, man. They're safe. You'll get them back, no problem. I just need to know I'm safe first.'

Verne chuckled, and then his chest wheezed, and then he coughed out red-hot phlegm. His lungs ached too. He felt like he was falling apart. Alan Ellis jumped up to get him another drink.

He supposed he would do the same, if he were the one with the power. There was no way he would give this man a gun, if he had found the man first. The man would be tied up, and he would wake to Verne holding a gun to his face, wanting answers. So really, Verne was lucky that this man was not made of the same stuff he was.

As if it had been in a queue, waiting to be processed,

Verne realised what Ellis had said, about this planet. *Not any more.* The phrase sounded like that of a local, rueing the day the neighbourhood went bad. A phrase of someone in the know, someone who had memories to which to compare.

'Were you born here?' Verne asked.

The man laughed. 'God, no,' he replied, bringing back Verne's cup with a new drink. 'Not at all, no.'

Verne took the cup, and waited for the man to continue. Again, nothing came.

'Then what are you doing here?'

Ellis had been smiling, still recovering from his amusement, but as Verne said this, the smile quickly faded. He sighed heavily, and he looked at Verne through dark eyes and leaned forward so that his elbows were on his knees, and he whispered even though Ballard was too near death to hear and he said, 'Listen, man. You gotta remember that I have your guns, I have your supplies, and I am the reason that you're both alive. I've been alone on this goddamn fuckin' wasteland planet for as long as I can remember and I am feelin' sick as fuck, man. I don't sleep. I spend half the day talkin' to my fuckin' self, I'm living every day thinkin' it'll be my very last, and then one day you show up outta nowhere and don't answer a single one of my very fuckin' reasonable questions. It's about time you gave me some answers. When did you come here?'

He was staring at Verne through eyes that burned white-hot and his hands were shaking, and though Verne had felt in control of the situation before, the man's sudden mood swing and his possession of the weapons and the words he had said had castrated Verne, and he sat motionless, feeling the pain from his muscles and the fear of being backed into a corner and the complete confusion of the situation all at once, and he too felt sick.

'Twenty-some days ago,' Verne said, his delivery measured and calm. 'We crash-landed in the desert to the west. We were lucky to make it out alive. Since then, we've just been wandering into the city, looking for intelligent life or trying to find out where it went. Where you found us, that was as far as we'd got.'

Ellis softened, took a breath, looked down at his hands as if he had woken from hypnosis and did not yet realise what he had done while he was under. He seemed shocked, ashamed by his own aggression.

'What, erm, what did you do before that? How did you get here?' he asked.

'We left Earth on May 17th, 2124, on *Conqueror 23*. We travelled for 967 years, but we slept for all but six Earth days of that journey.'

Alan Ellis was looking at the floor now, as if crushed by disappointment. He had, perhaps, thought that Verne would answer everything for him, or would solve his problems, whatever they were, if only he had given another answer; but Verne had given this answer, and Ellis's gaze had dropped, and so had his shoulders, and now he sat looking sad and empty.

'And all of this is true?' he asked, and Verne nodded slowly.

Alan Ellis smiled. He smiled, closed his eyes, and began to chuckle. He laughed and he shook his head and he stood and he squealed, giggling, and he slapped his knee and Verne just sat there watching him until he had calmed down, and then he said, 'I'm sorry, I'm so sorry, man. I lost it there. Just for a second. It's fine; I've got it now. Can I get you any food?'

Verne shook his head, and Ellis walked back to his little stove with its little stool next to his pile of personal effects, way out of Verne's reach in an alcove cut out of the curved wall of the tunnel, and started preparing a mixture of vegetables and pulses in another sloppy, brown liquid. As he stirred, he kept muttering things to himself and then chuckling, shaking his head and rolling his eyes as if conversing with an invisible man on his shoulder, reliving an argument he had had or a conversation where the best thing to say only hit him on the way out. Verne got the feeling, as he watched this man, that he had been here, alone, on this deserted planet, for a very long time. He pitied the man, with his mood swings and his bursts of excitement and his loneliness, but he also feared him, for reasons too numerous to list. Whichever of Verne's feelings was the greater, he knew that he was at the mercy of Alan Ellis for the foreseeable future.

And this he considered, as he noticed that the man's effects were stacked five feet high in sacks and boxes and crates, on top of one of the sleds that the Conquerors had lost in the desert, all those nights ago.

DAY 25

When James Verne reached up as high as he could, standing on tiptoes and pointing his fingers straight above him, he could touch the high ceiling of the sewer. But that helped little.

He would stretch this way and that, bend and grip his legs behind the knees and pull or place his hands on the small of his back and push forward, bending his body backward like a ruler ready to snap, but he still could not get rid of that niggling pain above his tailbone. It ground like a pestle or it pierced like a needle or it just ached dull and irritating all day, but it never felt comfortable. He could never perform any task without being reminded of its presence.

So he tried twisting his back, rotating left and right with his feet stuck in place, as far one way as possible, as far the other, pushing to the limit of what the tightness would allow, and then… nothing. Just more pain, more of that bone-on-bone grinding feeling.

He folded in half and put his hands on his knees, wincing. Panting, though he had not moved an inch. And Alan Ellis, who had watched him progress over the last two days from being unable to move to being able to stand, and from being able to stand to being able to hobble, put on hold his job of cleaning the gunk from under his nails to look up at Verne and say, 'Do you want me to help?'

Verne raised an eyebrow. 'How?'

'Here,' Ellis said, and he stood and walked to Verne, hunched over like a much more decrepit man, and draped Verne's arms over his shoulders, and put his arms around Verne's waist. To anyone watching, they might have looked like wannabe lovers caught in an awkward first-time embrace, mismatched in height as much as tenderness; but then Ellis began to squeeze, much harder than a lover ever should.

His strength was extraordinary. For a man who was so wiry, of such lean physique, he squeezed like an Olympic wrestler, fighting to the death. Verne's wind was taken from him and his back flooded with more stomach-turning pain, and he would have cried out if he'd had the gas, but within a few seconds, his back let out a crack that echoed off the walls and down the long tunnel and seemed to go on for miles, and the pain that had been plaguing him for days was gone. Just like that.

He laughed. He could not help it, the relief just hit him in the diaphragm like the cheesiest joke he had ever heard, and he giggled like a toddler, hearty and uncontrollable. He stood up straight and turned this way and that, bending and standing a few times, testing out the spine that felt so free now that it had nothing stabbing it on every movement, and he looked at Ellis like he was going to kiss him.

'Thank you,' he said, practically panting again, 'so much.'

Ellis beamed.

'Gnnuh,' Ballard grunted, twitching in his sleep on the bed from which he had not yet risen. The other men fell silent, and looked at him solemnly.

Verne stood tensing and relaxing the muscles in his lower back. This was a habit he had developed over the past twenty-four hours, but now that his back was free of pain, he enjoyed it even more. But his face did not show pleasure. His shoulders slumped and his brow drooped and he sighed long and hard as he watched his friend jolt in his slumber, grunting and moaning softly like a dreaming dog. Verne and Ellis had never discussed Ballard's fate beyond the next few hours, neither of them daring to voice the facts they could both see, and they were not about to start now.

'I know you don't like me mentioning it, man,' Ellis said, 'but you know we have to move on today, right?'

Verne had been hard on Ellis, grunting replies and meeting his kindness with stern looks or, sometimes, no acknowledgment at all; but now he had softened, partly in response to the release of the knot in his back and partly due to familiarity, time spent in Ellis's company.

'I know,' he replied, wondering how they would carry Ballard.

'I'll start packing up my things,' said Ellis. 'Could you fold up the bedding? We'll load ourselves up and move out as soon as possible.'

Verne nodded, and turned back to his bed, the damp and cold blankets laid across a thick pelt of rough but cushiony fur. It amazed him, as he folded the blankets and piled them neatly, that such poor quality materials had made such a comfortable bed, and that in this dingy tunnel without any good food or medical attention, he had healed so quickly. He felt a sense of achievement, as if he had done it all alone. He still had life in him yet, even if his much younger colleague might be struggling to keep his.

Which brought his thoughts back to Ballard. Everything did – it was impossible not to be thinking about him, when every turn brought the gaze back round to his body lying motionless in the centre of the alcove in which they were living and every thought of the past or the future flagged some concern over his fate. Verne had developed something of an anxiety around Ballard's condition since he woke in the tunnel – thinking about the boy never waking at all filled him with sadness, and thinking of him waking up a shadow of the boy he was when he fell unconscious cut even deeper, bringing Verne close to weeping. Because that was all he was: a boy. He was too young to be killed so far from his home, he had too much life ahead of him to be struggling against a severely damaged brain so far from his mother and father. Verne had felt no special connection to the man when they had been up on the surface, wandering through empty buildings looking for intelligent life; so for so much of his time to be devoted to worrying about Ballard now caught him off guard, which only made its impact greater.

Verne had limited knowledge of comas. He did not know how long a man could be expected to survive without assistive equipment, and without the attention of qualified, experienced medics, of which he and Ellis were not a pair. He knew that someone confined to a bed should be regularly turned, cleaned, checked upon, and they had been doing these things to the best of their abilities; but how to check where their patient sat on the Glasgow Coma Scale – or even what that scale was – was an unknown to the two strangers in the tunnel. What Verne knew, though, was that Ballard's brain had been badly damaged. He knew it because he had felt the flimsiness of the man's skull against the crook of his elbow, seen the blood spurting out in hot globs as he ran to the warehouse. He thought that if he had been able to see clearly past the screaming sand on that day, he probably would have seen Ballard's brain, exposed and delicate like a naked baby. He knew, therefore, that if Ballard ever woke at all, he would not be the same man who had fallen unconscious all those days ago. He would be reduced, and all that remained to discover was by how much.

So, while the barely-audible moaning and the subtle little twitches were encouraging, better than perfect stillness and absolute silence, they were also ominous to Verne. What if this was as far as Ballard would ever get? What would they do with him, if he depended completely upon them for survival, in this hellish place so far from home? Would they have time and resources to spend on caring for him, when their own stomachs were crying out for sustenance and their own survival depended on moving, constantly running from alien dangers? Would it even be fair to keep him alive, trapped in a body he could not control, a slave to the errant waves of a half-crushed brain? The answers to these questions were, unfortunately, just more items to add to the list of things Verne did not know. But he did know that sooner or later, they would need answers, and he would have to provide them.

Ellis sighed, and stood back to admire his handiwork. The sled that had come from Verne's ship had already been piled high with things that Verne had not yet seen Ellis use – fabrics and pieces of machinery and a misshapen shovel and pots and trays and all the bric-a-brac one would expect to see in the trolley of a tramp in any major city on Earth – and Ellis had placed the canister of gas he used for cooking inside his pot and wrapped it in his own bedclothes and placed it on top of this pile of things, and he had deconstructed his own bench and balanced the two ends and the plank of wood that joined them on top of the pile too, and the whole thing stood nearly as high as Verne and tilting precariously like the pile of presents on the Grinch's sleigh. He took Verne's folded bedding out of his hands and stuffed it into a gap in the pile, and grinned at his creation.

'That should do,' he said, half to himself, 'as long as we walk slowly. Hope you weren't thinking of running!' He laughed as if this was a very witty thing to say, and Verne just smiled at him.

Verne wondered if Alan Ellis had thought about how they were going to transport Ballard. 'Do we have a plan?'

he asked. 'Know where we're headed?'

Ellis's eyes darted to Verne like a lizard's to a scampering cricket, as if he had only just spotted him out of the corner of his vision. He still wore that overenthusiastic smile.

'Yep,' he said, 'to the food bunker.'

'The food bunker?' Verne repeated, and Ellis nodded quickly.

'Yep,' he said again. 'There's a bunker about a mile from here in that direction, which seems to be where some of the animals stash their food, just like squirrels with their nuts. We're running low, so we need to stock up.'

'The animals do this?' Verne asked. Having seen only the dogs for sure, he was doubtful that there was a species left on this planet that did not devour their prey on sight. Storing food seemed to be the folly of creatures that hadn't the power to murder a new meal every day. But then, he supposed, there must be a species on which those dogs were feeding. There must exist some food chain, even if he had only seen one link of it.

'Little rodent things,' answered Ellis, as if reading his mind, 'like rats the size of puppies, covered in leather. Fierce little fuckers, huge claws and teeth. I imagine they'd give a nasty bite, if they got ya. But they've never caught me, I'm too quick.' He chuckled to himself once again, patted Verne on the arm as if to encourage him to share the joke, and turned back to his pile of possessions on the sled.

Ellis had grown to like Verne, despite his coldness, over the past few days. This was, in large part, because Verne was the first human he had interacted with in a long time; but there was also a familiarity to him that the older man could not escape, no matter how hard he tried to be frosty and stand-offish. He was authoritative, strong and self-assured, all of which were attractive qualities in a land which made every human feel so inescapably unsure; and he cared deeply about people, whether he wanted to or not – Ellis could tell as much just by watching him watch Ballard. No, Alan Ellis no longer had any reservations about the man he had pulled from the rubble.

Verne noticed, as he stood behind Ellis, that his rucksack and his gun were on the floor next to the sled, and that Ballard's rucksack and gun were also there.

'Alan,' he said, 'I'd like to have my things back now. I'd be more comfortable on the journey if I had a weapon.'

Alan Ellis turned to Verne, wearing a very serious expression. 'Do you promise not to shoot me?' he asked, and contrary to Verne's expectation that it would break out into a smile at the silly question, Ellis's face begged a real answer.

'Of course,' Verne replied. 'I have no reason to.'

Ellis stared up into Verne's eyes for a long time, standing much shorter than the seven-foot-tall, five-foot-wide former Californian and much less accustomed to stand-offs, but nonetheless holding his gaze well; and then he giggled, genuinely tickled by the situation and by his only semi-serious request for a promise which had actually been granted.

'Aye, course you can have your stuff back, man,' he replied, chuckling, 'I don't want it. Besides, we might need your trigger finger.' He closed one eye and shot a few rounds from an invisible gun in his hand before giggling again, and walking toward the sled to collect Verne's things. Verne did not move.

'I was going to give you this shit before we left anyway,' Ellis said, picking up the bag in one hand and the gun in the other. 'You really asked just a second before I was gonna mention it myself.'

He stood in front of Verne holding the two items out in front of him, grinning like a dimwit. Verne smiled back and took them from him, but Ellis held tight to the rifle.

'Hey,' he said, 'remember your promise.'

'Yeah,' replied Verne. Ellis released his grip, and Verne

took the gun into his hands. He turned it over in front of him, inspecting it as if he expected some part of it to be missing, or as if he was buying it second-hand and was looking for imperfections. Once he seemed satisfied, he gave Ellis another smile, then hit him square in the face with the stock, hard and fast.

Ellis was on the ground before he knew what was going on, and blood burst from his nose like a sneeze of red paint. He was dumbfounded, caught entirely by surprise. 'Wh-what the fuck?' he cried out.

Verne stood on the man's ankle so that he could not crawl over to Ballard's weapon, and pointed the barrel of the automatic directly between his eyes. Ellis cried out again, under the weight of Verne's boot.

'Where'd you get that sled?' Verne asked, as calmly as if he was asking a friend, just out of curiosity.

'Huh?' Ellis said, holding back tears and gripping his nose.

Verne bent down and knelt on Ellis's thigh, staring a cold stare at the man on the floor, and hit him again, just as hard, with the stock of his rifle. 'Where did you get that sled?' he repeated.

Ellis began to cry. His voice shook with the tears. 'I found it. Up top. It was in one of the apartment blocks, leaning against a wall.'

'You found it in the city?' asked Verne. 'And you didn't think that it was strange that it had English words printed on it? You didn't recognise those space agency logos?'

Verne was menacing. That he could so effectively hurt someone who had spent so much time and energy caring for him was disturbing enough, but the calmness with which he did it was chilling. Ellis could hardly gather his thoughts enough to reply.

'Well, yeah,' he replied, stuttering, 'I mean no; I didn't think it was strange. I've seen plenty of English here. It's a novelty to them. They know all about us. I… I just didn't give it a second thought, I swear. I found it there; I thought it'd be useful, so I took it. I'm sorry, man, I'm so sorry.'

Ellis's mouth was turning down at the edges and his eyes were dripping slick lines down his cheeks. Verne applied greater pressure to his thigh, pushed the gun against his forehead.

'When was this?' he asked.

'I don't know,' Ellis replied through gritted teeth, his eyes closed as if he expected to be shot dead at any moment, 'about two weeks ago. If that. Eleven days, maybe. I don't *know*.'

Verne was silent for a moment, considering the man's answer. Verne had seen many people lie, and his time in the military had put him in situations where he had had to be a lot more merciless to force out the truth; but this was not one of those situations, and he was not witnessing someone lying right now. He could feel it. While he knew that this meant that what he had just done was unjust and was therefore just another item for his big long list of regrets, and that this moment would affect his life on this planet immediately and absolutely, he could not back down now. He still had adrenaline pumping through his veins, and his trigger finger was still itching to be tensed.

'You're going to get up,' he said to Ellis, lying there on the floor with tears in his eyes and blood from an already blackening nose drying on his top lip, 'and you're going to jettison everything you don't absolutely need from that sled. What is left, you'll stack so that it has a completely stable and flat top, and we're going to lay our bedding on top of it. We're dragging Ballard along with us, and from now on, he's our most precious piece of cargo.'

He stood, and held out his hand for Ellis to take, to assist the beaten man to his feet. But Ellis did not take the hand; he lay back on the floor and sobbed, heartbroken by the dog he had saved which had bitten him at the first opportunity. He had been alone on this deserted planet for so long he had actually questioned such unfathomable things as his own existence, his sanity and the kinds of jokes the gods would play; and as soon as that loneliness had ended, the moment he was joined out of the blue by members of his own species, one of them had beaten him and humiliated him for no reason at all. He thought he might never stop crying.

And so did Verne, after he had watched the wounded man deliberate over which items to leave and which to bring, slowly whittling away at the pile of half-useful items he had on his sled, until he had a sled that was half stacked and a nose still running and eyes still weeping. He breathed like a tortured toddler, all shaking exhalations and jolting, panicky inhalations, as he made a bed for Ballard atop the pile of his personal effects and equipment, and then he turned to Verne with his eyes on the floor and his hands by his sides, looking for mercy as much as approval. He stood next to Ballard's weapon and had no interest in picking it up or using it, and the significance of this was not lost on Verne.

Verne would have time to feel guilty about what he had just done. He would have many moons on this planet, many nights on which the darkness of the sky and the brightness of the stars would somehow goad his brain into deeper introspection than it had ever indulged in on Earth and the sorrow could come flooding in to drown him in that ever-growing list of regrets. But now was not the time to mourn his relationship with this stranger who had saved him from possible death in an alien sewer. Now was the time to move on, before the alien dogs or the alien rats found them and bled them dry. So instead of feeling guilty, and instead of apologising to Ellis, who looked scared and sad and broken, he just walked over to Ballard's body, picked it up gently, and took it to its new bed.

Laying his comatose friend on top of the sled gently, he said, 'Let's go', and took the reins of the sled over his shoulder, and began to pull it down the tunnel.

DAY 26

After a square meal and a long sleep, James Verne had had more than enough time to think on the way that he had treated Alan Ellis, back in the alcove. He had relived in his imagination the smack of his gun against the unarmed man's face, and the man's sobbing and flinching, enough times to cultivate a deep sadness within him that was unlikely to heal itself any time soon. But Alan Ellis was a forgiving man, and an empathetic man, and his understanding of why Verne had mistrusted him was just as strong as his desperation for them to be friends, to stick together in this foreign world. He had been alone so long he had nearly lost his mind, and now that he had found someone who might help him hold it together, he did not want to lose that person over two taps on the nose. So he had been quick to forget James Verne's transgression, and Verne was grateful for that, even if he had not shown gratitude for much else.

They were walking down a concrete tunnel that seemed endless, following a steady curve that Ellis said ran a wide circle around and underneath the entire city. Verne dragged the supplies and the third member of their group by a rope over his shoulder, the rollers on the underside of the sled making soft squeaking noises that echoed eerily down the tunnel; and Ellis walked alongside him, carrying Ballard's rucksack and gun. The gun was attached to the rucksack, well out of Ellis's reach, and Verne had spent many minutes wondering if Ellis would know how to use it, if he ever had cause to do so. He had held it in his hands only twice, but the way that he had done so spoke loudly to Verne about his experience with weapons, and what it said was that he had no experience at all. Having narrowly escaped death no less than three times in less than four weeks since his arrival on the planet, Verne had little idea how Alan Ellis had survived so long on his own, with no weapons and so little experience with anything practical.

But that was unfair. In truth, Verne knew very little about the man or his skills. Between nursing their comatose patient and fixing Verne's broken body, finding the food bunker and then searching for another safe place to sleep, they had had little time to exchange life stories. Verne knew that Ellis knew nothing about why the tunnels were still powered and the buildings on the surface were not, and Ellis knew that Verne's landing craft was half destroyed and totally unusable, lying miles away in a desert out west. Ellis knew that Verne could pull a sled weighing nearly 380 kilograms for miles and hardly break a sweat, and Verne knew that Ellis had been on the planet long enough to have an astonishing knowledge of the vegetation and its nutritional value, or lack thereof. But why Ellis was here, a human living where humans should never have stepped foot before, was still a mystery to Verne; and as he walked and considered this, he found cause to break the silence between them for the first time in an hour.

'I just realised,' he said, his deep, drawling voice rumbling back at him from the walls of the tunnel, 'that I still don't know how you got here.'

Ellis chuckled, and looked at Verne quizzically as if to

accuse him of forgetting an explanation he had provided.

'Are you sure?' he asked, scratching his chin.

Verne nodded.

'Huh,' Ellis said, surprised, 'I thought we'd talked about it.'

He shrugged, and they continued to walk down the tunnel in silence. Verne waited for a while, and then he said, 'Well?'

'Oh, yeah,' Ellis replied, his thoughts having drifted off. 'Well, the truth is that I don't know.'

Verne suspected that this was a joke and that he was supposed to laugh, but he did not. He said, 'Hmm?'

'I don't know how I got here. I can't remember. I find that the more time I spend here, the worse my memory gets. Whether I already had a bad memory and it's just getting worse, or this place has done something to me, I don't know. Could be my ship crashed like yours and I'm a little brain-damaged, who knows. I remember the last year, maybe a little more, and then it gets seriously misty. And all of that time, I've been here.'

Verne took a little time processing this. He watched his companion's face, expecting it to crack into that goofy laugh he often did. It did not crack – Ellis walked along in pace with Verne, his gaze fixed somewhere a few feet in front of him, his face sullen like a disappointed child's.

'You're shittin' me,' Verne said.

Ellis did break out into that laugh then, but not because he was lying. Verne's disbelief amused him somehow. Most likely because if he didn't laugh, he might cry.

'I wish I was, man,' he replied, shaking his head, 'I wish I was. It's not all gone; I can remember my name, obviously, and I remember how to walk and talk and eat and cook, and I have the vaguest memories of what life was like on Earth – like, I can *feel* it more than picture it – but the only vivid memories I have are relatively short-term. I don't remember why I came here or what the year was or who was the goddamn president of wherever I came from. Believe me, I'm as upset about it as you are.'

Verne continued to watch Ellis's face, waiting for the punchline. There was no punchline. He watched Ellis watching the ground, the man's face darkening, perhaps as he considered what he might have lost and how, now, he would never get it back; and as Verne began to accept that what Ellis had said was the truth, his heart ached. He had discussed memories with Ballard, and the way they could make one feel, and how there were some that he would give anything to erase; but losing it all, and living a life alone, in an inhospitable world, with no memories – happy or otherwise – to keep him sane sounded like hell to Verne. He was suddenly amazed that Ellis was as collected as he seemed to be. Under these conditions, Verne might have lost it a long time ago.

'Do you know where we're going?' he asked, to distract Ellis as much as to satisfy his curiosity.

'Aye,' Ellis replied, affecting a chirpier tone, 'this is a maintenance tunnel. Look up there, it says, *Supply Hall*. That's where we're headed.'

The words that he pointed to were written in the language of the city above them, the language that Verne had seen in all of their books and scrolls and road signs. This was the first time he had read it aloud.

Verne suspected that Alan Ellis might have been on this planet for a lot longer than he would care to realise, and that the truth of it could destroy the man this planet had adopted. He followed Ellis, deciding it might be best if he kept quiet for a while.

Ballard moaned loudly from the top of the pile of Ellis's things, stealing the attention of the two waking men. Verne did not know how long they had been down in the tunnels – he did not have the same perception of time that Ellis did, without the sun to tell him what was day and what was night – but he knew that Ballard had now been alive for a lot longer than he should have been. He was gaunt and his hair was dry, his lips cracked and his skin rough to the touch, but he was still alive. Despite all odds, Ballard was surviving the ordeal, fighting for his life without even knowing it. The previous day, he had even taken in some water in one of his half-waking stupors (though the difference between the amount he had swallowed and the amount he had dribbled or spluttered out was substantial); and this was of great encouragement to Verne, whose hopes for his own survival now rested upon his sleeping friend one day waking in full health.

If Ballard can make it, so can I. That was what he would think, when he lay awake and afraid in the dim light of the tunnels. And yet, only a week ago, he would have put money on Ballard not making it, and would even have been glib about his colleague's demise. A week ago, he would not have felt scared, because he had been prepared for anything. But now, he jumped at the sound of his friend's voice and ran to him at every movement, and when Ballard was neither moving nor moaning, he just feared for the future.

'We need to get up to the surface,' Verne said, noticing the paleness of his comatose friend's skin. 'He needs some sunlight. We all do. And we need to find the rest of our crew.'

'We will,' said Ellis, returning his attention to the cloth in his hand. He was sewing a patch over a hole in his overalls, wearing the concentration on his face like the black, swollen nose that Verne had given him. 'We need to find a ramp up that isn't blocked. The next two we'll reach are both cave-ins, and I can't remember about the third. It'll be two days, maximum. I promise you.'

'Will our food last us two more days?' Verne asked. He had no stitching to do, and he had cleaned his gun twice already, and he had no scrolls to read, so he sat idle, worrying and talking to let out some of the worry.

Ellis ignored the question. 'These friends of yours,' he began, 'how are we going to find them? It's a big city, man. We're a long way from where you fell down.'

'I know where we were walking, so we'll head there first, and see if we can track them. If Ballard is awake by then, he can contact them over his implant anyway.'

Ellis gave Verne a look that either suggested that he was familiar with implants and was confused that Verne had mentioned them, or that he knew not what an implant was – Verne could not tell which. Regardless, he did not pursue the issue, instead returning to his stitching.

'Where were you going, then?'

'We found a map in one of the buildings, pinned to the wall. A map of the city, looked hand-drawn. Anyway, there was a building had a tiny little picture of Earth drawn above it. Or at least something that looked just like it. So that's where.'

Ellis slumped his hands in his lap and looked at Verne with a knowing smile. He looked as if he had seen right through Verne, as if he suddenly felt smug that he'd had years of head start on the Conquerors.

'The Museum of Other Worlds,' he said, grinning.

'You've been there?'

'Yes, I have,' Ellis replied, 'and it creeped the hell out of me, man. Only God knows how many centuries these fuckers were spying on us, but they knew a hell of a lot about us before they died out. Studied us like we were animals, looked like.'

Verne felt, once again, like he was missing the joke. 'What's in there?' he asked, trying to sound less intimidated by the mystery than he felt.

'I don't want to ruin the surprise for you,' replied Ellis, 'but we'll head there first. We'll find your friends; don't you worry, big guy.'

Ballard moaned louder, and his moan echoed down the

hallway in which they were resting. The supply hall was another long alcove cut out of the main tunnel system, another dead end with one way in, which Ellis had adopted as one of his many hideouts. Verne liked the single entryway because it was easier to guard, but disliked that it meant they were cornered, should a pack of dogs come bounding down the tunnel looking for human meat to chew on. Ellis had already told him that the dogs hardly came down here, if they ever did at all, but Verne was hard to reassure. Ballard's shouting was loud enough to make it sound like there was a family of ghouls living in this alcove, and Verne was stirred enough now to stand and approach his friend.

'Tiiiiiiii-eeeeeee,' Ballard said, his arms flailing slowly like a sloth fighting off flies. 'Tiiiiiiiiiiiii… eeeeeeeeeeeeeee.'

'Is he saying something?' asked Ellis.

'I don't know,' said Verne, looking into the now-half-open eyes of his nearly-almost-half-conscious colleague.

'Tiiiiiiiiiiiillyyyyyyyyy,' moaned Ballard, his moans growing softer, his movements weaker. Once again, he seemed like he was drifting off.

'Tilly,' said Verne to himself.

'Tilly?' Ellis parroted.

'His wife,' Verne said. 'She was called Matilda. He's spoken about her before.'

'Fuck,' sighed Ellis, 'poor guy. She dead or something?'

Verne turned his gaze from the sled top and shot Ellis a stern look. 'No,' he said. Then he added, 'Well, yes, I suppose she must be by now. But when we left Earth, I think they were just divorced. He didn't say much more than that. I don't know.'

Ballard was still once again when Verne turned back to him, and the possibility that he might be dreaming, sad dreams of home and of love lost and of things he could never have back again, made Verne feel hollow, instantly drained. Verne could be hard, and glib, and mean, and ruthless, but there was a heart within him that was drenched in empathy, a soul as sensitive as a leaf in winter. That's what his wife had told him, and he had told her that it was all for her, that no one else would ever get below the surface because her name was written all over it. And until now, he had not really been lying.

But this was no place to be thinking about his wife. This was no place to cry, no time to be nursing his own wounds, when his colleague had so many still to nurse. He pulled his mind back into the room, and looked at Ellis, who had also slipped into a malaise, staring into his lap wearing only a sad frown.

'I've wondered, before now,' Ellis said, as if he knew that Verne was looking at him and wanted to provide an explanation, 'if I had a wife. I wonder if I had kids on Earth, if after I left I ever had grandkids. I wonder how happy I was, what I did with my time, if I was liked and if I was kind. I hope I was.'

Verne said nothing.

'I suppose I can't have been that happy,' said Ellis, turning the needle he had used for his sewing between his dirty fingers, 'because I'm here, aren't I? If I liked my life, I'd still be living it. Still, I hope I did have a family. I hope I had kids, and that they loved me. When I think about it, that's what I hope.'

Verne listened to the hiss of Ballard's stunted breaths, listened to the beat of his own heart pumping blood through his ears. He had spent the last few seconds talking himself back into being practical and sensible, rebuilding that shell around himself. Now, in the dim orange light of the tunnel, with one companion comatose and one engulfed in depression, he just wanted to sleep until he felt strong again.

'I'm sorry,' he said, unsure of where the words had come from before they left his mouth, 'about your nose. I'm sorry I hit you.'

Ellis looked up at him, and smiled. 'It's okay, man,' he said. He went back to his sewing as if he had already forgotten everything about the conversation they had just had.

Verne was woken by Ballard screaming at the top of his voice, over and over, howling like a wolf down the long, echoing tunnels, with Ellis standing over him hissing, 'Shut up, shut up, shut the fuck up, man, you'll kill us all.'

Verne had jumped to his feet and grabbed his gun before he even had control over his muscles, and he barked at Ellis, 'What the hell is going on?'

'He woke up again, moaning, and I ignored him at first, but it got louder and louder, until it was this. I don't know what we need to do, but he needs to stop. I have no idea what might find us down here, and we'll be trapped in this hall if we're found.'

'I thought you said the bigger animals don't come down here?' Verne said, pointing his gun down the corridor toward the tunnel that cut across it, as if a threat was already approaching.

'Well, I've never seen them, but then I've never been screaming my ex-wife's name as loud as I can down here.'

'*Matiiiiiillllldaaaaaaaa, stop,*' screamed Ballard, his movements ever so slightly more cohesive than before, as if he was making a concerted effort to sit up, or at least to lean up on his elbows and scream out his lover's name. His eyes rolled in their sockets; the eyelids open wider than they had been for days. He acted as if he were possessed by a demon that refused to be exorcised. '*Matiiiiiiiiiilllllldaaaaaaaa, nooooooo!*'

'What can we do, man?' Ellis said, panicking.

Verne sifted through ideas in his head, none of which were helpful because there was no way of thinking up a practical solution to their current predicament. He knew that their best solution was to hope that nothing came running towards the sound, and that Ballard would calm down within a few seconds. But the way Ballard was grabbing at air, twisting his arms and arching his back, screaming like Verne had never seen him do so before, it did not seem likely that he would ever calm down.

'*IIIIIdooooonnnnwaaaaannnaaaaaaaaaa*,' he screamed.

'We have to shut him up, man,' Ellis said, his stare into Verne's eyes intense and intimidating, as unhinged as the time he had shut Verne up on the first day they met. Verne had trouble deciphering what he was suggesting, if he was suggesting anything at all.

'I know,' Verne said, 'I know.' He continued to point his gun down the hallway, toward the tunnel, but kept his eyes on Jon Ballard. 'Fuck,' he snapped.

But Alan Ellis's eyes were no longer on Verne, and his stare no longer one of urgency and fury, but one of distracted fear. He looked past Verne and off down the tunnel, and the terror in his eyes made Verne's heart sink. Verne turned slowly, delaying the inevitable for as long as he could.

At the end of the hallway, in the tunnel that ran perpendicular to the supply hall, stooping to fit under the ceilings that seemed so high to the humans but so low to towering creatures, stood a beast that Verne had thought only existed in his dreams. Covered in hair as black as oil and with eyes that glittered in the dull lamplight of the tunnels, the creature's knuckles dragged along the floor while its shoulders pressed against the ceiling. It stood perfectly still, watching the men tremble in fear, listening to Ballard's screams, and its loud, angry breaths filled the gaps between those screams like an ever-present promise of impending doom.

The creature was a terrifying hybrid of bear, gorilla and dinosaur, grown larger than Verne thought any animal should be. He had seen one in the desert, reaching down into the crack they slept in that night, and he had seen one rotted down to a skeleton, half buried in sand, and he had hoped he would never see one again; but here one was, and its stare was menacing.

Ballard must have felt the change in the atmosphere too, because his moans grew softer. Though still loud, still desperate, still holding the attention of this giant animal, they were dulled, like his heart was no longer in it. Like he too was intimidated into quiet.

The creature took a step toward the men, into the hallway. It was in no rush to devour them, but it was clear that it had no intention of doing anything else. It knew, no doubt, that they had no chance; that it would not need to try. Like he had been in the corridor of the apartment block, nose-to-nose with hungry dogs, Verne was frozen to the spot, aiming his gun at the beast not because he thought it would save him, but because he had to, to prevent himself from fainting.

As the creature took another lumbering step forward, sniffing the air and growling deeply, Verne became aware of Ellis walking past him on his right, slowly edging toward the creature with Ballard's rifle in his hands. Verne wanted to whisper *What are you doing?* or *Stay back!*, but there was no wind in him to form any words. He just watched Alan Ellis pass him, and tried to concentrate on stopping his knees from shaking.

The creature picked up its pace, pushing itself forward down the tight corridor with its huge arms and snarling at Ellis, who kept approaching. Verne listened to Ballard moaning, 'Matildaaaaaaaaaaaaaaaaaaaaaaaaaaaaaa, comebaaaaaaaaa', now barely louder than his speaking voice, and he watched Ellis creep closer to the animal, and the animal grow more furious the nearer it got to the men, and he was sure beyond all sureness that they were all going to die.

When Ellis reached the creature, he stood in front of it with his arms by his sides, and the rifle pointing at the floor.

Verne was mystified, completely unaware of what Ellis hoped to achieve, apart from being eaten before Verne's eyes. He stood there facing the animal like he expected it to bow to him, tall and proud like he feared not a single thing in the universe. The beast towered over him and drool hung from its red lips as it growled a deep growl that vibrated the entire tunnel, and Verne was sure that despite his posture, Ellis was petrified; but still, he stood there, in front of the animal, and did nothing.

The creature bent forward and pressed its nose to Ellis's hair. It sniffed three times – loud, strong inhalations that ruffled Ellis's long hair and made the fearless man flinch for the first time. It seemed unsure of what it was seeing, what it was smelling, suddenly not so furious and hungry, but more confused. It sniffed again, pressing its face against Alan Ellis and licking his cheek and ear, getting a first taste of something it intended to swallow whole within seconds.

'Matil... da... Ma... til... da...' sighed Ballard, now calming.

The creature lifted its head and looked past Alan Ellis. It had sniffed and it had tasted and it had even brushed its knuckles against the man, and now it had lost interest. It locked its eyes on Verne once again, and snarled aggressively, as if angered that its time had been wasted on inspecting Ellis. It was not keen on tearing Alan Ellis to shreds, but it still looked like it wanted to try to tear Verne. As if Ellis was a chair that stood in its way, the creature pushed him to the side to get past, knocking him to the floor and stepping over him like he was a dropped coat.

But Ellis was not there to be stepped over, and as the beast's chest slowly passed over him, dragging those heavy hind legs behind it, he raised Ballard's rifle and shot five rounds into the creature's lungs. The beast recoiled, screaming a roaring scream that deafened as much as it shook, and hit its head on the ceiling of the hallway. Ellis shot again, the sound of the shots lost in the volume of the monster's wails. Hot, lumpy blood poured down onto Ellis's face and hands as the creature tried to back out of the hallway, run forward, turn around, do anything to get away from the pain; but it was no use, the wounds were mortal, and before ten seconds had passed the screaming had stopped and the creature was a lump of fur and muscles and bones on the floor, that pinned down Ellis's legs and bled out onto the floor of the hallway beneath it. In the silence that followed, only Verne's sigh of relief was audible.

Verne pulled Ellis from under the beast, and held his arms in a tight, grateful grip. 'How did you know it'd walk past you?' he said.

'I didn't,' Ellis replied, his voice shaking. Verne was suddenly aware of how scared the man had been, before he had murdered the creature like he was trained to do it. Ellis's hands trembled violently, as he wiped blood from his face with the sleeves of his overalls. 'It was an educated guess. The dogs have walked past me before, like I wasn't even there. I don't know whether it's because I'm wearing clothes that smell like their piss or because they can sense how I'd taste, but they don't seem interested in me, and obviously I'm thankful for it now.'

Verne laughed. Ellis joined him. They laughed the incorrigible laugh of the relieved, and slapped each other's arms as they walked back to their makeshift beds and their comatose friend. Neither of them really felt like the danger was gone, but they both felt like they had won the right to celebrate, even if only for a minute or two.

'He's calmed down,' Ellis said, when they reached the pile upon which Ballard lay.

'He has,' Verne agreed, watching his friend sleep.

But he had calmed too much. Verne realised, as he watched, that he had calmed to such a degree that he was no longer moving at all, not even the soft rise and fall of his chest. He wondered if it was his imagination, the heightened awareness of the recently threatened, and he took a step closer to check. But no – Ballard was not moving at all. He was as still as he would be if he were…

Verne threw his rifle onto the floor beside him and began pumping Ballard's chest, pushing the beat out, one, two, three, four, five; one, two, three, four, five; one hundred a minute. He listened for breaths and felt for a pulse but found neither, so he pumped again with his hands on Ballard's breastbone, desperation swallowing him and the world and the tunnel and Ellis and everything else melting away as he panicked for his friend and kept pushing on his chest to try and restart a heart that had stopped when no one was looking. Ellis was shouting something but Verne did not hear, and tears ran down his cheeks but he did not feel them, as he tried to push life back into his dead friend; and before he knew it he was on his knees, crying like he had not done for a thousand years, Ellis's arms wrapped around his shoulders and the energy draining out of him like the blood from the beast that Ellis had slain.

His friend had died so young and so far from home, and there had been nothing that Verne could do to save him, and for this reason, he felt he had failed. Yet again, he had failed someone he had cared for, just when they had needed him most.

The men would have to move on, this place was no longer safe; but first, Verne would cry for his friend, and Ellis would comfort him until he was done.

OCTOBER 20TH, 2122

When James Verne finally reached the restaurant, his journey delayed beyond reason by autocabs that never showed and traffic that would not move even when it could, his son was already sitting at the table, sipping whisky and staring absently into space. Verne had seen this look before – though he might appear spaced out and distracted, lost in thought or in the throes of an absent seizure, his son was most likely concentrating on his implant, reading a whitepaper or completing a crossword or speed-learning a new language, without ever lifting a finger. As Verne stood at the entrance to the restaurant having his coat removed and watching the boy staring at nothing with his mouth hanging halfway open, he imagined a future in which every human on Earth spent their time absent from reality, living on their implants, and the act of imagining forced a sigh from his lips as he approached the table.

His son did not stop doing whatever it was that he was doing when Verne reached the opposite side of their table for two. It was, for a moment, as if he was completely unaware of Verne's arrival. Verne spent this moment inspecting his son in that stained, tattered uniform of which

146

he seemed so fond – the steel-toed boots that looked two sizes too big; the skinny legs in baggy three-quarter-length jean shorts; the torn, faded *STOP THE WAR* T-shirt which mentioned no war specifically; all the tattoos and piercings; that ridiculous half-shaven head – and wondering if the office that this boy ran had a dress code at all. He was a co-founder, in investment more than implementation, of the company that was set to revolutionise the world of implanted computing ('implantables'), already floating on the stock market even though they had not yet released a single product for public consumption; and still, the boy could not seem to afford decent clothing, did not seem to care whether he ever made a good impression. It mystified Verne how the apple, on this occasion, could have had fallen so far from the tree.

He had speculated on the causes of his son's malfunctions many times before, and on occasion he would consider that perhaps – just perhaps – they were his own fault as much as the boy's. He had never been close to his son, even when the boy was a toddler, and no matter how hard he had tried it had always seemed like Tobias had considered him more of an inconvenience than a help, more of an ogre than a dad. Without a father whose love could break through those emotional barriers, and with what had happened between them since then, who could blame the boy for his aggressive attitude, his purposeful rebellion against his family name?

But no, it was not that simple either. It ran deeper than that, right down to the boy's core. Verne had seen him on news blogs and short video clips acting violent and dangerous, saying things that would never have been allowed in the house in which he had grown up. Behaviour that would have made his mother ashamed. The older man had had moments, as he watched his son gain notoriety and fame through controversy and wild outbursts in the public eye, in which he thought the boy was insane. It would explain some of the things that he had done, the way he had treated Verne and his mother over the years. But then, if Verne thought back on the psychopathic notions he had entertained and the nasty things he had said and the awful things he had done when he was a younger man which all formed the base of so much of his self-hatred and regret now, perhaps it was not too far a stretch of the imagination to believe that the boy was just following in his father's footsteps, that they had more in common than they thought, and that this route he was taking, though scenic and disorganised, might just end up somewhere that would make the journey worth it.

If only Verne could believe that his son would not crash and burn along the way, and never get to where he was going at all.

'I see you've already ordered drinks,' he said, unbuttoning his suit jacket as he sat opposite his son.

'Singular,' the boy replied, sighing and swiping down on his temple, reluctantly rejoining the room. 'I didn't know when you'd get here, if at all, so I didn't get you one.'

Verne smiled a smile that did not quite reach his eyes, beckoning a waiter to the table with a raised hand. 'I'll have a cranberry juice, please, in a tall glass, with a lot of ice. Thank you.'

'And another one of these,' the boy said, waving his half-full glass between two fingers, as the waiter turned to leave. It was the first time he had really focused on anything in the room since his father had taken a seat, and judging from the way his eyes glazed over when they met Verne's, it looked like he regretted it immediately. 'Cranberry juice. Don't want to join me?' He shook his glass in the air between them, rattling the ice within it.

James Verne held his son's gaze until the youngster found the contact too uncomfortable to stand, and resumed his disinterested staring out of the window.

'I've been sober five years. You know that, Tobias.'

'Please don't call me Tobias. Toby will do fine.'

'*Toby*, then.'

A silence.

'Are you eating enough? You look thin.'

'Yup,' Toby replied, smirking. The way he was looking out of the window, Verne was unsure if he was back on his implant, no longer listening; but then the boy's attention was stolen by the waiter's arrival with their drinks, and how he watched the waiter leave the table left James Verne uncertain whether his son was imagining fucking the waiter or pummelling him with the sharp part of a hammer. Neither would have surprised the older man.

'Are you still dating… *Mei*?' Verne's stomach quivered as he said the name, ready to drop completely if it was revealed that he had said the wrong one.

Toby's smirk dissolved. He took a long swig of his drink. 'Nope,' he replied, 'got rid of her.'

Verne was used to these answers, so carefully constructed from short, sharp words or phrases. This was the way that their lunches would usually go: the older man trying half-heartedly to extract conversation from the young man, and the young man cooperating as little as possible, both counting down the time until the meal was over and their monthly duty was done and they could go their distinct ways. In another world, at another time, perhaps they would have let their relationship go, accepted that no reparation was possible, cut their social ties and allowed blood to be the only thing that connected them; but neither was ready to do so in this world. There was too much left unsaid, that neither man could bring himself to say. Too much explanation left to give, and not enough courage left to give it.

'So, how's the firm?'

'The *firm*?' Tobias gave his father a look that made his heart sink. 'The *firm* is great. New batch of Initiates started last week. Could be production-ready by next July.'

Verne had watched his son's promotional videos, though he would never tell the boy so. He had read every article and watched every keynote, even though he had no interest in the technology and, if truth were told, found many of its applications repugnant. He knew what an Initiate was and why his son's company called their beta-testers by such a ridiculous New Age name, but still, for the sake of conversation, he asked, '*Initiates?*'

His son scoffed, rolled his eyes. Of course this old man would not know what he was talking about. The term was designed to exclude people like him.

Verne had heard the boy on soundcasts, explaining with polished enthusiasm what exactly an Initiate was. 'These are product testers,' he had said, 'for the latest implants. But they're not just testers – they're more than that. Because this isn't just a *product* they need to test, it's a *way of life* they want to adopt. They're media minds, industry leaders, CEOs, public servants, life coaches, holy men, fuckin' *baristas* who have integrated the implant into their daily routines so that we can tune the experience of a lifetime and they can shape the future of our software, our hardware, our *group*.'

Verne could probably have given the speech himself, the amount of times he'd heard it; and now, he half expected to see it live. He thought it was possible that the boy would open up, given an opportunity to talk about his passion – his life's work, the idea that had already made him a billionaire – and finally talk to his father like a human being, share something for the first time in years with the man who had created him. The old man allowed himself, just for a moment, to believe he had found his way in.

But all the boy said was, 'It's what we call our testers.'

'Oh,' he replied, unable to think of anything else.

'Yup.' Tobias grabbed a menu from the table and slouched back, reading it, sighing as if choosing a meal was a chore.

The waiter returned to take food orders, and Verne watched Tobias order the costliest meal on the menu, a signature dish from the flash-in-the-pan celebrity head chef who had recently taken residence here (he had been on cooking shows a few times – he looked filthy, like a drug addict), and then he ordered a steak, knowing that probably neither of them would touch their food. He had got this far, and for that he was relieved; but there was still time for the lunch to end miserably, as form had shown. From here, based on Verne's experience, they would either sit in silence, both running over the past in their heads and each stewing over all of the other's mistakes, or they would talk small until they broke out into an argument and one of them left before the food had even been brought to the table. Never a pleasant, father-son bonding session, like families had in movies.

The boy began scratching behind his ear, and Verne noticed for the first time where the tiny connector ports sat on his head. He saw the beginning of the dark line that ran across the back of his son's skull, the strip of wiring just under the skin that he had read about in his son's company's marketing, the strip that changed colour with your mood, your hydration levels, the vitality of your vital signs. Dark when you were unhappy or ill, light when you were content and well. He grabbed only a glimpse before his son caught him and stopped scratching. Tobias attempted the kind of nonchalant half-smile he might be wearing if he had never been scratching at all, so his father asked the unnecessary question.

'You've had the implant?'

'I was the first.'

'I see.'

The kid scratched his head again, clearly uncomfortable but trying in vain to hide it with an exaggerated simulation of ruffling his hair. A long time passed, the two men saying nothing, watching everyone around them, wishing that their food would arrive, if only so that they could make their hands and mouths busy. Watching his son watch the room and never deign to shoot a single glance at his father, Verne felt the bitterness within him build, a rising of resentment for which he hated himself as much as the boy, and he decided that he had to say something, just to escape his head. *Make a sound; let the energy out. Ask a question, engage him, even if you already know the answer.*

'What does it do?'

Tobias rolled his eyes, sighed loudly.

Elsa Verne was diagnosed with Lou Gehrig's disease when Tobias was just starting at Oxford. His father called him a few days later, slightly drunk and crying inconsolably, to tell him that his mother was dying, that the illness had her and it was as aggressive as it could possibly be and she would probably be dead by the time he had his degree. She wanted her son home, he said, and he wanted his son home too.

'Why don't you come back to the States, live with us again, put this college thing on hold, or else find one nearer to your family?'

Thousands of miles from home, young and stupid, receiving the worst news he had ever been given over a crackling transatlantic feed, Tobias gave in to some dark and cowardly voice within him, and he refused to return home that day, or any day for the next year. He spent his weeks avoiding his father's calls, or else answering and not listening to a single word about his dying mother, the yearning both his parents felt to have their son there with them. Not wanting to face the tragedy that was befalling the most beautiful woman he had ever known, the boy sunk into a pattern of studying, working, drinking, fucking, campaigning, rowing, getting high, studying… anything that would distract his mind from home, where death and sadness were slowly closing in to claim what was owed to them.

But in the summer after his first year, he found himself on a plane bound for San Francisco, only half aware of what he was heading toward, coming down from a year-long high so artificial that he could barely remember enjoying a second of it. He spent the hours on that flight drinking and leering at the flight attendants, unable to sleep; and when he got to the airport, it seemed to him that he was sitting in a cab on the way back to his parents' house before he had taken a breath.

Everything was happening without his consent. Moments bled into moments and everything in between was being managed by some subconscious process, some autopilot he could not remember ever having programmed, so that the entire journey from England to the USA ended up seeming more like a montage of someone else's life than an experience of his own. One minute, he had been debating whether to go home at all, and the next, he was standing outside his family's mansion, the house he grew up in, pressing his finger on the doorbell and trying to calm his panicking heart.

Cruz, the maid who had worked for the Verne family since Tobias was a toddler, answered the door, and her sweet brown eyes creased at the edges from the smile that immediately spread across her face. She had developed more lines, he noticed; her skin looked tougher. Living with a dying woman and her shattered husband was clearly taking its toll. She opened the huge wooden door all the way and held her arms out, offering a hug.

'Tobias!'

He smiled back, relieved that he did not have to face his father first. He stepped forward to embrace Cruz, but was stopped in his tracks when he noticed his old man stumble out into the hall behind her, looking to cause trouble for whoever was at the door. He was unshaven, bent over like an invalid, unable to focus his bloodshot eyes. The stench of alcohol clinging to him could be smelt from yards away.

When his eyes met his son's, they burned with a sudden rage.

'Cruz, close the door.'

He stood trembling, tapping his hand against his hip like he always had when he was mad, as Cruz looked between him and his son, unsure of what to do.

'But, Mr Verne, it's Tobias, home fr—'

'I said *close the fucking door*,' he slurred, hobbling to the door and wrestling it from her grip to slam it himself.

Tobias stood there for ten minutes more, waiting for it to be reopened, for the misunderstanding to be cleared up, before he went to find a hotel.

He visited again every day for a month, trying to gain access to his sick mother, but being denied every time, either by a tearful Cruz, or by the panelled face of that unopened door and the twitching curtains that preceded it. Gradually, his numbness was whittled down, the shell of passivity he had built to protect himself from the strain – and the guilt of having left his father high and dry to deal with it all – chipped away, until one day, he forced his way in, pushing his way past Cruz and running into the room where his mother sat stinking and neglected and his father sat drunk and self-pitying, wasting space. The old man threw a punch, tried to wrestle his young son out of the house; the boy, however, was stronger, and the fight quickly became a beating, until Tobias stood over a cowering Verne senior, sobbing as loud as the drunk, his knuckles stinging like he had been punching a cactus. He wheeled his mother out of the room, and apologised to Cruz as he left the house with her.

He took charge of his mother's care from that day, threatening his father with legal action, beatings, anything he could to keep him away. With his father being such a drunken old coward, he never needed to deliver on any of the threats; Verne stayed away for good, and only saw his wife once more – when she was reaching the very end, and her son decided to allow it.

When all was done, Tobias Verne had missed out on his degree, what should have been the best years of his life stolen from him, and James Verne had never got a chance to properly say goodbye to his wife. Both men had loved that woman more than they had ever loved anyone else in the world, and both men had hoped that they would never lose her, and when the thing they had always dreaded had happened, it had been so devastating that they had also lost each other. Each blamed himself as much as he blamed the other, neither could decide who he hated more, and both were too stubborn to admit it.

At the funeral, they stood at opposite ends of the hole in the ground, never even making eye contact.

Now, more for the sake of the woman they had both loved and lost than for either of their own, they met once a month, to eat and talk and remember the blood ties that bound them forever. Neither of the men would look forward to their appointments, and this was the first time in what seemed like a thousand attempts that one of their dinners had gone well – well enough, anyway; no skin broken – but both of them knew that they had to do it, because it was what she would have wanted, the very minimum she would have wanted, and she deserved to get what she wanted more than they did, since her heart had been so full of light and love and theirs were so dark, so angry, so hateful.

What would she say if she knew that this was all they could manage?

She would say that they were being morons. That they were proud, stubborn, angry fools and that they should apologise to each other and hold each other close and never let go. That she loved them, more than they could ever know. That they were more alike than she could say. That they should hold what they had with a tight grip, lest it slip away before they realised how much they would miss it.

That was what they had to remind themselves. That was the image Verne would put in his mind when he dreaded seeing his son, when he sighed ruefully at the thought of leaving the house to have dinner with the boy. But still, even after that reminder, and even after this successful lunch, there still existed a tiny, spiteful part of his mind which took pleasure in uttering the words that had brought him to arrange today's meal, the words that he had considered never saying, but had to.

'I've been offered a place on *Conqueror 23*.'

'Okay.' His son did not seem fazed, making a real show of picking spinach from between his teeth.

'It's a mission that will take a millennium. Not that I'll be awake for most of it. What's certain is that I won't be coming back.'

There was that spiteful part of James Verne, yes, which took that pleasure in letting his stubborn, unreachable son know that his actions had driven his father away for eternity; but a bigger part, a part that shouted louder but was heard less and less for all its screaming, ached for reconciliation, regretted already the decision to abandon Earth before it got a taste of catharsis. Looking at him, one would not have guessed that this battle raged within him any more than one would guess he was having a stroke or tap-dancing beneath the table.

'Yup. I know the mission. I've read all about it. I guess you weren't happy with War Hero or Celebrity Soldier, then. Now you're gonna be Legendary Astronaut. Go farther than any man has gone before.' Tobias picked food from between his teeth with his toothpick, stared out of the window, chose not to say any more, for fear of giving in to the choking lump that sat in his throat.

Verne found his heart to be fluttering, his breath quivering. He could see that the boy was unhappy, and far from tasting sweet in his mouth, this little victory over his son's disdain was sour and unpleasant. Verne experienced something like guilt, felt a hairline fracture developing in the concrete decision he had made to embark on his greatest mission yet, millions of miles from his only son. He sighed, a long and deep sigh that seemed to lift a weight just an inch or two off his shoulders, the weight of all that pride and all that stubbornness and all that resentment that had built up over the last eight years.

'Look, Toby, I know that—'

Verne was interrupted suddenly by a man at the restaurant's bar who was banging the wooden surface of the counter with his hand, shouting, '*Excuse me, everyone, sorry to disturb, please pay attention.*' Since he had sobered up and regained control, James Verne had never been a sucker for flashing lights, moving screens, loud noises, anything that grabbed the mind and dragged it forcefully away from what it needed to focus on; but on this occasion, his mind seemed instantly happier for the distraction.

'Sorry to interrupt your meals, guys,' bellowed the corpulent old man at the bar, his words melting into each other, a champagne bottle in his chubby right hand, 'but I have some very important news. Exactly seven years ago, my beautiful wife here set out to be a doctor. She went back to school, picked up all the books and the stress and all those horrible things the rest of us have completely forgotten about, and she studied her ass off for that degree. And today, she finally graduated – my stunning wife became a medical doctor.'

A light sprinkle of applause spread across the room, couples smiled at each other, the fat man's wife blushed and told him to shut up, though Verne could see it on her face that she did not want him to, that she was enjoying the attention. The whole display made James Verne sick.

The tubby husband continued, 'So I want to buy everyone in the room a drink. Every single one of you can have a drink on me. No, really, just bill them to me – let your waiter know what you'd like and I'll buy it. And now, a toast, to Dr Gretchen Meyer.' The fat man raised his bottle, nuzzled into his wife's neck, laughed his wobbling laugh, and after a round of applause, the room continued its chatter. Verne watched strangers pat the fat man and his dizzy wife on the back insincerely for a while, wondering how many of them would give a fuck if there was no drink in it for them, before turning back to face his son, who was gone.

On the table, atop Tobias' napkin, sat a fistful of crumpled bills, slowly unscrewing itself like a butterfly breaking out of its cocoon. A final *fuck you* from the son that James Verne would never see again.

Verne wished he could take the fat man up on his offer.

DAY 88

Kojima woke sticky with sweat, so hot she could feel her veins expanding under her dry, brittle skin and her tongue dehydrated like cured meat in her mouth. She pushed off her grimy covers and unzipped her tattered overalls and sat up, cross-legged, blowing cool air through her pursed lips at her breasts and belly. Before a minute had passed, she accepted that her effort was being wasted by the temperature of the room and sat instead just looking down at her body – her wrists, her ankles, the bones showing through the skin everywhere. She had always been slim, her height and her genes had secured that for her, but their meagre rations and the unforgiving conditions had her body now verging on ill health, tumbling toward dangerous malnourishment.

Shelley was worse. On Earth, she had been what many young women wanted to be – pretty and slim and youthful, with soft skin and softer hair – without ever having to make an effort to achieve it; but now, just weeks after losing their comrades (exactly how long was a mystery now – the women had lost count of the days), she looked twenty years older, one thousand sleepless nights more tired, and she had a scar across her face that tore through that prettiness like a bullet through brain tissue.

These were not the only tolls this planet had taken on her – her spirit had been gradually dampened, and Kojima had watched it happen. Shelley had learned to read the language of this city's people to an adequate degree just a couple of weeks after they had found the museum, with a little help from another translated passage they had found and a lot of help from her implant; and the more of their literature that she read, the less she wanted to read. She would now talk bleakly of their writings if she spoke about them at all, and far from being insatiable, her appetite to discover more about this world and its history was diminished to a vague memory, a folly she did not care to repeat. Watching her sleep, wearing that frown she had grown to always wear when she dreamed, Kojima would have felt sad for her, if she had the energy; but she did not, so she sat watching until she felt the desire to stand.

The women had taken to sleeping through the night, rather than guarding in shifts, after they came to the realisation that no harm had come to them at night, but much had been brought to them during daylight. They had not abandoned caution – they would barricade the doors of rooms that they slept in and keep their rifles close, but even these habits were fading, slowly being crushed by the weight of the women's apathy toward their own survival. Kojima foresaw a day in the not-too-distant future when they would leave their guns behind and forget to ever check their surroundings, so distracted would they be by their own hunger and exhaustion. She had even found herself hoping, in moments when her knees felt weak and her stomach was being squeezed in a vice that would not let up, that when they starved to death, Shelley would die first, so that the younger woman would be spared the distress of struggling for survival alone in this wilderness. But these thoughts were a slope she hated to slip down, so when they entered her head she did anything she could to distract herself from sliding into a bottomless pit of what-ifs and imagined doom.

She wandered to the window and gazed out at the river and the suspension bridge that hung over it, which they had crossed weeks before. The bridge was covered with creeping vines, like many of the leaning and burnt-out buildings they had seen, including the one they were in; and taking it in as it bathed in the first light of the morning, under waves and streaks of orange and purple and red like Northern Lights that filled the entire sky, she was reminded of just how beautiful this planet could be. They had become hostages of this world, slaves submissive to its whimsical destruction and wanton violence; Shelley had had her face slashed by its wild dogs, and Kojima had on one or two occasions been driven to fantasies of murder-suicide by its harshness. They were starved and bruised and gutted by its barren landscape and depressing history, deserted by their friends and also, by now, their hopes. They had been broken by this planet, there was no denying it; but if all that was true could not be denied, then it could also not be denied that this city, with its unusual real estate and scattered layout, its sprinkling of orange dust and stripes of green-black vines creeping their trails up leaning skyscrapers, was a breathtaking, captivating sight, and that this world so drab and devoid of life could wear more colours than a hundred thousand rainbows, and that if Kojima was to choose a beautiful place for her body to perish, this might just be as good as any.

But these were strange thoughts. And she was having those too often.

She turned from the window and found Shelley waking wearily from her slumber, rubbing her eyes and pushing off her covers, trying desperately to escape the heat in the room.

'Oh,' Shelley said, once she had calmed herself, 'we're

still here.'

'Yep,' replied Kojima, smiling softly.

Shelley yawned, stretched.

'Okay,' she sighed, climbing to her feet. Then, again, 'Okay.'

The women had been living in this building for three weeks. Their previous residence, an office block closer to the water, had a functioning plumbing system and much furniture and cloth with which to build defences and manufacture quilts, coverings and clothing for the colder nights. They had given up many weeks ago the exploration of the city for the sake of discovery, the desire to drink in this world's history and conquer its secrets as they had come here to do; and, by now, only explored to gather food, if they could find it.

It had been just as they were about to set out on one of these scavenger hunts that they had encountered the injured dog, limping into the doorway to take cover and rest in the shade. It had looked weak and tired, inches from death, as it dragged its useless hind legs into the building; but when it saw the women, it had lashed out like it had been feigning injury all along. The combined force of the women's rifles had won the battle, more through luck than skill; but with a six-inch gash across her face and one eye irreparably damaged, Shelley had not felt like she had won anything for a long while afterward.

They ate the dog that evening, and both spent that night vomiting, their stomachs now unused to the richness of meat, the texture of animal fat. When more dogs came looking for their lost comrade, or perhaps simply following the smell of meat and blood, the women decided it would be best to find a new home.

This building was one rung up from that one on this planet's property ladder. It was largely the same in layout, perhaps a little taller, again a probable office block;

however, in addition to the functioning plumbing system, it offered working hallway lighting, something they had not encountered in nearly one hundred days of breaking and entering. Shelley had dragged her feet into the building, tired and hungry, wandering like the undead in a low-budget horror film, and had been kicked out of her daze when the lights had buzzed on all the way down the hall. The lighting was dim and flickering as if powered only by some emergency source, and was therefore virtually useless to the women, whose eyes could be artificially assisted in darkness anyway; but still, it broke the monotony and made a promise that this world, though decrepit and crumbling on the outside, still held many secrets. They had lived here for three weeks, and a thorough investigation into the building's power source was still on their to-do list.

Their time had instead been spent on the roof of this building, tending plants they had never expected to find, which were growing in abundance at the top of the rotting office block. The women assumed that this had once been a roof garden, but how it had been maintained to this day was a mystery. When they found it, it was overgrown and bug-infested, weeds spilling over the edges of the roof and down the sides of the building; but still it hosted many of the root vegetables and wiry fruit trees they had occasionally stumbled across at street level, and even some new ones they had not seen below. Far from looking sorry and ill, it seemed that these plants had thrived without any help, and they gave Shelley and Kojima almost a week of respectable meals. Now, however, the story was not so encouraging. They had struggled to keep up the balance that nature had kept without them, and the plants seemed to be shrivelling in the sun and taking nothing from their soil, and the women had begun once again to feel weak with hunger, dizzy with abdominal aches.

It was in this garden that they spent their mornings, reintroducing some of the weeds they had removed and attempting to moisten the soil, hoping that this would restore equilibrium to the environment. Kojima would work until she felt sick and her back creaked and then rest in the shade of the shrubs until she felt better, and repeat this process until she could work no more. Shelley, meanwhile, would work for hours, with a glazed look and at a slow pace, working not because she wanted to but because her life depended on it. While neither of the women had been avid gardeners on Earth, they both knew the basic principles and filled in the gaps with common sense, but the little that they had learned from Earth's crops did not seem to apply here, as no amount of weeding and watering and keeping free of pests was helping this ever-diminishing garden of vegetables. But it would have to do, they supposed, until they found a book on cultivating this world's vegetation, which Shelley could absorb. Though the surface area of the roof was large and the garden covered most of it, to find anything edible growing in this garden was now a rarity.

'You'd think they would have given us survival training, or at least some flaming seeds to plant,' said Shelley, sitting with her legs tucked under her and cuttings of weeds in clumps in her hands. Sweat glistened on her skin, water running down her cheek from her bad eye. 'I haven't got a fucking clue what I'm doing here.'

Kojima looked at her from a few metres away, saw her ragged hair and her arms covered in tiny scratches and cuts from branches and thorns, and felt a sudden, irrepressible compulsion to laugh. Shelley looked pathetic and helpless, exactly as Kojima felt. The situation was not amusing, but the urge took her, so she laughed. And once she had begun to laugh, Shelley also started laughing. They laughed together until they had no more energy to do so, and then they left the garden to prepare some lunch out of the food they had found.

*

Weeks earlier, they had spotted their first example of this civilisation's version of advertising. A billboard, one hundred feet wide and just a little over half that high, faded into near invisibility, was mounted to the side of one of the shorter, stouter buildings near to the river; and upon discovery of it, the women were struck once again by that feeling of familiarity, that distinct wonder that a race could have evolved so far from Earth, but with so much in common with it. If they had advertising, what else did they have? Capitalism? Democracy? Philosophy? Taxes? How many of these concepts were designed for us, and not by us? If the probability of intelligent life forming on a planet was the same as a tornado tearing through a junkyard and forming an aeroplane, what was the probability of two planets growing up together, millions of miles apart? How many junkyard tornadoes had already happened, and how many were yet to be? The billboard, so long dead, had sparked much debate between its two living visitors, who could not decide whether this was proof of intelligent design, some higher being's will, or simply the logical course which society will always run.

They did not consider, at the time, that this society may have been mimicking Earth's, or if that theory might work the other way around. Exhaustion or apathy or something else entirely made them neglect, just then, to make a link (if, indeed, there was one) between the similarities they had spotted to their own culture, and this culture's study of humanity.

And Kojima was still not making this link, as she gazed upon the sign that evening, from the rooftop of the building. She was no longer looking to speculate about creation or evolution, no longer marvelling at alien marketing, but simply looking for prospects, places to which the women could move to have a better chance of farming effectively or hunting with ease. She had no real requirements for which she was looking, but she thought that if she found the perfect spot, she would just know. Besides, looking was better than doing nothing, as Shelley was doing and had been doing for hours. Sitting on the edge of the roof, rake-like legs dangling over the side, the younger woman cut a moody silhouette in the evening haze, completely silent and staring down at the roads below, in a solemn world of her own creation.

She would slip in and out of this malaise almost daily, one minute fine, if a little quiet, and the next depressive and morose and unwilling to communicate at all. Kojima had a feeling that it had a lot to do with this planet's extinction event, which the women now suspected to be a great war between believers in two different ideologies; a war which had ended, evidently, in mutual destruction. When Shelley had read the documents and texts that spoke of this war, and the suffering it had caused, she had grown more and more displeased, less and less eager to find out more, as if she had imagined a perfect scenario to explain the absence of life here, and the truth had betrayed it. She had become despondent and frustrated, as if she had expected the truth to have some deeper meaning, and had thrown down books and scripts and horrific photographs that refuted that, blaming them for her unhappiness. It concerned Kojima that the younger woman had taken it so much to heart, and during Shelley's sulky periods of sadness she would watch her with pity and feel helpless, wanting to comfort her friend but not knowing how, and knowing that even if she had some idea how, Shelley would still not be receptive. So she would just watch, and wait, and if Shelley caught her watching, she would feel guilty. On this occasion, though, she chose not to watch, instead continuing to look out at the horizon, the sky, the vines, the city.

'Do you remember the Disneyland bombing?' asked Shelley, breaking a silence that had lasted hours.

Kojima nodded, wondered how anyone could have forgotten that day. 'Yes,' she replied.

'I was eleven when that happened,' Shelley said, 'and it scared the shit out of me.'

'And everybody.'

'Yeah. But for weeks, I couldn't sleep. I just kept imagining all those innocent people killed, all those lives cut short just because they were in the wrong place at the wrong time, and a handful of sickos wanted to make a point. I was terrified, knowing that people like that could live among us, that there could be someone who wanted to kill me living next door, smiling at me in the morning and plotting my murder at night. I thought a war was going to start, and that every adult I knew was going to be sent off to die in it. I thought a lot of things, most of them irrational. But I was a kid, I didn't understand.

'Anyway, in the end it got so bad that my dad figured I needed some kind of intervention, so he picked me up out of bed one night and took me up to the roof of our apartment block. I'd been crying to him, telling him I was scared he was going to go away and that people were going to get me or blow my school up or something, yadda yadda yadda; so I was sniffling and blubbering in his arms, all the way up this staircase to the roof. When we got up there, he sat on some crappy garden chair that was up there, and sat me down on his lap. We lived in Melbourne, so looking out from the rooftop you could see the tops of so many buildings, apartment blocks and churches and shops and hotels, stretching for miles. Like this, but y'know... nicer.

'So my dad pointed out at all these rooftops and he said to me, "Wednesday, look at this place. This city is filled with millions of people, and tonight they're all going about their lives, dreaming in their beds or eating food or going out to work the night shift or whatever else. Some of them are as scared as you feel, and yeah, some of them are mean and angry and violent; but some of them are positive, and fighting for our future, and a lot of them aren't particularly angry or happy, they're just in their own little worlds.

They're thinking about how they'll manage to pay their bills next month, or the vacation they've booked, or something else entirely. The point is, there are so many people out there, and most of them just want to live their lives and not hurt anyone. You look out over any city and you can be sure that you'll be seeing more good people than bad. Many, many, many more people that don't want to hurt you than people who do. If the world is a matter of good versus evil, then good is winning. And all you have to do is make sure you're good too, and you'll be okay."'

Kojima looked back at Shelley from her corner of the rooftop and smiled. She wondered if this was what Shelley had been thinking about, all that time she had spent staring at nothing and sighing at intervals.

'That's nice,' she said. She worried that it would sound like sarcasm, but Shelley did not even seem to hear her.

'For the first few weeks here, I spent all my time thinking that everyone had just abandoned this city,' Shelley continued. 'I kept asking myself, *Why did they leave? What were they running from?* But now I just keep wondering if someone from this planet sat on a roof like this, looking out at this city, telling their kid the same thing, before the war tore their society down.'

Kojima could hear the sadness in her colleague's voice, and struggled for a moment with the discomfort it made her feel. Looking out at the river, her implant zoomed in, she watched a fat, hairless rodent-looking creature scuttle to the water's edge and wrinkle its nose at the river, as if sniffing for predators. It did this two or three times, then looked to its left and right, its movements jerky and quick, as had been the movements of most rodents on Earth. Satisfied that it was not being watched or followed, it dived into the water and just like that, was gone. The water calmed, and there was nothing left of the rodent.

From the corner of the building, four metres or more away from her friend, Kojima turned and replied, 'I gave things like that a lot of thought on Earth. I went through a phase – much later in life than you – of being very scared, spending most of my time worrying about why people do what they do, why wars and hatred and violence are such a huge part of our make-up, where we'd end up if it carried on that way. It was all-consuming for me. There wasn't a minute of the day when I wasn't thinking about it, and not many nights that it didn't keep me awake. Fear became my life, for a long time. And, really, most of the reason I came here was that I wanted to be free of that fear. I didn't have a nice childhood, and I'd suffered from anxiety in one form or another for my entire life, and I felt like I'd never really cure those things, only beat them into submission and make them my own.

'But in the end, I was so tired of feeling afraid of the world and all the things it could do to me, and so tired of trying to beat that fear into submission, that I just wanted to get away from it. *It can't get me if I'm a million miles away.* And when we got here and found the city like this, I wished I was back there, with that fear.'

Shelley looked at Kojima from across the roof.

'I don't know what I'm telling you,' said Kojima. 'I guess it's that what we had, that fear of war and violence and destruction, was better than nothing. At least we had homes to feel it in.'

Shelley nodded, then looked out at the city again. 'It's just so sad, to see a civilisation reduced to these ruins, isn't it?'

There was a short silence.

'Perhaps the sad thing isn't that this race managed to wipe itself out,' Kojima said, gazing out at the crumbling buildings, that ageing suspension bridge and the dark river that flowed beneath it, 'but that this planet survived its people. The plants weave their way up the skyscrapers and the animals wander in and out of buildings as if this has always been their jungle. I always imagined the logical conclusion of man's constant conflicts as an all-out, global nuclear war that would wipe out everything that man had ever created or known. But you look here, and you realise that man isn't as powerful as he thinks he is. If there was a war that extinguished our race, planet Earth would have forgotten about it within a hundred years. Maybe that's what's most depressing – we're a speed bump in history, and all this stuff that means so much to us, all these ideas and gods and countries, don't mean a thing once we're done killing each other for them, because by then, we're all killed, and those ideas and those gods have all been killed with us, and everything else just goes on as if we never existed.'

Shelley frowned. 'Well, thanks, but that didn't make me feel better,' she said.

Kojima smiled and gave her colleague a sideways look. 'No,' she replied, 'I suppose it wouldn't. But if the thing that upsets you is that it was war that killed these people, then tell me this: what would you rather have happened? That these people were all killed off by a meteor or a plague? Earthquakes? Famine? Forces of nature or forces of evil, the result is the same. Everyone dies.'

Shelley stood and placed the straps of her backpack onto her bony shoulders, still facing out at the city. 'I dunno,' she said. 'Seems better for it to be nature, doesn't it? Nature has no malice, it doesn't kill for any other reason than that it can.'

'Did the killers of Earth kill for any other reason than that? I always thought our world was covered with savages who'd kill civilians because they wanted to murder, not because they really believed in the causes they hid behind. They just wanted to see blood spilt by their hands, to feel as powerful as gods when they knew they were just men. Violence for the sake of violence.'

Shelley spent a few moments thinking about this, a frown on her face and her hands gripping the straps of her rucksack tightly, before saying, 'Okay. I get it.' And then, after a moment's thought, 'Honestly, though, I think you might be oversimplifying some complex issues, there.'

'Oh, I definitely am,' replied Kojima, not missing a beat, 'but I had to think this way. I couldn't have lived with the idea that murder was ever constructive and that there were so many causes worth killing for. The only way I could see *that* ending was… *this*.' She pointed out at the decaying city. 'Besides, if we pretend for a while that the world was as simple as it could have been, do I really seem that wrong? If the promise of Heaven turned out to be a lie, and the horrors of Hell were worse than we imagined, would there be any cause that was really worth killing for?'

'Well,' Shelley sighed, turning to her colleague, 'I still don't feel better. Let's get off this rooftop, before I jump.'

Then, over her shoulder, as she wandered away into the safety of the building, she yelled, 'There's always something to smile about!'

Kojima watched her walk away, and sighed. She had damaged her own mood by delving back into those thoughts she had intended to leave so far behind, but she was pleased that she had, at least, dragged Shelley out of her introspection. Talked some of it out, helped the younger woman get something off her chest. She stretched, picked up her rucksack, and followed her friend inside for the night. Tomorrow would provide more opportunities to farm, to hunt, to scavenge, and they would need their rest if they hoped to survive it.

Far off in the distance, James Verne and Alan Ellis crossed that bridge over the river, two dark lumps on a horizon toward which Kojima was no longer gazing.

Later that night, in a room as black as tar, a smell in the air just like it, when both women lay awake thinking the other was asleep, Shelley whispered to nobody, 'I bet you think I'm just a stupid little girl worrying about stupid, irrelevant things. Well, I'm not.'

And then she sighed.

And out of the darkness, Kojima replied, 'Well, I am. You never stop feeling like a silly little girl, and you never stop worrying about stupid, irrelevant things. Your hair goes grey and your back starts aching, but inside you're always pretty much who you were in your twenties, and you always carry those same concerns around with you, like weights around your shoulders. What matters is that you never stop caring, and that you don't let them beat you. You lose those fights, and all is lost.'

DAY 46

Verne watched a bead of blood swell in the mouth of the cut on his hand, a perfect scarlet sphere as hot and slick as melted solder wire, before it buckled under its own weight and trickled quickly down his calloused skin. Before the blood reached his cuff, his hand had reached his mouth, and he sucked the redness away from the wound, grimacing as he tasted the iron in his blood, the saltiness of the dirt on his palm. The cut stung, but somehow he liked the feeling of it. It surprised him, for a moment, how long it had been since he last felt pain. The men had been relatively free of danger for so long, he supposed, that he had almost forgotten he could bleed.

He had been making a snare with wire they had ripped from a wall a few days prior. Having taken a stretch of wire and made a loop at the end, he was threading the other end through this loop when the needle-sharp end he was pushing through entered his hand with almost no resistance, half a centimetre in before he even felt the sting. He must have made a hundred of these snares over the past two weeks to catch the rodents that lived near the river, which had become the primary food source for the men, and he had not once cut himself, with his blade or the wire; but today, he was distracted, never quite in the room. When it happened, he had been daydreaming about Ellis teaching him how to make these snares and telling him all about the habits of the rodents they were going to catch with them. Verne had been taught years before how to make a good snare, by his grandfather on his land just outside of Kermit, Texas; but still, he had listened patiently and with some level of awe at how much Ellis had learned about his new home since he had arrived. Whenever that was.

He removed his hand from his mouth and looked at it again. The cut was small and the bleeding had mostly stopped, but the skin around it was bright red and the pain was spreading across his hand like a rash. He frowned at his hand, opening and closing it to test the extent of the pain, before being dragged out of distraction by a memory.

Ellis had shown Verne what he called the Museum of Other Worlds on Verne's thirtieth day on the planet, two days after the pair had emerged from the sewers into the sweltering daylight. He had shown Verne the exhibits and had expressed disappointment that half the building was missing – it had apparently not been, last time he came – and he had promised that one day, he would show Verne the books he had found that proved just how deeply the aliens had studied their culture and that of other nearby planets; and Verne had listened and looked with amazement, shock, wonder – all of the emotions the women had felt days before them – but he had not remembered the drawing he had seen of the human hand. He had not thought to ask Ellis if he had seen that page, or the basement in which it sat. It had completely slipped his mind, until now.

He stood from the table on which he had been leaning, and walked into the corridor of the building they were in, stepping carefully between the debris and the cracks that lined the floor. The buildings they had been inhabiting the past few days had been filthy and wrecked, looking more like bomb sites than simply abandoned spaces; but Alan Ellis had said that they should stay here because he knew where the grizzly beasts liked to hang out and how to avoid them, and he must have been right, because they had not seen a dog or one of those huge bears since the incident in the tunnel. They had seen rodents, and bugs, and Verne was sure he had seen something like a snake; but he had not seen a single animal that he perceived to be a threat. As a result, they had become comfortable enough to split up, and explore their surroundings without needing to stay within shouting distance. So, to find Ellis and ask him about that drawing, he had to hunt through every crumbling room until he reached him.

When he found Ellis, he was in a room at the opposite side of the floor, facing away from the door, hunched over Ballard's backpack, rummaging through it as if time was of the essence and being detected might be catastrophic. Watching him from the doorway, Verne became concerned. If Ellis had asked to look through Ballard's things, Verne would not have cared – Ballard had no use for them now – but seeing him sitting in a dimly lit room, hunched over the bag and glancing sideways over his shoulder like a teenage onanist terrified of parental intervention, arose suspicion.

He looked on for a while as Ellis pushed objects aside and pulled some out for inspection, not seeming to find whatever it was he was looking for, and then Verne said, 'Ellis.'

And Alan Ellis froze for a moment, then sat up straight, and zipped up the bag as if he had completed his search. He turned to Verne with a smile and said, 'Hey, man.'

'You okay?' Verne asked, leaning against the door frame.

'Yeah,' Ellis said, maintaining eye contact and still wearing that grin. He was not blushing and his stance did not seem awkward or embarrassed – despite the circumstances, it did not seem that he felt at all caught out.

Verne supposed that maybe he had misinterpreted Ellis's rush, that perhaps he was not trying to be surreptitious and strange, but had done so by accident, and that he had not been caught misbehaving, just acting characteristically weird – being alone for so long, after all, would have an effect on any man's social skills.

Since he had saved Verne's life and only received a blow to the face in return, Verne was willing to give him the benefit of the doubt.

After a silence, Ellis hooked Ballard's rucksack onto his back and said to Verne, as if he already knew exactly why he had approached him, 'Wanna see some of those books I told you about? We can see if they're still next door.'

And he walked past Verne out of the room, without waiting for an answer.

DAY 90

When Ballard was a child, he had obsessed over the power of single moments. Whether it was the choice of whether or not to drop a bomb, pull a trigger, tell a lie or save a life, there were things in the universe that would take just half a second to do, but could change the course of history irreversibly; and this, he saw as unjust. More than the injustice of the skin into which humans were born, or the time or the place, or the ever-looming hand of death that haunted their every step, he often said that this inability to turn the clock back even a second to take back those things we immediately regret was the most unfair thing in the universe. He had said it to Kojima after three days here, in the heat and the sand, when they had all wished they could turn back time; and now, more than then, she had to agree.

The women had left their tower when its roof garden had died under their care, mere days after it had flourished under no care at all. Shelley's spirits had been lifted slightly after their talk on the rooftop, most likely because she had only needed to get her concerns off her chest and now that it was done she could get back to living; so she had been reading once again, and had found a map printed on a kind of leaflet, tattered and faded, which apparently labelled all of the city's shelters, where displaced citizens could have found food and warmth and medical attention during the war. Repurposed government buildings and warehouses mostly, they were dotted across both sides of the river and were probably the women's best chance of finding sachets of food like those they had found before, if there were any left in the city. The makeshift hospital they had stayed in weeks before was most likely one of these shelters, but that part of the city had been torn from this map. There was, however, another just two blocks from the tower they had been staying in, and the women had agreed that it would be best to trek there next.

But what they had not expected was to find in this building a pile of bodies taller than themselves, piled bones and rotten flesh so charred and blackened that it almost looked like a pile of coal on the black ground. This had been some kind of town hall or conference centre, circular and high with a ramp twisting up its sides like a screw thread all the way to the roof, and the entrance hall that this screw looked down upon in the centre of the building was a bonfire that must have burned decades, if not centuries, ago; and yet still, it smelt like smoke and looked fresh. The women had been hit by it as soon as they entered, and the whiff of hope that this building might sustain them for a few more days was overpowered by the stench of bodies before they could even enjoy its fragrance for a second.

And now they stood mourning that hope, rueing the moment they chose to come here.

As Kojima touched the writing on the wall, that same scrawl she had seen in the apartment block opposite the school, brown like dried blood and each character two feet high, she sighed and hung her head, remembering the ideas that Ballard had given her in the desert. *Perhaps there are a thousand other ways*, she thought, *that this could have turned out. It could have ended a hundred times worse or a hundred times better, and we'll never know because we made a choice that took an instant to make, and that instant changed everything. Maybe there's a universe where our ship blew apart before it even left Earth's atmosphere, and we never came this far. Maybe we don't know how much worse it could have been.*

Maybe there's a universe where we arrived here and it was Heaven, and there, we're living like kings, worshipped like gods.

If only she had chosen not to follow Shelley to this building, she would not be feeling this way again. If only she could turn back the clock to just that moment, looking at the map, perhaps she could have protected Shelley from this discovery too. Suggested a different direction, another shelter.

Or maybe there are no other possibilities; maybe there was never a choice at all.

'How could they do this?' Shelley said, on her knees by the pile of bodies, piling ash into her hands as if trying to resurrect those who had burned. 'Fucking hell, it's the same here as it is everywhere else.'

Kojima approached her friend from behind and placed a hand on her shoulder. She said nothing.

'Look at these bones. Some of these were kids. How could they do this? What cause could ever mean so much that everyone has to die for it?' She was close to tears again, as if she had known these people, been a part of this race. The scene made Kojima feel nothing more than fear – she felt no sadness for the lives lost in this room or this city, but she did feel sick from the smell of death that hung around even now, and the malice that still clung to the walls. She and Shelley felt just as strongly, about different things.

A time passed, with Shelley staring at the ash in her hands and Kojima holding her shoulder.

'Can you read what it says on the walls?' Kojima asked finally, pointing at the message as if it needed pointing out.

Shelley sniffed in her sadness and wiped her eyes, but

did not look at the wall. It seemed that despite her claims, there was not always something to smile about. 'I don't know,' she replied, 'give me a second. Christ.'

Remembering something, Kojima walked back to the wall and took a tattered, torn notebook out of her rucksack. She flicked through its pages, past notes from years gone by and others from days ago, drawings and doodles of things that she feared and notes of all of the things she thought she would always need to remember, to the page with the drawing of those hanging mummies in the block of flats and the message on the walls. She held it up to her eyes next to the wall, tried to see if the patterns matched, if the messages were the same. She could not quite tell, her drawing proving not to be that good after all, but she suspected that they were different. She felt disappointed by this, as if she had been close to climbing a ladder but had in fact slid down a snake to the beginning again; but really, it meant nothing at all if the two messages were different or the same. They could hardly be changed now.

'I think it says, *DEATH TO THE GODS*,' Shelley said, appearing next to Kojima out of nowhere. 'I think.'

'The gods?' Kojima replied.

'Well, that's the word I'm not sure about – this character isn't clear enough,' Shelley said, wiping her nose on her sleeve. 'But if it isn't *gods* then I don't know what it is.'

'So theirs was a religious war?' Kojima asked, though from the way she mumbled and the way she did not turn to ask it, she could have been asking the wall or herself as much as Shelley.

'I don't know what the war was about. I've read what seem to be newspapers, journals, notes pinned to sideboards, and all I've read about is how scared everyone was, and all the death, and the destruction, and how everything was falling apart. No one wrote, *and by the way, we're fighting over whose god is the best.*'

Shelley's tone was irritated, her body language defensive.

It seemed that she was taking this discovery personally, that she was once again becoming depressed by the state of the city, the fate of its people. Kojima did not want to explore this territory again, so she made to pack her bag, and was going to suggest that they leave the building to move on to the closest alternative shelter, when Shelley saw the notepad in her hand and asked, 'What's that?'

'It's a journal,' Kojima replied, closing it and shoving it into her bag hurriedly. 'I have a few in here, you've seen me writing in them before.'

'No, what you wrote in there. I saw that page you were on. I saw their writing on it.'

'Yeah,' Kojima replied, unsure of whether to be honest about what was drawn there or hide it from her colleague. 'Just some writing I saw somewhere. I thought I'd compare it to this.'

'Have you seen a scene like this before? Here?'

Kojima sighed, kneeling by her bag, and as she zipped it up and stood, she said, 'Not like this, no', and began to walk away, trying to affect a casual stroll.

'And you told no one?' Shelley persisted, ignoring Kojima. 'When was this?'

Kojima turned back to her friend and forced a smile, shrugged as if nothing was wrong. 'It was nothing,' she said, shaking her head. 'Really, I'm not keeping anything from you.'

Shelley narrowed her eyes, and stood for a few seconds tapping one foot with her arms crossed and her brows furrowed like a suspicious wife waiting for a good explanation. After a while, she shrugged, threw her backpack onto her back, pointed at Kojima and said, 'You know what? I'm sick of you thinking you're protecting me by treating me like a fucking child. You need to start being honest with me, because I don't need your protection. What would I need it for, anyway? Because you're scared all the time? You think that I'm scared too? You want to save me from that? Well, fuck, yeah, I'm scared. We're all fucking scared. All the fucking time. Everyone on Earth was scared and here I'm doing no better. But lying to me won't make me less scared, it'll just make me scared that if what I know about is scary enough, then what you think you need to keep from me must be really fucking terrifying. So… fucking… *fuck*, mate, I'm out of here.' And she stomped past Kojima, out of the door. She had ranted like this before about something fairly trivial, and though Kojima was shocked and a little upset, she suspected that like the last time, Shelley would be over it within a few hours; so she saw little value in spending energy trying to placate her angry colleague.

'Have you recorded this display? Taken photographs?' Kojima asked quietly, as Shelley walked away.

'I don't want to remember this,' Shelley replied, without turning back.

And Kojima felt relief, as she imagined some future Shelley browsing the photographs she had taken on her implant – as she was sometimes wont to do, in downtime – and noticing just how human some of these bones appeared, just how familiar were a lot of these skulls. She sighed once again, the thought sending a cold shiver down her aching spine, before she followed Shelley out of the building and back into the street.

The women found another shelter, and a meagre handful of edible goods, before nightfall, and slept without saying another word to one another for the entire day. When the sun rose again, Shelley was gone, and so was the food.

DAYS 61–63

'This is incredible,' muttered Verne, gazing over Alan Ellis's shoulder as the machine which would read the contents of the Conquerors' computer drive booted up. 'You built this from scratch?'

'No, man,' Ellis chuckled, shaking his head and creasing his face. 'The machine is unchanged; it's one of theirs. I've used a few of them; they're surprisingly simple, once you know the language. I just had to rework some of the wiring to plug your drive in, and then teach it how to read the files.'

Verne knew that Ellis had used these machines before – he had done so casually, without even thinking about it, when he had enabled the buzzing, flickering lighting system in the building they had entered fifteen days before, where he had shown Verne the documents he had found on the subject of Earth, and what these people knew about it.

'This is just the tip of the iceberg,' Ellis had said, as he showed Verne the drawings of human skeletons and the descriptions of human behaviour. 'They had books going right back to the beginning.'

But Verne had been more interested in what Ellis knew

about their computers. He had reached into Ballard's bag and pulled the ship's black box out of it, and he had said, 'This is the log from the ship that brought us here. Ballard had been trying to get it working, but without power and without knowing if it was even salvageable in the first place, we didn't have much hope. Do you think you could do it? I want to find out why we crash-landed, why it wasn't controlled like it was supposed to be.' And Ellis had grinned, like he had been waiting to be given a task all along.

'You did all of this in two weeks?' Verne asked, as lines of text scrolled down the semi-transparent sheet glass screen, petabytes of log data loading smoothly, as if the machine was built specifically to do it.

'Well,' replied Ellis, shrugging, 'yeah. It's really not that impressive though, anyone could have done it if they just knew how this thing worked.'

'But nobody did,' Verne replied. The log data was streaming onto the screen at an astonishing rate, and he knew already that he would not have a clue where to start inspecting it, so he began to walk away from the screen to leave Ellis to it. 'Where the hell did you learn so much about this place?' Verne asked, though he had not intended for this reminder of Ellis's lengthy residence to come out of his mouth.

'Honestly, I don't remember,' Ellis replied, chuckling again, 'but I imagine it was this place.'

While Ellis worked on the logs, analysing hundreds of Earth years' worth of data in the search for one, or two, or one hundred, or possibly zero, things that might have malfunctioned or been miscalculated or else just come out of the unknown to cause the Conquerors' eventual belated wake-up call from cryosleep and subsequent crash-landing on this planet, James Verne continued to hunt, and sleep, and clean his gun and reorganise his bag.

He was not prone to boredom like some other men, and could sit in silence without moving for many hours without losing his mind or finding cause to busy himself, so he did not yearn for something to occupy him when he was alone and there was no hunting to be done and he had completed all of his tasks; but after this long just existing in a concrete desert, he did occasionally wish that he had brought a book. Perhaps something to occupy him during downtime might have kept his mind off those images that appeared before him and would not go away, ruining his mood and lengthening his sleepless nights. His frail wife covered in that patchwork blanket she loved so much, or more upsettingly, young and laughing and not frail at all. His son, standing over him, blood on his knuckles. His dog, lying on the porch, wearing that glum face he always had toward the end, refusing to bark at squirrels or cars or anything else that would excite other dogs, flinching from human touch.

Perhaps having a book, or an implant full of them, might have kept him from going mad over these memories. Maybe it would have saved him from the realisation that this was the stupidest mission anyone had ever signed up for, and would still have been even if it had gone to plan and the four humans sent here had been ambassadors for a planet eight light years away, celebrated as heroes in a land to which they would never return. If he had brought something to keep his mind busy, perhaps he would not have spent two days cleaning his nails with his knife, cleaning them until they bled and the skin around them was scabs and the only way to fix it was to clean them again, just like it had been on Earth, just like he had done and taught himself not to do so many years ago when he could no longer use his hands because they were riddled with cuts and bruises and his mind was a cage and he had lost the control he had always been so good at keeping and the love of his life was gone and—

'Verne!'

Verne looked up from his bleeding nail; the sudden movement springing a pain down his back, like a Slinky tumbling down the staircase of his vertebrae.

'Verne! Come here!'

Ellis's voice was far away, muffled, as if heard from underwater. Verne stood and wiped his hand on his clothes as he followed the sound, using his other hand to finger his ear, pushing hard and twisting rapidly to fix the volume problem.

'Where've you been, man?' Ellis said, grinning, as Verne reached the doorway to his room. Verne realised, as he entered, that he had not seen Ellis for two days. Ellis could have died, and he would not have known. For that matter, Verne could have, too.

'You called,' Verne said.

Ellis kept grinning, and Verne was struck once again by how clean his teeth were, how closely shaven he remained. Verne had grown a large beard in his time here, and his mouth tasted like garbage. His gums ached and even after washing, he never felt clean. The only thing he shared with Ellis, in terms of hygiene and grooming, was the habit of tying his hair in a bun behind his head, though Verne's was considerably greasier than Ellis's.

'How far is Earth from here?' Ellis asked.

'Eight light years,' Verne replied, adding, 'or nine. Eight point six, or… something.'

'So your journey should have taken…?'

'Uh…' Verne said, scratching his head with one painful fingernail, '967 years.'

'Were corners cut on these missions? Did they buy their computers *preloved* or sutt'n?'

Verne sighed, impatient to get to the point. 'I'd say it was probably a stretch to do all they wanted to do with the money they had, but we got here. What have you found?'

'Hmm,' Ellis said, smiling and pointing at the screen, 'your equipment fucked itself within a hundred years of you leaving Earth. Everything was logged as it happened – look, second by second, with Earth dates, in case you were wondering – but after sixty-seven years, the timestamps go wrong. Look here: suddenly you're in 1989, then you're in the year 3000, and here you're going at twice the speed of light! There's a minor impact registered at fifty-three years – maybe it knocked something out of place, who knows – but either way, something went wrong with the devices that were measuring this stuff. Oh, and obviously the system clock too. Hey, it's not all broken; look at the temperature gauges, they always seem to report well, and there's obviously no problem with the actual writer saving the logs – but the data is unusable in this state. If you had the full computer maybe we could troubleshoot those devices and, by accounting for their individual malfunctions, fix the data; but like this, I can't tell what happened and when. Sorry, man, but if this is to be believed, you travelled about four miles, at a million miles an hour, and it woke you up when you reached Mississippi.'

'I see,' Verne replied, rubbing his eyes. He was not sure whether or not he felt disappointment. Why was it, again, that he had wanted to know what had happened? Had he really wanted to know, or was this one of Shelley's passions?

Which reminded him. Shelley and Kojima. He wondered, sometimes, if they were still alive; but he had not done so for days now. Why was that? Why was he forgetting to look for his friends, his kin, the people with whom he had travelled across the galaxy?

He felt tired. Hearing Alan Ellis speak had relieved some of the stress he had been feeling in those two days alone, but he still did not feel strong or comfortable.

'There's nothing useful in there, then?' he asked.

'I mean, I can see that you were woken up late, the logs acknowledge that – it says here that the expected cryosleep deactivation distance was ten million kilometres, and you were woken at two million. But it doesn't say why, and that was logged, apparently, in 2018, a century before you launched. So, no, I'm sorry, but there's a piece missing, and this means nothing to us, until we know what that is.'

'Thanks for looking,' said Verne, placing a hand on his companion's shoulder, sighing heavily.

Ellis looked up at his friend, standing above him sighing and sad and so much stranger than when last they had been together. 'Are you okay?' he asked.

'Yeah,' said Verne, 'I'm fine.' And he walked out of the room as if he was dragging an IV behind him, returning to his hospital bed.

That night, they ate on the roof of a building four storeys high, the skyscrapers looming over them and casting shadows across the city with their thick trunks, their twisted vines hanging down like dreadlocks from their heads tattooed with faded neon paint. They ate a stew of rodent meat and root vegetables, which Ellis said was his favourite meal, and which he therefore only prepared on rare occasions, so that he would never grow bored of it. Verne conceded that it was indeed delicious, though he was unsure of whether this judgement was relative to other meals he had eaten on this planet or to the meals he had eaten throughout his life. He had resolved not to spend days without human contact again – the more time he spent sitting with Ellis, a small fire burning and warm stew in their bellies, the less tightly wound he felt, the more he felt himself returning to some degree of health he had not realised he had lost.

'I don't know how long I would have survived,' he said, looking up at a grey building streaked with black and brown that reached all the way up to a wispy cloud, touching the sky like Jack's beanstalk, 'if you hadn't found us.'

Ellis scoffed, barely audibly. 'I'm sure you would've managed, man,' he replied, shrugging. 'You're bigger and stronger and more intelligent than I am. I can't see it being too much of a struggle. The size of you, I reckon you could've wrestled that thing in the tunnel to death and eaten it for your supper.'

Verne smiled and looked down at his body. He had lost much of the muscle and all of the spare body fat that he had come here with, but he was still much larger than Ellis. Ellis was lean, exactly six feet tall, in every way the most typical man one could ever gaze upon. Verne imagined Ellis pictured in anatomical textbooks, the diagram example of how the human male looks and will always look. Unlike Verne, whose shoulders were broader than many children were tall, and whose hands were like shovels and whose nose was crooked and whose head was almost a perfect cube. Not that he cared how he looked – it had not been a disadvantage to him yet, and it was unlikely to be in the future. His size had always been one of his greatest strengths, but what Ellis had said was wrong – it was no advantage here. Being able to lift a car did not enhance one's ability to hunt rodents, or know which vegetation was safe to eat and which was not without gadgets to help identify them. These were things that only Ellis knew, and things that not even Ellis knew how he had learned.

'I'm not sure about that,' he replied, after what was nearly too long a pause for the reply to be relevant. 'I would probably be dead by now if I'd had to survive alone, but instead I'm eating square meals and sleeping comfortably, knowing we're not in the part of town where dogs eat you in your sleep.'

Verne wondered once again, as he said this, what Shelley and Kojima were eating, and where they were. The two men had searched for them for weeks after leaving the underground tunnels, and were technically still searching for them, but had yet found no trace. Without Ballard to attempt contact over the implants and without any sign of them on the horizon or in any of the abandoned neighbourhoods that the men had visited, it was a mystery to them whether the women were even alive. Thinking about how hopeless survival would be if it was left up to him made Verne wonder in what state the women were, and whether he should have made more of an effort to find them, to help them, or whether it was too late already.

'Well,' Ellis said, interrupting Verne's thoughts, 'at least you know how you got here, and what you're doing here. You win *that* one.'

His tone was jovial and he wore a smile, so Verne chuckled and nodded; but soon enough, Ellis was not smiling, and he was leaning on his knees and looking at the floor.

'I spend so much of my time wondering,' he sighed, 'what God is doing with us. What are we, toys? Does He just want us to fight and struggle and slowly die for His entertainment? Forgive me if this offends you, man, but I think these things so much. It seems like all He ever does is take things away from us. My memory, my life, your friends, this place… It's like He's playing a game with us, and we're the losers. But, y'know, I get that it's all part of a bigger plan, it's just hard for us to see. I get that, most of the time.'

'A game?'

Ellis paused, thoughtful, before saying, 'What are the chances that you'd survive the journey here? And then that you'd survive a crash-landing? And that the air would be breathable? And you wouldn't catch some horrific exotic disease that didn't exist on Earth, or eat something poisonous, or get murdered by the natives? And that, after all that, you'd make it through days in the desert to reach the nearest city? To do all that, and then find that the city is abandoned, it's like God hates you. Like He's playing a pretty mean trick. What are you doing here? What am I doing here? Why can't I remember a fuckin' thing? It takes a lot of effort to keep the faith, mate; a hell of a lot.'

Verne realised, in that moment, that they had not

spoken of faith. He had assumed, for whatever reason, that Ellis was an atheist; or at least, that it was irrelevant here. He was amazed that they could have gone so long without discussing it. But then, there was so much they had not discussed. Married couples could go decades without touching on a subject even once, so perhaps it was not that surprising that they had not touched on this one in the space of forty days.

'You believe in God?' Verne asked.

'You don't?'

Verne gazed out at the decaying city, watched a rock fall silently from the top of a tower all the way to the cracked street below, leaving a trail of falling dust in the air as it dropped, and finally replied, 'There's a lot of suffering in the universe, for very little reason. Being a good person doesn't prevent you from developing painful, degenerative, terrible illnesses, any more than being a bad person makes you more likely to face justice. If we're the result of intelligent design, then I wonder how it can be so hard to live inside our minds, knowing and feeling and being so terrifyingly aware of our own mortality and the futility of everything. I wonder how the human condition could ever be an advantage to us. We're promised a plan by men who claim to be holy, but it never becomes apparent; and all the while, those men doing the promising become richer and the ones believing suffer more. Without end, on and on. All of this being said, I don't honestly see how there can be a god. I think that we were accidents, there wasn't supposed to be a species that grew as intelligent as we did, and now we're paying for it. And maybe that's what happened to these guys. They paid for nature's mistake.

'That's what I believe. If that's not so, and there is a god who treats his creations like this, and watches all this pain without ever intervening, and still demands that we worship him… then no, thanks. I can do just fine without him.'

He paused, then added, 'And then there's the fact that, if

you really think about it, a god like that, and a universe with mankind at its very centre, sounds a lot like the arrogant fantasy of a terrified man, doesn't it? Exactly the kind of story you'd create, if you needed to make yourself feel better or others feel worse.'

'Fuck, man,' Ellis said, shaking his head. He was smiling, but in his eyes there was sadness. He continued to shake his head slowly for a long time, as if processing what Verne had said, before adding, 'I feel for you.'

Verne did not feel like he needed to be pitied. He had not felt that way since he drank, since he spent all of his time pitying himself for something that was happening to someone else. Since he wasted the chance to care for the most beautiful, charming, intelligent woman he had ever known, in her final months in this universe. He thought about that time, and all that it meant, and how he had promised himself so many times that he would never again abandon the ones he cared about, and how many times he had broken that promise, and it made him feel empty, like there was nothing that could redeem him.

He sighed, and he said, 'I want to start looking for the women I came here with again. I mean looking properly.'

And Ellis just nodded, an enthusiastic grin creeping across his face like a Mexican wave. 'Yeah, I know,' he said. 'We'll start tomorrow.'

'Okay.'

'Aye, all right.'

Ellis placed his bowl on the floor and sat back to stare at the sky, and watching him do so, Verne noticed for the first time that what Ellis had been eating out of looked like it was made of ivory, a sort of jagged-cut dish of smooth, rounded bone, like a large cranium sanded and cleaned.

He pointed at it and said, 'Are you eating out of a skull?'

Ellis looked down at the bowl and shrugged. 'No idea, man,' he replied, then laughed that enthusiastic laugh of his. 'I bloody hope not.'

'Where did you get it?'

'Oh,' Ellis said, shrugging again, 'I found it.'

DAY 91

James Verne sat for a long time with his overalls undone and his boots untied, listening to the sound of his breathing and wondering to where Ellis could have disappeared. The Scot had done this several times recently, vanishing in the night and returning in the morning with very little explanation for where he had been. When pressed, he would simply say that he occasionally sleepwalked, and could not remember a thing after he did so. He said that as long as he always found his way back, that was what mattered to him, and Verne had accepted that.

But with Ellis complaining of more and more frequent headaches, and their ferocity increasing, Verne found himself spending a little more time each day worrying about his companion. What he would do if Ellis collapsed and stopped responding when one of those headaches stopped him in his tracks, or if he disappeared in the night and never returned, Verne did not know. He felt like he should have a plan for such instances, but he could not come up with one. Even after this long, he could only take it one day at a time.

He had felt so much more together on Earth.

He laced his boots and zipped up the overalls which had

been issued to him before this trip, and which he had washed the day before. He had a respectable bundle of clothing now – Ellis's apparent ambidexterity lent effortless skill to his needlework, so he had made Verne some clothes out of fabric they had found along their travels; and he also still had some of the more primitive coverings that Kojima had put together for him before their ways had parted. With these and what remained of the clothes he had brought in the ship from Earth, he had more than enough to last two weeks without having to do a wash, if they ever had to go that long, which they had not yet. Ellis knew where they could find water wherever they were in the city, and knew which sources were safe to drink and which were not. He knew the signs of when a sandstorm was coming, and he knew before it had even risen when the sun would burn hot enough to cook their clothes dry in minutes. If there was something in this world about which he did not at least know something, Verne had not yet found it.

He stood and stretched, turning his back this way and that, testing the ache that still whispered down his spine from time to time. Satisfied that he was now ready to move around, he picked up his backpack and his gun and left the room, leaving the rest of their possessions for collection after he had found Ellis.

The building they were in had been a prison and then a museum, and finally a hospital for those wounded in the war that tore this city apart. Ellis had advised that they come here because it had running water and was built from stone – a rare thing for buildings in this world – so it would be cool. There was also a room in the back, Ellis said, which was alive with some kind of mushroom which, when sautéed until soft and put in one of Ellis's stews, tasted like bacon. They had eaten some the night before, and Verne did not believe it tasted like bacon any more than it tasted like faeces; but he had agreed with Ellis's assessment all the same.

He looked down the row of cells, all of them communal, huge rooms that would each have been a squash court on Earth, and wondered where exactly he should start. If Ellis sleepwalked like Verne's late brother, he would have woken in his own wardrobe, having pissed his pants. Or in the street, hugging a lamp post. Ellis could be anywhere.

He decided to return to the sled first – it was in the cell directly below the one in which they had slept, and was as good a place to start as any. If Ellis had woken in the street, perhaps he would have returned to it first, to drink from one of their large water cartons or to change into clean clothes. Verne descended the ramp with slow, lumbering steps, still feeling tired and groggy, reaching the door to the cell before he knew he was on his way, as if he had been out and autopilot had taken over for the entire journey. He was woken from his daydream instantly, when he heard the woman's voice coming from inside the cell.

'Where the fuck did you get this?' it said. Then, without waiting for an answer to its first question, 'Who are you? How did you get here?'

Verne waited outside the room, back against the wall, for reasons unknown even to himself.

'Where did you get this? Where did you find this sled?' she repeated. Her voice was croaky and shaking, her nerves audible. Verne realised then what he had missed, the first time she had spoken: that this was a voice he knew, one he had not heard for nearly ten weeks.

When he entered the room, gun resting by his hip and hands by his sides, Kojima moved the aim of her rifle from Ellis to Verne, her movements jittery and her wrist bones poking through her skin like horned cufflinks. Her face looked drawn and aged, her hair thin and her eyes grey. She looked like one who should have been on her deathbed, barely recognisable to her old comrade. The room stank of smoke, and the state of her clothes and skin left Verne in no doubt as to who was stinking it out. When she realised she was looking at Verne – a much hairier, thinner Verne than the one she had known – her eyes filled with tears, and she lowered her aim to the ground.

'Verne,' she said, the relief palpable.

Ellis lowered his hands, which he had held in the air, and grinned. Kojima raised her rifle at him again, realising that she had let her guard down, and retrained her gaze on the stranger.

'You know this person, Verne?' she asked.

Verne found it hard to speak at first. He too was overcome, perhaps by emotion, though he had never thought he would be; and apart from that, he struggled, for a moment, with a sudden wave of relief that Alan Ellis was not, after all, a creation of his mind.

'Y-yes,' he stammered, realising he had left it a little too long without replying. 'This is Alan Ellis.'

'What?' Kojima snapped, as if surprised that not only had she found a human on this planet, but also that he had a name.

'Alan Ellis,' mumbled Ellis, his smile gone.

Kojima wore a confused sort of acceptance on her face this time, and kept the barrel of her gun pointing at Ellis as she turned her head to Verne and said, 'Where's Ballard?'

Verne sighed. He did not reply with more than a shrug; he could not find the words.

'No,' Kojima said. Her eyes were sunken and dark; black flowers atop the slick stems of tear tracks that had run down her cheeks.

Verne hung his head. He felt the knot of failure in his stomach once again, the guilt of letting his young friend die in a sewer. When he lifted it again, he asked, 'Shelley?'

Kojima sighed this time, shrugged, and said, 'I don't know. She disappeared in the night.'

'Last night?'

Kojima nodded.

There was a long silence, as Kojima struggled to keep

her heavy rifle pointed up at Ellis's head, and Ellis held his hands up, and Verne stood with his white beard and his long white hair, staring at the pair of them like a former World's Strongest Man waking up in a retirement home.

Finally, he said, 'Kojima, it's okay. Lower your gun. Come here.'

Kojima lowered her weapon slowly, cautiously, and then finally let it drop completely and hang from its strap. She ran to Verne in two long strides and fell into his arms sobbing, and he cried too, silently, and Ellis stood watching them next to the sled piled with the men's possessions, relieved that the woman was Verne's friend, and not another strange human who didn't know how she got there.

Kojima spooned the stew that they gave her into her mouth like her stomach was landfill. When she finished, barely a minute after she had been handed the bowl, she was breathless, and she wiped the liquid that ran down her chin with the back of her hand, and then licked it off. She smiled at the men gratefully, though her smile was tired and her teeth yellowed and rotting within it. Verne sat opposite her, no less worried about her than he had been when he was not sure she was alive, and Ellis sat shifting uncomfortably, unable to handle the way she kept staring at him.

'So… you're human,' she said, after a few moments of enjoying the aftertaste of her meal.

Ellis laughed, more nervously than usual, but just as eagerly. 'I think so,' he replied, nodding.

Kojima did not laugh. 'What are you doing here?'

Ellis fell silent. She had already asked him the question more than once, and so had Verne, but still his nerves held his tongue.

'He doesn't know,' Verne said for him, after too long a silence. 'Ellis hasn't got much of a long-term memory. He's here, but he doesn't remember how he got here. He can recall the… *feeling* of Earth, but has no real memories of being there.'

'Aye, and I don't know what the, erm, memory thing is all about,' Ellis interrupted. 'Whether it's medical, or environmental, or what. Maybe I had a knock to the head, but I certainly don't remember that.'

'I see,' said Kojima, still eyeing him suspiciously. 'And how did you find each other?'

'Ellis cared for Ballard and me after we lost you. In the sandstorm, Ballard hit his head, and by the time I'd picked him up you were gone. When we did find shelter, we fell through the floor, I don't remember how, but the next I knew I was waking up in a sewer, and Ellis was looking after us. Ballard never recovered from his injuries. But without Ellis, he would have died much sooner than he did.'

'I see,' repeated Kojima, staring at Ellis with less suspicion now, but staring all the same.

'We should find Shelley,' said Verne, going to stand.

'You don't need to,' Kojima sighed, stopping him mid-stoop, 'I've sent her my location, and if she's receiving audio, she's hearing everything we say anyway.'

Verne sat back down. He had forgotten the capabilities of those implants, so long had he been away from them. 'I thought she disappeared?'

'I think she needed space,' Kojima replied, tired. 'I kept something from her that I shouldn't have. She was angry with me.'

'Okay,' replied Verne, unsure why that meant that she should not be looked for. Even if she was on her way to their position, he did not think the city safe enough for her to come alone. But something kept him seated, whether it was Kojima's certainty that he should be or his own certainty that Kojima would not have the energy to walk around in the heat of the morning, combined with his unwillingness to leave her here alone, to risk losing her again.

'So,' Kojima said, sitting back as if to relax, 'I suppose we should fill each other in. Who's going first?'

By the time they had finished exchanging stories – Verne's about Ellis and the tunnels and the books he had seen with human drawings inside of them, and the rodents by the riverside that they had hunted and eaten by the sackful and the logs from the ship that had nothing to say, and Kojima's about the difficulty of finding food when they knew not where to look, and Shelley's passion and subsequent dispassion for reading about the history of this world, and the dog attack that had left the young woman scarred and the bodies they had found, burned and tarred and rotting in a pile – Ellis had slept away one of his headaches and returned to prepare dinner, and evening was falling, and Shelley was a silhouette in the doorway that shook with sobs and ran to hold Verne as soon as a gap appeared in the conversation.

She was thin as a pole and she felt brittle in his arms, but he held her tight and close like she was his long-lost daughter, as she cried and cried and eventually tried to compose herself, before crying again. The Conquerors realised, now that they were together, that they had subconsciously presumed each other dead, though they had not had the courage to face that presumption consciously, but now, being together, and alive, they had never been happier to be wrong.

After Shelley had regained her composure, she approached Ellis, who had been busying himself boiling more root vegetables and more rodent in more plain water, and embraced him too. While the two remaining Conquerors watched, she squeezed him tight and he tried awkwardly to hug her back, and she said to him, 'Thank you, Alan,' before she took a seat with the others.

'It's the funniest thing,' Ellis said, pausing over his pot. 'I just had terrible déjà vu.'

*

Though she was not yet truly rested, after she had washed herself thoroughly and eaten her first proper meal in weeks, Shelley was in good spirits and ready to quiz Alan Ellis on his knowledge of the city and the fate of its people.

Sitting around a dying fire, the same one he had cooked their meal over, she spoke over its crackle and hiss to say, 'Alan, what can you tell us about what happened here?'

Kojima and Verne remained silent. Kojima shifted anxiously in her seat, aware of Shelley's volatility when it came to this subject; and Verne watched the man think up his answer, secretly wondering why he had never asked Ellis this himself, or whether he had but he had forgotten.

'Well, what you see here,' said Ellis, 'is the complete and utter collapse of civilisation.'

He continued to wipe the bowls and utensils with which they had eaten their dinners, silent, as if that alone would be a satisfactory answer. When he had finished with his wiping and set down his tools and he looked up to find the others staring at him, their stares begging for more information, he continued, 'I'm no expert. What I know, I only know from what I've seen or read or worked out, and I can't even remember all of that. But it wasn't just war or environmental destruction or famine or whatever that made the place like this, it was loads of things at once. It had to be.

'But the way they behaved, the way their society was structured, it never looked like it was gonna work anyway. The way I've read it, there was a very clear class system: you were born wealthy and noble, or you were born poor and low, and there was no mobility at all. The low-born were treated like dogs, slaves to the high-born, and they were expected to be grateful for it; and for their part, the high-born were violent and cruel, wasteful and careless. But, y'know, not getting off on being nasty or anything. Just behaving how they thought they should, convinced they had things the right way up. They were the few and the low-born the many, but those elite still managed to near enough destroy the planet with their disregard for the environment, and all their wars that they sent their slaves to fight for them, for fun more than for survival. Their arrogance is obvious in everything they did – the engraving above the door of their city hall, which is now burnt down further up the river, used to say *HOME OF THE MASTERS OF THE UNIVERSE*. From the looks of it, they were real shitheads, man.'

'Masters of the universe…' repeated Shelley. 'We saw some graffiti yesterday that said *DEATH TO THE GODS*. Were they ever called gods?'

'They called themselves that, aye,' said Ellis, nodding. 'The word they used is somewhere between *master* and *god*. Someone so powerful and noble that they may as well be a deity.

'Anyway, as empires tend to do, theirs fell when the low-born realised that they were made of the same stuff as the masters and that they outnumbered them ten to one. This is guesswork on my part, but wherever you look, just like what you saw yesterday, there's evidence to support it. What it seems like is that many of the poor just fled the city as soon as the fighting began, trekking north or west through the desert to find a new home. Of the rest, they seemed to have had to choose between fighting for the masters and protecting their way of life after probably being convinced that change would be scarier than slavery, or rising up and risking it all for their freedom. There were certainly low-borns fighting for their masters' power, I've seen it written on the walls and the scrolls.'

'And the ones who ran, where did they go?'

'Into the desert. This species didn't mate or migrate like ours – you've probably noticed from your wee world map there, there were about three large cities on the two continents of this planet. The rest is barren desert and wild jungle. I read a letter that said the city to the north, Hnnkuh, was only taking in refugees if they agreed to fight for the masters. The size of their population, the appetite for war, the advancement of their tech, what they'd done to their planet… it's little wonder that the only winner of this war was Death.'

Shelley's brow was furrowed and her jaw hung limp. 'How did you know how to say that?' she asked.

'Say what?'

'The city to the north. You just said its name. I wouldn't know how to say any of these words, I can only read them.'

'Oh,' said Ellis, his gaze dropping to his torso, as if he might have an answer in his breast pocket, 'I don't know. Maybe I guessed its sound at some point, and I don't remember doing it. I might have made up a sound for every word and just never thought about it.'

'Sounds a lot like home, doesn't it?' said Kojima, unaware that the conversation had veered off. 'I wonder if this is how Earth has turned out, by now.'

'Does it?' asked Ellis.

'Well, our society relied on a delicate balance, and on everyone knowing their place and sticking to it, too. We had the illusion of social mobility, but it was rarely demonstrated. Those in power only ever wanted more power, and more wealth, and they would kill and start wars to get it, but they'd manipulate us into thinking that it was for our own good, or for a worthy cause, and all the while the normal people just suffered and had their lives disrupted by the decisions of the few.'

'Ugh,' sighed Shelley, shifting in her seat and rolling her eyes. 'Are you serious?'

Kojima continued, 'The world was falling apart when we left it. We were overpopulated by about fifteen billion, we were making more and more species extinct each year, and no one seemed to want to do anything about any of it; they were happy, as long as they could still watch the news on their holographic TVs and sleep with their favourite camgirls through their implants' VR. Half the world was on the brink of war, and had been for a century. It could have toppled at any moment, and the only thing that was stopping it was the collective sanity of a few good people. That doesn't last forever – look at this place.'

Shelley raised her hands in dramatic despair and gave Kojima a pitying, patronising scowl. 'This strange, fearful talk again. You sound like an insane person right now. The kind that spouts those conspiracies about there being a handful of people who run the entire world behind the scenes, like it's their own personal chess game. I feel like you might start saying the king of England is a lizard dressed as a human. You need to realise that the issues you had on Earth, the way you saw things through your fog of anxiety and fear, was not the way the world was. The world was okay. It wasn't great, there were a lot of bad people, but on the whole, we weren't ripping each other apart and burning each other in bonfires for the sake of a class war, or a race war, or a religious war, or whatever else this might have been. The world might have been a terrifying place for someone who believed everything their paranoia told them; but for the rest of us, we were enjoying the best time there ever was to be a human. We had the best quality of life, the best technology, the best entertainment, and the lowest chance of dying before reaching 110 that humanity had ever experienced. We were damn lucky to come from the time and place that we came from, and all you can do is sit there and say shit like that. And worst of all, you say it here. Christ.'

Kojima was silent now, and so were the others. Ellis felt the guilt of an onlooker to an argument, worried that he may have in some way contributed to its beginning. Verne placed his hand on Kojima's shoulder, not to take sides but to assure her that she was not alone.

Awkwardness stalked the room for a long time, and then

Shelley stood and physically shook it off.

'I'm going to sleep,' she said, her tone softer, perhaps more regretful, gathering her covers to sleep in the corner of the cell in which they sat. 'It was good meeting you, Ellis. Verne, I'm glad you're back.' She touched Verne's hand as her parting gift.

'O-oh,' Ellis stammered, caught off guard, 'you, too.'

Kojima did not speak again before she too fell asleep right where she sat. Ellis followed shortly after, having wiped clean the pot in which he had cooked dinner and packed away his things, ready to leave the next day. Verne stayed awake until a long while later, watching them sleep and listening to the sound of his breaths and feeling less worried than he had in weeks, a weight having been lifted from his shoulders that was so heavy it might have broken him, had it been left there any longer.

DAY 101

'You know,' said Kojima, 'I just realised we let our one hundredth day here pass us by yesterday.'

'Christ,' said Shelley, 'time drags when you're hungry. I thought we'd been here twice as long as that.'

They were on the pitch in a circular arena in the east of the city, a kind of coliseum surrounded by seating that rose steeply, half of it missing and the half that remained so rotten and ruined that it might as well have been gone. The sun burned down into the stadium hotter than it had felt even in the desert, so Kojima and Verne sat in the shade two rows of seating away from each other while, metres away, Shelley and Ellis played catch with a soft ball that Ellis had made out of rodent hide filled with the seeds of an extremely sweet fruit. Kojima had decided to teach herself how to read the planet's language, just as Shelley had, so she sat reading a passage of English next to a passage of their text and knowing not where to start; Verne, meanwhile, was sitting in silent meditation, having just finished cleaning his gun.

'All right,' Shelley said, throwing the ball over Ellis's head into the dry earth behind him, 'I've got a good one.

Who's been keeping track of what day it is in their head?'

'It's Tuesday,' Ellis said, bending to pick up the ball. 'I've kept track as long as I can remember.'

Shelley grinned. 'That's so weird,' she said. 'Because of when I started, it's Thursday today.'

'Friday for me,' said Kojima, smirking.

Everyone looked expectantly at Verne. He shook his head. He had not thought about it.

'I wonder how long their months were, here,' said Kojima. 'Or their weeks. Or if they even divided time like that. They must have had some system; it's hard to keep track of how much you owe to the past if you can't put a date on all of your borrowings. Do you know what they did, Alan?'

Ellis remained silent, distracted by something above Shelley's head. As she finished speaking, Kojima was struck by just how quiet it was in this stadium, how well the sound travelled when she made it. A thin layer of dust was blowing across the surface of the ground, but it made no sound. She knew from the previous day that outside the stadium, a skyscraper burned like the largest torch they had ever seen, its white-hot flames licking the sky and heating the city for blocks around; but from inside this arena, no one would know it. Only the sound of her voice could be heard, and apart from that, there was silence so loud that it rang in the ears and drowned out all else.

When Shelley had had enough of the silence and of waiting for Ellis to respond, she said, 'What gives, swagman?'

Ellis was still suffering from excruciating headaches, but now they were accompanied by a feeling of déjà vu that he experienced at least thrice daily. Combined with the absent seizures – times when he would drift off and respond to nothing for a few seconds before abruptly snapping out of it and acting as if nothing unusual had happened – and the ever-increasing episodes of somnambulism, these symptoms gave the impression that there was something going horribly haywire in his skull, and the Conquerors were all worried, though none of them would mention it for fear of worrying Ellis too, or making their worst fears real in their utterance. But this was how he stood now, absently staring into space, his body hanging limp, while Shelley waited for it to pass and for him to speak or throw her the ball.

The crew had been lucky, they knew, that only one of them had fallen ill on this journey. They had been sent with as many tablets and ointments for all sorts of different ailments as any average human would ever need for a lifetime, and given enough vaccinations for known diseases to make their immune systems near enough superhuman; but many of their drugs had been lost in the crash and the rest had been lost when their sleds were taken, so if one of them had fallen ill, they might have deteriorated quickly with no hope of repair. But apart from Ballard, they had not, and whether it was because of the amenability of the atmosphere to human sensibilities or the relative rarity of life forms from which to catch infections, they had largely escaped anything worse than a mild case of the sniffles.

Which made Ellis's predicament all the more worrying.

'Ellis!' shouted Shelley, tired of waiting. Ellis jumped and looked around, disoriented like a sleeping man kicked awake.

'Oh,' he said, 'sorry, man.' He threw the ball to Shelley.

Shelley's general mood had, by now, improved dramatically since the dip on the rooftop and the other at the pile of bodies. She now seemed more like a survivor than one who had just happened to survive, more like she had a brave face than like she was just putting one on. She had been feisty and determined when they arrived, and during their time alone together, Kojima had watched that erode away gradually until she had become what Kojima had felt like on Earth: a dark, paranoid, unhappy husk of a human who feared all and embraced nothing. She had obsessed for so long over the war about which she had read that this uptick in her emotions, this period of relaxation she seemed to be enjoying, lifted the worry from Kojima's shoulders a little and allowed her too to enjoy a slightly less anxious life.

But worry blew on the wind on Planet 127-001. If Shelley was not worried about the civilisation and its extinction then she was instead worried about how much food they had and how much they would need to survive another week. If Kojima was not worried about Shelley then she was instead tangled in a web of existential worries, lost in a hall of mirrors in her mind that asked her what she was doing here and where they were going and why she had not called the whole thing off when she had a chance. If Verne was not worried about the women and all their worries, he was instead worried about Ellis and his malfunctioning brain. The only one among them who did not seem to be riding up and down on a roller coaster of high and low emotions, pulled taut one day and slack as a hammock the next, was Ellis. Perhaps, having been here so long, he was immune to the world's infectious angst.

But today was a good day for all of them, and good days were to be enjoyed, and as groups of people are apt to do, they had made an agreement that was and would always remain unspoken, that no one should ever deliberately ruin someone else's good mood, for they were too rare to squander.

Shelley threw the ball at Ellis, and it glided past his shoulder onto the dirt beyond once again. He stood there, staring at the sky, as if his previous mental absence had never gone on hiatus.

'Ellis,' hissed Shelley, 'bloody hell, mate.'

Ellis raised one finger to his lips, not absent after all but rather distracted, genuinely captivated by something. 'Shhhh,' he whispered. 'What the fuck is that?'

And though he had whispered, and though the older two humans in the stands had been busying themselves with their own unrelated tasks, they all heard his question, and followed his pointed finger to the awning above the stadium, where there stood a creature that looked like a beetle the size of an Alsatian, scuttling here and there and flapping its large wings in quick bursts, before hiding them again under its exoskeleton. It had been there a long while, and Ellis had been unsure of whether he was imagining it or not; but now that it moved so often and so excitedly, he was sure enough to mention it.

'Christ,' said Shelley, backing away from the roof, tiptoeing in the opposite direction to the giant bug. 'Have you seen one of those before?'

Ellis shook his head. 'I don't think so,' he said. Up on the awning, the bug turned to face them, and stood there looking down on them like it was listening to their words.

'I have,' said Kojima, touching her temple to zoom in on the creature, holding enough nerve to stay exactly where she was. 'There was one in the display case at that museum, the one with the human skeleton. They had it on display like it was an alien.'

Shelley zoomed in too, and she looked at the creature's smooth body and its insectoid legs, its eyes on the sides of its head moving independently like a chameleon's and its mouth soft and pink down the centre of its face like a human vagina with razor-sharp teeth.

'Jeeeesus,' she whispered, 'you're right.'

'I think we should move,' said Ellis, as Verne took aim at the creature, 'slowly, and as quietly as possible.'

And as if to answer him, the bug took off from the awning, flying high into the air before nosediving toward them, swooping past them with loud, rapid beatings of its massive beetle wings before turning back and hovering above them, not ten metres off the ground, watching them like it was waiting for them to do something, challenging them to try moving before it got to them. The crew stood frozen, watching the bug, trying not to move a muscle for fear of incurring its wrath. Verne dared himself to pull the trigger.

Seconds bled into each other and the half-minute that passed felt like it could have been ten or fifteen or twenty minutes, as the Conquerors' hearts beat like hummingbird wings and the real-life wings of the insect filled their ears with their hideous *flap-flap-flap*, and its gross legs hung like jagged ornaments from its unforgivingly ugly body, and it hovered before them, destroying all hope that there was a god that loved humanity and created all this beauty and did not do evil.

But just like there had been for the beast in the tunnels, there was a human among them who gave the insect pause. It hovered above them menacingly and they imagined the damage that all its sharp edges could do to their soft skin, and this fear and loathing thickened the air and slowed down time so that the stadium looked like some waxwork advertisement for a twentieth-century B-movie in which no one could possibly survive, but all that really happened was that the bug's eyes scanned up and down Ellis's body, standing there staring back; and just like that hairy monster that Ellis had murdered, it did nothing to hurt him.

Instead, it landed, its four barbed legs thudding loudly onto the hollow stadium floor and those horrid wings retracting into its shell, the whole thing a lot smaller on the ground than it had been in the air, when its legs had been hanging limp below it and its wings stretched out to the sides. Now it was more the size of a tricycle or a small shopping trolley. Still far too big for a bug.

The Conquerors watched nervously, each waiting for another to make a move, as the creature stood dead still on the dusty ground, just watching Ellis with its bulbous eyes, slowly opening and closing the jagged teeth on its glistening face. Whether it was trying to threaten or communicate or do something else entirely, none of them knew. But then it took a step toward Ellis, and another, scuttling steps that were quick as a flash, creepy and jolting, and there was no longer any time to speculate.

Verne grunted loudly and tightened his grip on his gun, forever trying to bring himself to pull the damn trigger; but Ellis just held up his hand.

'Wait,' he said, and stepped toward the bug, reaching out with his other hand to touch its rubbery-looking exoskeleton. Shelley whimpered, fearful of the thing and what it could do to Ellis if it really wanted to.

But it did not want to. As soon as Ellis's hand came within an inch of the thing, it launched itself into the air again, the crack of its shell opening and the heavy unfurling of its huge wings thunderclap-loud in the humans' ears, making all of them jump out of their skin and forcing a yelp from the mouth of Shelley, who could no longer stomach the alien insect's presence. It scanned them all again from ten feet off the ground, and took another long, hard look at Ellis.

Then, after a time, it seemed to decide that they were no longer worthy of its attention, and it turned in the air and flew off over the side of the stadium. Gone as quickly as it had been noticed, buzzing its loud buzz more and more softly until no sound or sight of it remained.

The sigh of relief echoed from all of the humans off the walls of this great coliseum, and only Ellis remained enthralled by the beast, even after it was gone. Only Ellis walked in the direction it had flown, wishing it would come back.

'Fuckin' 'ell,' he muttered to himself. 'I've done all this before.'

When the beating of the creature's wings was no longer audible and its presence just a memory, Shelley fell to her knees and cried on the hard ground of the stadium floor.

Something inside of her just gave, the tension that had built in just a few seconds suddenly dispersed by the creature leaving without making the kill she had felt so sure it was here for. Relief, just as much as fear. But after the tears had been shed and the relief had passed, her mood would not repair itself – she would feel sad for the rest of the day, and that fear would stick around for a couple more nights; she could tell by how deep within her it was worming, even now. And this just made her cry all the more.

She looked around at her companions – the two older members of the group returning to their seats, Kojima grabbing one of her tattered black notebooks to draw the bug and Verne beginning to pack his things into his rucksack so that they could all move on, and Ellis wandering slowly toward the edge of the pitch, staring up at the point from which the animal had come, as if in wonderment rather than fear – and she felt so alone, so isolated in her crippling depression. Now, more than ever, she felt a kind of regret that cut her in half, right down the centre of her gut, devastating and all-consuming and more real than the dirt that dug into her skinny knees below her.

Perhaps she had always felt this regret, ever since they arrived, and she had only just cracked enough to admit it to herself.

'What are we doing here?' she asked the ground. 'Why did we do this?'

Ellis turned to look at her, his face expressionless, his demeanour calm and relaxed. 'Because you're Conquerors,' he replied, as certain as if it was the obvious answer.

'What?' the crying woman replied, looking up at him with her once-pretty eyes darkened by sadness, her cheeks reddened by tears, her scar a backslash of violence that tore her beauty in half.

'You were chosen to come here. It couldn't have been anyone but you,' he said.

Shelley just knelt there, confused. If the older humans

could hear their conversation, they were not letting on.

'You've lived through an ordeal that very few others could have survived. You made it through all the training and counselling and conditioning required to take a journey like this, and then you survived a millennium frozen in space, during which you really could have hit any number of objects and been blown into a million bits, but you weren't. And then you got here and you kept yourselves alive in hostile terrain with barely any food or water, for *a hundred days*. This is the stuff of fiction, Wednesday; and here you are, living it. All of this happened for a reason.

'I've felt so strange the past few days. So disoriented, all the fuckin' time. Some mornings I wake up a hundred metres away from where I fell asleep, and most days I've got déjà vu so extreme I think my life is stuck on repeat. But it's starting to come together in my head. I don't think something's wrong, Shelley. I think this was all supposed to happen. I think something is coming to me, and all that's happening is that my brain is fighting it. You survived all that, you passed every test, and so did I, and now we've met, forever away from the planet we were both born on. Something bigger is happening on this stage, and we're the players.'

Shelley looked once again at Ellis, now squatting just a couple of metres from her, his elbows on his knees and his face filled with eager optimism.

'Ellis, I know your intentions are good,' she said, 'but you can fuck off with that shit.'

Ellis looked injured, as if he had poured out his heart and she had sent it back wrapped in a bin bag. He sighed, and stood, and looked out at the stadium seating, and shrugged.

'Well, whether I'm right about that or not,' he said, 'the rest is still true. You passed every test to get this far; tests that lesser people would have failed. And that has to mean something. Verne told me they used to say that they were sending humanity's very best minds on these missions; they wouldn't do that for nothing.'

'They didn't,' Shelley said, looking at him with pity, as one would look at a child who had made a fool of themself in public, the look Kojima had given her so many times. 'The tests that got us here were the ones they wanted us to fail. And we failed them spectacularly, and that's why we're here.'

'Eh?'

'Do you really think they'd send humanity's greatest minds on suicide missions to planets light years away? We're not here because we passed any tests; we're here because we failed them. We weren't humanity's best minds; we were humanity's most expendable mid-level scholars and engineers. Good enough to give the missions credibility, useless enough not to be missed. The world went on just fine without us, believe me.'

'I don't think… I think you're wrong…'

'Ellis, look at us.' She nodded at Verne staring at the sky, stuck in a position in which he could probably stay for hours without complaining, and Kojima, hunched over her notepad, one hand scribbling away and the other in her mouth, biting away at her nails like an exhausted mother of seven carrying on her shoulders every worry in the world. 'We're not Earth's finest, and we never were. We're not here because we're the most well-rounded humans in history. We're here because we're broken.'

JUNE 9TH, 2121

Wednesday Shelley stared out at the Danube from the bench by the Parliament Building, watched laughing children jumping metres ahead of their parents and young couples taking romantic strolls and old men standing with their hands behind their backs watching the world go by, and she wished with every gram of her being that she could be one of them, any one at all. She could imagine how it would feel to be outside of herself, to be a child on a family trip, or a teenager travelling the world for the first time: how today would feel so dazzling, with the sun shining down on this beautiful place; how the breeze would blow softly through her hair and into her thin clothing; how free she would feel just walking alone, exploring the city all over again.

But she was not alone, and right now, she was not free.

'I just… don't see… why you would do this… now…' Olena sniffed, barely able to catch enough breath between her sobs. Her eyes were puffy and glowing pink and mascara ran down her cheeks like thick black paint thrown in anger at a once-stunning masterpiece, and as Wednesday turned away from the river to look at her, she saw the flabby, balding old man with the thick, turd-shaped moustache staring at their bench from a few metres away with that same vacant stare he had previously been pointing at the Parliament Building, taking everything in without wearing even a hint of comprehension on his wrinkled old face, and she almost smiled, but managed to bottle it up.

'I know,' she said, sighing and looking down at the space between them, 'I know. It's fucked up. I didn't know what to do. I didn't want to ruin things. Ugh, I just… I don't know, I suppose I thought that…'

And then she gave up trying to articulate her frustration, and looked out at the river once again. She would have given almost anything, at that moment, to be somewhere else. To be someone else, just for a little while. For this to be done, without her having to do it. She would pay nearly any amount for that.

Wednesday Shelley and Olena Kuzmenko met at a party in Budapest, when Wednesday was travelling and Olena was studying, and had hit it off immediately. Olena had a boyfriend at the time – she was still attempting to convince herself that the feelings she had been having were a phase, and that the drunken encounters with fellow students were just forgettable mistakes – but after talking to Wednesday at a party for hours and never wanting to stop, and going back to Wednesday's hostel to listen to compact discs her grandfather had given her, and ending the night with Wednesday's head between her legs feeling the kind of skin-prickling pleasure she had only ever felt from a woman's tongue, the boyfriend was history, and Olena was infatuated. After six months of dating, Wednesday proposed, and now, they were three years in, returning to Budapest to relive the magic for Olena's birthday.

Which was why it was such an awful time for Wednesday to be revealing for the first time her plan to leave the planet forever.

'Can't you… drop out?' Olena sniffed, trying to regain

her composure.

'No, it's decided now. I couldn't, even if I wanted to.'

'But… you don't… want to.'

Wednesday looked down at her tiny hands, folding and unfolding a dry, crumpled tissue in her lap. 'No,' she replied.

This brought forth a new flood of tears from Olena's eyes, and she blew her nose loudly as they ran down her glowing cheeks and dripped tiny blackened puddles onto the bench and her clothes.

'I don't understand,' she said, her voice quivering, the lump in her throat refusing to be swallowed down.

It upset Wednesday to see Olena this devastated, but greater than that feeling was the one of embarrassment that walked hot footsteps across her neck and chest, so mortified was she to be sitting opposite a woman whose heart was breaking so incredibly… *loudly*. She had feared this would happen, so she had considered breaking the news in their hotel room; but there, she would have had no escape, no opportunity to leave if the situation spiralled out of her control. It needed to be somewhere outside, and there had not come a better opportunity today, so here they were, around all this beauty and all this splendour, and all Wednesday wanted was to be somewhere else.

'Why… are you doing this? Don't you love me any more? Am I not what you want any more?'

'Of course you are,' Wednesday lied, 'of course I do. But come on, Olena, you must have felt us drifting apart. Do you feel the same magic when I come home from a trip that you used to? Do you feel butterflies when you think about me? I haven't felt that way in a long time. Maybe the magic is just… gone.'

Olena's face flashed with anger, her wide eyes glistening with tears and a bead of snot peeking from her left nostril, ready to storm out with the dribble and the tears and all the emotion that was pouring out of its host.

'Yes,' she barked, 'I've never stopped feeling those things. How could you say that? I get so excited when I see you, and when you're away; all I want to do is be there with you. I count down the days until you return. How could you say that? How could…' And then she was no longer talking, but crying, freely and shatteringly, into her tissue.

'Oh,' replied Wednesday, once again looking away. She was blushing; she felt hot and crowded. She could not imagine, even if she had tried, how Olena felt, for she had always done the dumping, and never been the dumped. She did not know why that had been.

'Besides,' Olena said, once again in control of her voice, and once again angry, 'so what if the magic has gone? So what if it did? We're married now. This is marriage. Do you expect it to be sunshine and roses and trips to Legoland from now till we die? Things were always going to get boring. That's life. How could you say that?'

'This isn't that,' Wednesday replied, bristling that Olena had made her concerns sound as trivial as they probably were, 'this is deeper than that. You obviously don't understand—'

'No,' interrupted Olena, blowing her nose again, turning the heads of the very last couple within a twenty-metre radius who had not yet silenced to listen in on the argument, 'I don't understand. Christ, Weddy, I'm so fucking… angry. My parents were right about you. How could I have been so stupid?'

Wednesday cleared her throat, indignation rising in her belly. She knew exactly what Olena's family thought about her. They thought she was unfocused and scattered, that she did not have the attention span to live a proper adult life. When Wednesday had told Olena's father about the degrees she had decided not to finish, the handful of sensible jobs that could have turned into sensible careers which she had thrown away to get where she was, he had given her a look like talking to her left a sickening taste in his mouth. Olena's mother had raised her eyebrows and shaken her head, making no effort to hide her disapproval. It did not matter to them that she had completed a PhD in anthropology, or that, at that time, she had decided once and for all that her career would be spent helping people in developing countries gain the education they needed to escape poverty and starvation; what defined her character for them was only that which she had given up.

A year later, when she changed her mind, returned to academia, and had to accept a poorly-paid research role at a local university which demanded much more of her time than either she or Olena would have liked, she was in the room when Olena's father asked across a poor feed line from Ukraine why Olena was still wasting time with 'that idiot butterfly, always flapping from tree to tree with no ambition', in a language he did not know or perhaps did not care that Wednesday could speak.

So yes, she knew what Olena's family thought about her. And she was used to it – she had met too many people by now who could not understand a life lived in pursuit of happiness, rather than one lived shackled to the spot, for the sake of stability. Her own brother was the worst. He had scoffed at every decision and every revelation she had ever made, assuming they would be negated and forgotten a day later. He thought she was rash and unreliable, that she could not be trusted to sit still for an hour, much less hold down a job for a month. He had laughed when she told him she was going to join the army, and after he had met her first girlfriend, he had only said, 'So, how long until you're straight again?'

But where Olena's parents thought it was stupidity and immaturity that drove Wednesday's indecisive nature, and over the years, others had speculated that she was just insufferably selfish or that she liked the attention that flip-flopping between strange decisions brought her, the conclusion her brother Trent had reached was that her need to be forever on the move, her constant search for opportunities to change her life and keep it exciting, were all a product of her fear of responsibility. He said that she was a coward, that settling down with a family or a career or a home or all of the above would be too much for her, so she had no choice but to keep running to avoid them.

'Wednesday, please take a step back and think about whether this is actually what you want, or if you're just running again,' he had said, when she told him she had been provisionally chosen for the *Conqueror* missions. Playing the role of sensible, serious, caring brother, for one night only. 'You don't want to come to your senses when it's too late. This isn't a mistake you can undo by dropping out once you arrive or thinking up another plan when you've already taken off.'

It frustrated her, how many years she had spent trying to gain his approval, when he had not spent any trying to understand her any better. By now, she had given up trying to gain anyone's approval – Olena's parents', her own parents', her brother's, her friends', the list went on and on – when it never felt as good when it came as the excitement of her unpredictable life.

'When you proposed,' Olena said, sniffing loudly, 'you told me you'd follow me anywhere. You said you'd always be by my side, that I'd never look to my left again without seeing you standing there. Do you remember that?'

She looked up at Wednesday, and Wednesday nodded. She scrambled through her brain, but she could not find a memory that matched the situation that Olena had described; though she did not doubt that it had happened, and she wanted even less to reveal that she had forgotten something that Olena obviously held dear.

'And now, that's just bullshit. You'll be gone forever. I'll never see you again, unless it's on the news or in documentaries. You'll be some hero of humanity, while I'm left back here to ache over what you did to me…'

Once again, her sentence was cut short by sobbing.

'We won't launch for at least three years,' Wednesday said, reaching out to hold Olena's hand. The sobbing woman flinched, pulling away from her wife's touch, and looked at her hand intensely, as if inspecting it for burns or cuts. 'I'll still be here until then.'

'Oh, great,' Olena replied, looking up from her hand with fire in her eyes, 'so you'll be around long enough to, what, move your things out of our house? Get our divorce sorted? That had better be top of your list, because we're not…'

Her eyes widened and her chapped lips hung open for a second. A flash flood of realisation drowned her irises.

'Fuck,' she said, 'what about our family? Is that why you're doing this?'

Wednesday shook her head. She rolled her eyes, and looked away.

A little under a year ago, more to appease Olena than to follow any dream of her own, Wednesday had agreed to pursue adoption, to start a family with her wife. After much debate, what felt like hundreds of visits from social workers and assessors, and finally approval by the Adoption Applications Committee, they were on the list of prospective adopters, and their profile was being sent out to birth parents all over Eastern Australia for their consideration and approval. They could be chosen at any time; they could be parents within a month. But if Wednesday was honest, she had been distracted during the process by her secret application to join the *Conqueror* missions, and since the noise of the adoption process had died down almost four months ago, the memory that she had even taken part in it had slipped her mind, too. Perhaps it had dissolved in the pool of rash decisions she had made and then reversed. Or maybe she had remembered, and her subconscious had decided on her behalf that she should run, and run forever, and never burden herself with such a huge responsibility. Maybe that was exactly what this was all about, after all.

'No,' she said, 'of course it's not about that. Don't be ridiculous.'

Olena was already fighting back tears again. 'Fuck, Weddy,' she said, choking on her sadness and the tightness of her throat, 'we went through so much to be on that list. I changed everything so that we'd be suitable. I did so much, and you did so little. Now I know why. I noticed at the time, but I thought you just weren't as excited as I was, and that once it was all done and we had a kid, that you'd completely change. I thought you'd be such a good parent. I was so wrong about you. Fuck. Fuck. *Fuck.*'

Wednesday could not protest – she agreed with everything Olena had said. She *had* done so little to get them approved by the Adoption Approvals Committee. She *was not* as excited as Olena had been – she had been indifferent, concerned more with her own affairs than the affairs of her family. Olena probably *had* been wrong about her, especially when she thought Wednesday would change for her. She shrugged, and shook her head.

'You're right,' she said. 'I don't know what I can—'

But Olena interrupted her immediately by standing and gathering her things, and clumsily loading her handbag onto her shoulder, flustered and frustrated and causing one more scene, to finish the drama outside the Parliament Building.

'You know what?' she said, pointing at Wednesday. 'You can begin your life alone right now. I'm sick of having to change my mind as often as you do, just so that we can stay united. I'm sick of feeling like an accessory that you drag along on your journeys. We don't want the same things, we're not really in love; this is all a big joke to you. I feel like such a fool for coming here thinking it would be a romantic trip for my birthday, when really this trip was just a ploy to soften the blow of you ruining our lives. I'm going back to our hotel to pick up my things, and then I'm going to the airport. I don't care what you do, but I don't want you to follow me. This is over, as of now. Good luck in space, bitch.'

With that, she left, leather jacket over her arm and bag hanging low from her shoulder, oblivious in her anger and hollowing sadness to the stares of the audience that had watched her meltdown.

Wednesday did not follow her wife off into the maze of Hungarian streets, and she did not fly home early from Budapest. She spent the remaining time taking in the sights and wondering why it was that she felt so little sadness over the dissolution of her marriage. Why had she fallen out of love so quickly, so easily? What was it about her hard coding that made it so easy for her to forget on Saturday passion that she had felt so strongly on Friday evening? Perhaps she did fear responsibility, or perhaps she did like the attention. Perhaps she was still desperate for approval and validation, or perhaps she really was immature and stupid. All she really knew was that she always wanted to do what made her happy, whether that made other people happy or not. She would only get one life, and she did not want to waste it trying to satisfy the needs of others. If that made her selfish, or scatty, or childish, or cowardly, then so be it.

She would not live unremarkable and die unremembered.

DAY 102

The tight space in which they had slept, underneath the stage of that great coliseum, had not needed a fire to keep them warm, and when the women woke, even the thin layers that they had worn to sleep were too much, and stuck to their moist skin uncomfortably, making them feel dirty and crowded, itching to throw themselves under a cold shower. But there were no showers here, cold or otherwise – for the past hundred days, the best washes they had received had been in a rodent-infested river, using their own clothing as flannels. The days when they had not known the river existed or had not been anywhere near it had been worse – weeks of wiping themselves down with worn clothing dampened with the meagre water supplies their synthesisers could produce, or if their synthesisers could not produce any more than that which they needed to survive, then just days without washing, their skin turning brown and wrinkling with the scum, dirt breaking off their bodies like the dead skin of a lizard, shedding in the desert sun.

The toilet situation was far worse. All of the humans secretly dreaded needing the toilet when all that surrounded them were dry, rubble-filled streets and ruined, rubble-creating buildings. Though they had found sorts of faucets, sources of running water that could be turned on and off and which poured their water into large, knee-high sinks with finger-width drains, they had not yet found anything that took away waste or provided comfort like any toilet they had seen on Earth. Despite all they knew about this civilisation, they still did not know how the aliens' bodies had expelled the unnecessary, nor where this fit into their society or building design; and if Ellis knew where this kind had laid its waste, he had not yet pointed it out either. So they would excuse themselves, and find a private spot, and leak their dark yellow piss or their too-hard stools onto the dry earth, and then cover it by hand, if they had reached a point when they could no longer avoid doing it at all.

And this was how Kojima woke – desperate to piss, and too hot and uncomfortable to find the motivation to do it. She propped herself against a wooden pillar next to which she had slept, and looked across the room to find Shelley doing exactly the same thing on the next pillar along, turning a tiny wooden trinket in her hands as if nostalgic for a time when it was a treasure.

'What have you got there?' Kojima asked, looking for a distraction from her heavy bladder.

Shelley did not answer with more than a shrug. She had been sulky since the creature flew down from the roof the day before, and while Kojima sympathised with the younger woman's fear, she did not feel qualified to help her talk it out. Too many times, she had tried to halve a problem with her friend, and found instead that the problem either became completely hers or even, when halved, was too difficult for her to carry, and so Shelley would end up furious with her for having tried, leaving them both somewhere a few steps back from square one.

So Kojima just sat in silence, rubbing her eyes and allowing them to adjust to the dim light under the ground, the sunlight pouring in one thin slit at a time, through vents in the pitch above them. Verne was gone; no great surprise, since he would often rise earlier than the rest and wander off to somewhere quiet to perform one of his many rituals in private, returning when he was ready. Ellis was also missing, his covers strewn across the floor where he had slept, as if thrown off in a rush. Most likely, he had sleepwalked again.

The ceilings were low in this room, much lower than they had been anywhere else, and from the size of the natives in the photographs and drawings that the humans had found, they seemed too low for this to be a room, this hall that spanned the length of the performance area above them and featured only pillars for holding the stage up and vents for who knew what. Perhaps the vents were drains, and this was a sewer. If that was the case, then it was unpleasant to imagine what might have gone on above them, back in the days when this arena had been operational.

'Did Ellis say how long it would be until we reached this library?' Kojima asked. After the visit from the giant beetle and Shelley's subsequent slide into sadness, Ellis had promised that when the sun rose, they would go to the library that he had shown Verne, the one with all the books about alien worlds and the history of this one and the research this race had done and the fiction they had written and everything one could ever imagine printed on so much of that strange paper they always used, and on computer screens that only Ellis knew how to operate. Shelley had mentioned it once or twice, so he thought it would cheer her up to hear that they could visit; but really, he only wanted to go so that he could find information on that beast and discover why it rang such a huge bell in his head.

Again, Shelley did not respond with words. She grunted, but her meaning was not conveyed, if she had one at all.

Kojima grew tired of trying, and pushed herself up the

pillar she was leaning on, to stand. Her muscles stretched and her bones creaked, and by the time she had reached her feet, the ache in her bladder was nothing compared to the aches in her knees, her neck, her elbows, her lower back.

'Okay,' she sighed, turning to leave the young woman alone and find a place to make water.

'Did he bury Ballard?' asked Shelley, her voice a sullen whisper.

'Hmm?'

'Verne. Did he bury Ballard, after he died?'

Kojima paused halfway between turning away and turning back, standing like a hunchback to prevent her head from knocking on the ceiling, and stood cycling through her cloudy memory for a while.

'I don't know,' she said finally.

'Hmm.' Shelley lowered her eyebrows, dissatisfied.

Kojima knew she would be a fool to continue the conversation, and even more of a fool to continue it with what she was thinking. But she had been much more foolish in her time, and she was sure she had much foolishness left in her yet, so she said, 'I mean, out here, does it really matter?'

The look that Shelley gave her was the colour of fury. 'Of course it does,' she said.

Kojima nodded. She had no more to say, no energy to debate the value of spending time burying a body in a foreign land, where death could arrive as soon as one's back was turned, simply for the sake of honouring tradition. Kojima had seen enough dead bodies to know that the ground wouldn't fix them any more than clothes or make-up would. Without a soul, bodies were just meat and smells and sorrow.

As she turned away, she was stopped once again by Shelley saying, 'Life just gets cheaper and cheaper.'

Kojima sighed. She wished that she had something to say in response, but she did not.

Verne did. Out of the darkness, from a spot which was not lit and from which he had been listening to their conversation after he had returned unnoticed from his morning stroll, he said, 'There's nothing that's worth more than life. Life is the most expensive thing in the universe, because it's all we have. People like to imagine all the things that came before them and will come after, but really all we have are the hundred or so years that we live, and then we have nothing. Nothing before, and nothing after. I've taken lives before, but I don't know if I could ever do it again, the more I think of just how much it costs, and who pays. The price is far too high.'

He too turned to leave, to go back up into the daylight where he felt more comfortable. As he reached the door that led to one of the ramps up to ground level, he paused and added, 'And yes, I buried him. I didn't want the dogs getting him.'

When the humans gathered up top to set out for the day, retrieving the sled from underneath the seating and packing their things onto it for pulling along with them, the atmosphere had cleared a little; and though Shelley had not yet completely emerged from the shell in which she was hiding, she was at least no longer actively seeking to bring others down with her, which was probably the best they could hope for. The three Conquerors stood in a triangle, packed and ready to go, for minutes before anyone asked the obvious, and when it was asked, it was Kojima who asked it.

'So, where's Ellis?' she said, scratching her skin as it tingled unpleasantly in the heat of the mid-morning sun.

Verne shrugged. Shelley did not answer.

'We should look for him,' Kojima said, frowning and gazing off across the floor of the stadium as if he might be in here, wandering around like a gladiator who had not realised the show was over.

Again, Shelley said nothing. Verne answered by shrugging, crossing his arms, and leaning back on the sled and its contents, the pile of possessions tilting slightly under his weight.

'He'll find his way back,' he said.

'Are you not worried about him?' asked Kojima. 'Anything could have happened to him. This isn't someone just wandering the streets of California. This is a burning city filled with six-legged dogs and giant insects.'

Verne smiled a mocking smile. 'I'm sure he's fine,' he said.

Kojima sighed, defeated by his complete lack of concern. She squinted at him in the light, and noticed that he was not looking back at her, but past her, into the stands of seating. And just as she noticed it, a shout burst out from the point at which he looked, and echoed through the coliseum, frightening the wits out of Kojima.

'Hey!' it said.

She turned and looked up at the seating, the rows of benches and rows of holes where benches used to be and climbing plants creeping across it all, and saw Ellis near the top, running down toward them, excited like a child waking on the morning of its birthday. Verne must have seen him there, known before she did that her worries were unfounded. She turned to him and rolled her eyes, and he winked, rising from the sled.

'Fuckin' 'ell,' Ellis panted, as he descended the rows and rows of seats from where he had been, nearly at the top of the stalls, to the ground. 'I have had a mental night, I'll tell you that.'

'Where've you been?' asked Shelley, breaking her silence.

'Oh, only up there, man, only up there,' he said, pointing, as he reached the others. He stank of sweat and garbage and smoke and kerosene, and he looked like he had rolled around in the desert dirt all night long. 'I want to tell you something. Come into the shade, this is important.'

Alan Ellis took a seat on the first row of seating, and Shelley sat next to him. Kojima walked the couple of metres that were required for her to be covered by the shade of the coliseum's awning, but she did not sit. Verne stayed where he was, his arms still crossed and his smile now absent. He watched Ellis through concerned eyes, as the young man panted in his seat, shaking with excitement, wearing a version of his grin which was more crazed than ever.

'First, I was having this lucid dream,' Ellis said, animated and twitchy like a drug addict recounting his latest trip, 'where I knew I was asleep but I was still totally submerged in the, I don't know, the *dream reality*. Anyway, in this dream, I woke up down there, underground with you lot, and I could hear this rumbling on the floor above us, a kind of inviting thrum like the throb of bass you hear from outside a concert, y'know? So I followed it up the ramp there, opened the trap door that led to the stage, and when I got up here, there was this army of those giant beetle things just standing there, thousands of them, all staring at me, like they expected me to do something. And at the very front of this crowd, there was a podium, so in my dream, I walked right up and stood behind this podium to make my big speech, feeling like this was exactly what I was supposed to do, nothing weird about it at all. When I got up there, I had a look around and behind me there was a wife and kid, proper prim-lookin' First Lady of a wife and this sweet little bairn, and it felt so natural for me to be there in front of them all, with me being their king or president or whatever.

'I looked out at the crowd and I said to them, "Fear not, I will make sure you are safe now, tomorrow, and forever. I will take you back." And they all cheered, there was applause; you name it. Then they come and line up to shake my hand, every one of them wants to do it, but for whatever reason my hands are made of metal, they're like bionic hands, and they're buzzing and sparking, and every one of the bugs that shakes my hand is vaporised like it's flown into a bug zapper, and even though they see all the bugs before them being killed by my bug-zapper hands, they just keep coming. And I get to the end of the queue, and they're all dead, and I go to take the hands of my wife and kid and walk away, but when I touch them, they're vaporised too, and I'm all alone again, walking my way up the stalls toward the top.'

Ellis paused to let the dream sink in, as if any of the other humans should have gleaned some meaning from the story. Shelley laughed, a tickled cackle, genuinely amused by the dream; and Ellis grinned back at her, nodding as if to encourage her to keep laughing. Verne and Kojima exchanged looks of concern.

'Anyway, anyway,' Alan Ellis said, adding this new thought as if it was the point all along and he had only just remembered it, 'I woke up at the top of these seats, all dusty and aching, and I sat up, and I realised… I can remember everything.'

'What?' Verne grunted, uncrossing his arms and stepping closer.

Ellis nodded. 'I remember everything, man. Why I'm here, who I was on Earth, what I did, my family were. I knew it was coming back, I knew I'd found you for a reason, I knew this wasn't all for nothing. I remember *everything.*'

Shelley's laughter dulled and her eyes filled with tears, tears of shock that surprised even her; and Verne and Kojima exchanged another sceptical look. It seemed too good to be true, that a man so plagued by a rapidly diminishing memory should suddenly dream back his entire history and wake up with nothing missing from a section of his mind which previously had nearly everything missing. Perhaps it stood to reason that there had already been, for this group of people, so many things that seemed too bad to be true but which had nonetheless come true, that they had earned this one miracle; but neither of the older

Conquerors were of the kind that would readily believe such an idea.

'So, what do you remember?' asked Verne.

Ellis seemed surprised to be asked, underprepared to answer. 'Well,' he replied, losing his smile and gaining instead a frown of concentration, distracted eyes seeking the information as if it was written on the floor in front of him, 'I'm an electronic engineer. I have two kids, a boy and a girl. I went to school in Glasgow, university in Germany. I've been here for just over two years, this planet's time. My first girlfriend's name was Hilda. Oh, and I had a dog as well, called Scout. I'm divorced, but my ex-wife and I are on good terms. We just weren't right for each other. Um, I was born in 2406—'

'Wait, wait,' said Verne. He wondered if Ellis needed some time to iron out the details that had come to him overnight – they poured from him like Lego from a box, and just like those bricks, they were not magically falling into formation to construct the model of which they were intended to be a part, but were instead falling in a messy pile, as disorganised and unrecognisable as if they were a part of some other model altogether. 'Twenty-*four*-oh-six? Is that what you just said?'

Ellis nodded.

'You were born 282 years after we left Earth,' said Shelley, her frown heavy and her eyes taking their turn to search for the answer to a riddle in the air, 'but you got here before us. How is that possible?'

'That's the only part I can't work out,' Ellis replied, 'but I know that it's true. Don't look at me like that, Verne, please. This isn't just some bloke left alone on a planet for years, finally losing his last marble. I know that's what you're thinking. But you have to trust me, this is right down inside my head, more sure than anything I've ever known. Right down where your memory should live.' He tapped a finger on his skull so hard that his companions could hear the knocking.

'Okay,' said Verne, 'so why are you here?'

'Okay, okay, this might sound mental too, but hear me out, man,' Ellis said, taking a deep breath for dramatic effect, or perhaps simply to calm himself down. 'I'm here to bring you back to Earth.'

DAY 102

Alan Ellis took his time explaining the plan for getting the crew back onto their ship, *Conqueror 23*, which was now orbiting Planet 127-001, and setting that ship on a course for Earth.

The study of other planets was far from just academic to the civilisation that had inhabited this world – though the humans of Earth had not known it, the creatures that lived here had visited their planet, more than once, and taken relics and souvenirs, knowledge and biological samples back with them each time. If one followed the underground tunnel system far enough west, Ellis said, into the desert, one would find hangars filled with light spacecraft, much like the ones Earth tourists would pay hundreds of thousands to ride, to spend two minutes in space. Here, they were the kind of transportation that the masters would own for themselves, and take out on the weekend like rich men with their classic convertibles on Earth. So, since their own landing vessel was now destroyed, the humans would use one of these ships, Ellis said, to rejoin their interplanetary vessel, and from there, cryosleep through the journey home.

They had fuel cells that would not expire for millennia. They had computers that Ellis knew how to use, documentation written in languages that two of the company knew how to read, software so intelligent it would perform all the calculations required on their behalf. They had the way, if there was enough of a will. This race had built everything that the Conquerors and Ellis needed to get back to their home planet and their own species, and all the humans had to do now was cross this inhospitable city once more, re-enter that desert, and take a chance.

If only they could agree to take it.

'How do you know any of those vehicles work?' Verne asked.

'I don't,' said Ellis. 'I don't even know if the fuel cells are still there. They could have been stolen by scavengers or become unstable and exploded. But what's the alternative? Stay here for the rest of our lives? At the very least, they have communications equipment in that desert. Beyond those mountains you saw, there's a farm of satellite dishes bigger than any you've ever seen, I've seen it on a map. We could contact home, just like they contacted us all those years ago. Even if we can't be there, we can tell our people what we know about this planet, let them know we're alive. I don't want to rot here and be forgotten. Not now I know I'm a real person with a past and a future.'

'And if the vehicles don't work and the comms equipment doesn't work, what then?' Verne asked, stony-faced.

'Fuck, man, I don't know, we tried, okay? What's the problem?'

'The problem is that we'll then be further from the city than we've ever been, and we will have gone there for nothing, and by then, we might just be weak enough to die there.'

Ellis sighed loudly, and waved his hands at Verne in frustration.

'If we can work out exactly how we would need to take off, at what trajectory, time and velocity,' Kojima said, cutting in calmly, 'how will we dock onto *Conqueror 23*? Our landing craft was specially made for exactly that. Nothing else will do – we don't have suits to spacewalk our way in.'

'Um,' said Ellis, frantically scrambling for an answer, 'I don't know. I don't know. We could try building our own docking attachment. We can find the tools and the metal, that's all we really need.'

Kojima shook her head and laughed incredulously. 'We wouldn't know the first thing,' she said, 'it would be impossible. This is incredibly advanced stuff, and none of us are qualified.'

'What about the robot arms?' Ellis said, a light bulb sparking to life behind his eyes.

His exclamation was met with blank stares.

'There are maintenance robots in those hangars, huge metal arms that were used to repair the ships. If I can get them working and they have the kind of intelligence the other robots on this planet have, they'll be able to solve the problem with us. All we'll need is to give them your ship's schematics, which I have on your black box drive.'

He looked very pleased with himself, as though he was now just stacking up the problems he had resolved that day. But Kojima would not be satisfied by conjecture and imagination, when facts and knowledge were what was needed, if they were to make it back to Earth.

'What other robots?' Shelley asked, confused.

'Well, there are plenty of robots here. Before I found Verne and Ballard, I came across one of the dogs dying,' said Ellis, 'in a public bath, in the south of the city. Its skin was mostly removed, and it had suffered some kind of head injury, crushed its skull in. Anyway, once it had given up and I went to harvest it for meat, I found that most of its body was robotic. Metal bones, hydraulic muscles covered in some sort of rubber to give the illusion of real muscle texture, blood vessels in the skin carrying enough blood for realistic bleeding – real impressive work. There were organs, but they were synthetic; designed to perform the real-life function of organs, so that the dog could live a normal dog's life and eat and drink and piss and shit and never realise it was a robot. Honestly, this was such a convincing animal that if it'd had all its skin, I would have had no doubts that it was real. Even the dogs can't tell, though I'm certain the robots are the most aggressive and cannibalistic among them.

'The amount of machinery I've found with robotic components and AI in their programming is astounding. In terms of technology, they were way beyond where we were, when you or I left Earth. These people didn't really need to work any more; they had computers running their world for them. If we can't get one of their ships to dock with ours, I'll eat my hat.'

'I don't know,' said Kojima, leaning back on the stone row behind her. 'What do you think, Verne?'

Verne grunted, and looked out at the seating, the sky.

'It's a huge risk to take on hunches and the hope for blind luck,' he said. 'Our hardest days here were spent surviving that desert and the suburbs on the west of the city. I don't know if I want to go back there, to see if a machine that Ellis *might* be able to operate *maybe* still works, and could *possibly* get us back onto our ship.'

'Yeah,' replied Kojima, shaking her head with the difficulty of the decision. 'I don't want to die doing something foolish, when we're doing such a good job of staying alive right now.'

Ellis sighed. He would go without them if he had to. He did not intend to stay here, waste the rest of his days only just surviving on a planet where he did not belong, because the people he now cared for would not take a risk. He would return to Earth and find new people to care for, and he would live like he might never have lived again, had he not regained his memory. He would not give up, like these people.

'What are you two talking about?' said Shelley, flabbergasted. 'Are you fuckin' serious? Am I hearing you right? You don't want to take the only risk that's ever been worth taking in your whole lives, and return to the planet you've left behind, instead of living out an empty, pointless life here just to prove to yourselves that you could? You're being ridiculous. You're both just so… fucked up. What are you running from? What is wrong with you? Why wouldn't you want to…? Ugh, whatever. Alan, I'm coming with you.'

'What do you know about calculating orbital inclination, Shelley?' snapped Verne, now irritated. 'Or about the complexities of completing a space rendezvous with two completely incompatible spacecraft and no spacesuits? Do you know where *Conqueror 23* is now, and when it'll be in the perfect position for us to board? Do you know if it has enough fuel to get us home *and* power our cryosleep pods for the entire journey? Do we even know it's still up there? You know nothing. And neither do any of us. We weren't sent here to ever return, and you know it. They would've sent someone who knew what they were doing, if they ever wanted us back. We were sent here for publicity, advertising; a sideshow to distract everyone from the horrors of the world, just like everything else. We've served our purpose, and now we're alone out here. And I don't want to die running a fool's errand. I don't want you to die doing the same. Any of you.'

Although it was clear that Verne was angry because he cared, Shelley was hurt by his anger, and was silent for a while as she processed what he had said.

'I don't know any of those things,' she finally said. 'But I know that I don't want to die here, and I wish I'd never come. I know that you're only here because you're a brute and you have no friends at home. I know that Kojima's only here because she thought she'd leave behind her anxiety and all her weird obsessions, and they followed her anyway. I know that I made the biggest mistake of my life coming here, and I'll do anything to take it back. I know you regret it, even if you won't admit it. I know…' And then the tears in her eyes and the lump in her throat overcame her, and she sobbed into her hands, slumped over and shaking.

Verne sighed, and put his head in his hand. Kojima bit her nails. Ellis held Shelley, clenching his eyes closed and shaking his head.

'The only memories I have of being on Earth are hazy and broken,' he said, rubbing Shelley's back softly. 'I'm going to make new ones, even if that does mean that I'll die trying. I want you to come with us, but if you won't, then know that we're going anyway.'

Verne sighed again, scratching his scalp hard with both hands and growling deeply. After he was done sighing, he put his hands on his hips and looked up at the sky, and then after a while standing like this he said, 'Of course I'm coming. What else is there to do?'

Ellis grinned, wiped his eyes and laughed. 'I knew it, man.'

Kojima smiled too, glad they were in agreement. Perhaps Shelley was right that her issues had followed her here, and that she would never be free from them if she just kept running; but she did not feel so anxious any more. She had friends now, so her fears were not her only company. She had people who relied on her, so she did not have so much time to indulge her more creative worries. She had a purpose that felt worthy – not just interesting or exciting, but *vital* – so she could no longer wander through life, fearing that she would die tomorrow having achieved nothing and leaving nothing in her wake. If she had felt like this on Earth, she might never have come here.

It took flying to an alien planet to make her feel this human.

DAYS 103-105

The humans stood in front of the library, in which Ellis had shown Verne the scrolls and books and screens laden with drawings of humans and maps of Earth, the same library that held all the knowledge this dead race had accrued about hundreds of planets that span slowly around their suns all those light years away, and watched it burn slowly to the ground.

Flames as hot and bright as a furious star, a stink that filled the lungs and turned the air grey.

'Ugh,' Ellis sighed, averting his eyes, kicking a stone in half-hearted frustration.

'What was in there?' asked Shelley, apparently forgetting all the other times she had been told.

'Everything. It was like some library from the future – books that went back centuries, storage filled with data from floor to ceiling. Everything they knew was in that building.'

'To know that, you must already have read a lot of it?'

Ellis shook his head, ran his hand along his hair. 'I barely scratched the surface,' he replied, beginning to walk away. He was certain that if the building had survived, he would have found inside of it diagrams of the anatomy of those insects, data on their biological make-up, detailed explanations of their eating habits, mating rituals, everything. He had found as much about humanity in there, so it stood to reason that they would know the same about all the alien species they had stolen from lands far, far away. But now it was gone, so he would never know.

In its scrambling for reason, as his skin was grilled lightly by the flames that reached from that building and across the street and up to the gods, his mind hit upon the idea that perhaps the building was burning *because* he wanted to visit it. That maybe this arson was aimed directly at his hopes, and was not after all as random as they thought. But this suspicion was like a balloon, and without evidence to weigh it down, it quickly floated away, to be replaced by something new.

'Come on,' he said, as he walked away from his companions, 'the sooner we move on, the sooner we get back home.'

'Which way are we going?' asked Kojima, stopping a few metres behind.

Ellis sighed and turned on his heels, rolling his eyes. 'Of course, I forgot. Well, overground is quicker, but there are wolves in these parts, if there are still rodents to hunt; but underground is damper, and slower, and more like a maze.'

He shrugged and smiled. He seemed to have forgotten already the building he had wanted to visit, still slowly burning a few strides away.

Kojima turned back to what remained of her crew. 'Well, I'd say the tunnels,' she said, 'but I'll go with the majority—'

'Overground,' said Shelley, before Kojima had finished speaking. 'If we have to trek across the city again, at least let's not do it in the damp and dark.'

'Okay,' Kojima chuckled, nodding past her at the old man in their group. 'Verne? Have an opinion?'

'Not really.' He shrugged.

So Kojima turned back to Ellis, and raised her shoulders. 'I guess it's the streets,' she said. 'Let's move out.'

'How are you holding up?' Kojima asked Verne, as they walked slowly down a long, straight road just west of the river, later that day. Twenty or thirty yards ahead of them, Ellis and Shelley walked side by side, Ellis pointing at buildings or doorways or gutters or the sky, explaining to Shelley how the world worked or perhaps recounting things that had happened to him here, or else just pointing because he liked to point. They cut narrow silhouettes into the early-evening dinge, skinny like two road signs blowing side to side softly in a breeze.

Verne's physical condition seemed to be deteriorating. His knees shook and his back hunched and he winced when he rose and sat, and everything he did was that little bit slower than it had been just days ago and even though all of this was only slight, barely noticeable if one was not paying avid attention, Kojima had noticed it all. Yet he still pulled the sled alone, gathered much of their food, rose early and took guard duty even when Ellis assured them that they were in a neighbourhood – if such a word applied here – where a guard would not be needed because nothing lived to threaten them. He looked like he needed rest more than he needed to do all of this, but he was too proud or worrisome or dutiful to give up. When Kojima had suggested that he let her pull the sled, or make snares in his place, or do anything to lighten his load, he had just given her a certain look, shaken his head, and carried on with his tasks.

So she had not tried again since then, to lessen the load he carried. It was clear that he felt like it was his responsibility, so she made it hers to make sure he was well enough to carry it.

'Fine,' Verne grunted, adjusting the strap on his shoulder which tied him to the sled.

'What do you think of this plan of his?' Kojima asked, nodding toward Ellis.

'I don't know.' Verne gazed at Ellis's back like the younger man was a puzzle that he did not want to solve.

'You buying the hangar idea? Old spaceships that we can take out for one last trip?'

Verne laughed, dropping his gaze to the floor. It was one quick exhalation with a hint of a smile, and then it was back to that frown, the furrowed brow, the dark, tired eyes; the total absence of joy.

'Not a bit,' he replied, shaking his head, 'but that ain't to say I think he's lying. I believe they're there and I believe he thinks we can use them, but I don't think we got a hope in hell of starting one up, let alone doing anything useful with it.'

'Then why did you agree to it?'

'What else is there? We can die in the city trying to survive, doing the same thing every day, counting the days till we run out of supplies or time or luck; or we can die trying to make it right. When I got here, I would have happily settled for the former. But now, I'm not so sure.'

Kojima nodded, smiled. 'I don't think you could have denied him anyway. I've seen the way you look at him,' she said. 'Like he's your saviour or something.'

Verne looked at the floor again, adjusted the strap on his shoulder, slipping a thumb under it to stop it from rubbing him for a while. 'I never bought the whole saviour thing,' he replied. 'The way I saw it, only thing I ever needed saving from was myself. But that was before he appeared out of nowhere on a planet eight light years away from the rest of his species to pull me from a pile of rubble, then told me he was from the future and here to bring me back to Earth. I hate to be dramatic, but even if he's just a nut, I owe him my life.'

'So now, what, you've found faith? A sleepwalker with a man-bun is your saviour?'

Verne smiled.

'You found the messiah, and he's a Scottish man with overalls and chronic déjà vu?'

Verne laughed. 'I've no idea what I've found,' he said.

They walked further, smiling, glad to be next to each other, having conversations that were not about impending doom or Ballard's death or the strange, deadly-looking animals into which they kept running. But those conversations were never far away, because they were all that there was, in that wasteland. Those creatures that had threatened them, and the fates that could befall them if they let their guard down for just a few minutes, were always at the back of their minds, ready to be talked out again.

But Kojima resisted.

'Tell me about your life on Earth,' she said.

Verne gave her a short, sharp look from the corner of his eye. He could have been wondering how they had gone a hundred days without sharing much about their lives before this journey, or he could have been wondering why she wanted to share it at all, or he could just have misheard her; whatever it was, it was too short to process, before he looked again at the ground a few feet in front of him, and that frown returned.

And then, he was silent for so long that she thought he had decided not to answer. So she took the hint, and stayed silent too.

'I had a wife,' he began, 'called Elsa. We lived in San Francisco. I always wanted to move somewhere nicer, somewhere less dirty and with less crime, but it was the house we'd had since we first married; she wouldn't let it go. I had a son too, Tobias.'

'Had…?'

'Well,' Verne shrugged, 'no one we knew will be alive now.'

Kojima smiled nervously, blushing. 'Of course.'

'My wife died nearly a decade before we left Earth. And my son hadn't spoken to me in… two years, maybe. If you can call the angry grunting he did before that speaking to me. I didn't leave anything behind; nothing that wanted me there, anyway.'

'Are you sure?' Kojima said, before her internal filter had had a chance to review it. Her heart skipped a beat when she realised how insensitive it sounded, when said aloud. What did she know about what his life on Earth had been like? What right did she have to question his assessment of it?

She started to panic, until she noticed Verne smiling again.

'Dead sure,' he replied, all sad-dog eyes, 'but if I could go back and change it, I'd do it in a New York minute. I was an asshole. Always have been, I suppose.'

He paused. 'I was so angry at him for not understanding how it felt to be in my shoes, but I never put myself in his.'

'Oh,' Kojima said, unsure of how she should respond. She knew that many people would reassure the man that he was not that bad, that his actions had been somewhat justified, that he should not be so hard on himself; but she did not know what his actions were, or even how correct he was in his self-assessment. She certainly would not have called him an asshole, but that did not necessarily mean he wasn't one, and she had always hated disingenuous niceties. Instead, she said nothing.

'Ellis reminds me of him. When he was happy, when we were a little closer to being friends. He's always so enthusiastic about everything. So scruffy. Tobias was like that. I think. But then, Ballard reminded me of him too; so it might just be me.'

The old man smiled again. Kojima smiled too, a smile of real joy, warmed by the connection she felt to her friend.

'How about you?' he asked, looking at her for the first

time in a while. 'I'd heard of you, you know. I'd read a couple of articles on you. You're probably the most famous of us.'

Kojima smiled, rolled her eyes, brushed a strand of hair away from her face and took her own turn to look at the ground. 'Yeah, practically a Bollywood star,' she said, slightly irritated with herself for blushing. 'But it wasn't very exciting. I really lived a very lonely life. And all the things that were written about my adventures as a child, what I went through to break out into the free world, I hated those. I didn't want them published, I didn't want the attention, and when I read them, I was angry that they made it sound so much more like a Sunday afternoon children's film than the horror that it was. After going through that, I could never live a normal life. I was looking forward to this, by the end, even though... well...' She trailed off.

She thought that Verne might be embarrassed by her openness, as she had been by his; but from the look of him, he was not. She had always saved some of her anxiety for her conversations, in which she would worry about everything she had said, and pick it all apart later to find parts for which she could hate herself, slip-ups over which she could obsess and about which she could imagine everyone around her was laughing or cringing. So where she had been worried that Verne would be upset by the things she had made him think about, or offended that she was asking such intrusive questions, it seemed that he felt only curiosity and interest. She liked the look he gave her, like he was really listening to every word she said.

'Why were you looking forward to it?' he asked.

Kojima thought for a long time. She did not feel like discussing anxiety and paranoia, having to choose on the fly how much information she should divulge in each sentence, how vulnerable she should make herself seem or feel. She did not want to go into it again, but she wanted even less for this exchange to simply end. She was glad that she had made a connection with Verne, that he was having a conversation with her that was more than just his usual grunts and nods, and she did not want to waste that.

After consideration, she said, 'I was scared of many things. I was anxious, most of the time. It wasn't easy for me to live like everyone else.'

She nodded, placed her thumbs under her rucksack straps, watched her long feet and her skinny legs jut out in front of her, left, right, left, right. When she looked up, Verne was still looking at her with that same expression.

'Things like what?' he said.

Kojima smiled at him, gazed into his inquisitive eyes for a few steps; and he looked away, as if that one look had told him exactly how she felt. Like he already thought he knew, and her look had just confirmed it.

'War,' she said, after a moment of silence. 'War and terror and hatred. I feared that there would be another world war, that all of the hate and the ideas that people had were always just bubbling over and all it would take was one spark to blow the whole thing wide open. I used to lie awake at night scared that some idiot president would decide one night to launch a nuke, and start the war that would end our race. Futile worries, really. But I was obsessed. I would read these quotes from scholars and authors saying that war was necessary, that it was dangerous to talk about a world where peace was the norm, because we could only better ourselves through conflict; and I used to hate them for saying such things. How could they be so glib about the lives of others? The births and deaths and dreams and aspirations and loves of millions wasted because some leader of one patch of land wanted to prove a point to some leader of another?

'Once I got to thinking about it all, everything got dark and the walls felt like they were closing in and I couldn't allow myself to think about anything else because then I'd let my guard down and it'd all tumble down around me… I don't know. I'm sorry. I must sound so stupid. I feel stupid, talking about it.'

Verne frowned, unsurprised by any of what he had heard. He had known already.

'I lived for a time with my grandpa in Texas,' he said, 'when I was a boy with an attitude that needed straightening out. He used to have all these sound bites, all these little phrases he'd pull out for every occasion, as if he had a scriptwriter feeding them to him through an earpiece or somethin'. Armchair wisdom, my grandma called it. Anyway, one of 'em went like this. He had me imagine that everyone's worries were marbles in their heads, and the more you had in there, the more your head grew to fit 'em all in. He said there was only one way to get 'em out, and that was to talk out every little detail of each one, even if it was as embarrassing as being paraded down Broadway naked. Then he asked me how the world would be, if all our worries were marbles.'

Verne waited, perhaps for an answer, though he did not look at Kojima. After a second, she said, 'And…?'

'We'd all be walkin' around with heads like beach balls,' Verne smiled, 'and still none of us would talk about it.'

And with that, the conversation was done. They walked in silence for a while, Verne's mind wandering from here to there and Kojima's enjoying the small release that talking about her problems had provided. Happy, just to be strolling with a friend, in the sun.

'Do you think he's really from the future?' Kojima asked, nodding again at Alan Ellis.

'I don't know,' Verne said. 'Every day that passes on this planet, I feel like I know less. You know astronauts used to be geniuses? Write books and academic papers and all the things I could never do?'

Kojima grinned. She had done those things – she had written theses on a number of mathematical disciplines from chaos theory to cryptography, and she had taught at universities in several countries, telling her students that the pursuit of knowledge was intelligent life's true purpose and that all others were a distraction – but those days seemed like a lifetime ago, and moreover, she knew that most of the people chosen for the *Conqueror* missions had not, and that the criteria by which they had been judged were much looser than those by which astronauts of old had been. But that said more about these missions than their participants.

'I did know that,' she said. 'They sound like a bunch of smart-asses to me.'

Verne laughed. 'I'm a tourist compared to those guys,' he said. 'I'm a photograph, in a museum of watercolours.'

They slept in the lobby of a housing block built to contain the dead race's underclass – tiny apartments stacked as high and as densely as possible, maximum capacity at minimum cost. The walls were painted with gaudy art and the floor was lined with rubble, debris and dust, and Ellis said that this was a good sign, as signs of untouched decay meant that no one and nothing else was living here and likely to return to harm them.

When they woke, Shelley and Ellis sat on a window ledge on the first floor of this building with their legs hanging out into the morning air, cooler than usual, blowing a light breeze past their shins and feet.

'They loved art, didn't they?' said Shelley, looking out at the city and not at the walls.

'It covers all the places that the low-born called their homes,' Ellis replied. 'Haven't seen it in any of the classier joints.'

'Do you know if it had any meaning? If it was a code, or contained hidden messages?'

Ellis smiled. 'I don't know. Maybe. Can it not just be art, for the sake of art?'

'Well, yeah. But what if it wasn't?' She gave him a suspicious look, playing for a moment the caricature of a conspiracy theorist, before giggling and looking away.

'I like it,' Ellis said. 'It's a really… *human* thing, isn't it? The appreciation of art, seeing the beauty in something with no practical purpose. It holds no key to our survival, it doesn't help us to eat or mate, but we love it anyway. And, unlike life, it has a knack of being joyful even when it's sad or angry. I'm pleased that they shared that with us.'

Shelley nodded. She liked very much Ellis's childlike wonder, the simplicity with which he expressed ideas that came into his head. A millennium ago, back on Earth, when she called herself an anthropologist, she had studied human behaviour, she had written about social processes and gender roles, she understood the role of art in society, and she had read Fünke's paper which claimed that the Western world no longer produced art, but had by routinely compartmentalising, labelling and monetising it turned it instead into a pseudoscience, and therefore, the only art which remained truly artful was tribal and would remain unseen by the developed world; but without all that noise, without having read all of those books or taken any of those tests, with one sentence, Ellis had summed up what felt instantly, undeniably true: between the robots that could not feel and the animals that could not think, art, and the appreciation of it, was a deeply human thing, one that defined her and her species.

Or at least, it had been, before they found it here.

'Do you remember if you were into art, back home?' Shelley asked, aware that Ellis was still foggy on some of the details of his previous life.

He screwed up his face in thought. 'Not really,' he mumbled, 'but I feel like I liked music. I want to say it was something that I was a fan of.'

'Do you remember any songs you liked?'

'Not for the life of me, man.' He shook his head, smiling. 'I don't remember a single tune.'

Shelley put her hand on the window ledge and twisted to

face him a little more. 'Verne said you were humming a song that he knew when he first met you. What about that one?'

Ellis turned to look Shelley in the eyes, and squinted when he found the sun to be shining right at him, out there on the horizon. He raised an eyebrow, and said, 'I have no idea what you're talking about.'

'Come on,' said Kojima, standing at the door, 'Verne's waiting.'

As they reached the limits of the city centre the next day, once again crossing that line where densely-packed towers and skyscrapers slowly shrank into suburbs filled with blocks of flats and hostels, eventually leading to the sprawling slums through which they had passed all those months ago, they were struck by just how quiet the air became. The city had been roaring in comparison, even in death, with its fires that started from nowhere and growled through the nights, and winds that kicked up and blew hard and furious through the long, narrow streets. But now, here, the air seemed more still, quieter, and nowhere near as uncomfortably hot as it had been the first time they came. They had not noticed that the city had had a sound, a smell, a feeling that drowned the senses, but now none of them failed to notice that those things were gone.

In fact, it was a little too quiet. As they passed that invisible line and the city fell behind them and the noise faded away, Verne's ears pricked and his eyes darted from place to place, like a guard dog alerted by an echo in the night. He stopped in the street, and it took the others a few steps to notice.

'What's wrong?' said Kojima, stopping and turning to him.

'The atmosphere,' said Verne, as if this was an answer, turning to check behind him.

'What about it?' said Shelley, her hand covering her

brow, shading her eyes from the afternoon sun.

'I don't know,' said Verne, 'but I feel strange.'

'Me too,' said Ellis, holding his head. His headaches and déjà vu had still not subsided, though he complained about them far less often. (He suspected, probably rightly, that the others would doubt his claims that he had remembered his past, if the symptoms that preceded that remembrance were not cured by the remembrance itself.) 'I feel like someone's watching me.'

And just as he said it, Verne reached for the gun hanging across his shoulders, and had it pointed at Ellis' head. The movement was as quick as a blink, and Ellis was looking down the barrel of the gun before he realised that Verne had started moving, and he was about to cry out when he heard Verne shout, 'Down!'

Ellis dropped into a squat and braced his head in one panicked movement, curled up like a ball in the street, as the six-legged demon dog that had rounded the corner behind him leapt into the air with long claws bared, aiming for his head. Like every time Verne had ever pulled a trigger before this, the fraction of a section it took was time enough for a thousand fleeting thoughts. He remembered all the times he had faced one of these dogs, and the fear with which they had filled him. He remembered his finger hovering over the trigger, his heart racing, but no part of him rising up to do the deed. He wondered how different their lives would be today, if he had been harder, more willing to act, more decisive and strong. He wondered if he would even be here, if he had been that way before he left Earth. He wondered if he had cleaned his rifle today, if it was likely to jam. He wondered how he would feel if it did, and the dogs mauled them all. All this ran through his mind before the trigger was pulled; and then, when it was, the dog was gone, and in its place was falling fur, flying blood. The creature, now, was just a pile of meat, skidding to a stop along the surface of the road.

But there was no time to celebrate. Immediately, another dog came charging from behind a building on the opposite side of the street. Kojima turned to shoot it, but was not quick enough in aiming her gun, so Verne had to stop this one too. It hit Kojima as it fell and knocked her off her feet, but was dead before it had come within a metre of her.

There were two more dogs further down the road that came running at the smell of blood, their teeth bared in hideous snarls and tails pointing over their heads as if they aimed to use them as scorpion stingers, but they were too far away to be a threat, and Verne had them bleeding and yelping before they had picked up any real speed.

The last dog sat at the end of the road, licking its paws as if it had not been made aware of the action that had gone on around it and would not care even if it had. When the dust that the dogs had kicked up cleared and the humans were mostly calm enough to stand up tall and attempt to regain their composures, it sat there watching them, its back straight and its eyes narrow, and Verne stood aiming his rifle at it, doubting that he could hit it at such a distance with his shaking hands. This stand-off went on for seconds that dragged, and Shelley and Ellis stood nervously as Kojima too took up her weapon to aim at the beast from her position on the floor, before the dog decided that it was no longer interested, and loped away casually, disappearing round a corner without making a sound.

'I think we should probably go underground,' said Ellis, dropping back to the floor to sit, breathlessly.

The rest looked at each other and then at Ellis, each of them running on pure adrenaline, shaking or nodding or shrugging distractedly.

'We're going underground,' said Kojima, climbing to her feet, holding her side. The claw of the dog that had died on its way to her had sunk itself into her skin just under her rib, and though it had only entered by an inch or two, it hurt as if it had cut right through her. She had checked it briefly before she rose to her feet, and there had been just a small spot of blood on her clothing and skin, so she assumed it was a minor wound, not worth attending to until they had escaped the danger, left the street. But as she held it, it got hotter and wetter under her fingers, and burned like an iron held to the skin.

'You all right?' asked Ellis, noticing her pain. 'Let me take a look at that, man.'

While Ellis took a closer look at Kojima's new wound and Shelley stared off at the empty space where the surviving dog had once stood, Verne, silent and lumbering, like a Sasquatch in the murk, approached the dog that had pierced Kojima's side and began to carve off its hide and its meat with his long knife, the blade now so badly blunted that he almost had to tear the flesh away with his bare hands.

'This isn't good,' muttered the younger man, as Kojima lifted the thin shirt she was wearing to reveal her midriff, the blood trickling down her pale skin and congealing thick and dark around the ragged stab wound, 'this isn't nice at all.'

He walked past Verne to the sled behind them, to retrieve a first-aid kit from one of the rucksacks. Verne kept hacking away at the dead animal, skinning it in patches and removing any chunks of meat that his knife would take. He ripped at the corpse like its owner had ordered the deaths of his family – hateful and angry, hungry for revenge. He hated these dogs, because he saw no good in them, just darkness and evil, malice and corruption. They probably knew nothing of hatred or love, grudges or friendship, but Verne had assigned them personalities in his mind, and to his perception they hated him too, and this attack had been planned since they had lost him all those weeks ago, when the Conquerors had taken refuge from a pack of them in a school on the edge of the city. They had come today to claim only him, to drag him alone into eternity with their long, crooked teeth and those vicious, pointed tails.

But as he thought this through and tore at the muscles and sinews of the carcass, and Ellis rubbed alcohol onto Kojima's injury and Shelley tapped her temple, documenting the scene of the survivors of the attack, Verne heard a whimper, and stopped what he was doing to pinpoint its source, cocking his head to locate the sound.

The first dog he had shot, on its way to Ellis, was not quite dead, and looked at him pleadingly with big black eyes and a bowed head, pawing at the ground in front of its snout as if offering its hand to be held so that it did not feel so alone in its final moments. He watched the creature moan and brush its bottom jaw sadly to and fro across the hard ground below it, and he saw in its demeanour an emptiness, a regret, a sense of soulfulness that he had not seen before in these creatures he had imagined as demons from Hell, or some other world even worse than Hell. The animal breathed laboriously and the ribs that were visible under its dark, patchy-haired skin rose and fell with its shallow inhalations like some mechanical part of an iron lung, and its wet eyes stayed glued to Verne, begging for forgiveness or salvation or companionship or whatever it was that would make the creature feel at peace as it slipped into death, and Verne was struck by a sickening depression, and he hung his head as he could not look into that dying dog's eyes any longer. The dog kept looking at him and pawing the floor until its breathing had ceased and its heart had stopped, and then it lay silent and still and lifeless, ten stones of evidence that Verne had, once again, been wrong all along.

'Right,' said Ellis, admiring the dressing he had just applied to Kojima's wound, 'where're we going next?'

The others prepared themselves lazily, slowly, not answering the question that did not need to be answered.

'Do we have a plan, or…?' Ellis pressed.

Shelley raised an eyebrow at him, looked at him through

narrow eyes. 'Are you serious?' she asked.

Ellis stared at her blankly for a long time, before grinning and waving his hand and replying, 'Nah, c'mon, let's get going.'

But it was half an hour before his mind unclouded and his headache subsided and he remembered exactly where it was they were heading and what they were doing here.

DAY 110

'It's amazing,' Shelley said, as she stared into the dying embers of the fire which had kept them warm throughout the night, 'how I still have to remind myself every morning that we're on another planet. Sitting in a Starbucks in Sydney, you can fairly effortlessly imagine travelling across space and living on a planet just like Earth, but nothing could really prepare you for really, *actually* doing so.'

Ellis yawned and rubbed his eyes, before pulling himself out of his covers and scratching his scalp, looking around the room with tight, bloodshot eyes, confused, like a newly hatched lizard.

'Remember who you're talking to,' he said, without a smile, but not without humour. 'I barely remember *not* being here.'

'The universe is so huge,' the young woman continued, still staring into that blackening orange pile of ashes and twigs, 'and it contains so many things, and there are so many planets we could explore and stories we could hear and lives we could live, but wherever we go, we're always just stuck inside our own heads. I could be in the desert on Earth right now, or sitting on the moon, and my experience of it would still be the same, because my brain has built a reality for me that keeps me boxed in, and no matter what crazy shit I see, it'll always twist it to preserve that reality so I can keep my sanity.'

'What the fuck are you on about, man?' Ellis said, rubbing his eyes again, scowling at Shelley.

She giggled, looking away from the ashes to meet his gaze. 'I dunno,' she said, shrugging and pulling her rucksack along the floor toward her. 'I suppose I thought that coming here would change everything from the ground up, but I'm still seeing through these eyes and living in this mind and my left wrist still gets that pain it always used to get every now and then and nothing's really changed except for where my body is.'

Ellis shook his head. 'I want some of whatever you smoked this morning.'

Shelley began pulling vials from her rucksack and reading the labels, holding them up to the dim early-morning light and arranging them on the floor beside her according to some unknown system of categorisation. Ellis watched her doing this for a while, before he pulled his feet out of the covers and stood, stretching his entire body and grunting a deep, satisfied grunt. He placed his hands on his hips and breathed in the stuffy tunnel air – it smelt like smoke, steam, body odour, dried sewage; the same as usual.

They had slept in a room in the underground tunnels which Ellis had not visited before, and into which they had had to force their way past thick iron doors. It was large and mostly empty, but had several large grilles in the ceiling which led to the street and which let sunlight in and the smoke from their fire out. There were also smaller grilles in the floor, the crew assumed for drainage in the event of rain. There were two smaller rooms that led off the one in which they had slept, and one of those rooms had a door which they had barricaded before sleeping, in case an attacker lay in wait beyond. The other room seemed to be a storage cupboard, filled with technology and tools and chemicals in strangely shaped containers, none of which were of any use to the humans.

To get here, they had been following signs that said *STATION 13*, in the language of this land. Ellis had not heard of Station 13 and showed no enthusiasm about finding it, but the Conquerors were intrigued, and agreement to take this detour was reached without the need for debate.

'Verne told us,' Shelley said, still arranging her tubes and vials in rows, 'that you got the computer working again. I'd like to free up some space, and some weight, in this bag; so is there any chance we could have it analyse these samples, so I can ditch the ones we don't need?'

Ellis had been staring at the sky through one of the slotted grilles above them, but when Shelley asked this, he looked down at the floor and scratched the back of his head.

'Oh. I didn't get *all* of the computer working,' he said, like a child confessing a misdemeanour.

'Huh?'

'The computer was dead. I had to rip out a lot of its components to find the problem, and all that I left was the screen and the drive. I've got the drive, but the rest of it's gone. The hardware you'd need to load in those samples is back in some building near the river, if it still survives at all.'

Shelley paused for a moment, her shoulders slouching and the tube she was holding dropping to her lap in her limp, disappointed hand. She sighed and looked around at her categories once more, taking inventory of all her samples, wondering why Ellis had refrained from telling her before she had unpacked them all like this.

Finally, she said, in a voice that was not free of annoyance, 'Oh well, I'll just have to keep lugging them around for a bit longer', and began to pack them back into her bag, handfuls at a time.

When she was done, she looked up at Ellis from her cross-legged position on the floor and said, 'So, did it tell you what happened, whcn you read the log? Why the computer woke us up late, why it launched the landing craft before we'd even strapped ourselves into it?'

Ellis shook his head, and returned to staring out of the grilles in the ceiling. They had been underground for days now, walking slowly and steadily west toward the slums, where they would ascend to street level once again, to enter the desert. But what he was seeing through this grille was not the skyscrapers he was sure they were still near, or the hostels and apartment blocks he thought they would definitely still be beneath; he tilted his view this way and that, but not even the tip of a tilting tower came into view from any angle. They had gone further than they expected, and he worried that it was in the wrong direction. If that was so, continuing this way would only take them further off course. But he could not admit that he was forgetting his way around the tunnels, that he was no longer sure if they stretched as far as he thought; so he would not mention it, and would instead indulge the Conquerors' curiosity until it was quenched.

'Not really,' he said. 'There was a chunk of data missing, and a shitload of it was garbled anyway. I told Verne, my theory is that you got hit by something that fucked up your sensors, and the ship only repaired itself enough to do anything useful when it was already too close to here. At that point, all it could do was get you up and get you out, late or not.'

Shelley thought for a while, zipping up her bag and adjusting her seat. 'When you say garbled, what was actually logged?'

'Thousands of log entries of nothing at all. Time spent in space decreasing one minute; then increasing tenfold then next. Recorded speed faster than anyone has ever travelled.'

'I see,' said Shelley, her eyebrows furrowed and her mouth wide open, deep thought occupying her features. 'Is it possible that that was all accurate?'

Ellis raised an eyebrow, smiled mockingly. 'What're you on about?'

'What if we're not where we think we are? What if something happened to us on the way here that makes that data valid? I mean, how much do we really know about how the universe works? We could have passed through some celestial gate, teleported anywhere and never known we'd taken a wrong turn. I mean, you're here, right? And you said you left Earth after us.'

Ellis's smile disappeared, and his eyes narrowed. His reaction to this theory seemed almost fearful, as if it was something worrying which he had tried not to think about but now that it had been said aloud, he would have to face it. If Shelley was right, then how would they ever return home? That gate she imagined could be anywhere, its effects impossible to predict. Even if they boarded *Conqueror 23* as planned, and the ship was still functional, and they managed to slingshot it out of orbit into the direction of Earth, where they would end up could be anyone's guess. He considered this for a second, and then he shook his head, erasing the thought.

'That's ridiculous,' he said. Then, realising for the first time that their friends were missing, he asked, 'Where're the other two?'

'We need to talk about Ellis,' Kojima whispered, her voice ripping through the silence with which Verne had cloaked himself like a monster truck through a paper wall, startling him so that he nearly dropped his gun.

'Huh?' he grunted irritably. He continued his precious morning routines, refusing to indulge the interruption.

'I know that he means a lot to you,' she said, coming closer, taking a seat next to Verne, 'but I don't trust him.

Either he has malicious intentions, or he's losing his mind; and either way, it's not good for us.' She winced and grabbed her side, the bandage she had applied just this morning already red with blood, green with pus. Verne could not help but glance at it, concerned with the pain it was causing her, the way the dressing would not stay dry for longer than a few minutes. He was going to ask her how it was, how he could help, but she silenced him by sitting up straight and letting go of her injury and giving him a stern look that told him he was not about to distract her by changing the subject.

They were sitting in the next room, on a stone surface that might have been a seat or might have been a shelf, which ran the length of the far wall. This room did not have grilles in the ceiling, so the only light was provided by those dim electric bulbs that lined the walls of the tunnels and sewers, constantly radiating that dingy orange glow that made everything look so dirty. The rooms were sufficiently big that whispering in this one would not be heard clearly in the other, and besides, their two younger friends were talking in the other room, Kojima could hear the murmuring of their voices. The older people were safe to talk, for now.

'What are you talking about?' said Verne, putting the pieces of his gun down on the shelf next to him, giving up on his meditation.

'Haven't you noticed how strangely he's been acting? First he tells us that he's finally worked out why he was getting headaches and thinking he's reliving things, and that if we just follow him it'll all stop; and then even when we follow him here, it just gets worse. I've seen him holding his head as he walks, flinching in bright lights. His headaches are more frequent than ever. He retches when he eats, Verne.'

'I haven't noticed,' Verne lied.

'He keeps forgetting things, too,' Kojima continued.

'Important things. Like where we're going, and what's safe to eat and what's not. The other day, he showed me a purple berry and told me that they were extremely rare but extremely toxic, so we should never eat them. A couple of minutes later, I caught him offering one to Shelley. Even if that was an accident, it's too dangerous an accident to risk. And you've heard him ask where we're heading, as if he's not the one leading us.'

Verne had noticed some of these things, and if he was honest with himself, he did have doubts at the back of his mind that Ellis's mental state really was holding up. To Verne's mind, it seemed like there was a connection loose in Ellis's brain, and when the conditions were right, he was brilliant and vital, just as he had been when they first met; but every now and then, when that connection dropped, he seemed confused and lost, clumsy and forgetful, like his mind was ever so slowly slipping away from him. Thinking of the effects of a gradually fading consciousness filled Verne with dread and sadness, so he had tried not to think about it at all, hoping that if he ignored it with enough vigour it would eventually go away.

Besides, Kojima's wound was clearly giving her more grief than she was letting on, and the way Verne's body had been treating him lately, he was surprised he could still walk. Shelley seemed to be the only one who wasn't falling apart. He shuddered to think how she would cope if they all dropped dead and left her to survive here alone.

'Why are you bringing this up now?' he said, picking up the parts of his deconstructed weapon and reattaching them noisily, frustrated with the conversation.

'Because last night,' Kojima whispered, quieter than before, 'I woke up and caught him with his hand in Shelley's backpack. He was just sitting there, upright, rifling through her bag like it was his and he was looking for something he'd lost. I hissed at him when I saw it, and he just froze, like he was stuck in that position; then after a couple of seconds, he put the bag back and went back to sleep, as if nothing had ever happened. He didn't say a word to me.'

Verne frowned. He too had seen Ellis sifting through a bag that wasn't his, pushing through the contents with purpose, as if looking for something specific and unable to find it. When challenged, Ellis had changed demeanour, freezing, and finally deciding to act as if nothing had happened. What was he looking for in his companions' bags? What could his motive possibly be, on a planet where, without these people, he would be the only human resident? What else had he done while the Conquerors slept, which they would never know about? These questions tumbled through his mind, and only frustrated him further. They were not what he wanted to think about, first thing in the morning.

'He might have been sleepwalking,' he said.

'I doubt it,' Kojima replied, quick as a bolting hare, 'you didn't see his eyes. They were focused.'

Verne sighed, once more irritable. 'Look, what do you want me to do about it? The kid saved my life, and all I did in return was nearly break his nose. I'm not gonna do it again because he's been acting strangely.'

'No,' Kojima said, putting her hand on Verne's arm, 'but I think it would be wise to keep an eye on him. I think that you or I should keep watch each night, to see if he sleepwalks, or if he does anything else.'

Verne did not like the idea of spying on his friend. It was the first step to shared paranoia, he thought, and an ending where they all turned against one another so that rather than returning to Earth they just returned to the ground, each having planted a knife in the next one's back. He did, however, agree that something would need to be done, even if he was not inclined to admit it. He sighed, rubbed the bridge of his nose, and finally made eye contact for the first time that morning.

Kojima looked tired, withered, half the woman she had been when they landed here. He had not known her then, and really, he hardly knew her now; but he knew that the look in her eyes was caring, and not paranoid. She was not requesting that they waterboard the boy, or stick blades under his fingernails, to pry out information that was not there. She was just suggesting that they look out for him, look out for each other, work to fix something that might be at the top of a steep slope, ready to slip out of control quicker than they could anticipate, unless they got a hold on it now. He forced a smile, and briefly put his big, rough hand on her small, bony fingers.

'Okay,' he said, letting go, 'but you're taking the first shift.'

Station 13 was hidden beyond a maze of small pathways and tunnels leading far out into the slums, and as they spent the day working their way out to it, Alan Ellis became more and more tense, forever anxious that they would not find their way back when they needed to. They trekked through hallways pitch-dark and painfully narrow, unbearably pungent and inexplicably carpeted with animal hide, and the entrance, when they found it, was just another nondescript door in just another plain, concrete room. But upon entering, even Ellis abandoned his worries to stare in wonder.

It was a bunker as large as five football fields, lined from near wall to far wall with machinery, trailing cables, huge metal cauldrons attached to cranes and hoists, and, most strangely, pill-shaped tanks made from glass, each the size of a large van, and almost a hundred in number. Most of them were smashed open, and those that were still intact were empty; but still, they screamed to the crew, begging to be explored, as the four visitors looked down on them from the high balcony onto which they had stepped when they entered the hall.

To their left, the ramp down from the metal walkway on which they found themselves had been severed, so that jumping from it would mean a forty-foot drop to the hard, concrete ground. Heading the other way, following the suspended walkway anti-clockwise around the edge of the room, they reached a point where the poles fixing the walkway to the ceiling had buckled, and the walkway fell off steeply into a large machine with cruel-looking robotic arms and a conveyor belt that led into its dark belly and out of sight. Though the descent was steep and the metal pathway unstable and slippery, the humans had no other way of reaching the ground; so they each carefully climbed down onto the machine, and jumped the short distance from there to the floor. The impact when her feet hit the floor made Kojima yelp in pain.

'What the hell is this place?' Shelley mumbled, wandering off into the lines of empty and destroyed fishbowls, holding her rucksack straps with white knuckles, like a tourist entering a theme park.

Verne clung on to the walkway for a moment, questioning whether letting go was such a good idea. They had left the sled half full in that room before the entrance, bringing many of their remaining supplies with them, while they went to investigate Station 13; and he worried that if this walkway fell and they could not get back up to that exit by the balcony, the rest of their supplies would be gone forever. But the others had already forgotten about those supplies and were spreading like wandering cats, so eventually, the desire to stay with his crew prevailed, and he jumped to the floor and, once his back had stopped smarting from the landing, began to explore with the rest.

There were stranger things in this expansive bunker than just water tanks. There were operating tables and egg-shaped orbs the size of cars, robotic arms that held sticks aloft that looked more like long bones than parts of any product, and signs whose text translated to something like

BRAIN WIPE, with an arrow pointing into a doorway that was now blocked by rubble and shattered computer equipment. The machinery and cabling were as battered and strewn as the glass of those damaged tanks – the hall had clearly been ravaged by someone or something, destroyed to satisfy anger or to hide a crime, and what this place had been used for before that was something at which the Conquerors could only guess. With the equipment which looked medical in nature and the beds with straps to tie limbs down, the machinery with mechanised hands which looked so suited to toying with things that might struggle and writhe, and the unmistakable scratch marks of claws or fingernails on the insides of those tanks which survived, all the evidence pointed to the kind of experimentation that no living thing should inflict on another.

They had all heard about the kinds of experiments men would perform on each other. In Nazi Germany, a twelve-year-old boy had been strapped to a chair, and a hammer had been brought down onto his head at regular intervals, until he went insane with the pain. The CIA spent the 1950s researching hypnotically induced anxieties, and had wasted countless hours attempting to torture confessions out of prisoners using mind control. The Soviets opened laboratories to test poisons on human subjects, which were still operational even when Kojima and her crew left Earth. But this place they had found, this huge, sprawling floor with equipment the likes of which they had never seen before, flared their imaginations into picturing events they could never have stomached on Earth, and like a wife stumbling across her cheating husband's love letters, the more it disgusted them to imagine what had gone on here, the less inclined they were to look away.

That is, until Ellis started to scream.

'*No! No! Get out!*' he screamed, holding his temples and squeezing his eyes shut. 'Not this again, not here, *get out, I don't want you here!*'

The others rushed to his side from their remote positions in the huge hall, and they held him and they whispered and they fanned him, but try as they might to calm him down, he would not be still; he would not quiet.

He writhed around on the floor, pursing his eyelids and pushing his hands onto his temples and shouting, '*Oh God, I've been here, oh God, I remember things, get out get out get out of my head!*' So together, without the need to speak a single word, the Conquerors decided to leave, and they hauled themselves back up onto the balcony, Verne climbing the metal walkway with Ellis over his shoulder, and left the way they came.

'Please get out,' murmured Ellis. 'Please get out of my head.'

And Verne carried him back through those tunnels, all the way to the room in which they had slept the night before.

Within an hour, when the storm had cleared, Alan Ellis would not remember a thing about the hall or what had happened inside his head in there.

DAY 111

Before she boarded *Conqueror 23*, a symptom of Kojima's anxieties had been regular nightmares. Nightmares so real that she would wake up scratching her skin to beat off the spiders, or inconsolably scared of the boy who lived down the hall because of what he had done in her imagination the night before. They had plagued the short periods of sleep she had managed to steal, and began to blur the lines between the terrifying reality she had constructed for herself and the terrifying dream world she dreaded to visit, such that at one point, it would take considerable effort to work out whether a horrible memory had actually happened, or was just something she had created in her sleep.

Luckily, the nightmares were something she had, so far, left behind.

Verne dreamed vividly; he had told her as much, out in the slums, before the storm had split them up. Shelley dreamed too – Kojima had seen her frowning and fretting, tossing and turning in the night, when they had been stranded alone together. But Kojima had not had a single dream that she could remember, ever since they had arrived.

But that night, she dreamed. In her dream, they were preparing a ship to blast off into space, out in the desert in which they had first crash-landed. As if packing for a family holiday, they were squeezing their possessions into cases, piling them up in the ship and labelling them with luggage tags and rushing around making sure they had remembered every little thing, eager to leave for Earth, where they belonged. Kojima had never felt so excited as she zipped up her case and hauled it up by the handle; but that excitement turned to acid in her throat, as she turned to the spacecraft door to see it closing, the crew inside buckling up and getting ready to leave without her.

Shelley wound down the window – this vessel curiously taking a form more similar to a classic convertible than a spaceship – and made a face at Kojima that was halfway between a wince and a smile, a pitying look in her eyes.

'Oh, you didn't think you were coming too, did you?' she said. 'You have to stay here, Stella. I'm sorry, mate.'

And Kojima stood in that spot, her luggage in her hand, watching the ship roar away into the sky, leaving her behind to rot on this planet, with no chance of ever getting home.

She tried to scream, she tried to raise her arms, she tried to protest, but all she could do was stand and watch, motionless, trapped inside a body rendered useless by devastation.

She woke with a start, ready to cry, briefly unsure of whether what she had just dreamt was real or not. She was sitting against a wall, and at her feet, Shelley lay across the floor, snoring softly under her blankets and tattered sleeping bags. Kojima sighed softly, and rested her head back against the wall behind her. She swallowed down the heartburn that had built in her throat, the metallic taste she kept waking up with. She regained her senses, and then she swore under her breath, as quiet as if she had made no sound at all. She had not even been awake for two hours longer than the rest before she'd nodded off. And it had been her idea to stay awake and guard. She felt like such a fool.

She could make up for it, she supposed, by staying awake from now on, making an effort to keep an eye on the stranger they had found on this planet, sleeping on the floor not ten metres away from here.

But, lifting her eyes from Shelley to Verne and finally to Ellis, she entered a new wave of panic.

There was a creature kneeling over Ellis, its large, sinewy foot resting to his left side and its other knee the floor by his right. It leant one of its bony elbows on its right knee, and the other arm was pointed at Ellis's forehead, the long, thin limb joining the grey, dead-looking hand joining the bony, yardstick finger so that the whole thing could have been one lumpy bone, nearly two metres long. Its eyes were black and focused on Ellis, and from its finger came a faint glow that lit up Ellis's face softly; and Ellis stared into that light with wide eyes and mouth hanging open, as if amazed and entranced by what he saw. He was frozen in this position, unblinking and unbreathing, and it did not look comfortable. The alien's face was long and narrow and wrinkled, as was the rest of its body, and the animal hide that covered its shoulders was as tattered and aged as its wearer, giving the creature a ghostly appearance, like a very wise zombie. Skin like tissue paper, hair like white straw.

When she realised that she was watching one of this planet's natives, doing something to Ellis that did not look at all beneficial, Kojima mustered just enough wherewithal to say, 'Hey!'

The being's finger ceased to glow, and it jerked its head round in a quick movement to face her with a snarl that froze her bones and made her hairs stand on end. She wanted to say another word, or to move, but she felt too shocked or scared or whatever it was that pinned her down. So she sat there helplessly, as the being slowly stood, its curved spine and long legs unfurling so that it stood tall and broad above her, its arms reaching nearly down to its knees, even when it stood upright.

She would have to do something. The way it was looking at her through those all-black orbs in its skull, so far apart and menacingly narrow, as it licked the lips that ran down the centre of its face, like the openings on those dogs' heads that they had used for spraying scent… it could only be considering ways to kill her. It would, at least, be contemplating silencing her, so it could continue whatever it had been doing to Ellis. It breathed noisily, that bony chest rising and falling quickly, vibrating with anger, excitement, panic.

Its hands, each furnished with those five long fingers and two thumbs, twitched by its sides, like the hands of a duellist preparing to draw his pistol. It was going to make its move soon, Kojima could feel it; she would have to do something.

But when it did make its move, she did not need to do anything. After a few seconds locked in the stand-off, it turned and ran down the hall, bounding away in long, awkward, flapping steps that echoed off the walls like skin slapping skin. In just a few strides, it must have been nearly twenty metres away.

Kojima did not know what possessed her to make her next move, and if she had been asked, she probably would have said that she did not make a conscious decision at all; but as she watched the alien bumble away on its wiry, crooked legs, she reached for her rifle, and she stood, and aimed it at the creature's back. Without even thinking, giving control over to something in her subconscious which had already decided – without consulting her – to take decisive action before it was too late, her finger pressed the trigger, and the creature went tumbling to the ground, hitting the floor like a paper bag filled with wooden blocks, and remaining there, unmoving and silent, as Kojima regained conscious control of her body and mind, and took a look at her surroundings slowly and warily, like a victim of shock. The pain in her side shot through her like a new blade was being inserted into the old wound, and it was all she could do to stay conscious, and not fall to the floor.

'Fuckin' 'ell, man,' said Ellis, the gunshot waking him from his trance, 'what happened here?'

Beside him, the others were waking too, with varying levels of alertness. Shelley woke lazily, thinking the gunshot had been in her dream; Verne, however, reached immediately for his own rifle.

Kojima smiled at them, barely aware of what she was doing, before dropping to her knees, and spitting a thick pool of green bile and red blood onto the floor below her.

DAY 112

When Kojima woke again, her body hurting like a part of her had been removed in a backstreet butcher's shop and she had been sewn back up with copper wire, she was above ground, in what looked like a wet room or a communal shower, thick pipes lining the walls and the floor slippery with waterproofing and everything streaked black and yellow and green with mould and damp, in a rickety building in the slums. She rested on a thick bed of cushion and cloth, but still she throbbed and writhed like she had been sleeping on a bed of nails. The wound in her side was white-hot and agonising – just the thought of moving it turned her green with sickness.

Bound to the spot by pain, she stared across the room at the alien, sitting against the opposite wall in a similar pose, its right arm tied to a pipe with the rope that Verne had been using to pull the sled.

The creature's leg had been ripped open so mercilessly by the bullet that Kojima had fired that its lower half now clung to the rest of its thigh by just a few ragged strips of skin, muscle and ligament, and would never be usable again. Though it had bled copiously onto the floor around where the creature fell in that tunnel underground, this bleeding had since died down almost completely, and once the other humans had wrapped bandages around the wound and fed the creature some water, it seemed surprisingly sprightly, considering the circumstances.

Rain beat down against the thin roof above them, thick and fast and never-ending, and with this as the soundtrack to her awakening she noticed through the fog of her pain James Verne, who sat beside her, his hand on the side of her face. How long he had been like that, she could not have guessed.

'How are you feeling?' he asked, more softly than she would have imagined he could speak, with that deep, booming voice.

She smiled back weakly, but even the smile caused her discomfort. Her skin was so pale as to be transparent and at her wrists and neck, the blue and red veins under the surface screamed their colour into the morning dimness like fading tattoos mazing across her dry skin. To her right knelt Shelley, her cheeks raw with old tears, wearing that same expression of helplessness and fear that she had worn so many times on this godforsaken planet. Behind Shelley stood Ellis, torn between looks of concern toward Kojima and looks of disdain directed at the beast tied to the pipe.

'What did I miss?' asked Kojima, the room spinning in her eyes, her voice a distant melody, fuzzy and tuneless and dissonant in her ears.

'Here,' said Verne, lifting the rim of a water-synthesising tube to her lips. 'You've missed nothing, but you'll miss a lot if you don't get your strength back.'

She drank in sips, and even that felt like too much. Every swallow was a struggle, and every one brought with it a retch or a cough that tore through her gut like a blunt steak knife, snagging on skin and dragging tissue with it.

'Verne,' Shelley said, welling up with tears again, 'is she going to be okay?'

'Yes,' Verne answered, unsure but stubborn. 'She has to be.'

Later, when she woke again, not an hour had passed, but still, they all repeated this routine as if none of them remembered that they had lived it before – Kojima woke dazed and Verne nursed her with desperation and Shelley fought back sobs and only Ellis did anything different when he said, 'Look', and gestured to the alien, which was pointing at Shelley and saying something out of its hideous mouth, in a language of growls and whines so familiar it almost seemed human, but so unique that it could never have been spoken on Earth.

'It wants to talk,' Ellis said, stepping toward the creature, crossing his arms anxiously.

Shelley fought, for a moment, the side of her that wanted to turn away from her suffering friend to face the alien, and she knelt there in limbo, torn between watching Verne attempt to help Kojima and watching an alien trying to communicate with a race that had travelled eight light years to find it. When she noticed that Kojima too was focused on the thing, distracted from her agony by the noise from the other side of the room, her guilt left her, and though she remained close to Kojima, she turned to give the creature her full attention.

The alien spoke again, a short, sharp phrase repeated over and over, and pointed its long, grey finger at Shelley as if jabbing a spell through the air with an oversized, knobbly wand.

'Er…' Shelley said, and turned to Verne for help with understanding. Verne was disinterested, focused instead on helping Kojima get comfortable, paying the alien and its newfound eloquence very little heed.

'She wants you to give her the device,' Ellis said, staring intensely at the beast.

'You can understand it?' asked Shelley, her voice

shaking. As she looked up at Ellis from her position on the floor, her body straightened and her ears pricked, like a dog on the hunt.

'Aye,' Ellis said simply.

Shelley had forgotten the trinket was in her hands, what with worrying about Kojima and moving out of the tunnels into the town and everything that had happened in between, but now she gazed down at the thing she had plucked from the alien's hand as it had lain there unconscious and wondered why she had not noticed before that she had already found one of these things. The same kind of small, wooden, intricately carved toy had been sitting on a table in that crumbling hostel all the way back when they had just arrived here, and if Shelley looked in her rucksack, she was sure she would still find it there. But why would the alien want it? What did it do? What would she be giving up, by handing it over? She looked up again, searching for help in making a decision, but found none.

'Why does she want it?' Verne asked, after a time. His eyes were still on Kojima, but he was at least aware of the events that were unfolding around him.

The alien spoke without the need for Ellis to attempt relaying the question, its sounds coming between short, wheezing breaths that seemed painful to endure. It kept adjusting its position on the floor as it spoke, trying to find a comfortable way to sit on the hard ground; but by the time it had made its point, it had given up on this endeavour, and had chosen instead to simply slouch against the pipe to which it was tied, a resigned look on its wispy-haired face.

'She says she's going to use it to communicate. Says it'll help us understand her.'

Verne continued to attend to Kojima for a few moments, brushing hair from her face and plumping the pillows on which she already had her weight and offering her water she did not want, all of this met with sighs and waves of annoyance, as Kojima tried to bat him off so she could watch the creature speak, like an old woman trying to watch a television show while her husband vacuums the carpet. But when Shelley, lost, still could not decide whether or not the creature should be handed the device after a minute or more, he sighed and turned toward the rest of the humans, picking up his rifle and resting it on his thigh.

'Hand it over,' he said. 'Let's see what it has to say.'

He seemed unfazed by the events they were witnessing, as if he had been through it all before, and he was bored by now of the drama.

Shelley held the object out in front of her, at arm's length; apprehensive and reverent like a worshipper offering fruit to a statue of a messiah.

With the length of the creature's arms, she would have had a good chance of taking the device from Shelley's hand herself; but she did not attempt to do so, instead holding her right hand out, palm up, and allowing Ellis to play the middle man, taking the gadget from the young woman's fingers and dropping it softly into the bony, grey hand of the alien. In her unbound hand, the native took the object between one thumb and the next finger, and pressed it into a void that existed around where her temple would be if she were human. Perhaps this was her ear, or perhaps some weakness in the design of her skull – with her vertical mouth hole running down the centre of her face and a distinct lack of nasal cartilage or ear flaps, it was hard to work out which of her features performed which function, when her eyes were the only items that sat where the humans would have put them.

When the device settled into its spot in the alien's head, it glowed just as it had that morning, when it had been held to Ellis's forehead. Before the light from this glow had even reached her eyes, Kojima winced, suddenly feeling the same kind of shooting pain she had woken up to find in her abdomen, but concentrated instead in the front half of her skull. Across from her, she could see Shelley rubbing her eyes and sighing, perhaps because she too had felt it. Ellis, doubling over from standing, was holding his head with both hands, growling in pain.

Quick as a flash, Verne reached for his rifle and pointed it at the creature's head, standing from the floor and stepping assertively toward the beast. He had not missed this sudden shared suffering, and he would not allow this creature to hurt his friends, even for a second. The creature, in turn, held out her free hand at arm's length, shielding her face from the barrel of the gun. Without hesitation, as if playing a human mirror to the alien's movements, Alan Ellis did the same, shielding his own face though the gun did not threaten him.

'Please,' he said, 'don't shoot.'

His accent remained, but his voice had lost some of its life, some of the enthusiasm he had always filled it with. It was clear that he was no longer experiencing head pain – none of the humans were, that fleeting feeling now having passed – but his eyes looked dazed and completely unfocused, nothing like they had been the morning Verne had first met him, when Ellis was excited to meet the man whose life he had saved, and Verne was terrified of the overeager man who was trying to force-feed him soup.

'Huh?' said Verne, irritably.

'I mean you no harm. I was here to help.'

Verne looked uncertainly from the cowering Scotsman to the cowering creature, and finally to the perplexed, spaced-out Kojima. The alien closed its eyes, slowly turned her face away from the weapon, and within a second, Ellis did the same.

None of the Conquerors wanted to believe that the alien was controlling Ellis like a puppet, but it was what they were seeing.

'What's going on?' said Shelley, breaking the silence at last, while Verne kept his automatic aimed at the alien.

'How are you doing this?'

'This device,' said Ellis, still cowering in a similar, but not quite identical, position to that adopted by the creature, 'it does no harm. Your friend is safe. As soon as I remove it, he will return to normal. I cannot speak your tongue, and you cannot speak mine; this is the only way we can talk, if you wish to do so. I can help you, I know how to save you, if you only spare me.'

The women exchanged a look, and saw agreement in each other's eyes almost instantly. What choice did they have? They could trust the alien not to harm Ellis, and perhaps learn more about this planet – and how to get off it – in a day than they had learned in over a hundred before now; or let Verne shoot it, and carry on struggling blindly, like they had never found the thing. This could be their best chance yet to undo the mistake of coming here, or at least to get answers to the riddles they had come here to solve, but with which they had had no such luck. They had to take it.

Verne would not pull his gaze from their detainee, but he had murder in his eyes, so everyone knew the opinion he would have without needing to ask.

After a few seconds of watching him glare at the alien, Shelley said softly, 'Verne.' Then, 'Put the gun down, Verne.'

Verne tore his eyes from the prisoner to give Shelley a stern look. She smiled softly, her leg shaking like the wagging tail of an excitable puppy. She was too eager to quiz the alien to be trustworthy, her judgement too clouded. He looked instead at Kojima, who simply stared at the creature, her expression a cauldron of stewing fear, pain, sickness and sleep. Still, after a second or two, she nodded in agreement that Verne should stand down; so he accepted that he had been outvoted, and slowly lowered his weapon, and stepped back. His rifle did not go far – he would keep it in his hands in case the need arose.

He remained silent for a time, matching Kojima's stern, tired gaze at the creature with a hateful, intimidating one of his own. The creature stared back, her breathing laboured, her every jittery movement echoed by Ellis.

Shelley broke the silence, after a time, with questions that she had wanted to ask since before she even left Earth, when she had imagined that one day, she might just meet an alien.

'What can we call you? What did you call this place?'

The creature turned her head to face Shelley, and stared at her for a long time. She breathed loudly and slowly. It seemed as if the alien would never respond, until she opened her long, vertical mouth, and began to speak.

'My race called themselves the Antistites,' Ellis replied over the alien's stuttered mumbling, leaving Shelley unsure of whether the confidence in his tone was passed on to him by the alien or just a happy accident, 'but I am known as Dolas, as were all the females in my bloodline. This world is Tepeu, and the city under which we find ourselves is Igni.'

'Is this where you lived?'

'Where I *live*, yes. The city has been like this for generations. Because it is a shell of what it was does not mean that it is dead.'

'Generations? Exactly how long has it been like this?'

'Many, many years. I do not know.'

The alien shot a look at Kojima, and Ellis's eyes followed. Verne's trigger finger twitched involuntarily.

'So, I guess you've never known it any different? Did you ever see the city alive?' Shelley asked, the questions reeling off like she had an endless list of them in her head. Verne and Kojima were not surprised – she probably did have a list, and it probably was endless.

'No,' said the creature, returning her gaze to Shelley, 'I did not. It had been taken from us many years before I was born. But it will be great again; we still fight for it every day, though we do it from the shadows, by proxy, with mind games. This city has fallen before, and it will no doubt fall again. That could happen again and again, and it will always be reborn.'

Shelley swiped her finger across her temple, double- and triple-checking that she was recording every second of the conversation.

'So it was a war, that made this place like this?'

The creature made a gurgling noise in her throat, and Ellis seemed to translate this to a cynical chuckle. 'Of sorts,' he replied. 'But when brother turns on brother and nature becomes a weapon and everything that is sacred gets torn down for the sake of pride or land or power, it might as well be called folly, or stupidity. Giving it a noble name does not make it a noble act. It should never have happened, especially not the way it did. It was a massacre, in many places. An invasion in others. Life was cheaper than it should ever be, for a very long time. But I don't need to explain to you the mechanics of war. It was a game to your kind too.'

Shelley took her time thinking on how to word her next question.

'Do you come from the nobility? Was your bloodline wealthy and powerful?'

The beast straightened its back against the wall and flicked its shoulders in a quick movement. Ellis nodded.

'We were as powerful as was our right.'

Shelley looked at Verne and Kojima uncertainly. The look could have been a request for assistance or a search for approval for the questions she had already asked, or something else altogether. Whatever she was looking for, she did not get it – only Kojima met her eyes, and all she did was nod, short and sharp, before looking back at the alien.

Not one of the humans watched Ellis delivering the answers to Shelley's questions. Apart from the fact that he was not really the one giving them, it also sat uncomfortably with them that they should watch him being controlled like this. Without his permission. Without knowing if he knew what was happening, if he would even remember this when the alien relinquished its influence over him.

As if conversing with an inhabitant of a far-off planet was not already strange enough.

'When you say it was your right, what do you mean by that? What made you deserving of the wealth and the power, and others not so deserving?'

'We made this city. We built this world. We made everything. Our civilisation has been alive for millions of years, longer than your kind could ever imagine. We didn't create it so that it could be torn from us. Not by those who have created nothing, done nothing of worth.'

'Those you speak of now, are they the low-born? The poor?'

'I suppose. Them and their allies; the invaders, uprisers. Put simply, I suppose you are right. It was a war. It was them versus us. But as with everything, it was slightly more complicated than all of that. They were not like us; they could not do what we did. They were a separate species altogether, if truth be told. They should have worshipped us for how well we treated them and all that we had achieved. But gratitude comes hard to minds too narrow to realise the extent of their debt.'

The alien adjusted her position on the floor, uncomfortable against the hard, smooth wall. Ellis made the same movements against the air that the alien was making against the wall and the floor, and then he sighed out of frustration when the alien could not find a position she enjoyed. He looked fed up, and it was clear that this expression was sent to him directly from the alien's mind.

'So it was a class war. We read about this in your books, but we weren't sure. You say you fight every day – are they still out there, the ones you're fighting? Is the war still on for them, too?'

The creature flicked her shoulders out again, as would a man trying to flick the collar of his shirt into the right position without using his hands, and Ellis nodded in translation. 'Yes. And if they had found you first, or you were already among them, I would be dead by now. So would all of my loved ones. I'd be hanging, or burned alive, or eaten. They'll use any of our creations against us, to destroy our power. They're vile, sick, depraved…'

Her eyes dropped to the floor, searching for a description extreme enough for the villainy, and fell silent as she failed. Shelley shook her head.

'Sorry, what do you mean, *creations*? What would they have done to us if they'd found us? What have we got to do with your war?'

The alien's eyes bolted from the floor and back to Kojima's face. With Ellis's intense stare and the creature's black bulbs fixed on her, Kojima blushed, and felt that heartburn and sickness she had been fighting since she woke rise back in her throat. She felt hot and uncomfortable.

'With all that your friend here has seen and all that she knew before you even came here,' Ellis said, his tone now laced with malice, 'I would have thought she would have worked it out by now.'

Wednesday Shelley looked at Kojima with confusion and fear in her eyes, as if she suspected her of cavorting with the enemy and this was how she had found out. 'What does she mean?' she asked.

Kojima stared back with just as much fear, just as unsettled. She shrugged, though it required great effort, and with croaky voice and raspy throat she started to say, 'I have no idea—'

But Dolas continued, through Ellis's now-angered tone, his finger pointed at Kojima just as the alien's was. 'Play at ignorance all you want, but I know that you've seen the writing of the culprits in blood on the walls. I know you've seen familiar bones and familiar scenes, just like where you came from. You could have known long before you came here that the world was like this, if you had only opened your eyes. There would be no war without your kind. The cowards who did this to our city and our world did it not with their own hands, but with puppets of our creation. They used life forms that we created as science projects, to tear us down from the thrones on which we were born to sit. And those puppets loved their new enterprise – they went tearing down this world like it was what they were built to do, attacking even those who summoned them to bring this devastation. No race could have been more well suited to destruction than that one, no species more callous and cruel.

'This war was a fight between those who had next to nothing and those who had everything, yes. But those who had almost nothing did not risk anything in their fight against us, because they had proxies fighting for them. They had you, humans. And humanity is the cancer that destroyed this world.'

DAY 112

Having translated the alien's revelations with the precision and timing of a trained actor in a very serious and sombre Russian play, Ellis fell silent and stepped back and lowered his arms, and calmed and let what he had just said sink in, his chest rising and falling in time with the alien's, as if the thing had control over him all the way down to his nervous system, all the way into his soul.

Shelley gasped, her hand covering her mouth. Where she had been resting on her toes, she now dropped forward to her knees, and she shook, and the colour drained from her. Kojima looked panicked, and her long nails dug into the hard ground around her as if she was trying to hold the earth still, stop it spiralling out of control. The gravity of what the alien was claiming was lost on no one in the room. Entire worlds could be brought down by this assertion, whether it was true or not. Faiths could be destroyed; wars could be wrought. If true, the creature's words changed everything.

If Verne was shocked by what he had heard, his face did not show it. He continued to stare with contempt at the creature, just as he had since the beginning of the conversation.

'So… you're saying that… you made us?' Shelley said, her voice shaking.

'We made everything,' Ellis replied, now calmer, quieter. 'We were known as the masters, or the gods, because that is exactly what we were. There were once shrines, temples, cities devoted to our worship; now, like many of the civilisations we created, that all lies in tatters.'

'The masters…' Shelley whispered, her eyes scanning the walls as if she might suddenly find that phrase written on them, as she had seen elsewhere. Her eyes were wet and she shook with such might that Verne could see the trembling of her muscles from across the room. 'You, our gods? Here? How can that be?'

The questions were delivered so slowly that it seemed almost as if she had forgotten how to form them, such was the extent of her confusion.

'What better place would you suggest?'

She looked up at the alien and stared into its deep black eyes for a long time; so black that to look into them was to look into deep space, the darkest cave; death eternal. 'But,' she said, after a time, 'what were humans doing here? If you made us on Earth, how were we here? If you made us here, what were we doing on Earth?'

'Tell me,' said Dolas, through Ellis, adjusting her position on the floor so that she faced Shelley and gesturing with her hand toward Ellis, who in turn gestured at the empty space to his left, 'did you believe that your friend here was from the future? That he really came here from Earth? How did you think that he got here before you? I am aware that you tried not mentioning it, probably thinking that if you didn't give it too much thought it would not be a problem, but you must have considered it sometime. There was no way that he could ever have arrived here so long before you did. So what is the only other explanation?'

'He was always here.'

'He was *born* here. In that laboratory you stumbled across just three days ago; or at least, one just like it.'

Shelley gasped again, and tears rolled down her cheeks. Whether those tears came out of fear or sadness or just the weight of the conversation, she did not know.

'When we observed humans in their own habitat and understood their usefulness, we visited your planet to take our own samples; and when we saw first-hand how useful you might be, we were even more impressed with our own creation, so we started mass-producing you here. You lived among us, serving, helping, building. For a time. Until it was found that you could not be trusted or controlled as well as had been thought, at which time we stopped production and exterminated all the humans we could find. Those that we couldn't find were already in the possession of the others, and… well… you know how that ended.'

'Bullshit,' said Verne, his booming voice in the quiet room surprising everyone. 'We're expected to believe that you just made a species in a factory and sent them to another planet? And then you, what, planted fossils around the place and created some smaller animals to make it all seem like nature and evolution? Give the impression of an ageing planet? And all of this shipped from halfway across the galaxy, a thousand years per delivery?'

Ellis chuckled, mirroring the alien. 'I never said that that was the case,' he said, shrugging. 'I wouldn't expect you to believe that at all. In fact, I know what you believe, James Verne: that you and your species were just an accident. And you should go on believing that, because you were. We identified candidate planets many millions of years ago, and sent small samples of life to each one while those worlds were still young. We sent many different specimens to many different planets, and of all the worlds that we tried this with, yours was one of the few that managed to break through all the barriers to one day, many millions of spins around your sun later, host intelligent, thriving life. It really was evolution, and all those fossils and animals and plants you described were real. It evolved before our eyes, and all we had to do was watch.

'Then, of course, when you had evolved, we could study your cultures, watch your struggles, document your lives, all from afar. We could even visit you, if we so desired.'

Verne tutted, looked as if he was going to spit on the ground, then decided not to. He looked outraged, like he knew exactly how the god he did not believe in would look, and this was not it. He chewed, though there was nothing in his mouth, as if trying to break down with his teeth the ridiculous claims the alien was making, and then he stopped and sighed, rolling his eyes.

'You don't believe me.'

'Well, put yourself in my shoes. You're woken by an eight-foot-tall alien zombie attacking your friend, and then once you have it cornered it tells you it's the almighty god you've always been looking for. I've seen with my own eyes men makin' crazier claims than this to escape a bullet to the head. How much would you believe?'

Ellis laughed. 'Unlike the gods you invented yourselves, this can be proven.'

'All right,' said Verne, baring his teeth and stepping forward aggressively, regressing somewhat to adopt some of the demeanour of the violent, vengeful man he had been long before he had ever met his comrades, before he had a son, before his life began. 'Tell us how you got there, to Earth. These visits of yours.'

The alien grimaced hideously, and Ellis smiled another cynical smile in translation. 'From being inside this man's mind, I know much about what you think happened to your ship on the journey here. Again, this is something I had hoped you would have worked out for yourselves by now; but such is the incapability of the human mind. Your vessel's computers did not malfunction; they were, in fact, reading everything correctly. If my memory serves me, it takes around eighty-two Earth years, travelling at the speed at which you were travelling, to reach Earth from here. This is thanks to what you would call an Einstein-Rosen bridge, a portal which you passed through by pure accident, and which we created to visit your planet without losing too much time. This is how we visited you. And this is how you have arrived here not even a hundred of your years since you left your homes.

'At the hangar to which I was trying to lead you with the help of our mutual friend here, there are ships that could take you all the way there with very little trouble. Your planet was a tourist destination for us, a zoo in space, of our own creation.'

Shelley's ears pricked, and she sniffed loudly and said, 'What do you mean, trying to lead us?'

'I have watched you for a long time, through the eyes of your friend. Perhaps because he was born here, he is easier to control and to observe than the rest of you; so he was my choice when keeping an eye on your activities. It took me a long time to decide what to do with you – leaving you to die your own deaths left me and my kind open to the risk of you being turned by the enemy, and I am not as quick to cruelty as some that I know, so I did not want to have you kill each other. I decided to send you home, eventually, and the morning on which he told you his story about the dream and the hangar and his idea for getting you all off the planet was the morning after I had inserted the necessary memories and ideas into his head to make him do so.'

'You watched us… through him? Is that why he was getting the headaches?'

Ellis shook his head. 'The headaches are a symptom of something wrong with your friend. I don't know what it is, but that is what I was there to investigate when your injured friend found me and blew off my leg. I was hoping to repair it before you woke, so that controlling him remotely would be easier and I could have you on your way expediently.'

'Controlling him?' Shelley thought for a moment, slightly panicked. 'What have you done to us, without us knowing? What have you made us do?'

Ellis shrugged like a Frenchman, nonchalant and distracted. 'That was a misspeaking,' he said, 'a *slip of the tongue*, as you would put it. I merely observed, and helped you on your way. I did not influence any of you; your minds were too hard to enter. Now that I think of it, I wonder if perhaps it was his time spent around you which made him close up, which made his mind begin to turn on itself…'

Dolas then drifted off into thought, thought which once again seemed dramatised for effect.

'You mentioned the hangar,' said Kojima, her voice barely a whisper, as painful to hear as it was to speak out. 'Can we really go home? What makes you think your ships will survive the journey, or even be able to take off?'

'Like I said before, because this place is a shadow of the world it once was, does not mean it is dead. We can still make journeys. We *have* made journeys, since the city fell. We have brought back our own specimens from other worlds, to fight in our name, to watch the city on our behalf. I know that the ships could have taken you home, and I know that this man could have taken you to them, with my help. The sleep would have been different than the cryosleep that you endured to get here, but I imagine you would have found it more comfortable by a mile.

'But that is all true of a future in which you had my help. Now that I am chained to the plumbing in a decaying baths on the outskirts of the city, surrounded by violent captors and with a slowly rotting wound in my leg, my vision of that future grows cloudier by the second.'

The Conquerors, all of whom had stopped listening a while ago and had each begun instead to imagine that hangar and the green and blue of Earth, and how they would feel leaving this desert far behind, exchanged a look.

Shelley smiled through her tears and her eyes grew wetter and she clenched her fists as in victory, and Verne frowned because he hated to see her get her hopes up over the words of this beast that owed them no honesty and was most likely paying for their mercy with lies, or at the very least embellishments.

They sat in silence for a while, each of them considering what it all meant, the revelations of their captive and the possibility of returning home now made concrete by her confirmation and everything else that she had told them, and staring at her alien face to see if they could read the accuracy of her information on it, or staring at the walls for some answer, or at the inside of their eyelids to cut out the room around them.

Then Shelley's eyes lit up, and her mouth fell open, and she said, 'So this explains the museum. Those other races, the insect-looking creatures and the weird monkeys and all the rest, did you create them too? Was that, like, a trophy cabinet of your achievements?'

Ellis chuckled again, along with his controller. 'Yes,' he said, 'in a manner of speaking. We did create all of those things.'

'And the giant beetle thing that almost attacked us in the coliseum, I'm guessing that wasn't from around here either?'

'You are correct. That creature was also made here, as a replica of a being from another planet which we seeded. I was controlling that specimen – by that time, I had almost lost access to your friend and his errant mind, so I sent that animal to look for him and show me that he hadn't gone missing or perished. By the time it found you, I had reconnected to your friend, so the one I was controlling needed to take no action to fix things.'

'Christ,' said Shelley, piecing together the facts and seeing for the first time that she had been living inside of a puzzle with no real solution, 'how many species have you created?'

The creature sighed, and Ellis translated its actions by becoming more bored, more distracted, to the point of irritation.

'There is no way of knowing,' he said. Then, after a long silence, 'Many. Very many. All we knew was that humanity was the cruellest, the most violent. All of the other intelligent beings we created fought only for sustenance, for food, for life. They realised that cooperation was key to survival; that it was far better to plan ahead and solve problems together than to beat each other to death for not solving problems that didn't exist. Humans never realised that, and humans did not fight only for those things. Humans killed each other for such useless things as honour and belief, for the things their neighbours said or might have put down on paper. Trivial things. We spent long enough watching you do this that eventually it seemed to us that humans fought purely because they enjoyed it. Which is, of course, why you were so easy to weaponise, why you could be turned against us with so little effort. Why the city ended up like this.'

Verne spat, and shook his head. 'How much of your shit are we going to have to listen to before you get to a point here?' he asked.

'I only state the facts,' said Ellis, affecting an air of superiority, of calm self-assuredness.

'Well, I hope you've considered the facts of what we might have to do to you once you've outlived your usefulness,' said Verne, his temper beginning to get the better of him.

'Here it is,' said Ellis, matching the creature's open-handed gesture toward Verne, 'the rage of man, ruled by his emotions, a slave to the hunger for blood and violence. This is why your major cities were running out of space to house their ridiculous populations, between all the memorial plaques from tragic events. This is why your biggest nations were in a cycle of cold war and resolution, starting and ending once a decade. This is why you invented your gods and your rules and your scriptures, so that you had a noble name to hide behind to justify your indiscriminate killing. Your anger, your greed, your undiluted self-centredness, all of it sums up your race better than your words or your nations or your gods ever could. You are the scum of this universe, and even you know it. And you come here, calling yourselves Conquerors. Pah.'

With the raising of the voices in the small, echoing room, the level of agitation in all of its inhabitants also increased, and though Kojima was still bound to the floor by the pain she was in, her face flushed red and her scowl burrowed deep and she tried to lift herself off the floor a couple of times before giving up and dropping again, wincing. Shelley, meanwhile, rocked back and forth and began to sob, like a child willing her parents with all her might to stop arguing. Verne stood, and held his gun like a hooligan would hold a broken bottle, down at his side and pointing at the floor, but ready to be used at any moment.

'Shut up!' he boomed over the crying and clamouring of his friends.

But the beast carried on.

'But why return to Earth to observe your failures, when here we have three of your world's brightest examples of model citizenry? James Verne, who left Earth because he hated his son for taking his wife away from him in her final days, after he was too proud, too weak, too angry and bitter to admit that he needed help caring for her. And Wednesday Shelley, who left her lover because she was too much of a coward to follow through on her promises, too selfish to spend any time thinking of others when all her time needed to be devoted to her next exciting pipe dream. And Stella Kojima, mission commander, who knew long before you came here that this world was in deep trouble, but brought you here anyway.'

Shelley, who had whimpered and flinched when she heard her own name, as if the summary of her character was like a backhand to her face, now looked up, her face red with tears, as Kojima lunged at the alien, ignoring the pain it caused her, and began to batter it with her weak, shaking hands, her legs strewn behind her across the floor like the useless tail of a beached mermaid.

She yelled and she growled and she cried out, 'Shut up! Shut up! Shut your stupid fucking mouth!' and Verne considered pulling her off the creature, but did not want to hurt her, so just pointed his gun instead, ready to exterminate the alien whenever necessary. Ellis stood in the same position, across the room, still playing puppet to the creature, defending himself from strikes that were not coming his way.

But the hitting did not go on for long. After a couple of seconds, the alien lashed out, and with a single swipe of its bony arm, it send Kojima smacking against the opposite wall, with the hard packing sound of flesh on stone. Verne ran to assist her, and in the moment that it was unthreatened, the creature started up again.

'Look in her journals, like I have,' it said, 'and you will find the messages that were sent to your planet, which she knew about before you ever launched. She was what each of you are: a coward, a villain, corrupt and selfish and angry and fearful and pretending forever to be wise and noble and intelligent but just wearing those traits as a mask to hide the ugliness inside. You were our biggest mistake, and now you are a cancer on the universe. I should have had you kill each other. I should have killed you myself. I should—'

And then there was a series of deafening pops that drowned out all noise, and then there was silence.

Verne stood over the creature and watched thick brown blood pour from the open flower where its head once was for not half a second, before dropping his rifle to the floor beside it and rushing to attend to Kojima, who lay still and silent on the ground opposite. Ellis fell to the floor just like that rifle, limp and lifeless like a rag doll no longer being played with, and took a long time to wake up.

Shelley kept rocking, kept crying, kept wondering where and why and how it had all gone wrong. The alien had turned in an instant from helpful to furious, as if it wanted to be put out of its misery and knew that that would be how. And in doing so, it had been proven right about them all. Which made her wonder what else the creature was right about – had Kojima known what this planet was like before they left? Were they really a creation of Dolas, and her almost-extinct Antistites? Could the Conquerors ever make it home alive?

But once the ringing in her ears had died down and Ellis had sat up from the floor, rubbing his head and wearing more confusion than she had ever seen him possess, she realised that there were more pressing matters than these to which she should attend, for Kojima was bleeding onto the floor, and Verne was crying on his knees beside her, and suddenly the room was darker and smaller and infinitely more terrifying than it had been before.

DAYS 112–113

Kojima lay on the floor, limbs akimbo and damp with blood and pus and feverish sweat, spiralling further down the drain she had been circling for days so that the pain she felt now was like none she had ever experienced before, even if all the other times she had ever felt pain were combined. Her stab wound hot like there was a blowtorch stuck inside her, burning its way out. The rest of her cold, as if she were floating nude in deepest space, cold beyond coldness, so cold she could barely feel a thing.

Verne knelt beside her and tears rolled down his cheeks, and though he wiped them away with his filthy sleeve, she had already seen them, and she had never seen Verne cry, not properly, so at that second she knew beyond all doubt that this moment was the darkest she had ever lived, that this was the only true point of no return, that this was the end. She had always thought, had always been told, that when death came she would be ready for it, she would have prepared in some way for its arrival, and so it would not surprise her or upset her; but this was not expected even though it should have been, and its arrival was not prepared for or welcomed, and she was not ready even in a small way to die and be gone forever, and the fear and the sadness of it was overwhelming, and she too cried.

'I don't want to die,' she said to Verne, though the words came out in her native tongue and quieter than a sigh, so he could not have heard or understood her even if it had mattered.

She held his hand tightly and she thought about her life, and she thought about an eternity of darkness and about an eternity of not existing at all, which was so much worse than darkness and in fact made darkness look easy, and she felt so scared and desolate that she wanted to scream until it all went away, but instead she wept so hard that her chest hurt and saliva ran from her mouth, and her thin, wispy hair stuck to her wet face and everything around her fell apart so that all she could see was grey mist and shapes without outlines.

Hers had been a life lived in fear, a life spent just scraping through day after day trying not to crack under the pressure that her worries put on top of her. Fear of authority, fear of failure, fear of death. And though she had achieved things of which many could only dream, these were always the things that she thought that she *should* do, and not the things that she might *want* to do. She had never let her hair down and just spent a day having fun, doing whatever took her fancy, or doing nothing at all. She had only worked, taken steps toward goals, ticked items off a never-ending to-do list. She had pitied Shelley, when they spent all those weeks alone together and she had heard about Shelley's haphazard life, her flitting from idea to idea, her scattered approach to life planning; but now, on her deathbed, Kojima envied the younger woman. She had been freer than Kojima had ever been.

What did Kojima have to show for all her hard work, all of her fear? How had it helped her to make the most of her one life?

Kojima had been a captive all her life. First of a

dictatorship, then of work, then of self-consciousness, and finally of fear. And now she would die, with no memories that made her smile, no family to love and only one friend in the entire universe to hold her hand and weep for her.

There was nothing more crushing than this realisation.

'Verne,' she said, her throat filled with mucus and iron, 'go back to Earth. Don't stay here.'

Shelley knelt behind Verne, too upset to involve herself, and unsure of how she would do so anyway.

'No,' Verne replied, more to himself than in response to Kojima's command, 'please, no.'

And then he wept again, and he stroked his friend's hair, and Kojima held his hand with all of her strength, seeming calmer and more accepting of her fate by the second, though the fear in her heart had not yet subsided, and then within a few minutes, she was still and her grip on Verne's hand relaxed and all that was Kojima was gone and all that remained were the flesh and bones that used to house her and the friend who mourned her with howling moans and jolting sobs.

Verne continued to hold her hand for a long time, though he knew she was no longer there, and stroked her dry, bony knuckles and closed his eyes and whispered his apologies under his breath, like an incantation that would take it all back.

'I'm sorry that you had to go through all of that. I'm sorry that I couldn't save you. I'm sorry that I couldn't take away the pain; make it easier for you at least. I'm sorry that I could not have taken your place.'

Ellis sat holding his knees and staring at the floor, scowling at it like it had done him some wrong. He did not even seem aware of the other people in the room, so absorbed was he in his introspection. What had been world-changing revelations on a very general level for the rest of the humans had had deeper, more personal implications for him, and learning that he had never been to Earth when he had had such vivid memories of it the day before shattered him to his core. He felt furious at the alien for taking control of his body like that, for revealing those things with such malicious pleasure. He felt empty, robbed, flayed by the truth of his existence. He wished that the creature were alive again, so that he could kill her himself.

And Shelley sat in a no man's land between Verne's whispered mantras and Ellis's absent staring, all cried out and suddenly more tired than she had been in a long time. She had done nearly nothing for the entire day, but she felt like she had run a marathon in concrete shoes. She felt helpless and hopeless and completely lost. Like Verne, she mourned Kojima and had still not recovered from the shock of how things had spiralled so devastatingly out of control; and like Ellis, she was lost in a maze of thoughts about all the things the alien had said, and what this meant for her life and everyone she had ever known and everyone who had ever lived. She felt like it stood over her, all of this, like a tall tree or a tilting tower in the centre of the city, casting its shadow over her and not letting her think of anything else. It was too much.

She slid herself toward a wall and curled into a ball, and wrapped a thin, rough blanket around herself. She would rest until she was strong enough to deal with at least one of the things she needed to consider. Until she had the strength to do anything at all.

When she woke, Verne was sitting with his back against the wall next to Kojima's body, which he had straightened out and covered with a blanket, and he rested his elbows on his knees, his arms out straight in front of him and hands hanging limp from the ends of them, as if tired of holding themselves up. The way he sat there and the face he wore were not unlike those of a drunk on a kerb with an empty bottle hanging from each hand. He looked drained of everything he had.

Ellis was still in the same position he had been when Shelley fell asleep, still staring at the floor with that same darkness.

The room was lighter than it had been before she fell asleep, thin beams of daylight now creeping through the frosted windows around the top of the walls, so much higher than they would have been at home.

'How long was I asleep?' she asked, desperate for interaction, and feeling that it was as good a question as any.

'Hmm?' answered Ellis, barely broken out of his reverie.

'Few hours,' replied Verne. He did not look at her. 'Six, maybe.'

'Christ,' she said, sitting up and rubbing her eyes. Her back ached and she felt sticky and revolting. The stench in the room was appalling, and the corpse of the creature that Verne had killed still lay headless and wet in the corner, tied to the pipe. It felt in that moment as if all of this was a bad dream, and she would wake up at any moment back on Earth, in a comfortable bed, around people who loved her and were alive and well and would laugh when she retold the story of her ridiculous nightmare. She wished with all of her being that that could be the case.

But she knew that it was not.

'You did all you could, Verne,' she said, not knowing if it was the right thing to say or even if it was an appropriate thing to say, but wanting to say something all the same.

'I know, kid,' he replied, nodding. 'There was nothing could be done. Just wish it hadn't been like that.'

'Yeah.'

'Yeah.'

The room fell silent again, and seconds passed like minutes.

Shelley watched the two men staring into space at either end of the room, each one caught in his own maze of thoughts or dreads or painful memories, and wanted more than anything for them to open up and help her feel normal again, to explain to her the meaning of everything that had happened, to deal with it for her so that she did not have to. She did not know if either of them was any closer to dealing with any of it than she was, but she hoped and she would not stop hoping.

'Were we created here?' she asked.

Verne shrugged. Alan Ellis did not answer.

'She seemed to have the answers to everything that didn't add up before. And the things we'd seen, the writing on the wall that said *DEATH TO THE MASTERS*, and the museum, and...' She sighed, and slouched further, and looked down at her small hands. 'It's just mind-blowing, isn't it? Everything can be turned upside down, just like that.'

Verne nodded slowly, expressionless, probably not even listening.

Shelley grew sadder.

'She was right about Earth, wasn't she? We were always killing each other, trying to outdo one another, never looking for peace or cooperation. She was right about us. About me.'

She swallowed down the lump in her throat and a tear hit her hand as it fell from her cheek, and Verne sighed from across the room as if he was sick of her shit, and then he stood slowly and bent to pick up Kojima's body, one arm across her back and one under her knees, as if he was carrying a sleeping toddler. He turned and walked towards the door and he said nothing as he exited the room, and Shelley was left unsure whether to follow him or to stay where she was and wait for him to return.

He returned before a minute had passed, and he picked up his rucksack and his gun and checked the floor for anything he might have forgotten or dropped.

As he turned to leave again he said, 'I can't be in this room any more and I ain't leaving Kojima unburied, to rot in here with that thing. If you two wanna come with me, you can; if you wanna stay here, I'll be out burying our friend, when you're ready.'

And as he walked out, Shelley stood to follow, gathering up her things desperately, as if she only had a short time to do so before he would be gone forever. Dropping things, and dropping more as she bent to pick up what she had dropped, and getting more frustrated with every passing second.

Once she had everything bundled in her skinny arms, she was able to take only one step toward the door before Ellis stopped her by saying, 'She was telling the truth about getting home, you know.'

'Eh?' she said, halting with her rucksack and blanket and rifle all hanging off her arms like a pile of washing waiting to be hung.

Ellis looked at the floor. 'While she controlled me, I could see everything. It was like we were thinking with the same mind, the whole time. And she was right, what she said. You could make it home, if you made it to that bunker in the desert.'

Shelley slowly lowered her things to the floor again, and knelt beside Ellis. 'You're kidding,' she said.

Ellis shook his head.

'What about the rest?' she asked. 'What about being gods and creating all these worlds? Was that all true too?'

Ellis smiled sadly. 'I don't know,' he replied. 'She certainly believed it, but… I don't know. She had such a narrow view. She was just reciting the beliefs of her ancestors; she hadn't created a thing in her life. But she was right, when she said that I was made here, so…' He shrugged.

He looked down at his wrists and hands as if he was unsure that they were even real, and he opened and closed his fists a couple of times, as if testing their functionality. Shelley felt as if she was watching a man waking from a coma after twenty years, gauging his body's capabilities to see if anything had stopped working in that time. He looked so empty, so sad, as if he had lost everything he had. She wanted to hold him and tell him it was okay, but she was having a hard enough time convincing herself that that was the case.

'Go on,' said Ellis, 'bury your friend. I'll join you in a while, after I've thought about what to do next.'

After a moment of silence and gazing at Ellis, Shelley rose and gathered her things, and picked up Ballard's gun also so that Ellis did not have it. She placed her hand on his head for a second, and then left the room. She left her bag and her blankets by the sled in the next room, and as she turned to exit the building, she remembered what Dolas, the native of this planet, had said about Kojima and the things that she had known before they had even left Earth. She remembered Kojima's black books, and wondered exactly what they had hidden inside them that she had never wanted her crewmates to find.

So she did not leave the building. She turned back to the sled and to Kojima's bag propped against its side, and she unzipped the rucksack and stuck her hand inside, and from it she pulled the handful of tattered, ageing black notebooks into which Kojima had scrawled her notes and her thoughts and anything else she had chosen to jot down for the past decade or two. She checked the doorways of the room to ensure she was alone, and then she opened the first of the notepads and began to read.

In the next couple of hours, she forgot completely that she had intended to join Verne in burying their mission commander, and instead lost herself in the dead woman's notes. She found essays on the corruption of governments and the terrifying tide of religious radicalism, intended for no one's eyes. She found drawings of old-fashioned, human-driven cars, and recipes for jambalaya and all kinds of smoothies. She found a sketch of bodies hanging in an apartment, some of them Antistite and some of them human, with alien writing across the walls. She read diary entries recounting everything from upsetting personal betrayals to mundane journeys to work.

And finally, in an entry dated January 5th, 2123, she found cuttings from a document that changed everything, and turned all that Shelley had thought she knew about Kojima and thcsc missions completely upside down.

JANUARY 5TH, 2123

The hands which rested in front of the girl's face, pressed together as if in prayer but as limp and lifeless as those of one despairing in the knowledge that they are already forsaken, were not her own, and she learned this only after several baffled attempts to move them, to lift a finger, to brush away from her forehead the soaked hair that stuck to her face, tangling itself with her eyelashes and creeping into her mouth.

The hands belonged instead to the girl who lay above her head, the one whose breath streaming down onto the girl's face in regular hot blasts had stunk of illness, of rotting teeth and infected wounds, back when they had just set off. The girl would have known much sooner if she had been of sound mind, if she had noticed the way the hands sat in front of her, the direction in which the thumbs had faced; but by now, after three hours of drifting slowly and painfully in and out of dim consciousness, the simple task of saying her own name out loud would probably be beyond her, so stewed were her wits. Her nose no longer sensed the girl's foul breath, only the head-splitting stench of melted rubber and diesel fumes, that intoxicating cocktail that filled the lungs so deeply that she could feel it in her bloodstream and her muscles, her stomach and her tongue. She no longer had any grasp on whichever part of her mind held the rest together and made the whole sound; it had been destroyed by the heat, so hot it should burn off her skin if it was not already doing so, so close and suffocating that it was all she could do to stay awake. The pain which could not be contained; so spread to every part of her body like a scandalous rumour in a schoolyard.

She had had a bottle of water at the beginning of this journey. Where that was now, she had no idea. She would do anything to have it back.

She tried to move her skinny legs, but her foot nudged the boy curled up by her ankles, and her knee hit the top of another child's head as she flinched away from the first. Cramps ate away at her joints, and there would not be room to stretch them out even if there had not been five children squeezed into this space, and knowing this just made the pain more intense.

Her entire body was damp with sweat and condensation, her skin slippery with it. There had been a rubber tube of some sort on the bottom of the tank when they had climbed in, but in the heat of the space once they had set off, it had been reduced to a black puddle in the dark grey murkiness of the bottom of the container. It swam with the urine of the two children who had wet themselves earlier in the journey, and the thick steam that now made the darkness darker and the skin slick was probably made of all of this rubber and sweat and piss and old fuel whose fumes invaded all of the senses, and she thought about all of these things without feeling anything for them except complete indifference, as if they were now just a fact of life that she had accepted as unavoidable and about which she would spend no more time worrying, and all she could muster the enthusiasm to do instead was keep her eyes open and not close them, because the idea of closing them and never opening them again was terrifying, even if she did not know quite what lay beyond.

She thought about her father, tried to picture his face. His forever tired-looking face, his kind smile. The way his wrinkled eyes always looked sad, even when he was laughing. She thought about how strangely he had acted recently, tried again to get her poisoned mind around that which she had not been able to fathom even with the clearest of heads. The hushed conversations he had had in the kitchen when he thought the girl was asleep, with the fat, bullish-looking man with whom he worked. The way he had let the man smoke those disgusting vapour tubes in their kitchen, that stank the room out so much that she could still smell it in the morning. The money she had seen him counting, the weighty sighs and the long silences.

And then, earlier that day, the journey her father had taken with her, wordless and sullen, to the warehouse in the part of town to which she had never been before, to stuff her into an empty fuel tank on the side of a rusty old truck with four other children, and hand the driver a handful of notes to take her away forever. The way he had wept freely, loudly, as if it was not he himself who was doing this to her but some higher power who was doing this to him.

She had not understood it. She still did not. Her father was her only family, her only friend, the only person in the whole world that she could trust. Why would he want her to go away? Why would he have given that disgusting, bony old truck driver in the tattered baseball cap and stained vest all the money he had to squeeze his daughter into a fuel tank and take her away forever? Did he not love her after all? Was he punishing her for something? She could not remember having done something wrong; she had always tried to be well behaved for him. Until today, his disapproval had been her greatest fear.

All he had ever told the girl about her mother was that she was taken when the girl was just a baby. Had he done this to her too?

She felt so betrayed, so scared.

So hot, so ill.

If she had the energy or the sense or the moisture within her she would have cried just then, but she had none of those things, so once again she wriggled to stop her entire body from aching, and she whimpered for the sake of making a sound, and she tried to force her eyes to focus in the dimness of the tank, lit only by the sunlight creeping through tiny holes in its shell. She grabbed one of the grey, limp hands that lay in front of her face and held it tightly because her seven-year-old mind knew not how else to escape the sadness and the fear and the pain, and though the girl who lay pressed against her did not squeeze back, she felt slightly better already, just for the contact. She lowered her head once more onto the hard surface of the tank, and she was drifting back into that toxic, brain-boiling half-sleep before she had time to shut her eyelids.

The next thing she knew for certain was that the road was bumpy and the truck was struggling to traverse it, the engine roaring so loudly that it almost drowned out the sobbing and wailing of the children in the tank. The old man truck driver had told them with darting eyes and black teeth as he stuffed them into his empty fuel tank that they were to keep silent for the whole journey, because if they were heard screaming or talking or crying then they and he would be locked up forever; but the only times they had been silent were when they were all unconscious – for the rest of the journey, at least one child had been crying, or screaming, or begging to be let out, as if there were any other people in the tank with the power to free them. The noise now was so great that it seemed that the other children stuck in here with her were in competition with the engine for volume, as if they wanted to be caught by whomever was out to catch them.

It was too much. The heat, the smell, the noise, the pain. She felt like she might be dying, like she might swell until she burst, like she might dry out and wither away to nothing like a crisp packet in an oven.

She slid her hand out of the other girl's and realised as she felt its limp weight brush against her, unmoving and unfeeling, that there was at least one other child not hollering, just lying there sleeping instead, or perhaps wishing she was somewhere else. She tried to focus her swimming eyes on the other children in the tank: the boy at her feet, or the one whose gender she had not been able to decipher, curled up somewhere around her knees. She wanted to tell them to shut up, to calm down, to stop making her crippling headache worse. That headache was everything now.

But when she opened her mouth to speak, the movement stopped, and a second or two later, the rumbling of the engine ceased too. In just a few seconds, the tank had gone from roaring and shaking and swallowing everything and never letting up to suspicious stillness and a quiet that felt like silence even with the persistent sobbing and wailing of the other children, such a contrast it held to the deafening thrum of before.

The girl hoped that this meant that they had arrived, even if she did not know where it was that they were going. It could be anywhere, scary or strange or anything else, as long as it was somewhere she could climb out of this tank, dry off and feel real air on her skin again. She listened past her crying companions to the slam of the truck door and the slow, muffled footsteps on crunching gravel, the far-off voices and dim click of a distant car door, and she tried to piece together the clues to work out where they had gone, but without knowing anywhere outside of her house and her school and the single street between them, she came up with nothing.

She did not have to speculate for long. After a short

conversation in voices too distant and dampened to understand, the old man was unscrewing the tank once again, and attaching it to the contraption he had used to raise it to the side of the truck when they left, and cracking it open to let in a flood of blinding sunshine that silenced all of his passengers in an instant. His wrinkled face staring back at those of the wincing children was still as emotionless as it had been in that warehouse, and his vest was still as dirty and his body still as musty, when he lowered the tank to the floor and told them to climb out, offering no help and watching them with narrow eyes and hands on hips, as if disapproving of the way their knees wobbled and their backs cracked. As if expecting thanks for the horror he had put them through.

As they peeled themselves out one by one, shielding their eyes from the sun with their skinny arms and scratching at their withered bodies where their clothes stuck to them, sodden with sweat and piss and boiled rubber, they each noticed what the girl had noticed first – that there was a new man in this place, this wasteland of gravel and weeds which seemed like an empty car park that went on forever. He wore a suit and he leaned against a car that looked like a robot or a hairdryer, a car of a kind the children had never seen before, and he stood beaming at them as if he were a long-lost relative who had always hoped to be reunited with them, even though they had never met. Mystified, disoriented and tired, the children stood staring at him with apprehensive frowns and open mouths and limp tongues, and he greeted each of them in turn, softly and kindly, until he looked past the children at the tank behind and said something which the girl could not understand, but which she could tell was not good.

Over her shoulder, the old truck driver was pulling the girl with the foul breath and the hands held in prayer out of the tank like a man dragging a carpet out of a delivery truck. She watched him lay the limp girl on the floor and put his ear to her nose and his fingers to her neck and her wrist, and then she saw him remove his baseball cap and sit fanning himself and shaking his head, looking at the man in the suit like there was nothing that could have been done to help the girl, like this was of course just something that they all should have expected and could never have been prevented. He shrugged and knelt there, fanning his face and puffing air out of his mouth as would the victim of a great inescapable heat, and the children looked on silently, still struggling to grasp even the most minor details of the situation in which they found themselves.

Looking back at the man in the suit, the girl saw him take a handkerchief from his pocket and dab it at his eye, sniff loudly and sigh. He shook his head sadly and he looked at the floor and he stayed like this for a long time, as if contemplating a hard decision. After a minute or more, he waved his hand at the old man, and the old man set to work putting the limp girl back into the fuel tank and reattaching it to the truck.

When the man in the suit had composed himself, he opened the back door of his robot car and gestured for the children to climb inside. He smiled as warmly as he could and he said to them in their own language, with a thick foreign accent, 'I am sorry for what you have to go through to get here. I know how horrible that journey must have been, I see it many times, and I see it on your faces too. But you are free now. You might not understand it yet, but your lives have been saved today. Please take a seat inside so I can take you home.'

Then, when none of the four remaining children moved, he added, 'Please. You are safe now, I promise. We need to be quick, we can't come all this way to be caught here.'

The girl had not thought herself unsafe before today, and she stood, wary of the man and his words. She had been at home this morning, or yesterday, or however long ago it had been, and all that had happened in between was that she had been taken on the most uncomfortable and traumatic drive of her life; so if this man was just going to take them all home again, what was the point of all that? She suspected that when he said the word 'home', he meant somewhere different than the home that she knew. She stood dead still and watched the other children wandering slowly and uncertainly toward the car, looking at each other and at the man for encouragement and giving the girl quizzical stares that asked why she did not join them. She was not a fool – she had been top of her class for two years straight, a fact which had, for some reason, made her father proud and scared in equal measure – so she knew that she would have to follow them into that car in the end. She saw no alternative – they had no other choice presenting itself in this concrete field, nowhere else to go and no one else to trust. And besides, this man was friendly enough, and he seemed gentle and caring, so perhaps he was not one of the strangers her father had warned her about, whose cars she should not climb into. But still, she wished that she did have another choice, and that that choice was returning to the home that she knew, even if it did mean returning to her father, the traitor.

The traitor whose arms she so desperately wanted around her.

She walked to the car behind the rest and looked in cautiously without touching anything; unsure of what exactly she was checking the inside of the car for, but checking all the same. There were six seats in the back of this car, not two or three like all the rusty old cars on her street; and they faced each other in two rows of three and they were furnished with soft black fabric and thick cushions upon which the other children were bouncing and gazing with awe. Like her, they had never seen a vehicle in which the cushions had not worn away, in which the upholstery was not faded and tattered and holey. It looked as fancy as the government buildings she always saw on television, so clean and new. Two of the three spare seats had a bottle of water and a paper parcel sitting on them, and the children who already sat in the car held the packages and the bottles that had been on their own seats in their hands, and once they were done with testing the seats and exploring the interior of the car with their eyes, they set to unwrapping those packages; and when the girl noticed that there were sandwiches within them, that was what decided for her that she should climb inside and join them immediately. She had not known that she was hungry, but now that she had seen food, and the joy on the others' faces when they ate it, the hunger within her added its voice to the choir of needs and anguishes that sang their tuneless chorus within her mind. The thirst, too. She felt like she might drink that whole bottle of water in one desperate gulp.

However, when she sat and unwrapped the packaging and took a bite of her sandwich she found that that hunger had been a lie she had told herself, or at least had not been as great as she had thought. She felt full after just one bite and then she just felt sick again, and dizzy and achy. She drank the water instead and found that it tasted like diesel and rubber, like sweat and urine, and her stomach turned further, and she wanted no more of it even though her body still seemed to crave the lot. She looked up from these broken promises and noticed that the car was moving now, that fields and distant cities and a wide, unending highway were all rolling past their windows, and because she had not been aware that they had pulled away in the first place, she felt tricked. The man in the suit had tricked her into the car and onto the road with disgusting food and a bottle of poison, just like her father had tricked her into this whole thing with false love and lies. Suddenly, with a passion she could not have summoned just half an hour previously, she hated them both. She wanted to scream and cry and throw her food and her drink out of the window and kick and punch the man until he crashed the car.

But more than that, she wanted to sleep. Once again, that dizzy tiredness was creeping over her as if it had not held her captive for too long today already, and like those of a couple of the other children in the back of that car, her eyelids began to grow heavy and her neck less able to stop her lolling head slumping to the side, and before she knew how to stop it, she was gone again.

This time, she woke in a bed. At first, feeling the cotton pressed against her cheek and the distinct lack of a crippling headache behind her eyes, she thought that she might be at home, that it might all have been a terrible dream, and a deep joy rinsed her like cleansing rain, washing away all that sorrow; but as she looked around the room she was in, she noticed that it was completely unfamiliar, larger than any she had slept in before, not home at all, and the sorrow came flooding back. The covers were thick and comfortable and they smelt like flowers and perfume, and the pillow under her head felt so soft that she thought it might swallow her whole. The room was simple and white and sparse, but it had toys in an open toy box and eight colourful spheres hanging from the ceiling on poles that made them rotate at various distances around the great yellow ball at their centre, and a poster on the wall with a laughing cartoon schoolgirl below letters from a language that the girl had never read, and it was a long time before she noticed that there were two adults, a man and a woman, sitting by her bed, smiling softly and staring at her like she was an adorable puppy or a gift all wrapped up. She froze in position, staring at them like a cornered animal, and they stared back, looking happy and sad at the same time, desperate and ecstatic at all once.

They stayed like this for a while, the two adults and the terrified child in a stand-off in that white cell, none knowing what to do or when to do it, and then the man reached out his hand, to touch the girl's cheek, or to grab her, or to do what else she did not know.

She covered her face with the bedclothes and she flinched from the man's hand and trembled with fear, and for the first time in a long time, she found that she had the energy to cry, and scream, and beg for her father and her home and all the things she did not yet know she would never see again.

Kojima found herself reliving that day – or set of days, she was still not sure – in her mind, as she read through the files on Trusov's desk. At the time, it was the most traumatic and disturbing experience of her short life; but now, all these years later, she appreciated more than anyone who knew her story just how lucky she was. She had read about little girls just like her smuggled from their war-torn homes into sex slavery and gang warfare, into permanent imprisonment and the violent drug trade; but she had been adopted by a kind young Japanese couple, and raised well, and she had never wanted for a thing ever again. Her life truly had been saved that day, and though it had taken years for her to realise it, once learned, she had never doubted it again.

Instead, she had grown up to watch her home country and the insane dictator who ran it slowly crumble, starting wars that could not be won and sparking revolutions that would cost the lives of millions. From without, she had seen her motherland die, until nothing was left but a smoking radioactive wasteland and a feeling that her father had bought her a ticket for the luckiest, timeliest escape that had ever been paid for. She had developed an idea that she was the most fortunate person alive, and that armed with this knowledge, she would never miss an opportunity to jump out of an oven in which the heat was about to be turned up full. These chances, she thought, presented themselves only to those whose eyes were open to them;

and from that point on, her eyes were open. She would always be ready to drop everything and move, to escape while the going was good. She would never tie herself down for the sake of sentimentality or comfort; she would do anything to survive.

She had been wrong a few times. She had dropped everything and hopped onto a plane to a different country or a boat to a different continent, sure in her fearful mind that she saw the seeds of war being sown and violence coming into fashion like retro dresses reduced to clear, and then found when she got to her destination that that which she had feared had fizzled out over the course of her journey, that she now had to start again just because she had overreacted. She had overreacted more than once, she knew, and her theory had been tested more times than she cared to mention; but this time, she was sure. She had never been this scared, never seen a world this dark and hateful. Never before had death been so in vogue, war so sought after. Never before had she been plagued by such dark dreams, such gruelling sleepless nights.

The way she had been feeling recently, with the fear that was eating her up, nothing was going to stop her boarding this rocket and making her escape, to live out the dream of a billion children and adults who had come before her, to touch the sky and meet an alien race and never look back at the Earth and all its people, fighting and destroying and hating and striving endlessly for their own extinction.

So, as she read documents that said that no two grainy satellite images of Planet 127-001 were ever the same, that from one angle its surface could look populated and from another it could look obliterated, she did not feel scared. As she gazed upon images of scorched earth simulated from light years away, and graphs of estimated atmospheric toxicity and hazardous radioactivity, she did not flinch. She read the transcripts of messages from the planet and saw that they were directly translatable into English, and that they were conflicting and nonsensical as if written by a hyperactive schizophrenic, one minute welcoming and the next violent and threatening, and although she was surprised and confused by this fact, it did not show on her face, and it did not stop her from dropping the pages back onto the table as if they did not really matter, lifting her gaze from them and looking at Trusov and saying, 'Where did you get this stuff?'

'Where did I…?'

'Where did you get these files?' she asked again, pointing at them so that he was absolutely clear on her meaning. Her voice shaking, though she tried so hard to keep it still. 'Where did you find them?'

'In a box of Haque's things,' he said. 'In a file marked *CONFIDENTIAL*.'

'Have you spoken to Alphabet about them?' she asked. 'To Umbrella, or MegaFon? Are they aware that these files exist?'

'I alluded to them on a feed with Alberto from Alphabet yesterday,' replied Trusov, his voice cracking under the pressure, the coffee in his hand shaking, 'and he told me that if such files ever existed, the sponsors of the missions would have "dealt with them" as appropriate. They told me if anyone knew of any more information that might jeopardise the missions then they should send all copies over to the sponsors immediately for review.'

'I see,' said Kojima, retreating into her thoughts.

'I mean, he actually said any *more* information. Like there had already been some. These are the biggest space missions the world has ever seen, and it seems that there is hard data that might justify scrapping them altogether, and that the people funding it would happily just make that data go away, for the sake of the mission's continuance? It's unthinkable, Stella.'

Hearing her name broke Kojima out of her thoughts. She did not think she had ever heard Trusov call her by her first name. It sounded odd to her. She did not like when things were odd, when things that never happened ended up happening. It was events like that that triggered her paranoia; that fed her constant malaise. That made her even surer that she should run, and never stop running.

'Unthinkable,' she repeated, having only really heard the end of his speech.

She spent a moment watching Trusov staring at the files. He looked like they were something to be feared, like they were toxic or dangerous or too hot to touch.

'So,' he said, after a while, 'what should I do?'

'Hmm?'

'About the files. What should I do with them?'

Kojima looked at the pathetic man, skinny and pale, scared like a child, and knew that he would be crushed if she told him he should destroy them. That he had entrusted her with the biggest secret he had ever owned, and that now he expected her to save him from it with her wisdom and mercy, back him up and tell him that he had to do whatever it was that needed to be done to make everything right. To discover that she wanted them shredded and never looked upon again, and that she intended to climb onto that spacecraft at all costs, would be a sledgehammer to his expectations, a violent dashing of all the hopes he had had that she could save him from his fate and do on his behalf what he was too cowardly to do himself. She might be killing him by doing what she was about to do, but she was going to do it anyway. She had to.

'Is there another copy of these? A digital copy on the servers, or on a drive somewhere? Did you take photocopies?'

'Erm,' Trusov said, scrambling for answers to the questions being fired at him like foam bullets from a toy gun, 'no. Not that I know of. I found them just like this; I never copied them. Why?'

'I'm going to take them,' Kojima said, gathering the files

together and putting them under her arm, checking the desk and double-checking it to make sure she had them all, 'and I'm going to keep them safe. We can't have anyone finding these. The missions must go ahead, Trusov. I'm leaving this planet while I still can. I don't care where I go, I just need to go.'

'What?' replied the man, his eyes watering and his hands shaking with fear, with sadness, with something pathetic and all-consuming, 'No. What? No! We have to go public. You and I. We have to. We have to close them down… I can't… We can't…'

'Trusov, listen to me,' said Kojima, her voice hardening and her long, slender finger pointing inches away from his screwed-up face, 'the missions can't be jeopardised. Mohammad Haque worked for decades on putting these rockets into space and visiting planets we never even knew existed, and now we're only just over a year from it finally happening. Humanity needs this, remember. You don't want to be the one who took it from them, and neither do I. I'm taking these files and I'm going to… *destroy* them. No one is going to look at these, ever again.'

'No,' said Trusov, collapsing to his knees in distraught desperation, dribbling and sobbing and turning red with the panic, 'you can't. Please. We must stop… We can't…'

And that was how Kojima left him, feeling awful, rotten at the very core, for destroying such a fragile little man with her actions; but also fortunate, escaping once again, to watch from without her old home tear itself apart, as she began again, in a new one.

DAY 113

James Verne sat sweating and breathless next to the shallow grave in which he had buried his friend, all of him shaking like he was run by the tired engine of a creaking old bus or ill-maintained tractor. He sat on the floor though it was bad for his joints, and he did not notice the intense pain that it gave him, just the sun in the centre of the sky, in the very same position it had been when he came out here and started digging the hole all those hours ago, not setting and not rising, just hanging still over the desert as if time had stopped so that he could gather his thoughts and re-plot his course, take a step back and pick another fate from the big bag of them that the universe or God or whomever else had presented to him. His eyes and cheeks stung from the tears that he had shed and the sand and dirt that had attached itself to those tears, but he did not wipe his cheeks and he did not rub his eyes, he just looked up into that never-ending expanse of blue and white like an ocean above him, and meditated on everything that had come to be, and his part in all of it.

He wanted to hate the alien for the things that it had said and all the evil it had attributed to the humans. He

322

wished that he could blame it for the death of Kojima, the emptiness of the city, the waste of the journey, even the death of Ballard, which now seemed so long ago. But when he thought about it, he knew that the creature had not introduced any concepts that the humans had not already considered, but had instead just echoed ideas that the humans had brought with them, or else listed the crimes of which they themselves were guilty. Wednesday Shelley's selfishness, her wilful ignorance of the needs of others and the responsibilities she had. Ballard's notion that any wrongdoing could be excused, as long as one had an idea as noble as fate or forgiveness to hide behind. His self-assurance that mistakes of the past were not an issue, as long as the suffering they caused was temporary.

Kojima, and her obsession with war and violence. Her fear that it was written into the DNA of mankind, right down at the level of the soul, and that the only way that it could ever be vanquished was if all of men's souls themselves were vanquished. Dolas, the dead alien inside the building, had implied exactly that.

And, yes, Verne's cowardice, his weakness, all the pride and the anger and the hatred that had brought him here. The alien had known all about that, too.

These were the things that had given the Conquerors cause to pack their belongings and leave Earth forever. These were the crimes they had committed and the evils they saw in the society around them, and they had been so overwhelming or terrifying or sickening that the humans had not looked back when they boarded their ship and blasted themselves trillions of kilometres across space with no hope of ever returning. So why now, having had these ideas read back to them by a being that claimed to be their god, did it seem so wrong that they should be the reasons that they died so far from home, with no one to mourn them and no one to remember their names? Why did the idea sit so uncomfortably in James Verne's mind, as if these flaws were crimes for which they had already served their time, and any further punishment would be a great injustice?

He thought back on what he had said to Ballard, in the middle of the night, with the women sleeping in the next room, all those weeks ago. He had told Ballard that his mistakes were his alone, and that they were his to learn from or to regret, and if he was too cowardly to do either of those things then he had failed, and deserved all the mistakes he would make from then till the grave. When Ballard had died just two weeks later, Verne had felt crushed that he had said those things, convinced that the boy would have taken them to heart, and spent his last two weeks beating himself up over mistakes he was powerless to change, and a past he could not even revisit, much less revise. Verne had felt so ashamed of the views that he had loaded onto the dead man's back, so unsure of why he had ever believed them in the first place.

But after Ballard's death, Verne had been forgiven by fate or by providence or simply by blind dumb luck, and he had found his way back to the companions he had lost and they had made it all the way here, all but one still alive, still deemed worthy to fight another day. He wondered how that had been, what these things were judged on, for it to be judged in his favour, even after committing such a terrible sin.

Which made him think of his wife, and the beginning of the gradual decline in his own life, the root of all the sins that had led him here today. Elsa Verne had been his light, his happiness, the other half of his soul. She was the purest, most intelligent, most beautiful person he had ever met, and the only person with whom he ever really felt at home. It was only she who could get James Verne chatting like a schoolgirl on the night before prom, only she who could have him grinning like a drunkard in a locked-up brewery. Hers was the smile he had always hoped to see, and hers the hands he had assumed he would die holding. So when she had fallen ill so many years before she should have, when she had declined so much more quickly than the doctors had thought she would, Verne's world had been destroyed. His light had been snuffed out, and the very centre of his universe had slipped away, leaving everything to drift off into the darkness, cold and hard and without purpose. He had lashed out at everyone and destroyed everything, and when she was dead and buried and gone forever, all that destruction had solved nothing, and would never bring her back. It all just made the grief more painful.

And what was he left with? A son too angry to ever forgive him and to whom he was too proud to apologise, and very little else save bitterness and regret, which he wore like a weight around his neck.

What would Elsa have said about that? What would she think of what he had said to Ballard that day, those poisonous views he had carried around with him for all those years since her death, eating away at his soul like a cancer? What would she have said about everything that had happened?

What would she say right now?

She would say that Verne had been an idiot. That he was a proud, stubborn, angry fool, and that he should have stayed on Earth and apologised to their boy and held him close and never let him go. Then she would tell him that she loved him, and she would hold him close, and she would kiss him and ruffle his white hair and put her tiny head against his chest and tell him never to stop loving her.

She would think that the alien was wrong about everything. She would say that yes, there are times when all of that nonsense can seem true and the world can be a dark and scary place, but right at the very core of humanity, there is a light that cannot be extinguished. There is good in the heart of every man, and the bad that he does is learned and not born with him. She would have said this, and she would have believed it.

Elsa Verne had believed that everyone deserved a second chance; that no man was so evil that he could not be forgiven.

And that is what Verne had forgotten, when he had told Ballard never to stop regretting his mistakes. When he had pushed his son away and never stopped doing so. When he had travelled across the galaxy, to avoid forgiving himself.

But she was right, and staring out at the wrinkling horizon and the blistering sun burning all the previous day's rain off the sand and dirt, Verne knew it more certainly than he ever had before. Everyone deserved another chance to get it right, whether they were a lover who had never learned to love unconditionally or an excitable girl who never really learned to be a woman or a stubborn old man who could never forgive anyone or a world full of people who have all lost their way. Everything could be fixed, if there was enough desire to fix it.

Since he had lost that voice that kept him positive, Verne had lived his life by a set of rigid, suffocating rules. He had lived life hating everything and everyone as much as he hated himself. Hatred as a hobby, anger as a mask. He had lost his joy and all his purpose; he had forgotten what life was about. But now, thinking on his past and the things that he had learned here and everything that his companions had shared with him on this journey, he truly understood all the things that were important, as if the list of them had always been a part of him but had been locked away for some time in a box that had just opened up inside of him.

Freedom. Passion. Happiness. Forgiveness. Positivity. Love.

Most importantly, love.

These were the things that Elsa had given him, these were the things that mattered when all else was stripped away, these were the things that were worth fighting for above everything all the way to the bitter, painful end, and these were the things at which he wanted to give Shelley and Ellis one more shot, even if he died trying to do so. He would not let them live another day in the shadow of their pasts, living by someone else's rules, or scared of anything they could not control. He would fight to the death if he needed to, to make them free again.

Because Shelley deserved a chance to live again, to love again, to take back the world she had run away from and have another shot at living a normal life. She needed to be shown once again that there was always something to smile about.

And Ellis deserved to see with his own eyes the world that he had only ever seen in false memories, made up by false gods. He was the most deserving of them all.

Verne smiled, and shook his head, and rubbed the sting out of his eyes with dusty, calloused hands. He kissed his fingers and placed them on top of Kojima's fresh grave, though he did not know exactly why, and then he stood from the ground, his knees shaking and muscles aching, and brushed dust from his knees and torso. He inhaled a great lungful of alien air and sighed loudly, stretching his back this way and that, forgetting for a moment that he had just buried a friend and feeling more like he had banished a demon that had haunted him for years. He turned and went to walk toward the door of the building, but was stopped by Shelley, exiting with her arms crossed across her chest as if she were cold, her tiny frame trembling like a stick insect in the wind.

'Hey,' she said, trying to smile, a sad smile. Sadness blanketed her, and it was the kind of sadness that was exhausted, fed up with itself, desperate for any ray of hope to come shining through the clouds. She looked down at the fresh grave, and then up at Verne. Her eyes asked a question, and Verne's nod answered it. She smiled again, her chin wrinkled, and then she started to cry.

Verne took the young woman in his arms and held her tightly and she sobbed into his chest, and her muffled voice could have been saying, 'Why did we do this?' or 'I want to go home' or 'I want to die' or all of the above, but all Verne said was, 'Sshhh. Sshhh.'

'She knew,' said Shelley, her forehead pressed against Verne's sternum, dampening his clothing with her tears, 'she knew that the planet was dead before we came here. She knew that humans had been here before we met Ellis. She didn't tell us anything.'

'It doesn't matter now, it doesn't matter,' Verne replied, holding her head with his huge paw and stroking her filthy hair. 'She was scared, just like the rest of us. She was running away. Anything looked better than what she was going through at home. It doesn't matter now. We're alive, that's all that matters.'

As Verne held the young girl's head to his chest and petted her like a distraught child, Ellis too appeared from the gloom of the building, slowly, stepping out of the shadows like a ghost from a wall of smoke. The sleeves of his coveralls were rolled up to his elbows, and a gash in his right wrist drew a dead straight line all the way from the ball of his hand to his elbow. He held out the forearm as if showing off some amazing animal he had discovered, looking up at Verne and Shelley as if bewildered by what he had done.

Shelley gasped when she saw the bloody cut, backing away as if it might be contagious, whimpering like a beaten dog. She grabbed Verne and pushed him between her and Ellis. Verne did not react at all.

The gash had bled – that much was clear from the drying red liquid around it, slick and thick like red oil – but it was no longer bleeding. The reserves had been used up, and with no real arteries underneath to supply a fresh stream, that was all there would be until the systems inside of Ellis had had enough time and input to create new blood with which to make injuries more believable. Verne watched Ellis, knowing all of this, as the younger man placed his fingers into the incision and pinched the edge of the sliced skin and pulled it back like the top of a yoghurt pot to reveal the wiring inside of him, the false muscle covering the robotics beneath.

'The animals didn't avoid me because I smelt like their home,' he said, his voice slow, stunned, 'but because I smelt like nothing at all. I smelt like a machine. The alien was wrong, Verne. Everything she said about how we – how *you* – got here, she was wrong. They never created life; they made imitations of it so they could call themselves gods. So they could lord it over their own kind, live in big towers and order everyone around.'

'I know,' said Verne, nodding, approaching Ellis with long, careful steps. 'I know.'

'Wha…?' Shelley gasped again, pale and shuddering, from behind Verne. 'You knew?'

Verne nodded at Ellis, as if the younger man was the one who had asked the question. 'That thing could only control you,' he said, 'it couldn't control me. All it could do to Kojima and Shelley was give them a headache, probably because whatever it was doing to connect to you screwed with their implants. It was something electrical, radio waves or something, not anything mystical or magical. The creature I killed in there was either a fool or a charlatan, and either way, just another arrogant creature that thought it lived at the centre of the universe. I don't regret blowing it away.'

Verne smiled at Ellis, and Ellis stood blinking silently. He held open the flap of skin on his arm for a few seconds as if Verne had not understood or was yet to say the right thing in response, and then when he realised that the conversation was over and that Verne was not amazed or shocked or running for cover, he let go of the skin and just stood, looking at the other two humans, feeling self-conscious and exposed, like a stripper in an alley in the midnight rain.

The two humans and the android were silent for a very long time. They stood looking at each other, each waiting for the next to say something, and each of them unable to think of anything to say.

Eventually, Verne shrugged, and nodded, and walked into the building, patting Ellis on the shoulder as he passed him, his steps purposeful as if he were going about business he had been meaning to sort out for a long time. The two he left behind just stood in silence, confused by their companion's newfound inner peace and the utter ease with which he had received all their devastating news, each unsure how to act around the other. So much had changed in the past two days that neither of them could see how anything would be normal again. The future for them was shrouded in the darkness of uncertainty, the terrifying shadow of lives upturned. For Verne – the one who had always been so solemn and cautious, so slow to satisfaction in troubling situations – to be taking it all in his stride was discomforting, to say the least.

After a time, to break the silence as much as to quell her curiosity, Shelley gestured to Ellis's arm and mumbled, 'Do you… need to do anything to that? Bandage it up, or…?'

Ellis looked down at the cut and raised his eyebrows at it as if he had forgotten it was there. 'I'm not sure,' he said. 'I always have, because I thought I was…' He shrugged, rolled his eyes. 'I think I probably don't need to, but I will.'

'Oh,' replied Shelley, that being all she had to say.

Verne returned with the one remaining strap to the sled over his shoulder and the rest of the thing following close behind. He dragged it out to the dirt road and started to pack things onto it – the shovel he had used to dig Kojima's grave, the blankets he had collected from the tunnels and the wet room they had just been in, his own rucksack – concentrating on the task as if it was his only worry in the universe.

When he was done, he turned to his two companions and said, 'Get yourselves ready, and we'll go.'

'Go?' asked Shelley, her feet turned in to face each other and the fingers of each of her hands picking at the ends of the fingers of the other, the posture of a toddler lost in a supermarket. 'Go where?'

She looked back at Ellis uncertainly. Ellis shrugged.

'We're going to find this hangar in the desert,' replied Verne, straightening the pile of supplies on top of the sled, taking inventory of its contents in his busy mind. 'We're taking you two home.'

'But—'

'Look alive,' said Verne. 'We don't have much of the afternoon left, and we have a long way to go.'

He clicked his fingers at the pair, and this movement did more than his words to kick them into action.

The young woman and the android had very little to do to prepare to depart, but they took a long time about it. They packed their things into their rucksacks and put on their boots in a daze, still unsure of where they were going or why. Ellis wrapped a bandage around his wrist, and Shelley checked her bag for her samples, as if she had anything useful to do with them. They walked in and out of the building multiple times to check that nothing had been left behind, both staying well clear of the wet room with the rotting alien corpse inside of it. When they were done, they stood in front of Verne in the street outside the building as if expecting a briefing from him, another explanation of what they were doing next and why they were doing it.

Verne did not say a thing. He looked them both over, and he gave them a familiar half-smile and another short nod, and then he began to walk out of the slums and into the desert, dragging the sled behind him with no small amount of effort. The journey would be long, and the desert would be cruel. There might be trials ahead that would punish the remaining Conquerors and their newest friend until they felt that they could take no more. And all of this would have to be tackled before they could struggle with an alien spacecraft, take a journey through space and time, and attempt landing back on Earth alive and in one piece. But Verne's mind was made up – he was taking his two friends back home, whatever it took.

Not to live in fear, not to live ashamed or alone, not to live without compassion and empathy and art and friends and goals and all that made them human; but to conquer the darkness in their hearts, and have one more chance at happiness, one more taste of freedom, one more shot at unconditional love. Because once everything was stripped away, and there were no nations to war and no financial markets to crash and no rules to live by and no dark pasts casting a shadow over the present, and gods and conquerors were just characters in stories and not real tools of terror, these were the only things that mattered. The only things worth fighting to keep.

www.destroyedordamaged.com

23247230R00201

Printed in Great Britain
by Amazon

GODS
AND
CONQUERORS

AARON KANE HEINEMANN